THE LOST PRINCE

BOOKS BY EDWARD LAZELLARI

Awakenings
The Lost Prince

THE LOST PRINCE

EDWARD LAZELLARI

A TOM DOHERTY ASSOCIATES BOOK
NEW YORK

This is a work of fiction. All of the characters, organizations, and events portrayed in this novel are either products of the author's imagination or are used fictitiously.

THE LOST PRINCE

Edited by Paul Stevens

A Tor Book
Published by Tom Doherty Associates, LLC
175 Fifth Avenue
New York, NY 10010

www.tor-forge.com

The Library of Congress Cataloging-in-Publication Data is available upon request.

ISBN 978-0-7653-2788-8 (hardcover)
ISBN 978-1-4299-4743-5 (e-book)

Tor books may be purchased for educational, business, or promotional use. For information on bulk purchases, please contact Macmillan Corporate and Premium Sales Department at 1-800-221-7945 extension 5442 or write specialmarkets@macmillan.com.

First Edition: August 2013

Printed in the United States of America

0 9 8 7 6 5 4 3 2 1

To my dad, whom I miss . . .
for giving New York its passion

ACKNOWLEDGMENTS

Thanks and cheers to the folks who help me look better than I have any right to.

Paul Stevens, Seth Kramer, Chris Cooper, Evan Gunter, Rayna Bourke, Tom Doherty, Ron Gwiazda, Amy Wagner, Alexis Nixon, Patty Garcia, Irene Gallo, Christian McGrath, Seth Lerner, John McClure.

No one should come to New York to live unless he is willing to be lucky.

—E. B. White,
Here Is New York (1949)

THE LOST PRINCE

PROLOGUE

ONE FATEFUL NIGHT

1

MALCOLM

Malcolm sped his Porsche through the downpour in the dead of night, obsessed like a zealot in the midst of sacrilege. The sky was black. Drops of hard cold rain battered the windshield and the wipers couldn't keep up with the deluge. Every few seconds, the car hydroplaned, sliding along a kinetic sheen of water before it found asphalt again. The herky-jerky gusts buffeted the tiny roadster, threatening to slap it from the road. That Malcolm's window was cracked slightly open, letting the storm in, only added to Scott's anxiety.

Mal pushed the car to 120 miles per hour at times, far from its maximum, but wholly unjustified for these conditions. The Long Island Expressway was not made for this kind of driving even on the best of days. Scott had never seen him like this: Was he hurrying toward something . . . or running away? A hard gust and a slide would jerk them back to eighty miles per hour, a virtual slow crawl, and then Mal would push it up all over again. Scott was certain he'd be sick all over the leather before they made it to their destination—assuming they didn't crack up in a fiery jumble first.

"Want to slow it down?" Scott asked. Malcolm ignored him just as he had since they left the mansion.

The craziness began earlier that night. They were reading reports in their East Hampton home, dogs napping by a lit hearth against the backdrop of a dark ocean breaking on the shore. It was the type of moment they both cherished, private, peaceful, the type of serenity purchased by power and wealth. Scott was going over the coming week's schedule—meetings with congressmen, senators, generals, parts suppliers, and anyone else who could expand Malcolm's vast industrial empire. Then the seizure hit.

Mal fell to his knees, clutching at his skull. His eyes rolled back and he collapsed. Scott grabbed a riding crop and jammed it in Malcolm's mouth to keep him from swallowing his tongue. Their live-in maid, Rosita, rushed into the room to check—Scott told her to call an ambulance, then asked her to go back to her room . . . he didn't want anyone to see Mal this way. The spasm subsided as quickly as it came on. Scott stroked his partner's face. He removed the crop once he deemed it safe. White froth dotted Mal's copper-hued beard like drops of cream; he feverishly mumbled the same phrase over and over.

"And or what?" Scott asked him.

Malcolm recovered quickly, brushed himself off, and took stock of the damage. He had a slight nosebleed and he rubbed the elbow that had taken the brunt of his fall.

"Good thing you're so close to the ground already," Scott said, to lighten the mood. "Might have injured yourself, otherwise."

Malcolm stared at him as though seeing Scott for the first time. He walked away from his partner and locked himself in the study. Scott regretted his joke. The humor was more for his frazzled nerves than his partner, but that was no excuse for callousness. Here the man had nearly died and he cracked smart about his diminutive stature. But Mal had never been sensitive about his height; seldom had Scott met a person as comfortable in his or her own skin. Scott himself had only two inches on Mal, and their height had always been a good source of humor between them. Through the door, he heard his partner canceling the paramedics. Scott tried repeatedly to gain entrance to the study, but the door was solid mahogany, with solid brass knobs. That didn't stop him from shouting that Mal should see a doctor and that he wouldn't be able to help from *this* side of the door if Mal had another attack. The muffled tapping on the computer keyboard implied that Mal was on one of his obsessive streaks, tackling some new idea that had come to his brilliant mind . . . like the ideas that had made Malcolm Robbe America's greatest weapons builder.

"And or" had become Mal's new mantra as he drove. It was something from his partner's past, and they were hurtling toward it at breakneck speed.

Two-thirds of Malcolm's life was a complete mystery to him. He'd seen neurologists, psychologists, psychiatrists, and every other quack between Washington, DC, and Boston. He'd even resorted to the arcane, much to Scott's disapproval. One charlatan explained that he was a former Christian missionary whose sins among native peoples were so heinous, he had blocked them from his memory. A gypsy woman claimed that he was not of this world, and that the memories he sought were from *another* plane of existence. The wealthier Malcolm had become, the more those con artists charged, but neither doctors or hacks had cracked his amnesia. The wall around his mind was as thick as the armor Malcolm built for America's tanks.

Scott had been sleeping on the leather couch outside the study when Mal finally emerged hours later.

"I'm going into the city," Malcolm said.

"In this weather? Can't it wait until morning?"

"I'll be at our suite at the Waldorf."

"What about tomorrow's appointments?"

"Cancel everything for the next few days. Tell them I'm not feeling well."

"You're *not* well," Scott stressed. "You just had a grand mal seizure. Pun intended."

A smile cracked the industrialist's dour veneer, and dissipated just as quickly. He put a hand on Scott's shoulder indicating his thanks for Scott's solidarity.

Mal grabbed the car keys and his coat.

"You're not going alone," Scott said, grabbing his jacket as well.

The billionaire considered it a moment, and just when Scott thought he would argue the point, Mal said, "Suit yourself. But you've no idea what you're getting into."

"Malcolm, what's going on?"

Leading toward the Porsche in the driveway, he said, "The gypsy was right." It was the last thing Mal had said to Scott that night.

Ahead loomed the Midtown Tunnel. Beyond it, the diffused lights of Manhattan eked through the dark, rainy mist.

2

ALLYN

Michelle calculated the tithes in the back office as her husband pounded the pulpit out front with fervent oratory. The office's hollow pine door was no match for the reverend's passionate deep tenor. His voice commanded attention—he was, after all, God's proxy on earth. Allyn worked his special appeal late into the night to help find two children who had gone missing from their community.

Michelle clicked away at the adding machine under the watchful portrait of Jesus on the wall; the strip of paper snaked across the table and off the edge to the floor. She breathed a sigh of relief because the First Community Baptist Church of Raleigh, which was technically located in Garner, would be able to keep the heat and power on for another month. Not so certain were roof repairs, new tires for the church van, or the monthly donation to the regional NAACP chapter. Her husband had promised her a new computer and accounting program, but money was tight, with more parishioners unemployed each week and asking for help instead of donating funds. There was always someone in the community in desperate need.

Michelle worried about their daughter, Rosemarie. Her college savings were underfunded relative to her scholastic aptitude. She knew the reverend loved his daughter, but it often seemed as though her needs came second to starving families or those who'd lost their homes. *The Lord will provide,* the reverend told his wife. Allyn Grey was as confident of that as he was that gravity would not let him fly off the earth.

The reverend's passion swept all before him into his fold. He had a resounding conviction that there was more to this universe than what they could see, such as his uncanny ability to heal people by laying on hands and praying. He succeeded often enough that many came from miles just for the chance at curing their diabetes, gout, or cancer. Allyn took his failures hard, blaming himself when he could not cure an ailment.

"We are all connected," Allyn's voice boomed through the office walls. He told the story of old Agatha Crowe from their former congregation, who awoke in the middle of the night at the exact moment her son had been shot dead in Afghanistan. Her son came to her in a dream and said he was in a place surrounded by their ancestors. "A link that binds us all," the reverend drove on. And it was in the spirit of that connectivity that he worked so hard on his parishioners' behalf. Two of them, the Taylors, were in the midst of a tragedy—despondent over their children.

The family had been carjacked that morning by robbers at the Piggly Wiggly, and the thieves took the children as insurance. The police retrieved the car at the edge of the Uwharrie National Forest and captured one of the men, but the children, a six-year-old boy and his younger sister, had run into the largest and most secluded part of the forest trying to escape. One of the thieves went after them, no doubt to retrieve his bargaining chip with the authorities. They were still lost in those woods. The reverend said that if the Taylor kids had been white, the media would be all over the story and the amount of help overwhelming.

Allyn was trying to get the community to put pressure on the governor and the local stations to increase resources for the search. The sheriff and the state police were good men, but money and people were stretched tight all over. A hint of racism was still the best way to stir politicians to action—and it would be for as long as those who remembered segregation still lived. Rosemarie's generation would know a different, better South. Michelle had just finished her calculations when Rosemarie rushed into the office.

"Something's wrong with dad," she said frantically.

"Wrong . . . What do you mean?" Michelle asked. She hadn't realized that the reverend had stopped speaking.

"He jus' standin' behind the pulpit with a blank expression."

"He*'s* jus*t* standin*g*," Michelle corrected. She hated the local dialect's influence on Rosemarie. She rose from her desk, ignoring the pit of fear that planted itself in her stomach. "People with our skin don't get into Duke talking that way," she told her daughter, in a somewhat absent tone. The word "stroke" pushed other conscious thoughts to the rear of Michelle's mind.

"Whatever . . . you coming?" urged her daughter.

A small crowd had gathered around the pulpit. Her husband was sitting on the floor looking older than his forty-one years; his yellow coloring took more of a beating in the southern sun than Michelle's dusky russet tone. Gray strands that had woven their way into his short, tightly cropped head these past few years shone brighter beside the blank stare that had descended on him.

"Allyn?" Michelle said, pushing through the crowd. "Everyone back. Please give him air."

Someone in the assembly shouted, "His eyes rolled back."

"We thought he havin' a heart attack," a blue-haired old lady said.

Blood and drool pooled at the corner of Allyn's lip and trickled down his chin. He had bit his tongue. His large brown eyes were moist and stared blankly ahead. His breath came quickly, short, and shallow.

"Allyn, say something?" Michelle asked. She turned his head to face her. He looked at her with accusing eyes. He shook ever so slightly as though someone were walking on his grave. Rosemarie handed Michelle a paper towel to wipe the blood from his chin.

"I'm okay," Allyn responded in a coarse whisper. "It hurt for a moment, but I'm okay."

"What hurt? Why are you sitting here like this?" she asked. "We need to get you to the emergency room."

"No," he said, grabbing her wrist. "No doctors. Doctors won't know what to do."

Michelle was confused. She was at a loss as to what to do next.

Allyn started to weep, which scared Michelle more. She wanted all the eyes in the church to go away.

"Everyone, please go home," Michelle ordered. "Thank you for coming out tonight. Remember to call the governor's office and the TV and radio stations to help find the Taylor kids tomorrow morning. We need help now. The forecast said a cold front is coming day after tomorrow . . . we don't have long."

She beckoned to the janitor to help. "Randy, please . . ."

Randy began herding the congregation. They looked back over their shoulders with concern as he shuffled them out. Allyn was the church's rock. They drew strength from their minister. They had never seen him cry . . . never seen him afraid.

"Let's get you to the hospital," Michelle said.

"I am not ill," Allyn insisted.

"Well, then what are you? You are certainly not well."

"No. I am not well," he acquiesced. "I am overwhelmed. I am . . . sad."

"Why?" Michelle asked. Her first thought was about the Taylor children. "Allyn, did—did you get news about . . . Did someone die?"

Allyn thought about it a moment, and upon reaching a conclusion said, "Yes."

"Who?" Michelle asked.

"Me."

"Daddy, you're not making sense," Rosemarie interjected. Her tone was anxious.

"My darling Rose, it's very hard to explain," he said. Michelle recognized Allyn's teaching tone. The man believed that every moment of life was a learning moment. "When we are happy we forget God's grace because we are living in the pleasure He has bestowed on us. Sorrow, however, brings us closer to Him." He took the paper towel from his wife and patted his mouth. "In grief we seek out God," he continued. "We need Him to lighten our burdens." Allyn stopped. He made a fist and clenched his teeth, fighting the urge to weep. "But I have found a new thing in my soul," he told them both.

"What thing?" Michelle asked.

"It pollutes me, like the fruit Eve gave Adam—it separates me from His grace."

Allyn shivered. Michelle put her arm around him.

"Allyn, it's okay. You've been pushing yourself so hard to help the community . . ."

"I am in the depths of a sorrow from which I know not how to ascend," he said. "From which none of the gods can save me."

Michelle's fear escalated. Did the seizure cause damage to his brain? He wasn't making sense. "Allyn, there is only *one* God," she said, struggling to remain calm.

Allyn held her gaze like a lifeline on a stormy sea.

"In this universe," he said.

3

TIMIAN

Babies Ate My Dingo performed their hit on the main stage at Madison Square Garden. They were the opening act for Bon Jovi, a huge break that had catapulted their song "Karma to Burn" to the iTunes Top 10. The logo that Clarisse had designed, happy vampire infants chomping on the remains of a dog, was prominently centered behind the drummer on a huge banner in dual-toned red and black. Clarisse was in awe of how far the band had come in a few short months. Sales on the song had already paid for the home in La Jolla she shared with lead guitarist Timothy Mann, and the tour would set them up for a good long time. Tim's stage presence was magical—almost unworldly—as he rocked lead guitar in front of twenty-five thousand fans. Life was great.

She snapped away with her Nikon, collecting her favorite shots, the ones from behind the band with the crowds in front of them. That composition would throw a light halo around the band members and give them an angelic vibe. The band had finished the second chorus and was about to start the bridge when the song fell flat. She put down the camera and searched for the cause. At first she thought the power had gone out, but it soon became clear that Tim had completely blanked. The band recovered well, revving up the lead-in to the bridge a second time, but Tim missed his solo again. He stared out blankly at the audience who, knowing the song intimately, could tell something was wrong. One of the stagehands whispered, "Drugs," but Clarisse knew better. They only smoked the occasional grass.

The band stopped. The lead singer, Rick Fiore, approached Tim. His eyes had rolled to their whites. Rick braced the back of Tim's head as the guitarist fell backward onto the stage. The audience's collective gasp echoed through the arena. Moments later, some in the audience shouted about not taking the brown acid and snickered. Other fans told those people to go back to Jersey, and a fight broke out. Clarisse grabbed a bottle of water and a towel and ran onto the stage.

Rick turned off their microphones and asked his guitarist, "What's up, dude? You dying?"

"Here, sweetie, have a sip," Clarisse said. She pulled his shoulder-length brown hair away from his face and put the bottle to his lips.

Tim took a large swig and shortly caught his breath. "Just had my mind blown," he said, shaking his head.

"You dropping acid, Mann?"

"No." He took the towel from Clarisse and patted the sweat from his forehead and neck. "It's just . . . I just remembered I'm a lute player from an alternate universe on a mission to raise a prince that some dudes in another kingdom are trying to kill. I swore an oath and everything."

Clarisse laughed. Rick was not as amused.

The sound of the crowd's impatience rose steadily in the background.

"Mann, we're on the verge of being the biggest band since U2, and you're pulling shit like this during our big number?" he asked.

Clarisse seldom found Rick Fiore's talent for hyperbole and drama amusing. That, and his bottle-blond David Lee Roth coiffure, was why she dumped him for Tim, who was as cool as a mountain lake. Tim would never mess around with their success, and if he was cracking jokes, it was his way of saying he'd be okay. "Lighten up, Flowers," she said. It was the nickname she created for him just before they broke up.

Rick pursed his lips and ground his teeth. "You dumped me for a dude that falls on his ass in the middle of gig?" he said. "You can get his ass off the stage without me." Rick stormed off to brood in the wings.

Clarisse turned to her significant other. "Seriously, Manly-Mann, you okay?"

"I wasn't joking. That amnesia about my early life . . . all of a sudden, it was like a wall of memories hit me out of nowhere. I came here years ago with other people to protect a baby prince. I don't know what happened after that."

"Uh, that's great," she said, not really sure how to react. Clarisse wondered if Tim *was* on something after all. They swore never to go down that road. She could put up with the occasional groupie, but not hard drugs. Cocaine had torn her parents apart; that was her deal breaker. The audience started to hiss.

Rick and the drummer were talking in the corner, shooting dirty glances at them. The paramedics finally showed up and were heading toward them with a stretcher. "Can you finish the show?" she asked him.

"Heck yeah," Tim said. "I'll do five encores. It's been thirteen years. One more day won't make a difference. I can get back to that other stuff tomorrow. As he stood, he pumped his fist into the air and yelled, "ROCK 'N' ROLL!"

The audience cheered.

4

BALZAC

"What can be said of Lear's fool?" Balzac Cruz threw the question out to his Elizabethan literature class. He wore a triangular red, yellow, and green jester's cap with three protruding appendages that ended in small bells and jingled as he moved. Tufts of his gray hair stuck out the sides of the cap. Under a dark brown sports jacket, he wore a cream-colored rayon knit turtleneck that protruded subtly at the waist, green and brown plaid trousers, and oxblood leather loafers.

Balzac performed as he taught because an entertained mind was the most receptive mind. At least that was what he told the department faculty. But actually, he relished the attention. He received high marks as one of the department's most favored professors. This was the first year he had taught Elizabethan lit as a night class, though, and he was sure it would be the last. It cut into his nightlife, which for a single man of fifty was generously rich at the university.

"Lear's fool saw things clearly," a female student answered. It was only their second class and Balzac had already pegged her as the overachiever. He suspected her name was Rachel.

"Clearly?" Balzac asked. "As in he did not need glasses?" Jingle, jingle.

"He saw things Lear couldn't or refused to see," an eager young man wearing the school's lacrosse jersey said. The boy's hair was a curly brown tussle as though he'd just rolled out of bed. Balzac licked his lips at the image of him sweaty and hot at the end of a game. *Perhaps the night class isn't a total loss,* he thought. Balzac's hat jingled vigorously.

"And . . . ?" Balzac prodded.

"He was loyal," the overachiever cut back in, annoyed at having her moment usurped by a pretty-boy jock. "The most loyal of Lear's servants."

"True," Balzac agreed. "But also . . ."

A white haze descended upon Balzac's view of the room, as though everything were behind a sheet of gauze. He was aware that he had stopped talking—couldn't move his hands or feet. His students, on the other side of the gauze wore worried expressions. The last thing of the room he saw before everything turned solid white was the handsome lacrosse player rushing toward him. Another world took its place before him; a beautiful gleaming city made of marble, brick, and oak. His mother, his father, his teachers, lovers, masters—all came back to him. His mind was the pool at the end of a waterfall as memories of Aandor rushed into his head.

Slowly the gauze lifted. He was on his back, his students hovering around him, concerned. The strong arms of the lacrosse player cradled him—his hand supported the back of Balzac's head.

This lad has earned his A, Balzac thought.

"Are you okay, Professor Cruz?" the overachiever asked.

Balzac stood up and brushed himself off. He wiped the sweat from the top of his balding head with a kerchief. "I think we might cancel the rest of tonight's class," Balzac said. "I'm not feeling quite myself."

His students returned to their seats to gather their belongings. "Someone should see you home," the overachiever—*probably Rachel*—said.

"Perhaps you're right, my dear." Balzac turned to the Lacrosse player. "Would you mind terribly seeing me to my flat, uh . . ."

"Rodney," the young man said.

"Yes, Rodney." Balzac threw him a grateful smile. The overachiever practically stomped the treads on her shoes flat as she returned to her seat.

Balzac spied his fool's cap on the floor. He picked it up. It jingled as he brushed off some dust.

"The fool . . . ," he said to the entire room . . . stopping everyone in their tracks—books half packed.

Balzac gazed at the cap, seeing more in it than anyone in the room could ever imagine. He looked up at his students and smiled a devilish grin.

". . . as is often the case in Shakespeare, is a commoner with tremendous clarity—and usually the wisest man in the world."

CHAPTER 1

DREDGING THE PAST

Callum, Catherine, Seth, and Lelani drove into the town of Amenia, New York, weary from the events of the past two days. A fresh dusting of snow had descended on the small locality, which emanated three blocks in all directions from a center traffic light. The Sunoco gas station tucked in one corner was the intersection's largest presence, joined by a bank, salon, and empty lot on the remaining corners. Its citizens, dressed mostly in overalls, jeans, flannel, and construction boots, went about their business in that contented manner only those far removed from the fast-paced and worried centers of the world could. Nothing was a rush and no one was out to get them. This was the third town they'd visited that day in the vicinity of the portal that Callum and the other guardians had come through thirteen years earlier. Agriculture was a large part of the local economy. Street signs steered tourists to the many vineyards that dotted the region—Cat was always telling Cal how wonderful a winery day trip would be. Today was not that day. Today, Cal hoped to find his lost prince.

At stake were the lives of millions of people. The Kingdom of Aandor had been invaded by the maleficent war-happy nation of Farrenheil. Callum MacDonnell had come to this alternate universe to save his infant prince from execution. With the prince came his guardians, a ragtag band of servants and soldiers sworn to protect the boy and raise him to adulthood so that he could one day reclaim his throne. But Farrenheil also sent agents to this world, and now they hunted the prince as well. It was a race to get to the boy first.

Guiding the car, Cal scrutinized each teenaged boy he passed hoping to recognize in their manner some thing that would reveal the prince—his gait, Duke Athelstan's sharp profile, Duchess Sophia's ocean-green eyes. It was a long shot, and perhaps they had used their quota of good luck just surviving the attack in the woods. Cal was exhausted—stretched thin by the mishaps, mistakes, and tragedies of his life that had culminated in the past two days. The most personal of his challenges had yet to emerge from its chrysalis; the secret of his betrothed back in Aandor that he had yet to share with his wife.

I have to tell her was the new mantra that nested in Callum's thoughts. He had never kept secrets from Catherine before. The past few days had introduced several new firsts in their marriage, but no revelation so far constituted the threat to his marriage that his betrothal would. His wife sat in the passenger seat and serenely took in their surroundings, unknowing of the turmoil in Callum's heart. The weather had warmed a bit, and the sun cut deeply into the snow turning the ditches beside the road into babbling brooks. The crisp daylight brought out the gray in Catherine's eyes, and where the light touched her raven tresses it shone blue. She inherited her light skin from the Dutch branch of her family, but Cal always encouraged her to dress as a Native American for Halloween because of her Sioux heritage. *You have the cheekbones for war paint,* he often teased. In this moment, you would not know from looking at her that their lives had recently been upended. Cal's elusive past finally caught up with him.

Cat was understanding of his mission and willing to do her part, to a point. But that point was poorly defined . . . a hazy dot on the horizon whose distance neither spouse could gauge. They would only know it when they smacked into it. Cat had accepted that Cal was from a feudal kingdom called Aandor in a far-off alternate reality—that his role in that society was to defend the world order, of which his family resided near the top, and that his mission here was to protect and raise a young prince who would one day rule his kingdom. But the betrothal to another woman—a woman he owed a great debt to and that he realized he still loved as much today as he did thirteen years ago—that was the bomb under their bed.

"This Podunk town makes the *other* Podunk towns look far less Podunk," Seth moaned from the backseat. The punk had mastered backhanded compliments. Cal was certain the delinquent knew no other kind.

"Concentrate," Lelani scolded. Seth sat in the backseat of the Ford Explorer, and Lelani in the rear cargo area with her upper torso hanging over the seat back. A pile of salt lay in her palm, which she held before Seth. They'd been going over rudimentary sorcery all morning as Cal hopped from town hall to town hall, trying to find records of the events that split his group apart years earlier. It was an important thread to finding the prince.

"How can I concentrate when you keep yelling 'concentrate'?" Seth responded.

"I am not yelling," she said, though Cal heard the strain behind Lelani's calm response. Seth had a talent for testing the limits of patience.

The backseat bickering chafed the sheath on Callum's last nerve. They seemed to be growing on Cat, though, evident from the smile she tried to hide from her husband. She had always wanted a larger family, and now they inherited two teenagers—a seventeen-year-old centaur that acted thirty-seven, and a twenty-six-year-old porn photographer who behaved sixteen. Cal wasn't sure if Cat's acclimation was a good thing. His negative feelings about Seth had not subsided and were at best mixed. If it weren't for Seth, they would not have lost their memories and spent the better part of the past decade unaware of their real identities. They would never have lost the prince, who had been put in Callum's charge. Tristan might still be alive, as probably Ben Reyes and a score of others. The hardest point to resolve, though, the part that disturbed Callum to his core, was that he would never have married Catherine. He would never have pursued another woman if he were cognizant of his betrothal to Chryslantha. She was as much a part of him as his heart and lungs and he would have stayed true. But then his daughter, Brianna, whom he loved more than life itself, would never have existed. For all his incompetence, bellyaching, and pessimistic rhetoric, Seth was the reason Cal had his family.

Cal once believed his love for Chryslantha was the most powerful force in the world, breakable only by death itself. Noble houses in the kingdom paired their offspring to gain land, status, and power; girls of fourteen betrothed to old men, couples with nothing in common except their parents' desires to grow their holdings. His father was not enamored by the game despite the advantages that paired him with a wife twenty years younger, but Cal's mother, Mina, was a different story. She was a master at the matchmaking art.

Cal had been impressed with Chryslantha since they played as children. At seven, she looked like a princess but climbed trees like a squirrel and spit farther than a wharfie. Her father was wealthy—a duke with only an arm's-length claim to Aandor's seat of power. They had written to each other as children when family business took them to opposite ends of the kingdom. A union with Chryslantha would raise Callum's status and land holdings considerably, but he was already in love with her before the first inkling of a match occurred to their parents. His friends taunted him, jealous that he valued her counsel over theirs . . . What kind of a man had a woman for a best friend? Chrys had more common sense than any of them; if she'd been a man, she would have been a force to be reckoned with at court, and she would still have been his closest friend.

When Callum was sent to quell the Mourish queen's rebellion at Gagarnoth, Chryslantha could not accept that he might die before she knew his love. The night before he embarked, she gave him her maidenhood, knowing full well the risks that it entailed. Callum had known women before Chryslantha, but it was different for men . . . they were expected to start young and be worldly in these matters. But had Callum changed his mind about marrying her she would have been scandalized—even if he died on the mission, her reputation would have suffered. Her father's enemies would paint her as soiled and wanton. Because she had brothers to inherit the bulk of her father's titles and lands, only families of lesser repute would have offered their sons for a union and they would leverage her shame to increase her dowry. Many poems had been written about the virtues of chastity—virginity was worth a woman's weight in gold.

Chrys gave Callum the silk garter she had worn while they made love, and knotted a small braid of her golden hair to it. *I'll try especially hard not to die,* Cal had promised her, clutching the fetish as though it were worth more than all the jewels in the kingdom. For only in death did Cal imagine his life would not be spent with his beloved. He did not anticipate the consequences of a transuniversal expedition, skewed time lines, and incompetent wizards. Some impediments were too powerful for ordinary human love. And yet, he'd found love again. Was his bond with Catherine as fragile? The thought of losing Cat filled Cal with as much dread as confronting Chryslantha with the news of his marriage. He pulled the SUV into the town clerk's parking lot with a mind in turmoil.

"You kids stay here and practice," Cal told his sorcerers. "We'll check this out."

The town hall was an old wooden firetrap, and also served as post office, court, and records office.

"At least it's not made out of pink bricks like that other post office," Cat said.

"We're lucky this place hasn't burned down yet," Cal responded.

The floorboards creaked under Callum's weight, but not so much under his petite wife. There was a hint of mold mingled with old paper and dust in the air—the type of place you expected to find a long-lost manuscript from some long-dead, but brilliant, writer. A tired wooden counter barred admittance to the small office area behind it. A man in a white short-sleeved shirt, square buzz haircut, and about fifty extra pounds sat at the rear desk reading the morning paper. The woman was in her early forties with a bobbed hairstyle. Her name tag read *Gloria Hauer*.

"Can I help you folks?" she asked.

Callum flashed his NYPD badge. "I was wondering if I could look at your police records from about thirteen years ago?" Callum unfolded a piece of paper from his pocket. It was a printout of a short newspaper blurb that Cat had found online about an accident involving Galen and Linnea Ashe. The newspaper had long ago shuttered its office, a victim of the Internet era. "Is this the jurisdiction that responded to this incident?"

The woman looked at the paper blandly. "Nope. This was in Wassaic. Sorry."

The man at the desk put down his paper and walked up to the front desk. His square puffy face, black horn-rimmed glasses, and pocket protector gave him the appearance of a NASA employee from the early 1960s. His tag said *Hank Meier*. He looked at the printout. "Well I'll be darned, Glory. Yeah, this was us—there was another feller in here the other day asking about the same incident. Why so much interest in a decade-old pair of roadkills?"

"I can't talk about the case," Callum said. A sinking feeling nestled in his gut. "What other fellow?"

Gloria checked her watch. "You take this, Hank," she said. "I have to get to the bank before they close." She grabbed her coat from the hook and left.

Hank said, "Some private gumshoe from the city. Wore a trench coat like Bogart, if you can believe it. He looked like hell. I guess those types have to work through the flu. Thank God for paid sick days," he said knocking the wooden counter. "But I'll tell you what I told him. The cops that worked that night are either retired in Florida or dead. Only thing we have is the file."

"Can we see your file?" Cat asked.

Hank escorted them back to a desk and left to retrieve the file. He returned, shortly, perplexed.

"I can't find it," he said. "I know I put it back."

Cal bit his inner cheek—a habit he'd given up in his new, calmer life here that had reinstated itself with the return of his memories. Every time they caught a break, something shoved them back a step. He must have put on quite the expression because Hank then said, "Don't have a cow. We're in the process of updating all our records onto the computer. That one wasn't scheduled for scanning yet, but since I had it out anyway, I did it. All the documents are in here," he said tapping the monitor.

Hank opened the file and offered them some coffee and Danishes. Cal scrolled through the documentation. It was all there. On a dark, stormy October night, Galen and Linnea were killed instantly when their car hit a tractor-trailer head on. They were driving south on Route 22. They had stopped at a local diner, where an employee named Mitch Sweeny gave a statement about talking to the couple just before the accident. The authorities could find no history for the man and woman, no point of origin for their journey, and they were officially listed as a pair of Does. There was no mention of a child in the report.

"What's that?" Cat asked, pointing to a photocopy of a coin.

"That's a Phoenix Standard," Cal answered. He stared at the picture with a modicum of awe.

"Cal?" Cat nudged.

"It's our money," he said. "All the kingdoms use the Standard, but mint their own sigils. The sigil of Duke Athelstan's house is the phoenix. It's almost pure gold. This is it," he said emotionally. He almost couldn't believe it. Ever since Lelani's spell deciphered his memories, Cal hadn't felt quite himself; it was like halves of himself lived in different universes, neither one of which was right on its own. The entire mission was a bad dream. Cal expected to wake up in his bed in the Bronx at any moment and realize Aandor didn't exist, there was no prince, and he was only in love with one woman who might be carrying their second child. Either that or he was a patient in a mental ward, wrapped up like a Russian newborn for his own good, and everything he knew about Aandor was an elaborate fantasy of a deluded mind.

But this was it—proof. Aandor existed in the computer records of a town clerk in upstate New York. He turned to Cat and smiled. "We've found the trail."

"Do you have these coins?" Cat shouted back at Hank.

Good question, Cal thought. He scrolled the rest of the file—nothing at all about an infant. Was it possible the prince wasn't with them the night of the accident? Galen and Linnea were the agreed-upon caretakers. Proust's spell had their identities written to be the child's parents, so even if Seth's miscasting of it overpowered them, they should still have come away thinking they were responsible for the baby.

Hank returned holding a plate of Entenmann's Danishes.

"What happened to the items from the crash?" Cat asked the clerk. "Are they in storage?"

"I don't know. I wasn't full-time back then. But I've never seen them around. Probably stolen."

"We should interview anyone that's still in the area," Cal said. "Does this Sweeny still live around here?"

"Yeah. He's up there in age, but still works at the diner. It's about a mile down the road."

The clerk who filed the report was listed on the corner of the original page: *G. Manning.* Whoever had pilfered the gold coins would not be forthcoming. That might not matter, though. Cal decided to run a hunch—he loaded Google and searched for local coin collectors.

"What are you thinking?" Cat asked.

"I'm thinking you can't buy groceries with twenty-four-karat-gold coins," Cal said. "Not exactly something you can throw into the Coinstar machine at Pathmark. And unless you absolutely have a love for obscure, yet impractical, seemingly ancient coinage, you might want to cash in on such a thing, right?"

"Right," Cat agreed.

"So whose hands would something like that eventually fall into?"

The search hit on a Web site called the Numismatist run by a collector named Nathan Dumont. A link on the site led to a blog he wrote called Exonumianiacs.

"You think he's involved?" asked Cat, not really following the thread. "There might be bigger collectors in the city, or even Hartford."

"I don't know," Cal said. "But these types, they like to share knowledge of their scores—brag and taunt. Otherwise, there's no glory in possessing something rare if no one knows you have it. Whoever took those coins thirteen years ago, it probably ended up in the hands of a guy like this. He may have brokered a deal, know the people who have the coins, or at the very least heard rumors in his circles, all of which can put us one step closer to the trail."

Cat planted a soft, wet kiss on his cheek.

"What's that for?" he said.

"So sexy when you use that brain."

"I *am* a cop," he pointed out.

She grinned. "Please, don't ruin the moment."

CHAPTER 2

SCHOOL DAZE

Seth walked to the edge of the parking lot and lit his last cigarette. He drew in deep, savoring his last rush, and exhaled a mix of smoke and winter breath. Around the clerk's building, the air was quiet and crisp with only a hint of frosty sting—peaceful as only winter could be. A mix of birch trees and pines surrounded the lot, and covered the distance to the nearby hills. The occasional squirrel or rabbit skittered over fallen logs. It reminded him of that Stallone movie, *First Blood.*

He contemplated his place in the universe, and more specifically, this mission that'd been thrust upon him. *Why him?* For the part of his life that Seth could remember, there was nothing special to set him above other men; the opposite was true. He was crude, base, common—his acts had been childish, vindictive, preemptive in the way of brats that won't be ignored and force reactions from others. But as it turned out, he was handpicked for this secret mission to protect the future of an entire kingdom. He even had a protective field cast about him, shielding him from magic.

Seth pulled down his zipper and relieved himself against a tree at the edge of the lot. Lelani approached behind him. He closed his eyes and concentrated on the sound of her steps—one, two—three, four . . . once you knew, you could push aside her illusion.

"Shall we try again?" she asked.

"Can I finish my business—in private?"

Lelani folded her arms and arched her eyebrow, broadcasting what she thought of his privacy. *Probably pee wherever you want to, just like a horse,* Seth thought. Lelani appeared to all like a typical six-foot-something gorgeous redhead, but was in fact, a four-footed centaur sorceress from another reality. Her long athletic legs were part of an elaborate illusion of light and sound she wove around herself to fit into this reality. Seth thought about male centaurs, and how they were likely hung like horses—literally. Last thing he needed was Lelani snickering over his wee human willy.

Then again, that was not her style. Lelani was all business. She had been on him all morning, parading a pile of salt under his nose, unwavering in her pursuit to squeeze magic out of his . . . What did one squeeze magic out of? The brain, the heart, the gonads? Wherever it came from, his reservoir was as dry as a ninety-year-old's cooch. He shook, tucked, and zipped and took another drag from his cigarette.

It wasn't as though Seth wasn't interested in learning about magic. Who wouldn't want the ability to do real magic? Then he'd never again fear people like Carmine, who had goombahs combing the five boroughs of New York for his kneecaps. But Seth felt boxed in—almost suffocated—and unable to tap into the vast reserves of power Lelani kept telling him were out there in the world. It was like someone had wrapped him in magic-blocking cellophane, and he'd only just begun to notice because his new awareness of real magic emphasized how cut off he was. Seth wondered if it had anything to do with the spell of protection around himself—something he had nothing to do with. In how many ways had it affected his life?

"What's the deal with this protective shield?" he asked her.

"It's complex," she said. "Really, several spells working in unison. One is a molecular lock. It prevents you from transforming into another type of creature, like a rat or a dog."

Interesting choice of examples, Seth thought. Why not a horse or an eagle? Was he so bad, he didn't even warrant "noble" animals in an example?

"Another spell prevents an outside mind from bedding upon your own, able to see through your eyes, controlling you like a puppet," Lelani continued. "And a myriad of other spells to stop poisons and such."

"You said this was heavy mojo."

"If 'heavy mojo' means advanced wizardry, then yes. The enchantments have to be harmonically synchronized."

"Why have I got one?"

"Excellent question. There are few wizards I know of who could cast this type of enchantment. It's expensive. This lends credence to my theory of your parentage. In Aandor, rulers are born with a natural resistance to magic. They pass this trait on to their children, in some cases, by breeding with members of their extended families. Once in a while you end up with a child as susceptible to magic as any commoner. Sometimes the 'ruler' isn't the true father. That's why the court's wizard and cleric administer a test during the child's infancy. The result for a trueborn is only a slight burn on the skin shaped into the sigil of the ruling house. The prince's sigil is a phoenix."

"And if a kid's not legitimate?"

"Its fate is sealed. The test would kill it. Born of a commoner mother, you likely did not inherit the resistance. It's not unheard of for the very wealthy to purchase such protections—fathers love their bastards, too."

Seth didn't feel like a duke's bastard. He certainly never felt loved. Could the shield be the reason Seth spent a lifetime wallowing in loneliness? Is love a type of magic that Seth was physically cut off from?

Lelani poured some salt into her hand and held it before him—like she was waiting to rub it into the open wound that was his life.

"You're obsessed with this salt thing," he said.

"Fundamental molecular redistribution," Lelani said.

"I feel like I'm trying to push a boulder up a hill with one hand."

"It is the most rudimentary magic," she said. "A spell's complexity equals the time and effort put into casting it. This is why wizards want to choose the time and place of their battles. A wizard on the run is at a disadvantage. Big spells require focus, time to conceive of the effect in the mind's eye, to build energy, allow transformations—some have elaborate hand movements and chants. But we always start learning with the simplest spell.

"Few bonds are as precarious as the one that holds together sodium and chloride. If you cannot accomplish this, there is no hope for anything else. We call it 'threading the needle.'"

"I call it 'annoying the Seth.'"

"The initial step is the hardest part of premeditated magic," Lelani said. "Confidence is key, but so is state of mind and inner calm. You have to invite the magic, let it settle in you. Anxiety, insecurity, anger, fear, depression, even too much elation, muddles your resonance, repels the energy."

"All wizards are happy wizards," Seth said sardonically. "What if you stub your toe . . . uh . . . hoof and make a pouty face?"

"After a wizard masters the simplest spells, he or she attains the ability to cast regardless of emotional state. Most with a proclivity toward magic never evolve to the premeditative level. Half of Magnus's academy applicants wash out."

"How do evil wizards get past the inner peace part?" Seth asked.

"Evil wizards don't believe they are evil, Seth. They are at peace with their natures and feel justified in their actions. This exercise is not a judgment of your character. You are trying to invite this energy into you—to accept you as a station on its journey through the multiverse." She held a pile of salt before him. "Concentrate."

Seth attempted to pull apart the elements that comprised it. In his hand, Seth couldn't yet draw magic from the environment, so he tried to pull it from a palm-sized smooth stone talisman Lelani had given him. He chanted the words. The salt refused to budge.

Seth couldn't focus to save his life. Concentration had never been one of his assets even in the best of times, but now, he wrestled with anger, sadness, and fear while harangued into learning one of the universe's greatest arts. Old Ben Reyes kept popping into his head. Ben died saving his wife from a pack of gnolls because of the trouble they had brought to his door—the same trouble that still threatened them and the life of a young boy somewhere. The things Seth had seen in the past few days challenged the laws of reality. Now he was thrust into the role of a reality bender himself. As usual, the universe was not cooperating. But it was more than that—he had not cooperated with the universe for years, acting out in ways he knew were wrong deep down in his bones. Seth was always in pursuit of the easy buck. He owed money to a lot of friends, ruined the reputations of women who were naïve enough to trust him—abandoned girlfriends when they needed him most . . .

The mistakes of his former life piled together into a tsunami—a merciless wall of past regret set to fall upon his remaining days. "How am I supposed to achieve inner peace?" he whispered.

"What?" she asked.

"There's no calm in me," he said, louder. "I'm anxious—a jumble of regret. I've been angry for so long, I've no idea how to turn it off. Now, I have to fight a psychotic sorcerer obsessed with killing us. Except I can't turn salt into sodium and chloride, and *that's* the easiest spell in the universe, apparently." Seth was hyperventilating. He closed his eyes and tried to control it. The cigarette had lost its allure, so he flicked it into a snowdrift. Thirteen years of his life spent ignorant, exploiting others as punishment for his crappy existence. The rude awakening that he caused all that misery to himself and others put a crick in his neck no less painful than if someone had jammed a chopstick in there. Now his future depended on achieving inner peace. This was a task to be measured in months, not days. When would he find time to untangle the mess? The present situation was so desperate. It was a catch-22.

"You are in the throes of imaginings that have no bearing on this lesson," Lelani said, frustrated with him.

"No duh," Seth quipped. Was she trying to be his friend? Unlike Callum MacDonnell, Lelani at least acknowledged Seth's desire to do better.

"You have no wife, no children, no job," Lelani said, framing his life's situation in a way that suggested fewer distractions were to his advantage. It had the opposite effect. It only confirmed that at twenty-six years of age he was beholden to no one when he should have been obliged to many, and they to him. "No true obligations here outside of your service to the duke," she continued.

Correcting Lelani's misread of his situation was pointless. He couldn't stand to give her more reasons to think badly of him. The patterns on a nearby birch became infinitely more interesting than Lelani's lecture at that moment.

"You should not let the actions of your unfortunate past influence inactions toward an unfortunate future," Lelani warned. "We need every advantage. Unfortunately, you are one of them." She did not mean this as a rebuke. Seth saw in her eyes an understanding of the pressure he was under. Lelani would lift this burden if she could. Her risks, her struggle to travel across dimensions and awaken the guardians to the dangers they faced only strengthened Seth's resolve.

"Are you even sure I can do this?" he asked.

"I saw you do it when you were twelve."

He stared at the salt. Seth said the words again and tried to separate them with a thought. Still nothing. "Shit!" He threw the salt on the asphalt. "There isn't any mojo here! Only way to separate this is with a glass of water."

Lelani waved her hand over the salt and the grains sprang from the ground. She stirred them into a white granular circle in the air on the tip of her finger. When she pointed up, the salt shot up in a white line and then dived into a pile in her hand. "If you pull these elements apart, I will buy you a pack of cigarettes," she promised, resorting to the carrot-and-stick approach.

It occurred to him he'd never seen sodium or chloride. "What's the end result supposed look like?" he asked.

Lelani gazed at the salt and the pile separated into a pale yellow-green gas and some silvery metal dust.

"That," she said. "Chloride is an ion form of chlorine."

"An ion form of . . . I didn't like high school the first time I went," Seth complained. "Isn't magic about waving wands and silly phrases?"

He picked up a stick and waved it at a tree. "Expelliarmus!" he shouted. Nothing. A cold wind continued to blow; a squirrel looked at them and, deciding they were of no importance, skittered up a tree.

"I am not familiar with that spell," the centaur said. "What was your intent?"

"To avoid retaking organic chemistry. Magic looks easy when you do it. You just say some words, wave your hands."

"Magic relies on communication," Lelani admitted, picking up on Seth's track. "Wait here a moment."

She went to the Explorer and pulled a six-foot-long branch from a bundled stack on the roof. Seth wondered why she'd tied them there in the first place. She tossed it to him.

"Many wizards use staves to focus their spells," she explained. "Staves, wands, amulets, rings, and so forth are walking aids or decorative accessories for the best of wizards, and a crutch for the rest. You are hopelessly lame and, I believe, in desperate need of one."

"Did we stop at Wizards R Us?"

"These branches are from Rosencrantz. Wizard trees are very rare, and staves made of their wood even rarer. Magic from the lay lines has seeped into the wood over the years. It will not be difficult to draw magic into the finished staff from far-off sources."

The branch was hardly straight, still had bark on it, and was pretty thick and heavy in his hands. "Really?"

"You must whittle your staff from that branch," said Lelani. "And take care to save the shavings—they can be used for potions and other enchantments."

"I don't know diddly squat about whittling."

"I'll teach you my technique," Lelani said. "But your bond to the staff is determined by your mind-set as you craft it. Put some thought into what you want to accomplish. I'll help you with the runes when it's ready."

"Runes? I have to learn a foreign language, too?"

"Magic *is* language, Seth—verbal and nonverbal, thought, knowledge, and will merged into a single action. When we cast a spell, we're communicating with magical energy to produce an effect—rearrange molecules, speed or slow kinetic movement to change temperature, and in more advanced stages, altering the smallest particles of creation—even brain neurons that influence the mind. The more powerful the wizard, the smaller the particle he can manipulate. But you have to have a fundamental understanding of a thing, both in what it is and what you intend to create. And, most importantly, we are *asking* the energy to undertake this change."

"What if the hocus pocus says no?"

"The things a caster asks are in harmony with the energy's nature," Lelani instructed. "Just as a bee wants to make honey, the energy *wants* to affect things. It is oblivious to the ramifications of those changes at our level of understanding. If a wizard turned you into a mouse, the magical energy he used to rearrange you is not aware that you think being a mouse is inferior to being a man. It does not realize that it is changing you from the version of yourself that you hold superior. The magic was asked, in the proper cipher and form, to rearrange you in a particular way, and its nature is to do that."

"Does the energy think?" he asked.

Lelani smiled. Was this what geeked her out?

"The sentience of magical energy is a matter of great debate,"

Lelani said. "Scholars, sorcerers, and clerics have had passionate arguments—even coming to blows. Some clerics believe it is the lifeblood of the gods coursing through all creation. They become incensed when wizards use the power outside of what is prescribed in their dogma. The true source of the energy is a mystery."

"So Dorn is using the same magic we are . . . the intent is what makes magic dark, not the spell itself?"

"Dark?" she queried. Her eyes thinned and settled on his contemplatively.

"You know . . . black magic. Casting spells for devils, turning people into mice to feed their pythons."

"Seth, that is not dark magic. I told you, the energies pass no judgments on the spell caster's intent. Such spells, constructed to convey a sense of evil or foreboding, serve really to fuel the caster's self-image. The magic doesn't care if the caster prefers to wear black robes instead of white, spiderwebs over roses, or pentagrams to circles. All that is required is access and communication."

"But your reaction just now . . . ?"

"Dark magic is a perversion—banned in Aandor. It forces the energy to act against its own well-being. After you render a spell, the energy you used continues through the multiverse in some form or another. Dark magic, however, wrests control of the energy, captures it, or destroys it." She turned serious, solemn. "You do not want to provoke or harm the magic . . . it could curse you."

Cat and Cal emerged from the clerk's office in better spirits than they went in. "I'll have you know there are plenty of brilliant police officers," he overheard Callum say to his wife.

"Mostly on television," Cat responded.

"Where to now?" asked Seth.

"To talk to a man at a diner," said the cop.

CHAPTER 3

THE TIPPING POINT

1

The examining room conveyed to Dorn a cold, antiseptic feeling of death. Its bright red hazardous materials box blared radiantly against the room's mint hue. Posters under the fluorescent lights illustrated unique maladies—a travel advertisement warned of inoculations to stave off the dangers in Africa. This lord of Farrenheil, nephew to the archduke, could not remember a more humbling experience—even in the earliest days of his youth, when his nascent susceptibility to magic subjected him to his family's contempt. Dorn was cognizant of their distrust of his abilities. Magic was simply not the attribute of a prince. Sitting naked in a paper gown, it was clear there was nothing to be done about his ailing health on this earth. His only chance to live was to return to Aandor, and the only way to return to Aandor was victorious. *Victorious or not at all*, were his aunt's exact words. He had to complete his mission. He had to murder his cousin, the prince.

The debilitating migraines and voices plagued him more each day. So desperate was he to stay this coming tide, he had turned to the quacks and charlatans of this universe for a local remedy. His servants pretended not to notice, but his periods of incapacitation and irrationality were growing more frequent. *How long can a man plagued with madness retain their loyalty?*

Medical implements lay before him on the counter. If he thrust the scalpel into his temple, would it stay the pain, cut out the voices?

No inoculation would have prepared Dorn for this trip. That his group was ill prepared was an understatement. Who knew the court mage of Aandor, Magnus Proust, had discovered a bridge between universes? Dorn often remarked that Proust's reputation was bloated—the endless accolades simply enthused hyperbole. And yet Proust, with his power and great knowledge, was impotent against Farrenheil's invasion. *Invasion?* It was an onslaught. They took the capital and most of the kingdom in a single day. This last trick of sending the prince across universes was the final desperate gasp of an extinct house.

Dorn offered a small fortune to have his examination and blood work rushed. But here he waited yet again. The doctor had skittered off to tend other patients and left him alone to rot. In Farrenheil, Dr. Korensteen's family would cower for their lives until he successfully healed a member of the archduke's family. Dorn toyed with the idea of converting the doctor into a minion instead of paying the promised exorbitant fee.

Not to waste a period of clarity, the bored lord of Farrenheil retrieved his iPad and opened a file with the scanned parchments of forbidden magicks that he'd stolen during the invasion. These sorceries had been sealed and guarded for centuries in a vault on the border of Aandor and Nurvenheim. All requests to study the scrolls had been turned down—but war favored the opportunist. Chaos made an excellent cover, circumventing powers that might have been brought to bear protecting the scrolls. Many sorcerers had died defending their citadel. Dorn did not see wizardry as a brotherhood—*the fewer, the better.* True magic users were rare; one in ten thousand had any sensitivity to magical energies. Of them, maybe one in a thousand could willfully wield the energy.

One scroll contained a spell that could suck an entire city into a singularity no larger than a grape seed. A black snake on a scarlet, hexagon-shaped field was stamped in the corner of that parchment; all the scrolls had this mark—the symbol for forbidden knowledge.

Like most of these spells, it required a radioactive element. Destructive weapons existed in this reality through scientific means, but in Aandor, where men still fought wars by hacking at each other with swords and spears, such a spell would be interpreted as an act of the gods.

You are a god, said the voice. He ignored it. Talking only encouraged madness.

Dorn read over the singularity spell and wondered what the point of war was if there were no spoils. Sword fighting was messier and less efficient, but one could not rape or enslave cinders or plunder a singularity. One could not farm a field burned to ashes.

You would be the farmer of death . . . your crop a bountiful row of corpses.

The other spells were just as impressive. A few could be utilized to hunt down the prince. They would not be necessary, though. His indentured detective, Colby Dretch, was hot on the lad's trail. Using forbidden spells at this point was like swatting a fly with a trebuchet. These spells would have to wait until they returned to Aandor. Perhaps he would wipe out that postage-stamp kingdom of Jura—always cowering behind Aandor's skirt. A miscreant breed of ass kissers if he'd ever met any.

He opened the locket with the image of Lara. She was only a few years older than him, and could have chosen any lover in the Twelve Kingdoms. Their affair was the worst kept secret, made scandalous only by the fact that she was his mother's half-sister. But her reputation as a vengeful witch kept their detractors' tongues in check. Dorn suspected she had enchanted him, heightening his passions for her. It was ironic that those best able to utilize sorcery were also most susceptible to it. Resistance to magic was the sole commonality among the rulers of the Twelve Kingdoms. It was why Dorn could never rule.

He wondered about the love spell that Lara may or may not have cast on him. These spells were complex, dangerous enchantments and difficult to remove. The enchanted has no desire to remove the spell even when he or she is aware they'd been afflicted. It was like a drug. Intense longing came over the subject when parted from the object of the spell. Dorn had not been prepared to be away from Lara for so long when he crossed over into this universe. He wondered if this was the root of the migraines, the dementia that had grown increasingly worse since arriving on this dimensional plane. "I'll be home soon," he told his aunt's portrait.

The doctor walked in without announcing himself. It irritated Dorn to no end. This world excelled at rebukes, and all seemingly set against Dorn's superiority. "Have you diagnosed the cause of my headaches?" he asked bluntly.

"The causes of many migraines are a mystery," the doctor said, sidestepping the question. "May I call you Rudolf?"

Another slap; he was required to fill in his full name on the office indemnity form. "No," said Dorn flatly. The doctor continued regardless.

"You're exhibiting symptoms similar to decompression sickness, otherwise known as the bends. Do you scuba?"

"No," Dorn said.

"It can also occur during travel when an aircraft isn't properly pressurized. Have you traveled recently?"

"Yes," Dorn said. *Perhaps it's not the love spell after all.* "But, my companions do not share my symptoms."

"You could simply be more susceptible than other people."

The doctor was a never-ending line of insults, and he had graduated from rude manners to direct affront; implying that Dorn's ragtag band of half-breeds and peasant bastards were better suited to survivability than a member of the house of Farrenheil. Dorn couldn't see himself suffering this man's presence too much longer . . . his usefulness was becoming marginal at best. "And what, pray tell, is to be done?" Dorn asked.

"Like I said, you show *similar* traits to people suffering from this.

Your blood work came back negative for dissolved gasses. There are bubbles forming in your blood though. I don't know what's causing it. It does not seem to be pressure related, you have no joint pain or breathing problems despite the staggers, so I don't think a hyperbaric chamber would do much good. Frankly, I am stumped."

"Is there anything you can do for the migraines while I search for a more competent physician?" Dorn said, pondering the doctor's imminent demise.

The doctor was shocked at Dorn's directness. He pulled a prescription bottle from his lab coat pocket. "Treximet will help," he said, handing Dorn the pills. Dorn swallowed his dosage while the doctor watched, clueless that the medicine only bought him a reprieve contingent on its effectiveness.

"It should allow you to focus," Dr. Korensteen continued. "I'm also setting up an appointment with a neurological specialist at New York Presbyterian. Can I inform the neurologist that you'll be offering a similar cash deal for payment?"

Dorn agreed, but with the detective close to finding his little lost prince, he hoped to be back in Farrenheil before the appointment. The doctor left to let Dorn dress.

As Dorn put on his Armani suit, there was a knock at his door. He thought it was Korensteen again, until he realized the doctor would not seek permission to enter. "Come," said Dorn.

Oulfsan, entered—tall and thin with a fair complexion and impeccably dressed in a tuxedo of gray pinstriped trousers, white shirt with bow tie, and black long-tailed jacket. Oulfsan's outdated attire reminded Dorn how far they'd come since arriving in this reality.

They'd crossed the transference point following the prince's party expecting to find themselves somewhere outside Aandor City. It was a similar spell that allowed Farrenheil's armies to sidestep Aandor's border forts and deliver crushing blows to the capital city's support garrisons. But the transfer point Proust created actually led to another universe . . . this universe. Dorn's company had been unprepared for the differences in this reality: language, customs, currency, and so forth. They also believed they were only a few hours behind the prince, only to find it was years.

When they arrived at the transference point in upstate New York, they took refuge from the storm in a bookstore. With shelves of images and language from which to draw, Dorn thought it a stroke of good luck. He and Symian were able to concoct crude language spells from the texts and give everyone a passing knowledge of modern English. They utilized photos from the books to create new garments, but unfortunately, did not realize at the time the wide range of eras covered in all the books, and that fashions on this world evolved rapidly. Oulfsan and his fraternal twin, Krebe, searched for servants' attire and had become enamored with a book on Victorian England. The desert sorcerer K'ttan Dhourobi fancied fashions from a tome on cinema from the 1970s. Dhourobi had been killed in a duel with the centaur mage Lelani Stormbringer, and, Dorn had to admit, he was grateful not to have to suffer K'ttan's swagger or powder-blue leisure suit any longer. Any fool that lets an acolyte, and one from an inferior race at that, defeat him in open battle was too incompetent to remain in his service. The rest of his crew eventually came in line with their choices of contemporary styling. He didn't care so much about Oulfsan because he was not expected to be out in the field like the others. And yet, what was so important that the man ventured the six blocks from their suite in The Plaza hotel?

"How fare you, my lord?" Oulfsan asked.

"We shall know shortly," Dorn said, shaking the bottle of pills. "What news?"

Oulfsan fidgeted uncomfortably.

"Well?" Dorn said curtly.

"Our devoted taxi driver, Salim, has gone missing."

"Missing?" asked Dorn, incredulously. "He has no family, no green card. I hold the man's heart in a velvet sack. Where could he have gone?"

"Lhars saw him in the elevator this morning, looking more miserable than usual," Oulfsan said.

"And what of our other heartless? Are they of a mind to defect?"

"The specialist is set to his task and awaits the proper opportunity. The other, Tom, remains at the hotel. He is far less ambitious than the others and seems to be content, so long as we allow him to watch the Devils play hockey. I've never seen someone less concerned that he is missing his heart. He doesn't realize he should be more worried. He may have been mentally deficient prior to our converting him."

Dorn's sour stomach competed with his migraine for the greatest discomfort. Half of their contingent had been lost in a battle upstate two nights past. What remained were idiots, freaks, and half-breeds with only Lhars, Gunther, and Hommar his last three human soldiers from Farrenheil. They were loyal and trustworthy, if not particularly bright. A new migraine struggled against the medicine he just took. He rubbed his temples and hoped Korensteen's treatment would kick in. "Our heartless minions are dropping like flies," he pointed out.

"Perhaps, my lord, if we restored one minion to health, Tom perhaps, it might inspire the more able servants," Oulfsan said.

Dorn laughed. Oulfsan wasn't seeing the humor.

"Creating a minion is an act of sorcery," Dorn said. "Restoring one to full life is an act of divinity. We can *return* their hearts, but only a cleric can return their breath. Do you see any clerics in our party?"

"Then we . . ."

"Lied," Dorn said. "Hope is the chain that binds our thralls to their purpose. Speaking of which, what news of our fair detective?"

"Krebe has followed him to Baltimore. The boy resides in a suburb, but . . . there was some type of incident at the home. The police have sealed the scene and he could not get closer to investigate."

Another stab of pain cut across Dorn's stomach. If the migraines didn't kill him, the ulcer surely would. "What type of action?" he asked.

"It looks as though the prince was involved in a murder, and . . . has fled."

With no warning, Dorn backhanded Oulfsan across the cheek. The man broke his fall clutching the edge of the examining table. He was shocked, frightened. Dorn's agitation accumulated in his temple, feeding his migraine.

"You waited to tell me this?" Dorn said. Another wave of pain restrained his rage. He backed off cradling his forehead.

"I-I w-was concerned a-a-about your health, my lord," Oulfsan stammered.

"My health? My health will improve when I am attended by true healers and not these pill mongers! *Where* is the detective?"

"He searches for the boy still. His car is parked at the motel where he took a room. He has not called in over a day."

"In other words, we've lost him as well."

"My lord, he found the prince once," Oulfsan pointed out.

Dretch was indeed a godsend. His detective business in ruins, under indictment, desperate, Dorn could not have found a more valuable asset at a time when they could not buy a lead on the prince for a million dollars. The man was a master sleuth.

"He found the boy's trail upstate when it was cold and no one else could," Oulfsan continued. "And unlike Tom, Dretch has a very healthy survival instinct. He has been out of communication before. His methods are—"

"DAMN HIS METHODS! Dretch is the slyest, craftiest, and most intelligent person we've encountered in this gods-forsaken universe!" Dorn never could abide by any person capable of doing anything better than he could. It vexed him to need someone so. "We should be watching him like a hawk, always!"

Dorn was of a mood to kill everybody that worked for him and start over from scratch. He'd create a thousand heartless minions and tell them only the one who brought him the prince's head would get their heart back.

Symian popped his head into the room nervously. As part of his clothing upgrade, he had ditched the trench coat, scarf, and large brimmed hat for more contemporary blue jeans, black hoodie, sneakers, and Mets cap, under which he hid his yellowish eyes. He carried a large duffel bag. "You told him?" he asked Oulfsan.

Dorn waved Symian in. Although it turned his stomach to think that a human woman once copulated with a troll, the boy's nature made it difficult to dislike him, even with his large, sharp canine incisors and disturbing yellow eyes. He was innocent of the rape that produced him, and almost as pure as his father was evil. Oddly enough, this half-breed worked hard to bring about Farrenheil's vision for the empire. Symian wanted no woman to suffer at the hands of a troll or any other creature as his mother had. The lad hated his troll half more than Dorn did.

"Salim just pulled up to the Midtown police precinct on Fifty-fourth Street," Symian said.

Everyone knew what Salim intended to do.

"Give it to me," Dorn said.

Symian reached into the bag and handed Lord Dorn a thumping velvet sack. Dorn motioned for Symian to leave. Oulfsan stood quietly in the corner staring somberly at the floor; he was a proficient killer in his own right, but his brother Krebe was the true artist at death. Salim's defection came at a good time . . . Dorn had wanted to kill something ever since he entered the waiting room three hours ago. He put the bag in a curved steel medical tray. This was the heart he had promised the detective—young and healthy with no blockage or arterial sclerosis—Colby's eyes had lit up at the prospect of living decades longer than he had any right to. In one of the drawers he found a large scalpel sealed in plastic. He unwrapped it, and without ceremony, impaled the bag with the scalpel. It lurched like a struck animal, thumping faster and causing the pan to bounce on the counter.

He stabbed at it a second time and it soon stopped moving. The velvet sack absorbed the blood. Dorn pulled the organ out and examined it—indeed pink and healthy. *At least we know the detective still lives,* he thought to himself, amused at the prospect of possibly killing the wrong man. That left him only Dretch, the specialist, and Tom. He would need to replenish his magical supplies and make more.

Dorn spotted a container for medical waste. He wrapped the dead heart in a plastic bag and stuffed it in the bottom of the container. Then he washed his hands, and handed the scalpel and the metal container to Oulfsan to clean.

Dorn was tired. As he finished dressing, his options for the next steps rolled through his thoughts. He picked up the iPad and looked again at the scans of the forbidden scrolls before putting the device to sleep. Perhaps the trebuchet approach was not unwarranted. He hated this world. He could not wait to be rid of it. What did he care what happened to it after he left?

It was time to retrench, retool, and begin preparations for an alternative approach. They needed insurance against the detective, who was the most pivotal piece in this game at the moment—too important to allow a free run. Dorn did not like that the detective vanished for periods at a time—thralls should be on a short leash. A trip to Brooklyn looked unavoidable. He would have to split up what was left of the men; Kraten to Brooklyn, Symian to collect the components for an ambitious bit of sorcery—the kind banned from Aandor for over a thousand years. Hesz will take the remaining men to Baltimore to assist Krebe and put pressure on the detective, and more importantly, retrieve from the prince's home the necessary components for the spell he wanted to cast should the worst come to pass.

A good plan, thought Dorn. He was pleased. It had been some time since his thoughts crystallized so easily. It was then he became aware of his clarity. The migraine had subsided considerably. With his ability to strategize again, he could end this task and be home in time to stave off death from this unknown malady. The doctor had bought him a fighting chance. Korensteen had earned another day.

2

Hesz looked up from his book. Symian hovered before him, reading over the top. Hesz doubted the half-troll would understand its contents right-side up, much less inverted. They were in the alley adjoining the doctor's ground floor office. Hesz, in only his stylish suit and fedora despite the chill, had found a sturdy milk crate to sit on. As alleys went, this one beside Manhattan's famed Fifth Avenue was cleaner and better kept than most of the streets of the world.

"What have you there?" Symian asked.

Hesz tilted the book to reveal the cover.

"*The Tipping Point*?" Symian said. Hesz had hoped the lad would take the gesture as a sign that he wanted to continue reading. Dorn's doctor visit afforded Hesz a generous piece of downtime.

"Does the story recount a great battle or romance? Or a quest?" Symian continued.

Hesz had some affinity for Symian, who was a mixed breed like himself and therefore a second-class citizen of the kingdoms. Unlike Hesz, though, Symian relished the comforts of Lord Dorn's service. *A master's favorite dog is still a dog at day's end,* the frost giant thought. It was beneath Hesz's dignity to beg for scraps.

Hesz was one-quarter frost giant. He stood eight feet when he didn't hunch, his arms were thick as telephone poles—when he had his custom suit fitted, the tailor's measuring tape would not reach around his chest. He tried to sit as often as he could since he resented hunching in human company; a book was often on his person.

Hesz debated with himself how much he could he share with his young companion. How much would the half-troll understand of his ideals and goals? Symian was not even aware of the extent to which Dorn's incompetence had cost them many advantages and put their lives at risk. The enemy was now aware they were being hunted. They had fought back successfully, cutting Dorn's numbers by half. Hesz checked his watch and wondered how much longer the lord of Farrenheil would be.

"You are always pensive and sulking, my big friend," Symian said. Despite Symian's shortage of worldly thoughts, the young half-troll was amiable. Hesz could see how his friend had charmed his way into Magnus Proust's academy in Aandor, despite his dark lineage.

"Have you ever wondered what happened in our universe?" Hesz said. His deep voice rumbled from the depths of his chest like a rolling black storm.

"What in particular?" asked Symian. "The war against Aandor?"

Hesz would take a risk—test where the lad's thoughts lie on the subjects dearest to his heart. "What happened that gave men dominion over all other races?"

"I have never thought of it," Symian admitted. "What does it profit me to think of past events? I look only ahead. Fortune and glory." He smiled.

"'Fortune and glory'?" Hesz repeated. "What corner of the world of men have you found where they turn a blind eye to your grayish hue and jaundiced eyes? Or to my size and jutting lower cuspids?"

"Gold is the color that matters most to men, Hesz. With enough gold before them, they are blinded by its radiance and men and maidens will see what they want to see."

The boy was daft if he believed any father would let his daughter consort with the issue of a troll rape. Even whores would shun him. The boy was annoyingly positive. His expression, Hesz realized, had betrayed his thoughts. Symian returned his best impression of mock glum, with pouty lips and frown.

"You are in a foul mood today, Hesz—which is to say, you are completely yourself. I will humor your diatribe." He smiled. "Tell me of the sins of men."

Hesz looked up and down the alley to confirm their privacy. "Man has drawn lines on a map and created kingdoms to rule with banners of griffons, krakens, phoenixes, and so on," he said. "Within these lines on their maps are centaur villages, dwarv mines, troll hives, gnoll camps, and so on. Who gave the humans leave to draw these lines and say to all others that they exist within *their* kingdoms?"

"Most races pay no heed to the maps of men, Hesz. And men also draw on their small maps those places where they fear to tread . . . where they know better than to push their luck."

"Those places are fewer in number each year, my young friend. The kingdoms of men should be abolished, and only the old boundaries observed."

"You talk treason," Symian whispered. He looked around nervously.

"Ah . . . so much for your interest in my lecture," Hesz said and returned to his book.

"No, pray, do continue, Hesz. I would know more of the thoughts that keep you perpetually foul of temper."

Hesz folded the corner of his page and closed the book. He needed Symian's friendship for his own purposes. "The lords of Aandor, with their squabbling, do not want us to talk of such things because they wish us to believe their rule is absolute," he said. "But it had not always been so. Tell me, in a battle between a centaur and an unarmored man, who would be the victor?"

"I would wager on the centaur," Symian said. "I would wager the centaur even if the man were armored."

"Agreed. And between a man and a frost giant?"

"The giant, of course."

"Of course," Hesz repeated. "And a gnoll?"

"What is your point, Hesz?"

"Man is a fragile creature—glass and sticks held together by twine and spit."

"And yet they rule?"

"And yet, they rule," Hesz pointed out, his index finger aimed upward as though the inference were marked in the sky above them. Symian's comment pleased him. The lad had a good mind. Hesz pointed to alley door that led to the doctor's office and said, simply, "Wizards."

"Yes," Symian said. "Better to be with them than against them. Only a soon-to-be-dead fool goes into battle against a wizard." Hesz noted that Symian did not include himself among that group, though he was quite proficient at magic in his own right.

"But it was not always so," said the frost giant. "I have read the histories in various libraries of the masters I've served—long ago, man did not wield magic. Man was equal to, or more accurately, *inferior* to the other races of our world. The giants of Nurvenheim have tales of the days when they would enter a human settlement at will and take what food they wanted. They gnawed on the bones of men in the dead of winter when there was naught else to eat. Before wizardry, humans lived behind wooden walls in fear of everything. And then, about six thousand years ago, all changed. Why?"

Symian scratched his head. "I can barely conceive of six years ago and you ask me to ponder six thousand. Does this tome have the answer?"

"This tome speaks of thresholds—of epidemics and rapid change. For what is man's rise in our world if not an epidemic—a disease? And what changed once, might yet change again."

Symian looked nervously again at the doctor's back door. "Why do you serve Farrenheil?" he asked. "Your heart is so clearly set against the world of men—and yet, they, more than any other kingdom, have wronged those who were different from men."

"They are Aandor's enemy," Hesz stated. "Aandor is a wretched nation that placed its hand over the world. It forces the rule of Man's law upon all other kingdoms. It deigns to offer equality to its betters," Hesz said. "It is no gift at all, for how can you change those into something they already are? How does one offer what he does not possess? Think of the arrogance. Magic allowed the old world order to succumb to the age of men?" He waved *The Tipping Point* before Symian. "What will turn it back is another epidemic."

"Or a revolution," said Symian.

"Aye."

Symian was quiet.

Hesz was never quite sure how much of his beliefs he should divulge. He had no love of Farrenheil's cause either, but war created opportunities, and when the nations of men attempted to destroy each other, they were all left weaker for it. Farrenheil was a stick with which to beat a dog . . . it was a means to an end for a larger plan, though even Hesz did not yet know its design. It might well be that Hesz would live and die without effecting any real change, but chaos and mayhem among the kingdoms served his desires nevertheless. Killing the boy prince would add years of anarchy and infighting.

"You are a very odd giant," Symian said. "Most live for their bloodlust—battle and flesh. You devour books and speak of history like a scholar."

Everyone expected Hesz to be the lumbering fool, ready for a brawl, even those closest to him. With a thick low brow, large jaw, and jutting cuspids, almost vestigial tusks really, protruding from his thick rubbery lower lip, everyone assumed he was stupid—a natural bully, vying for an opportunity to smash and grind bones.

Hesz's grandmother, Gerda, was human—the daughter of landed gentry in northern Farrenheil and a remarkably tall woman. On the journey to her wedding, highwaymen attacked her party, killing every one else and kidnapping her. She was passed among the raiders for pleasure. Because of her resistance to entertain and her height, they dubbed her "Frosty Giant," claiming that a woman beyond six feet must have some giant ancestry. When they grew bored of Gerda, the raiders threw her, naked, into a cage with an actual frost giant that they kept for pit fights and wagering. As tall as she was, she was no true companion for an actual mountain giant. The one in the cage was rumored to be thirteen feet tall, but that did not prevent it from forcing his pleasure on her. When Gerda gave birth, it was no mystery whose seed had taken root; Hesz's mother, Ylva, arrived into the world already the size of a three-year-old, with a downy coat of blond fur. She shattered her mother's hips in the birthing, killing her.

The highwaymen, in an uncharacteristic act of guilt or mercy left the baby on its grandparents' doorstep. But Gerda's parents wanted nothing to do with this abomination and gave her to the Sweet Sisters to raise. Ylva had a frost giant's wildness in her. To say she was a tomboy would be like calling a vulture a chicken. No sane man would ever have her for a wife. When she was fifteen, already taller than a grown man, the Sweet Sisters turned Ylva over to a brothel where an endless parade of degenerates could try to feed her insatiable lust. Ylva birthed fourteen whelps, of which Hesz was eighth. All were large children, but most came out relatively human looking, more so than Hesz, and blended into the general population. Hesz was large among most races but puny among the true frost giants of Nurvenheim. He was an outsider no matter where he made his bed.

Hesz, answering the young troll's query, said, "I lack no skill in the ways of death. What I lack is knowledge. In Aandor, only the sorcerers, knights, clerics, and scholars have access to it. Dorn's spell here has given me an understanding of English, and information flows in this world like ale at a summer fair. You should avail yourself, my young friend. Learn what you do not know."

"You are perpetually unhappy," Symian said. "If knowledge leads only to dissatisfaction, then I prefer to remain happy."

Lord Dorn emerged from the doctor's office with Oulfsan in tow. He smiled, a good indication that something had been done for the debilitating migraines. A twinkle in his lordship's eye said Dorn had an idea. Hesz was about to embark on a new mission. He hoped it was to retrieve the prince. Hesz relished the notion of breaking that young neck—feeling the bones crack and splinter in his massive hands as he crushed all of the lad's notions from his skull. He was almost happy—almost—at the idea of perpetuating the war between kingdoms for another quarter century. Perhaps somewhere in that time of squabbling and distrust, Hesz could find his epidemic, and set the world of men afire.

CHAPTER 4

SHE'S GOT LEGS . . .

Daniel sat with his back against the tree sketching the calm blue lake in his pad. Like a perfect mirror, the water brought a portion of the sky's celestial peace down to earth. Colby watched from a respectful distance, allowing the boy to work and drink up the scene's tranquility. The prince's recent buzz cut bought him some anonymity . . . at least in the boy's own mind. He'd never worn his hair this short, so the police would not have any photos of him looking as he did. Unbeknownst to Daniel, the police and his father's murder were the least of his worries. The kid had more pressure on him than a submarine navigating the Marianas Trench; he just wasn't aware of it. Daniel was of hearty stock, though. Colby couldn't help but admire him.

They were staying with Colby's half-sister and her daughter in a double-wide trailer off Route 64 in Nash County. The trailer was a bit claustrophobic. Autumn had been holding on by its fingernails in North Carolina, refusing to concede to winter, which resulted in blocks of warm and cold days. Colby prayed the weather would hold out a little longer so that Daniel could spend his days outside in the woods behind the park. Otherwise, cooped up with those two crazy chicks in an aluminum box might make the boy contemplate prison as an improvement. Colby needed to act before the weather turned for good.

Most of the people Colby had come across in his life as a detective deserved prison more than the young man before him. True, Daniel killed his stepfather, a mean-spirited, drunken waste of a human being—but it had been in self-defense, after years of being a punching bag. Yet, the circus that the kid would be put through until he proved his innocence would ruin him. His own mother would have testified against him. And then there was the matter of those people in New York who wanted Daniel dead. Daniel might never get to his kangaroo trial alive.

The boy had a price on his head of which he knew nothing about. A distant cousin who was a powerful sorcerer had traversed universes to find him—a prince of a great kingdom—and end him. Colby was collateral damage in that mission. Lord Dorn had taken his heart, literally, and was keeping it hostage in a velvet bag. Colby existed in a sort of static state. He was an undead thing of some kind, unable to experience many basic pleasures all people take for granted. The price of his heart's return was Daniel.

The first few days of the transition were the worst. His body voided all its gas and solid waste. He felt oily and smelled awful. But as the days passed, he achieved some sort of equilibrium. Colby could not think of it as an improvement. He did not eat, did not drink—he was inert matter, existing like furniture at room temperature. He worried that the longer he remained in this state, the harder it would be to return him to the living . . . if Dorn intended to at all. That was the crux of this whole situation. The boy was his. All it would take is one phone call and Dorn's men would be down in North Carolina ending the whole matter. But Colby didn't trust Dorn.

Lord Dorn was an elitist sociopath who used everyone to his own ends. Once someone stopped being useful, he couldn't care less about them. The most Colby saw getting out of this current situation was the money Dorn promised, and his heart handed back to him in the thumping velvet bag. That was unacceptable. Colby wanted to live again . . . more than he ever did before.

"You're looking better," Daniel said from under the tree. The kid was a true diplomat. What he really meant to say was: *Colby, you don't smell like a reeking piss-ridden bum anymore.* Colby didn't *look* too much better. He'd changed into fresh clothes, but his skin was still sallow and the dark circles around his eyes had become permanent fixtures.

"Thanks, kid. You're looking better yourself," Colby said, referring to Daniel's bruises from his conflicts back in Maryland. "Whatever bug got me before is working its way out. I just needed a shower and a hot meal."

"You call what Beverly serves a hot meal? I swear, it tasted like vanilla Pop-Tarts smothered in Ragu."

Colby laughed. His sister was a terrible cook. It was probably how his niece stayed so thin when everyone else in this county was packing on pounds.

"How long are we staying here?" Daniel asked.

"A while. No one's going to find you in this bum-fuck trailer park off a sleepy country road. Right now you're a hot ticket in urban areas. Don't overestimate your transformation," he said, pointing to Daniel's new haircut. "But give it a week or two and there'll be dozens of new rapes and murders to take up law enforcement's time. Time's our friend—the more the cops dig into your family life, the more sympathetic they'll be."

"I'm bored out of my mind. I already filled one sketch pad. I wish I had a book. Is there a library nearby?"

Colby arched an eyebrow that told Daniel he should know better than to go waltzing into a municipal building with closed circuit security while on the lam.

"We can ask Luanne," Daniel suggested hopefully.

"I don't think my niece has ever seen the inside of a public library," Colby said. "It's not her scene. They'd probably launch a federal investigation to find out why she walked into one."

"Jeez, Colby, she's in high school. There's not one book in her room. Doesn't she have English assignments?"

"Hang tight, kiddo. I'll see what I can scrounge up. Just draw the pretty pictures for now. Won't stay this warm for long."

"It's always warm in Central America," Daniel said.

That was the kid's plan. Some Central American country with no extradition and no questions asked. Start life over. It actually wasn't a bad plan. Colby himself intended to move to Costa Rica or Chile when Lord Dorn first offered him millions to find the kid. Colby was in trouble with the law himself—under indictment for extortion, embezzlement, tax evasion, and a few other charges. It was tough finding credible reasons to keep the kid from taking off. They'd only just met. If the kid had more street smarts than book smarts, he'd be more suspicious of Colby's altruism.

Colby headed back to their temporary home. Beverly had saved enough to move into a double-wide, which for her and Luanne was definitely a step up, though to hear Luanne tell it, you'd think they were rich or something. Their trailer was on the edge of the lot, with a stretch of grass behind them that ended with trees and the lake. On the other side of them, families of four and five were crammed into single-trailer homes bunched up next to one another like drawers in a mausoleum. It wasn't Luanne's fault that she didn't know any better . . . the girl had never been to a city bigger than Raleigh, and even that barely met the qualifications of a city. In this trailer park, she was a princess and she had it good.

From the rear deck, Colby could still see Daniel under the tree. If he hovered or stayed close too often, street smarts or not, Daniel might get suspicious. Right now, the kid thought that staying was *his* idea. He wished he could chain Daniel down. They were partners on the lam. But Colby needed to leave North Carolina. He had to find the kid's people without tipping off his current "employer," and see if they had the same abilities as Dorn. There was no guarantee they were any better than Dorn's lot, but it was a chance he had to take. The devil he knew was not to be trusted.

On a bench by the glass sliding doors rested Daniel's other sketch pad. Colby thumbed through it. He didn't know a Picasso from a Dalí, but he did know the kid had talent. He sketched everything in the trailer: appliances, table settings, and Colby's sister in a smock. And then there was Luanne. There were three pictures of his niece in the pad, and they were clearly ones that the boy had worked on the longest. One full-body pose of the girl reclining while watching TV was so detailed as to be almost photographic, the way the television light highlighted the ringlets in her blond hair. Colby could even see the rivets in her Daisy Duke shorts. Careful attention had been given to the lines of her long legs and the way her breasts fell across her chest in the reclined position. Something clicked in Colby's brain. *A pretty girl and a thirteen-year-old boy with a fixation*, he thought. *Who needs chains?*

He slid open the door and entered by way of the kitchen. It was a relatively large open space with the living room adjoined on the far end in the second trailer. The living room had faux wood–paneled walls, a large beige couch in front of a high-def TV, and a big La-Z-Boy recliner against the far wall by the window. A green shag carpet covered everything except the linoleum on other side of the breakfast counter where the sink, fridge, and stove were. Beverly was getting ready to make supper. She wore a new blue Adidas tracksuit with yellow arm stripes. She'd gained a lot of weight since he last saw her fifteen years earlier, and her hair, which she wore very short, had gone entirely white. Colby paid her two hundred dollars a day to put him and the kid up, and Beverly, who never made more than seventy dollars a day after taxes, got it in her head that it included board. For the kid's sake, Colby was inclined to offer her another fifty not to cook. The counter had egg noodles, Hunt's ketchup, garlic powder, Polly-O string cheese, and Kraft shredded Parmesan cheese.

"What are you making?" he asked.

"Thought I'd whip up something ethnic," she said. "Baked ziti."

Colby's dead stomach almost woke up enough to turn over at the thought of her ziti.

"Kid said he wanted to order some Chinese tonight," Colby lied. "I'll pay."

"We ain't got Chinese in these parts," Beverly said. "Does this look like New York to you?"

"You got a barbecue place nearby?"

"Heck yeah. Doug Sauls'."

"Then he'll have a pulled pork sandwich."

"What about you?"

"Not hungry, thanks."

"Jeez Louise, Colby, you look like death warmed over. You need to eat, hon."

"You know Bev, it's bad enough that you don't realize you need actual pasta and not noodles to make baked ziti, but when you play southern hen with that drawl of yours, it's hard to believe you grew up with me in Brooklyn of all places." Colby smiled and walked out the front of the trailer.

"Noodles was all they had left," she shouted behind him. He could see her giving him the finger in the reflection on the window by the front door. There was still some Brooklyn left in the girl after all.

Luanne was on a beach chair on the front "porch" filing her nails, feet up on a wooden table that used to be a large cable spool. Her dirty blond hair was pulled back in a ponytail. If her Daisy Dukes frayed any higher, there'd be no point in her wearing the pants at all—unless it was to warm her abdomen.

Colby looked around the trailer park—he was sure any one of these neighbors would rat him or Daniel out for a buck. He wondered how long it would take for Dorn's tail to pick up the trail again. The man was a piss-poor spook, but Colby assumed they had magical means to track him, and probably a phone tap on his mobile as well. He didn't turn on his cell phone in the trailer park. He needed to go back north to Baltimore and find his shadow again, the short stout man in shabby butler's clothes with the bowler hat that reminded Colby of Jack the Ripper. That's where he'd put the battery back in the phone and place his call.

"Hey," Colby said to his niece.

Luanne popped her bubblegum and kept right on filing.

He noticed a tattoo by her ankle that read *Cody & Luanne 4EVAH* on a little banner flying over two red hearts. If she was willing to let an illiterate tattoo artist stick needles into her, what else might she be letting Cody do to her? He wondered if Bev knew—or even cared. Bev was a notorious flirt in her youth as well. Colby realized Luanne's free spirit might be just the thing to help him out of a jam.

He lifted her feet off the spool and put them down gently. Then he took a seat on it in front of her.

"What are you doing?" she said. "This is *my* house."

"And a lovely *house* it is, but I have a proposition for you."

"A what?"

"An offer. Hear me out. Where do you want to be five years from now?"

"I don't know."

"Here?"

"Heck no," she said with a dash of attitude.

Colby was tempted to say, *What, and leave all this behind?* but decided to stay on message.

"What do you make at the Walmart?" he asked. "Hundred a week?"

"About." Luanne perked up. She figured out that this was about earning some money. Colby had her attention.

"Know that kid I'm with? Daniel?"

"Mama says he's in some kinda witness protection. I thought the cops put people up in hotels for that."

"They do, but this is a very special case. Not quite as official, but just as serious. Point is, I'm his protector. But I need to be in two places at the same time. I have to go north and follow up on some elements of the case. He's okay here; no one's going to find him. But I can't take him, and I can't have him leaving here on his own. He's antsy, like all boys are."

It took a moment for Luanne to process what her uncle had said.

"So what do you want me to do?"

"First thing . . . be nice. Second . . . don't let him find out I put you up to making sure he sticks around. He needs to *want* to stay. Third . . . keep him away from your mom's cooking. I'll pay for meals out of my pocket."

"Well, doesn't he know he ought to stick around for his own good?" she said. "I mean, if people want to hurt him . . ."

"It's complicated."

"I don't know what you expect me to do, Uncle Cole."

Colby pulled out a roll of money—part of the operating budget Dorn had given him. Luanne was fixated on the money. She'd likely never seen so much come out of a man's pocket before.

Colby began pulling out hundred dollar bills and laying them on Luanne's thigh, starting at the frayed ends of her shorts and stopping at her knee. When one leg was covered with fifteen bills, Luanne scooped the money before a gust of wind stole it. He handed her another fifteen bills. She made a neat stack of the bills, folded it, and stuffed it into her ample bosom.

"That should get you to California or wherever you want to be five years from now that's *not here*. Keep him in this trailer park by any means necessary short of hog-tying," Colby said. "And if nothing else works, then hog-tie him."

"But what if—"

"He's thirteen," Colby cut in. "A pretty sixteen-year-old says 'boo' to him, he'll follow her like a puppy trailing snacks until he grew some sense. If Daniel's still here when I get back, there'll be another forty of these bills for you."

Luanne was trying to calculate how much that would be. Colby waited for the ding in her head when she finished. Her face beamed.

"If he's gone, however," Colby continued, "I'm taking back what's in your bra. Do you get me?"

Colby could almost hear the whirring and clicking in her young mind. The tumblers of a plan were falling into place. When she smiled, he knew that she had gotten it.

CHAPTER 5

CHILD OF A LESSER GOD

1

The reverend had spent the wee hours of the morning restless, staring into the space above his bed, reflecting upon the multitude of revelations that accompanied the return of his memories. His origins in Aandor, his temple—how would he coalesce the two belief systems, their cosmology that had dominated the two halves of his life? Would it even be possible to incorporate the past with the present? His two lives were diametrically opposed to one another, and he had never abandoned his first one willingly.

Wizards . . . there are sorcerers on this world now. This world! In Aandor, the Wizards' Council maintained order among the overly ambitious—education was available and threats were neutralized, but this world? It was defenseless and ill prepared against amoral power brokers with the ability to pervert nature at their whim—like the spell that had robbed Allyn of thirteen years of his true identity.

Quietly, Allyn left his bed before sunup, still unsure whether these new revelations were in truth a well-disguised bane. The truth in this case, contrary to setting him free, had burdened him with doubt and confusion. As so not to disturb Michelle, he dressed downstairs, pattered into the garage to get his wheelbarrow and a flashlight, and went into the woods behind his home. Each time the wheelbarrow was full, he deposited its contents behind the church, which was next door to his house. As the sun rose, he surveyed the patch of grass that had hosted many church barbecues and baptism celebrations now littered with the pickings of his treasure hunt. His next actions would be considered sacrilegious by most of his congregation. It could not be helped. He took solace in that his motivations were entirely Christian.

At about 8:00 A.M., the drapes of his kitchen window across the driveway rustled. He held his breath, hoping that Michelle or Rosemarie would not come out and ask him what he was building. His luck seemed to hold, and he continued to work until eight thirty, when Michelle's brother pulled into the driveway in his black GMC Terrain. When Theo stepped out of the SUV, the vehicle jumped up six inches. He'd been a defensive linesman for Alabama's Crimson Tide—a sweet-natured kid with massive shoulders and arms. Allyn chuckled, suddenly comprehending Theo's college nickname—"The Mountain That Rides." It supposedly came from a popular novel.

Despite the cool air, Allyn's undershirt was moist. It stuck to his skin—a clammy adhesion made tolerable by the honest labor that produced it. He wiped his brow with a handkerchief to keep the sweat from his eyes, and resumed working as Michelle, Theo, and Rosemarie approached.

"Allyn, should you be exerting yourself so soon after your . . . episode?" Michelle asked.

"Episode" was what the girls decided to call the event from the previous night, since neither could agree on what it actually was. Michelle thought it was a stroke. Rosemarie insisted it was an epileptic seizure, because they had just studied how to identify one in her health studies class and it matched the symptoms she had looked up on WebMD. The janitor insisted it was bad pork. None of them would ever guess the right of it—not in a million years.

"What are you doing, Daddy?" asked Allyn's daughter.

Allyn surveyed his work, a group of stones about two feet high, standing on end, arranged in concentric circles with an outer diameter of about fifteen feet. Outside the circle was a dirt bank with a concentric outer trough next to it. A heel stone stood at the end of a makeshift avenue that bridged the trough and bank a few feet away from the circle facing east. At the east edge of the trough and bank on the avenue was a slaughter stone. On the north and south ends of the dirt circle were barrows with station stones within. Within the ring he had constructed a circle of blue stone and within that a small U-shaped group of sandstone trilithons surrounding three sides of the center. At the exact center was an altar stone of high iron content, slightly bigger by comparison to the rest of the setup. Allyn didn't know how to begin to explain it to his family.

Theo offered an opinion. "It looks like that place in England," he said. "Stonehedge."

"Henge," said Allyn, grasping upon the observation. He would never question the value of an athletic scholarship again. "Yes, very good. It is a miniature henge," Allyn confirmed.

"Like in *Spinal Tap,*" Theo added.

"Why are you building a henge?" asked Rosemarie.

"To draw energy from a nearby lay line," Allyn said matter-of-factly. "It's the pattern of the stones and their elemental content, you see. The henge will draw the flow."

"The flow of what?" asked Michelle. An edge had inserted itself to her speech ever since the previous night, not just because of his episode, but because of the things he had said about gods and other universes. Allyn had explained it with the same conviction he preached the Bible on Sundays.

"This energy I'm drawing, it is the gods'—it is God's life energy circulating through creation," Allyn responded. "The power of my blessings comes from this."

Michelle's severe look warned Allyn he could not put off a long and complicated explanation for much longer. Michelle normally bore the aspect of a schoolmarm—she had good posture; her speech came near formal, but often contained a kind word or vital information; her skirts always fell below her knees, her blouse always buttoned to its apex; and though she was by no means a large woman, she was thick in that healthy way that promoted a good image for young women.

Nevertheless, Allyn returned to his work. He placed tea light candles on each stone of the sacred circle surrounding the center and a votive candle on the altar stone and lit them. On the diminutive altar sat their wooden salad bowl filled with distilled water and next to that their stainless-steel mixing bowl. In the water floated a long piece of quartz tied to a birch twig by a vine. Using a hunting knife, Allyn chipped pieces of roots, seeds, and plants into the metal bowl.

"What are those?" asked Rosemarie.

"Althaea root, angelica root, bloodroot, caraway seeds, and star anise. Remember that herb garden I tried to start a few years back? In frustration, I discarded what was left of it in the woods behind the house, and some of them took root. The star anise is from our cupboard."

Allyn used the bottom end of a steel ladle as a makeshift pestle and ground the pieces up in the bowl. He emptied a bottle of lavender oil into the bowl.

"Is that my lavender oil?" Michelle asked. "Lord, Allyn, what are you doing?"

He cut his palm with a knife and let the blood drip into the bowl. His family cringed and cried out in unison.

"Everyone, please stand back outside the trench," he asked. Using a candle, he lit the inside of the steel bowl full of roots, blood, and oil.

"Oh Jesus, Allyn!" his wife cried out. "You've lost your mind? Theo, do something."

Theo hesitated at first. When he decided to act, Allyn motioned before him, a single wave as though wiping a windshield. Theo remained outside the circle.

"Theo, do something!" Michelle repeated.

"I can't," Theo said. "Feel like I'm standing at the edge of a cliff and I can't take the next step."

Allyn pulled out a child's drawing from his coat pocket—a crayon depiction of Jesus creating bread for the five thousand. It had been one of many on the display in the church's vestibule. He read the line scrawled under the picture: *When I broke the five loaves for the five thousand, how many basketfuls of pieces did you pick up? Twelve, they replied.* The children loved that story. They always loved the magic in the Bible. The bottom of the drawing was signed *Zach Taylor, age 6*. He threw the drawing into the bowl and watched it burn.

Allyn raised his arms over the flame and the water bowl. *"By the powers of Moon, Sun, Earth, Air, Fire, and Sea what has been lost, be known to me,"* he chanted. He repeated the line—drawing the power into himself—thinking of Zach, imagining the boy's face, the sound of his voice, his laugh, and then he switched the chant to his religious order's sacred language, summoning an elaborate cadre of elemental forces. The trees bristled loudly, whooshing as the wind whipped through them. His family huddled together, anchored by Theo, as the wind whipped all around them.

Allyn felt the surge of energy and delighted in the rush he had missed for thirteen years; the divine energy's caress of his mortal form. The fire dwindled. He poured the ashen contents of the steel bowl into the wooden one, and swirled it with the ladle. Lifting the bowl he observed the quartz fetish carefully. It pointed confidently west. He turned the bowl and jostled it, and still it pointed west. Satisfied, he said to his family, "Let's go into the church."

2

"You're a what?" Rosemarie asked.

The eyes of Reverend Allyn Grey's family bore into him like a drill. Jesus watched, too, from his portrait in the corner. Allyn would tell the truth—all of it. He didn't see any other choice; strangers might begin showing up from his past, for good or for bad. He could not leave his family ignorant of the facts.

"A cleric," Allyn responded. "A prelate in the temple of Pelitos, the Golden Son."

His words rolled out softly, without the confidence of his oratory. Jesus judged him unflinchingly from His picture. Under Christ's gaze, Allyn confessed about his home in another universe and his role in bringing up a prince, a savior to his kingdom that he had sworn to protect. Allyn kept his voice low and steady, and spoke in a tone no different than if he were confessing to gambling away the church's budget. He tried not to look as much the charlatan as he felt for not being who they thought he was. Except for Michelle's occasional comment, his family remained in stunned silence.

"Oh Jesus . . . he's gone and lost his mind," Michelle said to her brother. Turning to Allyn, she asked, "Do you expect me to believe my husband, the Reverend Allyn Grey, a minister of Christ, is a pagan?" Her inflection rose on the word "pagan," the way one would say "drug dealer" or "pimp."

Theo looked uncomfortable, and not because he barely fit into his pew. Allyn was the older brother he never had. But if the reverend did not convince Michelle he was all right, she would instruct her brother to bring him to the psychiatric ward by any means necessary. Allyn continued, nevertheless.

"Thirteen years ago, I attended the naming day celebration for Prince Danel of Aandor," Allyn said. "It was a huge affair. A prince of the empire had been born, a symbol of peace and reunification for a fractured kingdom. Before the celebrations commenced, a massive army attacked our nation. Enemy soldiers appeared within the castle. It was mayhem. I ran with a group of priests through the castle looking for sanctuary from the bloodshed, but the enemy was in all places at once. Some who pretended to be part of the celebration turned out to be agents of other kingdoms. The screams of dying men came from every corner—loud crashes—my brothers were cut down. I would have been, too, if soldiers from the Dukesguarde hadn't appeared and fought them off. I followed the Dukesguarde to a room near the pantry. The grand magus, Magnus Proust, had a plan to save the prince and was thrilled to have found a cleric. He said the boy would need a spiritual protector, teacher, and healer. He asked if I would go to another realm to help raise Prince Danel away from his enemies. He used that word, 'realm,' as one would say 'we were going to the next county'—a mere wagon ride. Of course, I agreed. No sane man would have remained in that war zone."

Allyn stared at the painting of Jesus, looking much farther away than the portrait. The memory of his last moment in Aandor was crystal clear. "The wizard opened a hole in the universe," Allyn said, incredulously. "Inside a large silver picture frame a portal appeared from which no sound or light emanated, no air flowed through—I could not even describe the color . . . it was a dead place outside of time. I did not know any man had acquired the knowledge to unravel the threads of creation. No one should have such power."

"You are the rock of this church," Michelle cut in. "Are you going to throw your life away on this fantasy?" Her expression weighed on Allyn's conscience. She was a practical woman, dignified, but with a store of passion that she reserved for mourning the dead. Her argument was to be expected—his claims placed his church and his community leadership in jeopardy. Allyn knew better than to take her plea at face value. His wife was coming to grips with the reality that the man she married and bore a child for was a complete stranger to her.

He wanted to comfort her, but he could not stop now. If he did, he would never finish the story. "My task was simple," Allyn continued, "to be the boy's spiritual tutor and raise him morally and ethically to manhood."

"As a heathen," Michelle said, disgusted.

"Yes," Allyn responded. "Does that matter now, Michelle? Insofar as the prince is concerned, I have failed. I do not know where that child is . . . or if he's even still alive. I don't know if any of the guardians are alive."

"Why do you remember all this hokeypokey stuff now?" Theo asked.

"As I spoke to the congregation last night, a spell ignited my memories."

"Something certainly touched your mind," Michelle said. She grew more agitated with each explanation. He had always been her rock.

It pained Allyn to see her like this. Michelle prided herself on her demeanor—calm, thoughtful—she was always mindful of the image she presented to others. Allyn reached out and held her wrist. He closed his eyes and drew energy from the henge. Michelle's heartbeat slowed, her eyes turned serene. She became calm.

"What did you do to me?" she asked.

"It's called a *soothe*," he said. "Clerics have gifts beyond simple oratory." It was the lightest touch. Had he pressed harder with his will, he could have converted her—shown her the euphoria of the gods and rid her of all secular pains—rid her of all choice. Many in Allyn's vocation believed such an act an atrocity; Allyn was one of them. Conversion was a cleric's act of defense—the paths a person chooses to take in life are what should bring them to their faith.

Michelle pulled her hand away, as though Allyn were something rancid. She stood and left the chapel through the office door.

"What's *that* called?" Theo asked, pointing to her departure.

"That was pure Michelle," Allyn told his brother-in-law. A headache hit him right between the eyes. He squeezed the top of his nose. "She needs time to take this in. How are you doing, Rose?"

Rosemarie looked contemplative. She had inherited her mother's intellectual capacity, but at twelve years old, was far more flexible. "Is that how you fixed Mr. Jackson's gout?" she asked. "You soothed him."

"In a way," said Allyn. "Mr. Jackson's house sits on top of the lay line. Although I didn't know my true identity, I must have channeled the energy subconsciously." Allyn's proximity to the rivers of energy was an important factor. It explained why his healing was inconsistent.

"You a wizard?" she asked.

"No!" Allyn snapped, sharply.

Rosemarie and Theo's shock caused Allyn to pause. His old prejudices were back, too. Rose was simply trying to come to terms with her father's unorthodox past.

"I'm sorry, Rose," he said. "Wizards and clerics use the same energy, but wizards have no regard for the soul or the greater good. They are pure secular intellect. They unravel the secrets of the universe for their own benefit, and their spells are abominations." *And wizards are on this world,* he thought.

"So what's your job then?" Theo asked.

"A cleric works in harmony with creation," said Allyn. "We pay homage to the Makers and weave blessings of healing and protection. We exult the soul. We mark and celebrate the phases in a man's life from naming day to last rites.

"Wizards, on the other hand, create spells for the sake of creating spells. They celebrate when they've acquired more power for themselves, with no regard for how they bankrupt the culture, the ecology. They are selfish, secretive, manipulative, and destructive. The one who stole thirteen years of my life was barely a teenager—following the orders of his master."

Theo pointed to a pink-colored scar on his forearm. "I got this burn a few years back when I stumbled into a hot tractor pipe. Can you fix it?"

Allyn heard the question as it was truly meant. *Heal it, or we're going to the crazy house.* Allyn put his hand over the scar and chanted in his order's language.

"Ouch," Theo complained.

"What?" Rose asked.

"Like a lit cigar being put out on my arm," her uncle said. He bucked. "Ahhh!" he cried. But Allyn would not let go. Theo couldn't take it anymore and broke free of Allyn's grip. "What the hell," he said looking at his arm. His scar was gone—replaced by slightly reddish, but whole skin. The linebacker stared at it, mouth agape.

"Lord Jesus almighty," said Michelle, who had watched from the office door.

"More like Lord Pelitos almighty," Rosemarie corrected.

"Rosemarie, please," her father implored. The last thing he needed was to push Michelle any harder.

"What does all this mean, Daddy?" she asked. "Are we leaving the church? The universe?"

That question troubled Allyn most. He didn't have the answer. *What did it mean?* Allyn owed the prince of Aandor his allegiance. But was it more than he owed his own family or the community that had come to depend on him? The kings of Aandor expected their subjects to put their rulers' needs ahead of their own. But that was not the way of this world. It was not in keeping with Christian teachings.

And what of wizards? Who would protect this world from their games if not Allyn? Exodus 22:18 said *Thou shalt not suffer a witch to live.* In the Catholic Bible it read "sorceress" instead of "witch," but the meanings are clear in all translations; by Calvinist interpretation, Allyn was considered a witch. Was this God's plan . . . to bring him across universes to serve here, in this town, this church, with these people? Maybe that was his true calling, and the prince's escape merely the vehicle that brought him to his vocation. Or was Christ's father merely the god of one universe. If so, he genuinely was all-forgiving to accept such a flawed intruder into his house. Or perhaps the Mormon cosmology was closer to the universal truth than anyone suspected.

A loud knock came at the front of the church. Miles Jackson and

Fred Gibbons from the church board of directors walked in with Maurice Taylor, the uncle of the missing children in Uwharrie Forest.

"I hope we're not disturbing anything important," Miles said at the sight of this impromptu family meeting. Allyn lied and warmly invited them in. His family also seemed relieved at the interruption by the "real world."

"Any news?" Michelle asked regarding Maurice's niece and nephew.

"No," said Maurice. "We have thirty volunteers ready to join the police at nine thirty. There's a cold front coming in tonight bringing the temperature down to the twenties. We're out of time."

"Allyn, how you feeling?" Fred asked.

"He's tired," Michelle said before Allyn could respond. She challenged her husband to contradict her with a subtle glare. Allyn knew better. "He won't ask you himself," she continued, "but he needs some rest before resuming his ministerial duties."

Miles and Fred nodded in agreement. Maurice looked exhausted.

"Have faith," Allyn said. "I will join the search."

"The hell you will!" Michelle said.

Allyn walked the men out and reassured them he would help them search later. As he walked back down the aisle, he saw that Michelle was about to launch into a litany of objections. He put his hand up to stop her. Michelle flinched at the gesture, as though Allyn were about to do something otherworldly again. Allyn put both hands up in a nonthreatening posture and then motioned to the bowl of water, which was resting on the church altar. He picked it up and showed it to them. The quartz fetish pointed west. He jiggled the bowl and still the fetish continued to point west despite the waves.

"This crystal points toward Zachary Taylor," he said. "And it will continue to point toward him all day, which I hope will not be necessary. I will take Theo and go on this search. I will find these children, Michelle. I am still their shepherd, and nothing that you say will dissuade me from doing this."

Michelle acquiesced. He was, after all, functioning in his role as the leader of this church. Allyn saw that it brought Michelle some comfort—perhaps as sign that the man she's known and loved for twelve years was still present.

"I need for you and Rosemarie to do me a favor, though. You must locate some people for me—a couple named Galen and Linnea Ashe and a man named Callum MacDonnell."

"We ain't got no magic," said Rosemarie.

"*Have*," corrected Michelle. "We *don't have any* magic," she emphasized, keeping her husband in her sights. She was suspicious of the request.

Allyn placed a hand on Rosemarie's shoulder and smiled. "That, my child, is why God invented Google."

CHAPTER 6

NAKED AMBITION

The weather had turned cold with the setting sun, and Daniel was tired of sketching the lake. He tried to find peace in this tranquil setting, but the vision of his stepfather, Clyde, choking on his own blood from a broken table leg jutting through his gut had pushed all other thoughts from his mind. It was all that occupied his thoughts when he wasn't otherwise distracted. Even in death, Clyde would not give him peace. He told himself it wasn't his fault—he didn't want to fight his drunken stepfather, he didn't have a choice—but some part of him wasn't buying it. Daniel had wanted Clyde dead for so long, it was as though the universe heard and granted him his wish with no regard for the spirit in which he'd made that wish. *Be careful what you wish for.* The incident weighed heavily on Daniel—he hadn't had a solid night's sleep since the fight. He wondered if he ever would again.

Daniel opened the trailer's sliding back door, and the smell of tangy barbecue assaulted him. The kitchen counter, an L-shaped breakfast nook that divided the living room from the cooking area, was packed with corn bread, ribs, pulled pork, sandwich bread, coleslaw, macaroni and cheese, a tub of pickles, and jars of extra barbecue sauce. It was a feast compared with the fare Beverly had been serving. Luanne sat on the other end of the counter working on a plate piled so high with food it belied her thin figure. She wore a gray, low-cut cotton tank top that highlighted her ample cleavage.

Her mouth was covered with sauce, as were her fingers, which she kept licking clean. Daniel felt a stirring at the sight and quickly turned his attention to Beverly.

"What's the occasion?" he asked, as he shoveled food onto a plate.

"My brother the food critic," Beverly said. "We hadn't talked for fifteen years until he showed up. You'd think he'd tread more delicately than to insult my cooking." Bev's smile conveyed she knew how bad a cook she really was. "Look, hon, I have to cover for someone on late shift at the bar tonight. So you dig in and just hang tight with Luanne."

"Uh . . . okay. Where's Colby?"

"He had to run an errand up north. Said he'll be back in a day."

"An errand?" When Daniel met the man just two nights ago, he could have sworn Colby was a down-on-his-luck transient barely scraping by. Now he had out-of-town errands and enough clout with his estranged sister to have her put Daniel up while he avoided the authorities.

"You know what I know, hon . . . the man has *always* lived secretly."

Luanne finished licking her fingers and picked up the sketch pad Daniel had just brought in. She started thumbing through it, leaving light barbecue smudges on the edge of the pages. Daniel felt Luanne should know better than to do that without asking. At the same time he was flattered she'd taken an interest in his work.

Beverly grabbed her purse and coat and headed out. "There's some good stuff on the HBO tonight," she said. "New *Entourage*. You two be good, now." She shut the door behind her.

Daniel delicately lowered himself onto a counter stool; his bruised rib throbbed whenever he shifted his weight. He wolfed down the pork, some mac and cheese, and two pieces of corn bread. Luanne had gotten up to the drawing of the lake that he had just finished.

"You're good," she said. "Is that all you draw? Trees and stuff?"

Daniel looked around subtly for his other pad, but it was nowhere in sight. "Uh, yeah, pretty much," he lied. "Stuff."

Luanne gave him a smoldering look followed by a wicked smile. She slowly pulled the other sketch pad from its hiding spot on the stool next to her, the one with the drawings of her.

"I think you're a liar," she said, waving it in front of him. Daniel flushed. He had to eat his own criticism from a moment ago about asking permissions.

"I should have asked," he said. "Sorry. I do that a lot. Stealth sketching. It's the only way to draw a subject in a natural pose."

She threw him a wicked glance and opened the pad to the first sketch he did of her. It was a close-up headshot of her on the phone. The pencil lines on the tightly rendered ringlets of her blond hair were delicate. He put great detail into the reflections in her eyes, catching both the primary and secondary light sources. He softened her jaw line and made her nose 90 percent of actual size to give her the hyper feminine look of a Disney heroine.

"Dang—I don't remember sittin' still long enough for any of these," she said.

"I blocked them out while I had you in front of me—outline, contour, lighting, shading, and other details—and then tightened the details from memory later. The strokes in your hair are just pencil techniques I can do in my sleep."

"You took classes?"

"A couple. I'll take more after I leave." *Hopefully not in prison,* he thought.

"Leave?" Luanne said quizzically. She looked mildly startled at the prospect. Since he was sleeping in her room, Daniel thought she'd be happy at the prospect of getting her own bed back. "You leavin'?" she asked cautiously.

"Well, yeah. I mean not at this moment. But soon enough . . . I can't stay here."

Luanne looked at him for moment and then turned her attention back to his drawings.

"How come you ain't got no neked people?" she asked. "I thought artists always drawed neked people."

"Not in public school. At least not in Maryland."

"So you ain't had a chance?"

"Someday . . . maybe in college." What was he thinking . . . what college? Life as Daniel knew it was over. He was moving to Central America to work on a banana farm, soon as the heat on him died down.

Luanne studied the picture of her reclining on the couch. "I like the way you draw me," she said. "I look pretty."

"You are . . . uh, pretty," he said.

"Why, thank you, Danny," she said with a southern grace.

The way she called him Danny reminded him of Katie Millar. He missed Katie, his former best friend and lifelong crush. Her boyfriend—captain baseball—had assaulted her the night that Daniel ran away from home. He was up to his neck in his own troubles and still he went out to help her at the sound of her sobbing. It was there at that ballpark Daniel revealed to his stepfather he'd discovered his infidelity. And now he was on the run because of the fight that followed. Being in love sucked. It put you at a tremendous disadvantage with no guarantees that it would be worth it. And despite all that, Daniel still felt guilty he couldn't be home to help Katie cope with the aftermath of her assault—not that she'd even let him. Katie wanted to bury the crime like it never even happened. He couldn't blame her—he felt the same way about Clyde's death. Daniel hoped Katie was doing better with her own demons.

"Thanks," he said to Luanne.

Luanne left the counter and plopped herself on the big La-Z-Boy recliner in the living room. She sat there lotus style for a good minute, contemplating the kitchen . . . more specifically, Daniel in the kitchen. In one bold move, she pulled her tank top off and threw it on the floor. There she sat in her bra, having put on only a wicked smile to replace the shirt.

Daniel looked around, panicked that he'd find Beverley watching. "Uh . . . what are you doing?" he asked Luanne.

"Draw me," Luanne said.

"You serious?" Daniel couldn't begin to understand the workings of a sixteen-year-old girl's mind—nor what factors might have led to Luanne's losing hers.

"Yep," she said. "No one's ever drawed me before. Figure it's a nice way to thank you. Just this one time."

"That's very nice," Daniel said, flattered. "But, totally unnecessary." Daniel looked around again to confirm they were alone. He realized both the living room and kitchen shades were up—nothing to prevent passersby in this tightly packed park from peeking in.

Luanne reached back and unsnapped her brassiere. Her unfettered breasts popped the bra forward. She pulled the straps down and threw the bra next to her shirt. Her breasts hung freely, smooth and round, the fading tan lines of her skin perfect except for a few beauty marks. She had large pink areolas and thick flat nipples, much bigger than Daniel had seen in art books. Though mentally numb with a mixture of disbelief and excitement, Daniel managed to find his pad. Subconsciously, he placed it over his lap.

Luanne pulled down her Daisy Dukes next and threw them onto the bra and shirt. The little pile grew into its own landmark of Daniel's life, one he would remember well into his dotage. She was nearly naked—Daniel was more cognizant than ever of Luanne's hourglass figure, the type that had been in vogue in past eras before the emaciated fashions of the 1970s.

The seriousness of the situation cut through the young man's hormonal fog; Daniel was really worried now. This was a dangerous situation . . . he had nowhere else to go and didn't want to do something that might get him and Colby in trouble with Beverly. Luanne wasn't the least concerned about onlookers—maybe she just didn't think that far ahead. For all Daniel knew, she gave the neighbors a peep show every night. She sat lotus style in deep contemplation (at least for her) wearing nothing but her white cotton smiley-face-print panties with lace frills on the edges. Daniel wondered what she was debating, until she hooked her thumbs into the waistband and unfolded her legs.

"No," Daniel said, trying to stem the momentum. "You don't need to take off . . ."

Luanne whipped her panties off with a swish and tossed them on the growing tower.

"Nope!" Luanne said confidently. "Neked is *neked*. Now draw," she said, pointing fingers at him like a gunfighter.

The dark blond tuft between her legs was a bit thicker than most porn stars'. Daniel kind of liked it. On the Internet, models were trimmed or completely shaved. There was nothing phony about Luanne . . . at least not physically.

Daniel walked over to the living room window and lowered the shade, keeping his pad over his thighs the whole way. Then he brought a stool over from the kitchen counter and placed it about nine feet in front of Luanne.

"Don't you need to be closer?" Luanne asked. He moved the stool a little closer while she shifted in the La-Z-Boy, trying to find a pose she liked. She kept flashing Daniel in the process. He concentrated on clean thoughts, failing miserably. The blood was rushing out of his brain and into other areas of his body. *She expects me to concentrate?*

Luanne had no concept of what constituted a tasteful pose. She settled on a sitting crouch with her feet planted on the chair in front of her butt cheeks, and her knees under her armpits; her pink rose flashed him in all its feminine glory.

Daniel stared, transfixed by the beauty of her womanhood. No picture could ever capture the complexity of one in three dimensions.

He shook his head to break its spell and resumed breathing. He said, "Uh . . . no. Legs down, fold them over each other and flop them to your right, and put your arms on the rests. And turn your head three-quarters to your right and focus on that picture on the wall." Luanne seemed less impressed with the new pose.

It took about ten minutes for Daniel to stop seeing the naked girl and start seeing a subject. His first live nude taught him a lot about female anatomy—the way body parts hung, the way bony landmarks and creases appeared on the skin—things he only guessed at in the past, proved or contradicted. Despite this being one of the more comfortable poses a model could take, Luanne began to fidget after ten minutes.

"How much longer?" she asked.

"Five more minutes, and I'll have what I need to finish the sketch."

"Have you burned me into your memory yet?" she teased.

"That's an affirmative," he said, trying to sound as clinical as possible. The *subject* struggled to become a hot naked girl again. He didn't know where her interest was coming from. She practically ignored him for two days, making him feel more like an alley cat that peed her shoes. Daniel put extra concentration into the last bits he needed to finish the rendering.

Luanne put on her underwear and tank top and moved to the couch to watch TV. "Make some popcorn and we'll watch a movie," she said. She held out her hand in the *give me* position and said, "I want to see my picture." With her drawl it came out, "mah pik chure."

Daniel handed her the sketch pad and went to make popcorn. "Uh," he said, pointing to her Daisy Dukes.

"Puh-leeze. What *ain't* you seen already, city boy? You some sort of prude?" she asked, narrowing her eyes. Luanne studied the drawing carefully. Daniel waited, hoping she wouldn't hate it. How a portrait looked depended on what aspects the artist focused on. You could soften a hard nose, thicken a thin lip, shrink a large forehead—basically it was within the artist's power to beautify any subject with his choice of line, shadow, and light. The same subject could be rendered a hundred different ways. Luanne was already beautiful, but that didn't stop Daniel from pulling every trick in the book to give her the most beautiful rendering he knew how.

"This is great," she finally said, engrossed. Luanne studied every line twice as though she couldn't believe the drawing was of her. "Let me know if you need me to pose more," she said.

Sexy naked trailer-park girl, on demand, Daniel thought. The microwave dinged. Daniel singed his fingers taking the bag out of the oven. He stood behind the kitchen counter for a little while longer. Like the searing puffed up popcorn bag before him, the boy needed a minute cool down.

CHAPTER 7

CORPSES CORPSES EVERYWHERE, AND NOT A GHOST TO FINK

Sweeny had not come to work that morning. The diner manager said it was unusual—yet another omen that Cal trotted along an already rutted path. The girl confirmed that Sweeny had met with some colorful characters from the city a few days earlier. The blond man, who she described in great detail, fit Dorn's description. If Cal didn't catch up with the detective soon, he would find only the corpse of his prince at the end of this journey. The manager had given Cal Sweeny's home address without much fuss. The ease with which rural folks gave out personal information bothered him. Cal hoped otherwise, but it probably had cost Sweeny his life.

The sweep of the police emergency lights cut through the trees before their SUV rounded the corner to Sweeny's home. It was a dirty yellow two-bedroom ranch style with a worn-down periwinkle-blue porch; two officers were unspooling yellow tape across the front marking the crime scene. Lord Dorn was ahead at every step. Cal needed a break—something to help leapfrog him two steps ahead. Otherwise, the prince would be dead before Cal reached him.

His crew looked exhausted in the car. The last forty-eight hours had been a marathon of violence and tension. "You guys stay here," Cal said, exiting the Ford Explorer.

He approached the senior officer, a sergeant, and flashed his NYPD badge. "Looking for a missing kid," he said, matter-of-factly. "I need to interview a man named Sweeny."

"Only questions Sweeny will be answering are St. Pete's," the sergeant said.

"Natural causes?" Cal asked.

The sergeant shook his head. "Not even close."

"Mind if I look?"

"It's a bit foul. Bad luck that he had yesterday off, so no one even knew until today. My sister's the cashier at the diner and asked me to check in on him. We've lost about thirty-six hours. Might need your help if the killer took off toward the city."

Cal clipped his badge to his coat lapel and walked into the house. Everything was worn down, last decorated in the eighties, but it had dignity. A picture of Sweeny in uniform taken in front of the U.S. embassy in Saigon hung above his Purple Heart medal sitting on a bureau. Cal found the man in his bathtub. A junior officer snapped photos and took samples. Blood was splattered on the walls. A sharp cut ran across Sweeny's neck from ear to ear. The victim's mouth was filled with dried caked blood. His tongue lay on the floor next to the tub, with a numbered evidence marker next to it.

"They cut his tongue out?" Cal asked.

"*Before* they killed him, it looks like," the cop said. "He pissed off the wrong guy."

There was nothing more for Cal there. He needed to follow up on the coin collector, Nathan Dumont, a slim lead at best, but the only one left.

Twenty minutes later, the group pulled up to Dumont's home, an impeccably kept burgundy Victorian with white trim and empty flower beds on the sills, on what passed for a busy road in Dutchess County. They all got out and stretched their legs. Immediately, Cal sensed something was off. Dumont's mailbox was full. The garage door was open with the car still in the driveway. Dead leaves and snow had blown into the garage, contrary to the immaculate order of the tool racks and garbage bins and property in general. Everything about this man's home said he would not have left the doors open and car out for several windy days. The raccoons had gotten into his trash.

There were no children's or pet toys lying about and the grass behind the house was as perfect as the front lawn. The man probably lived alone. The back door was unlocked. It led into the kitchen and they entered shortly after knocking. The rank smell hit them immediately. Cal followed it to the living room where Nathan Dumont lay motionless on his black leather couch, his head twisted slightly more than normal human mechanics allowed. The man's pants were soiled with his own feces and he had begun to bloat. Cat took a whiff and clamped her hand to her mouth and nose. She ran out the backdoor gagging. She made it to the yard in time to retch in Dumont's bushes. Cal wanted to follow her out there to see if she was okay, but they were pressed for time. He gestured to Lelani to go in his stead.

"We're racking up quite a body count," Seth said, once they were alone.

Cal wished it weren't true, but what could he say? They *were* the reason the trail was being covered up. They could just follow the bodies . . . all the way to the last one, a dead teenaged boy with no clue as to why anyone would want to kill him. Cal checked the contents of Dumont's wallet. In it there were business cards for local shops and one for a Manhattan-based private detective named Dretch. Cal stared at the card a long while.

"Know the guy?" Seth asked, reading over his shoulder.

"This card's still crisp," Cal said. "Not worn, dog-eared like the others. The man that went into the Amenia clerk's office a few days ago was also a private detective. But why leave his business card with a man who was about to be murdered?"

"What do you mean?" Seth asked.

"Nothing about this detective indicates that he's sloppy. In fact, he's meticulous and creative. So why leave behind something that could tie the corpse to him."

"He's rubbing it in? Or it's a setup."

There was the weight of truth to Seth's words. Killing the prince was Dorn's primary objective, but bringing all their heads back as well would be icing on the cake. Farrenheil no doubt considered them insurgents. Feudal societies had no tolerance for rebels. And Dorn was a vindictive, scary bastard. Cal had the displeasure of meeting the man once during a diplomatic function Archduke Athelstan hosted at his country palace. One of Cal's guardsmen found a bruised serving girl running half naked from the guest apartments late in the night. Cal was still green as a company leader. He should have handled things better to protect his guardsman. The guard reported that Dorn and his aunt had lured the girl into their chambers and performed perversions she could barely recount. Both Dorn and his aunt had been barely dressed and smelled of sex and alcohol. Dorn had denied all of this and accused the guard of lying. Cal believed his guardsman and conveyed the story verbatim to his superiors, but should have let the matter rest there. Such was Farrenheil's power that the guard was transferred from his cushy palace duties to some hot dusty corner of the empire to please Dorn's uncle. The serving girl soon disappeared as well. The aristocracy protects itself.

"Shouldn't we call the cops?" Seth asked.

"Not right away. Dumont's the only piece of this puzzle I have. Look around."

Cat and Lelani returned.

"Sorry," Cat said. "The smell was . . . too much."

Cal shot his wife a concerned look that asked if it was morning sickness. She hunched her shoulders to indicate *who knows?* Cat's pregnancy test had been ruined the night Dorn's henchmen attacked their Bronx home. Cat strongly suspected she was pregnant.

The house seemed quite normal except for the dead body. It was clean and painted in warm yellows and mint greens, with hardwood floors, antique cherrywood furniture, lots of knickknacks from Crate & Barrel, Pier 1 Imports, and a healthy supply of lace doilies beneath table lamps and other tchotchkes. Cal looked in the drawers of an old-style secretary desk, but there was nothing of note in there. No one had rummaged through Dumont's belongings.

"They must have gotten what they needed from him before they killed him," he said.

"My lord," Lelani said, beckoning him.

The group converged on Lelani's position in the pantry. She stood before a locked metal door.

"All the other doors in the house are wood with brass or crystal fixtures," Lelani said. "This one is steel with a lock normally reserved for front doors."

"Probably keeps his coin collection down there," Seth pointed out.

"Can you open it?" asked Cat.

"Yes."

"Are you going to blow it apart with a whammy? Or kick it down with your horsey strength?" Seth asked.

Lelani pulled a bronze key out of her bag and blew hot breath on it. She stuck it in the lock and rubbed the bow for a few seconds with her thumb before turning the key. The door clicked open. She removed the key, which looked different than it did when she put it in. She held it directly in front of Seth's nose so that he practically went cross-eyed to see it.

"Subtlety is the hallmark of all good magic," she said. "And I am not a horse."

It was a finished basement, strangely nonmusty, and as comfortably decorated as the house above. Behind a large antique desk was a bookcase built into the wall lined with books on antiquities, mostly coinage and stamps. A large dehumidifier sat silently in the middle of the room. The other walls were wood paneled. There were several lit display cases of the type one found in museums, full of old and rare coins from around the world. One display sat atop a series of long flat steel drawers, the type a jewelry merchant might put his wares into after closing up shop. Cal tried the first drawer, but it was sealed. Lelani used her key to unlock the flats and pulled open the top drawer. On black velvet liners lay ten Phoenix Standards laid out in a row.

Seth whistled. "That's a few thousand dollars if those are real," he said. He picked one up and turned the half-dollar-sized gold coin around. The profile of a man with a long face, hawkish nose, short curly hair, and large ears adorned the other side. "Whose face is this?"

"That's Archduke Athelstan, Danel's father," Lelani said.

"Who's Danel?" Cat asked.

"Prince Danel the third, future archduke of Aandor, prince of the realm, regent to the future king," Cal said. He took the coin from Seth and became lost in its brilliance. "If we succeed, it'll be his face on all newly minted coins one day."

Cal pulled open the next drawer down. He froze. What lay in there was a miracle; he never thought to see it again. Disbelieving his eyes, he took the sword by the hilt and lifted it out of the drawer. His mind raced with long-ago memories—the sound of his grandfather pulling the sword out of its scabbard when he taught him to duel. The smell of whale oil on the steel as the old man taught Cal how to clean the blade. The tales of how his grandfather did the same for him, and that one day it would be Cal's to wield. What little light the basement had magnified off the blade, tiny flares erupting like small suns on its edge.

"Whoa," Seth said.

The blade part was three feet long and gleamed like polished silver. Ancient runes were etched into the steel. It had a double fuller. The hilt was brushed bronze with brown bull leather suede wrapping on the grip. The cross guards and rain guard were ornately engraved with a vine motif, and the grooves were stamped in gold leaf, which reflected brightly against the bronze.

"It's Bòid Géard," Cal said. "It's *my* sword."

"You named your sword?" Cat said incredulously.

Cal motioned in the air before him, slicing, thrusting. The air whipped around the blade. The weapon was part of him—an extension of his arm and his will. It was an instrument of his duty. It was his family . . . it was Aandor.

"Swords are handed down from generation to generation," Cal said. "My grandfather gave me this blade. His grandfather gave it to him."

"You're not giving Bree a fucking sword," Cat said. Then she added, "*My lord.*"

"Don't be ridiculous . . . ," Cal said.

"Right," Cat agreed.

"Girls don't inherit swords," he added. "If we have a son, we'd bestow Bòid Géard on him after my father relinquished his sword, Sìth Géard, to me. That's the symbolic sword of the MacDonnell clan. It's finer than even this one; made of Murano steel. Slightly lighter than this with a single deep fuller, but perfectly balanced and slightly more ornate."

Cal's delivery may have been more serious than he intended, based on his wife's reaction. Cat's jaw hung in disbelief, but he wasn't sure if it was because a child of hers would inherit a weapon, or because Bree would be excluded from a birthright due to gender-biased traditions.

He winked at her and smiled. Cat was ready to sock him.

"Porn stars name their swords, too," Seth said. "The guys, that is."

Cat looked ready to transfer that punch to the photographer.

"Aren't we men silly?" Seth added quickly.

"Shut up," Lelani told him.

The sword still retained the nicks of every battle Cal had ever fought. But Dumont had treated it well—oiling and polishing the steel to a luster Cal only remembered seeing at ceremonial occasions. He looked around for the scabbard and spotted it hung from its straps in a dark corner. Dumont hadn't stored it, thinking it was a less valuable thing. Most who did not know weapons did not appreciate the artistry in a great scabbard. The wood is shaped and sanded, the leather stretched just right. For a sword like Bòid Géard, it would be a custom-made fit. He took the scabbard from the wall and looked it over, thinking for sure that it couldn't still have . . . ah, but there it was—the tiny leather pouch was still looped on the belt. Cal looked over his shoulder. Cat was occupied with other items in the collection. He unclasped the pouch and stuck his finger in. It was still there . . . the silk and lace of Chryslantha's garter, and the strands of her hair she tied to it; his good luck charm. Until this moment, Aandor remained a distant dream, but now, laying fingers on his betrothed's hair, more than just recollections flooded back. Now he remembered the scents of leather, hemp, steel; the taste of the food; the feel of the clothing; the sounds of knights on horseback and the smell of their mounts—the scent of bedsheets after he and Chryslantha had made love. Real . . . all real.

"Find anything?" Cat asked.

His wife's voice pulled Cal back to reality. He pushed the fetish back into its pouch and said, "My scabbard." He sheathed his sword and threw it over his shoulders, buckling the belt across his chest. The weight was negligible, more like something returned that had been missing from his life.

"There's a light blinking on Dumont's message machine," Cat said.

The desk was the real working center of Dumont's operation. Dumont used an old-fashioned telephone message machine. A light blinked, indicating two messages. Cal pressed play. A woman's voice said, *"Jimmy, why aren't you answering your cell? Call me as soon as you get this. It's important."* Beep.

Cal suspected there were a bunch of messages on the cell phone in Dumont's pocket, too.

"Is it me, or did that voice sound familiar?" Cat said.

Beep. *"Jimmy, it's Glory. Where the heck are you? More people came in today asking about you-know-what from you-know-when. Why are people dredging up the past all of a sudden? This is a nightmare. Call me!"*

Cat studied the photos of friends and family on the wall and pointed one out to Cal. He took it down and they looked at it closely. Cat pointed to a woman in the front row. A thinner, younger, but very familiar uncooperative county clerk appeared in the picture. Cal pulled the photo from the frame and read the back. *Me with Gloria's family—Manning family reunion, Millerton Rec Park, '96.*

CHAPTER 8

COMING OF AGE

Daniel sat up in bed finishing his rendering of Luanne. It was the best of all his drawings. He was quite pleased, and yet had a foreboding that nothing good could come of it. The intellectual part of his brain said to put a match to the whole sketch pad, but the tiny little corner that still yearned to impress Luanne overruled it. It would be rude to the subject to destroy the work after she volunteered her time to pose for him. A willing model was easier to work with, he convinced himself. His brain was most definitely not a democracy—a tiny selfish minority overruled common sense. He enjoyed looking at her. She was—bouncy. No degree of equivocation would erase that fact from his consciousness.

Daniel and Colby were there on Beverly's good graces. Bev was a gracious host and shared what little she had openly with them. Luanne had even given up her bedroom and slept in her mother's king-sized bed. The trailer park was a safe place to hide until the authorities found other crimes to distract them. Daniel's good behavior was paramount to continuing this arrangement. Breathing space was vital to coming up with a long-term plan of action; it was worth more than some short-term titillation. Talk about timing—meeting Colby at the bus station in Baltimore was a brilliant stroke of luck for Daniel—he had no history with the boonies of North Carolina, no ties to this community that the cops could trace back. There was no reason to look for him here, and the trailer park inhabitants were too distracted with subsistence living to poke their nose into his business. No one there suspected the sweet, well-groomed, articulate thirteen-year-old was wanted for murder.

When Luanne turned off the shower, the beleaguered pipes reverberated through the trailer adjusting to new pressure. The bathroom was across the tiny hallway opposite his door. She'd need to use the hallway to get to her mom's room at the end of the trailer. He convinced himself to stay put—no midnight trips for water, snacks, or to walk the dog they didn't own. Her footsteps padded into her mother's room. He imagined her wet, wrapped in a towel; an alien force had taken control of his mind; he couldn't stop thinking about her with that overly stimulated brain of his.

Why did she suddenly take an interest in me after ignoring me the first day? Luanne was selfish and self-indulgent—not the type to seek out friends unless it improved her status. There was nothing in it for her to make nice with Daniel. Was she really that impressed by the drawings? It nagged at Daniel, but his little brain, aided by his ego, bullied the big brain into acceptance.

Daniel put away his sketch pad and turned off the light. His head hit the pillow but sleep eluded him—he was too revved up. The whole room reminded him of Luanne. It smelled like her. He grabbed a wad of Kleenex from the nightstand and reached down beneath the covers—the teenaged boy's Ambien since before recorded history. He tried to think of Katie Millar, except somehow, she kept morphing into Luanne. *So much for loyalty,* he thought. He succumbed to his mind's insistence for Luanne and finished off quickly. With his vitality dispelled, Daniel drifted toward slumber. *This can't go on,* he thought as his mind settled down. The morning would bring a clean slate. Luanne will have lost interest by then—girls like that always did.

Daniel awoke to a sharp chill nipping at his nose, cheeks, and shoulders. The clock said only forty minutes had passed since he dozed off. The room had dropped in temperature and he could see his breath. He pulled the thin timeworn sheets up to his nose and folded into the fetal position to preserve body heat. There was a knock at his door—Daniel realized another knock had preceded this one while he slept, and it was why he'd awakened. The door creaked open.

"Danny?" Luanne whispered. Her breath misted against the weak light in the hallway. Daniel couldn't understand the point of her whispering. They were the only ones in the house, and she clearly intended to wake him. Wouldn't normal volume make more sense? Luanne tiptoed into the room wrapped under a large comforter. Upon reaching the bed, she took it off and threw it over his blankets—in that second he glimpsed an extra-large Brooks & Dunn T-shirt that draped over her like a short dress before she crawled underneath the combined covers, pushing him to the far edge of the mattress.

"What the heck are you doing?" he asked. Panic, confusion, and even a bit of elation vied for control.

"Mama forgot to pay the propane man," Luanne said. "She's a scatterbrain. Scoot over."

"Scoot? It's a twin mattress."

"Move over!" she insisted. "It's thirty degrees. We'll be warmer this way. Mama and I do it all the time."

Daniel straightened out from his fetal position to make room. "Do I look like your mother?" he asked.

"Ain't you ever been campin'?"

"What if Beverly comes home?"

Luanne giggled. "No room for her here." She lay on her side facing the door, and away from him.

"Seriously," he said.

The thought of Beverly catching her little girl in bed with him gave Daniel stomach knots. *That's how Luanne gets rid of me,* Daniel thought. *Mom comes back in the morning, it freaks her out, Luanne gets her bed back.* Now it made sense. He had no car, Colby was gone, and they were in the middle of nowhere. He'd be lucky to get the kitchen floor.

"She'll thank you for not lettin' me freeze to death because she was too scatterbrained to pay the propane," Luanne said, as though reading his thoughts.

Daniel doubted it, but it *really* was cold. The windows had crap insulation—no better than being in a school bus with furniture.

She took a healthy helping of mattress, forcing him to the far edge. He turned on his side facing the window and away from her and instinctively bent into a fetal pose, which turned them into two butting bookends and made less room in the bed.

"Turn—the—other—way," she said, like scolding a puppy that just didn't get it. Daniel flipped over so that they were facing the same direction. She squeezed against him to spoon.

"We could have spooned the other way, too," Daniel pointed out.

"Then I'd be on the outside," she said. "The girl goes on the inside. Don't you know nothin', Danny Hauer?" It was also the warmer position. Daniel swore he could sense her smiling, even with no view of her face. As he tried to settle in, Daniel didn't know what to do with his arms; one was bent and pressed between him and her back—the other kept wanting to go back or forward from his side, but neither was comfortable. He held his arm in the air until it started to ache, trying to decide.

"What are you doin'?" she asked impatiently.

"Can't figure out—uh, my arms . . ."

"Put it around me, dummy. Least you can do for kickin' me out of my bed is keep me warm. Jeez Louise, ain't you ever bunked with a cousin when you was little? Gone campin'?"

Daniel was fairly certain cousins north of the Mason–Dixon over the age of ten would get smacked for bunking like this.

She pulled his lower arm through the space under her neck. Then guided his upper arm over the curve of her waist. His hand settled naturally on her stomach. When she was entirely in his embrace, she closed the space between them tight. *This seal would impress NASA,* he thought.

Daniel was acutely aware that but for the T-shirt, she was essentially naked. The hem had ridden up with her fidgeting and her bare bottom was now pressed against his crotch, separated only by the slender margin of his Fruit of the Looms. Things stirred below.

Luanne wrapped her ice-cold feet around Daniel's shins. The shock spazzed him out, and he thrust against her tighter.

"Sorry," she said, giggling. "That feels sooooo good, though. You're hot as a teapot."

Her hair was still damp from the shower and smelled of strawberries. She smelled clean and fruity overall—he wanted to take a bite out of . . .

Stop that! he thought to himself. Daniel was in deep. Perhaps Luanne does this with all her friends—and more power to them—but his loins, despite his conscious wishes, approached DEFCON 1 in a subversive act of rebellion. *She's going to tell her mom and Colby I'm a perv,* he thought, panicking.

He lay as still as he could, hoping she'd fall asleep, and more importantly, to keep a bad situation from escalating. But her scent and her heat overrode his effort to calm down. He couldn't get the image of her posing naked out of his mind—he tried everything—imagining the Orioles' starting lineup; intricate stacking designs for cereal boxes; and in an act of utter desperation, he even tried to imagine old people, like William Shatner and Joan Rivers, completely naked . . . but nothing worked—her clean scent corrupted his resistance. His heart pounded like he'd just run a sprint.

Luanne absorbed Daniel's body heat like a thirsty succubus. It was getting hot under the covers. She hadn't moved for a while; he prayed that she'd fallen asleep. Daniel wouldn't get any sleep tonight—there was no way for him to *take care of business* a second time.

Luanne gyrated her butt against Daniel. "Well at least you ain't a gay," she mumbled into her pillow.

"Sorry," he said. Beverly was going to KILL him.

He waited for the eviction. And waited . . . they lay, unmoving.

"That thing ain't goin' anywhere, is it?" Luanne said.

"Uh . . ."

She reached back, searching for his briefs, and took the problem in hand.

Whoa! he thought. It was the first time someone had done that.

Daniel's resolve waned before her tender strokes. Luanne's logic, if it could be called that, baffled him: Her presence kept him up, which in turn kept her up, so for both their sakes she was going to take him down. He'd have said something . . . if it didn't feel so amazing.

Luanne's stomach was hot to the touch. Daniel didn't remember how his hand got under her shirt, or her raising an objection. He moved it upward; her nipples were as erect as he was.

Luanne probably expected this solution to be a quick fix. It would have been, had Daniel not already taken care of business earlier.

"Sure can hang in there," she said, puzzled, but also a bit impressed.

"Sorry." It was the only word left in Daniel's vocabulary.

"Elastic's scratchin' my wrist," she complained.

Daniel kicked his briefs down to alleviate her suffering.

Another minute passed, and she whispered, "Damn!"

Was he already screwing up? Daniel was in uncharted waters— as lost as Columbus four weeks into the voyage. He seldom understood girls when fully clothed and in command of his faculties.

"You're makin' me hot," she said.

Luanne shifted her leg to position him in closer. She steered him to between her legs. Daniel gulped. She was very wet down there, and he realized he was on the cusp of a special moment. There was no rational part of Daniel's mind left—only instinct. Gently he pushed, expecting her to stop him. Luanne's only protest was an inviting moan. The heat she radiated couldn't compete with the warmth inside her. Luanne and Daniel exchanged their body heat—like a symbiotic transference as primeval as the first mitosis. He pushed deeper until he thought her body would swallow him whole.

"Yes!" she moaned.

Daniel never imagined it would feel this fantastic—why would people ever do drugs or race sports cars? This was all man and woman had been created for. It was too hot now; he kicked the comforters back and they continued.

"I'm only doin' this so we can get to sleep," she panted playfully.

Luanne could make any excuse she wanted; she could no more control him now than she could a runaway train. She was his and he was hers. They continued for a timeless stretch until Luanne grasped his hands and pressed them harder into her bosom—a teacher, guiding her student through the most important lesson of his life. Luanne's cries grew louder until she arched her back and shuddered.

Daniel thought the whole trailer park could hear them.

"Don't stop!" she cried.

Pressure built inside him—like a wave on its cusp, he held her so strongly they became one. She cried out a second time, a long feral sound as they exploded simultaneously, his body a crescendo of pleasure.

They stayed spooned, shaking, as waves of heat emanated from them. Even now, Daniel refused to grow soft. He kissed her on the nape of her neck and on her cheek.

"Dang! What's it take to put you down?" she said, breathing heavy. Despite the complaint, she squeezed herself around him, locking him in. "Cody's usually done in two and snorin' at three."

Daniel pulled her T-shirt off all the way. It excited him to feel her completely naked against him. He situated himself on her missionary style. She wrapped her calves over his legs.

"Let's find out," he said.

She ran her fingers through his hair and down his back.

He kissed her passionately. This time he didn't go gently. Luanne uttered a sharp, "Oh," and bit his lower lip. She grabbed the back of him with her hands and pulled him into her. Daniel couldn't remember the last time he'd been this excited about life—been this happy. He believed that in his dotage, despite whatever else he might accomplish, this night would still rank at the top of the list of best things that had ever happened to him.

Somewhere in the recesses of Daniel's long-abandoned rational brain, a tiny molecule cried out for attention. *Who's Cody*? it asked. Luanne kissed him. That voice, drowned out by more pressing matters, faded into the background.

CHAPTER 9

IN THE NAME OF LOVE

1

Danel. Cat turned the name around in her head. Before today, the prince was a concept—an abstract—a storybook character Snow White awaited to save her from a witch's curse. Now he was real—flesh and blood with parents who loved him and a guardian in the form of Catherine's husband sworn to protect him come hell or high water.

They were a block from the clerk's office waiting for Gloria Hauer to finish work. Lelani paced the sidewalk; Seth snored softly across the backseat. Callum sat pensively in the driver's seat, one arm on the rest, the other wrist hanging over the steering wheel ready to move. His breath came out in soft white puffs; the cold didn't bother him. Cat was adept at reading the subtle changes in her husband's moods—but you'd have to be blind deaf and dumb to miss how sullen and tightly wound he'd become these past few days. Two worlds rested on his shoulders, and the fates of his families were stuck between them. It was too much for any man. Cat turned up the SUV's heater and sipped her mochachino.

He was *still* the person she married and loved—still the father of her baby, even if he answered to "my lord" these days. He had whipped Bòid Géard around skillfully in Dumont's basement. His movements had been pure poetry, cutting the air silently, like the sword weighed next to nothing in his hand. She thought of him jabbing that thing into men in a fight, hacking out bits of their flesh—their blood running all over his arm with bits of bone and intestine splattered on him. This was her gentle giant: a man who, after a decade in the NYPD, had never drawn his gun in anger, never killed anyone. Brianna's father was the kindest most truthful man she'd ever met—and lurking underneath, perhaps all along, a *butcher*. Cat felt nauseous—a sudden burp of hot foulness made its way up her chest. She cracked the window to get at some of that country air.

Cat placed her hand on Callum's arm. The muscles were tight as steel coils, but at her touch, the tension abated. A good sign that even with all that'd happened, he still welcomed her caress. He took her hand gently and laced their fingers together.

"I should bring you on all my stakeouts," he said.

"You'd lose all your marks," Cat answered. "Only reason we're not steaming up the windows is we have 'the kids' with us."

Seth grumbled, "Ewwww," from the back.

Cal's phone rang. It was the local police. Cal had told the sergeant as much of the truth as he could at Dumont's house. Lelani's silver flower pin, imbued with a truth enchantment, helped push the few white lies through without much effort. Cat wondered if the pin's effects had worn off. Cal would have to be careful on the phone since the pin's enchantment didn't travel over cell phones.

When he hung up, he told Cat, "Local PD is looking at Dumont and Sweeny as related homicides. There's a suspicious third death as well. A local named Steve Hauer was found dead in his pool."

"Steve . . . *Hauer*?" she said. Cat looked at the clerk's office and then again at her husband.

"Yeah—same as the clerk we're trailing," he said. "Story is he was sweeping dead leaves around the pool, slipped, got tangled in the winter tarp, and 'drowned.' Coincidence? I'd lay money the autopsy won't find water in Hauer's lungs."

"You think the gumshoe's covering his trail," Cat said.

Cal shrugged. There was no evidence of anything. What they did know was that Gloria Hauer had lied to them—she was involved in whatever happened thirteen years ago. People around her were dropping like flies. Was she a murderer hiding evidence? *Did Dorn steal her heart as well? Or was she a potential victim?*

Normally, Cat would not be concerned with how Cal went about his work but the personal nature of this investigation had changed her husband. *And not for the better,* she thought. He'd misplaced that reserve of patience she found so endearing about him, and in fact, depended on to counter her own quick temper. At six foot five, Cal could be intimidating even when calm. As tense as he was now, coming off nonthreatening was unlikely. And what if Gloria was innocent? What if this was the worst day in that woman's life, hearing about the deaths of people she loved? And what if she was scared out of her mind?

Gloria exited the clerk's office early. She was visibly upset and looking over her shoulder and down the street on the way to her car. There was no doubt news of the double murders had reached her. Cat's gut instinct told her the woman was no murderer, but she was neck deep and on the wrong end of whatever was happening. Cal put the car in drive and Lelani squeezed into the rear compartment. The centaur's illusion couldn't fool the Ford Explorer's suspension as the weight of a small horse tipped the back of the vehicle down. The thought that they'd need to get new shocks entered Cat's head.

From a discreet distance, they followed Gloria home.

"Cal . . . ," Cat started in.

"Mmm," he grunted, focusing on Gloria's car.

"What are you planning to do?" she asked.

"In what way?"

"How do you intend to confront her?"

"Don't know," he said.

Cat waited a moment to see if that was all he had. She took a deep breath and steeled herself. "You are not going to barge in on that woman's family."

"She knows where the prince is," he said. "Every instinct I have says so."

"I understand. But, keep things in perspective. Gloria Hauer is not some all-powerful villain. She's not from an alternate universe. She is a clerk in a small town in upstate New York, driving a beat up Chevy Cavalier. Don't assume she's all knowing. There's no proof she benefited from your group's misfortune—you might want to think through how to approach her. Her family may know nothing of what she's involved in. There could be children . . ."

"Cat, I am a step behind Lord Dorn and running out of time . . ."

"Damn it, Cal! We're not breaking into these people's house like Dorn's monsters did to us!"

Cal drove with the silence of a man knowing his spouse was right. The silence of the woods around them belied the mood in the car. Seth was fully awake and sitting up at this point but, for once, he was smart enough to keep his mouth shut. Cat turned around to see what Lelani was up to. The centaur was looking right at her with a guarded expression. It was hard to tell if she was sympathetic to Cat's wishes, or in favor of Cal's no-holds-barred approach. Did it matter? She was a soldier and Cal was her lord.

2

Gloria Hauer's Chevy turned into the driveway of a prefab ranch-style home on a two-acre parcel secluded from the neighbors by a healthy smattering of trees. It was hard to tell the color of the house in the dark. The mailbox had *B&G Hauer* in big vinyl letters on the side. Through their large bay window, Cat spied Gloria falling into her husband's arms and he hugged her tightly. Their daughters were in tears, and the two dogs barked at the emotional outpouring. Steve Hauer and Nathan Dumont must have been very close. Cat was grateful for the seclusion the Hauers' property afforded them. Whatever Cal needed to do, Cat was certain she wouldn't be proud of it, and wanted to be spared scrutiny from the neighbors.

"I could just knock on the door and say I'm running a police investigation," Cal said.

"If a six-foot-five Viking came to our home to interrogate me, would you stand idly by while I squirmed?" Cat asked. "Even if I were guilty?" She turned to the centaur in back. "Is there magic that can put everyone asleep except for Gloria?" Cat asked.

"I can put everyone to sleep—then revive the woman."

Before Lelani could start the spell, a scream emanating from the house cut through the night. Everyone jumped out of the vehicle, unsure of what to do and looking to Cal for their next move. He had pulled out his pistol, but didn't seem to know the next move either. The lights went out in the home and only the shadows of a struggle came through the window. More screams, and the front door burst open. A terrified girl, no more than eight, ran from the home crying. Sounds of fighting followed through the door. She stopped short when she saw Cal and the group.

"Please don't hurt me!" she begged.

"We're here to help," Cal said decisively. He reached into the backseat and grabbed his sword with the other hand. "Cat, stay with the girl. Everyone else, come on."

Cal and Lelani charged into the house. Seth, however, stood frozen in place.

"Seth? What's the matter? Go!" Cat insisted.

"I—I—uh . . . ," Seth stammered. He had lost his nerve and silently implored Cat not to force him.

"Fine!" she said in frustration. "Stay here with the girl. Don't let anything happen to her."

Cat heard gunfire. As she headed into the house, she drew her Colt .32 from her jacket pocket and clicked the safety off. She wasn't a cop or a fan of cops in general, but suddenly understood the appeal of that kind of work to some people. The rush from holding a loaded weapon in the pursuit of danger had her heart thumping a mile a minute.

The front door afforded her a complete view of the living room to her left. Gloria Hauer was on the floor with her other daughter beside her, cradling her husband's head. He was either unconscious or dead. She heard the clang of metal in the back of the house, perhaps in the kitchen. She was about to head back there when the hairs on her neck stood on end. Something was behind her—in the shadows. She spun around in time to get knocked on her back. Two very golden feline eyes stared into hers. It was a woman, covered in orange fur, with a tail and a very catlike face. Cat's gun hand was pinned under a paw. The cat thing was about to rake her with a healthy set of claws when a wooden staff whacked her on the head.

The cat thing rolled off Catherine. It sprang up, bounced off the top of the wall near the ceiling and changed trajectory toward Seth. Two hands tipped with razor talons reached out, ready to dice him like an onion.

An arrow struck the creature in the ribs and it dropped short of the petrified novice. The creature gasped for air, coughed up blood, and then stopped moving. Lelani walked into the living room.

"I've been chasing that felidae throughout the house," she said. "Very quick—thanks for distracting it."

"Who are you people?" Gloria cried. "What's going on?" The clang of metal grew louder; Cal and his opponent emerged into the dining area. Cat's fear welled at seeing her man in danger but she was also transfixed—fascinated. He maneuvered the sword through the cramped room avoiding chairs and furniture and positioning it confidently where it needed to parry a blow or swing at his attacker. The steel had become an extension of his body. He looked in his natural element . . . he looked like a killer.

Lelani moved around Cat and retrieved Cal's gun by the couch. "The felidae surprised us and knocked it from his hand," she said.

"Should we shoot that other guy?" Seth asked.

The other guy, an Aryan type as tall and solid as Callum, had his back against the wall. When he spotted the dead cat-girl, he realized he was short a partner and badly outnumbered.

"Yield," Cal ordered at sword point.

The man made a show of dropping his sword—but with his other hand, he threw down several black shiny marbles. A bright flash filled the room. When it dissipated, Cat saw white spots everywhere. Everyone else shared the same effect. The man was gone.

"Blinder spell," Lelani said, rubbing her eyes. "Pursue?"

"No," Cal said. "Our night vision's going to be iffy for a while. But shut all the doors and windows."

Cal stared at Seth rubbing away the spots in his vision with a most unkind expression. Seth must have sensed something because he looked up at that moment.

"Where were you when we rushed the house?" Cal asked him.

Despite Seth's help during the fight in Rosencrantz's meadow, Cat's husband had not forgiven him for wrecking their plans all those years ago. His patience with the porn photographer had been exhausted. They needed Seth to take on a sorcerer of Dorn's caliber—except the boy had yet to cast so much as a Fourth of July sparkler under Lelani's tutelage. Cal had said to Cat that watching Lelani instruct him was like watching a chimp trying to understand a computer. It was not in Cal's nature to say something so cruel, but the kid brought these things on himself. He contributed little more than complaints and sarcasm. It was odd to think of Seth as a "kid," but at the same time, it was accurate. Men Seth's age led troops into battle and ran Internet companies. At twenty-six, he was a classic case of arrested development—like those grown men who still dressed like teenagers and attended comic book conventions.

"I asked him to stay back," Cat said. She didn't know why she did it. He hadn't earned any cover from her, and yet Cat felt she needed to do it to keep her husband's temper in check. The whole world really must be turning on its head if *she* was the one promoting calm.

Gloria and her daughters had managed to get her husband on the couch. He was still out cold, but not cut or bleeding. Lelani said his bruises were superficial and that he would recover. The family looked vulnerable—an image that disturbed Cat. They had charged in as rescuers, but Cat knew this night could have gone differently . . . they could have been the invaders.

Gloria reached for her telephone, probably to call the police, but Cal depressed the switch to cut off the connection. He shook his finger side to side and silently told Gloria *No*. There would be no cops.

Cat felt criminal violating the sanctity of this woman's home. Was this what Cal did in Aandor? How many homes had he barged into in service to his duke? This was the United States, though; there were no vassals or peasants, at least not officially. Here, every home was a castle protected by God and law.

"Please," Cal asked Gloria, motioning her and her daughters to the dining room. "I need answers."

Gloria sat at the head of the dining room table. Cat and Seth took seats to her right, with Cat closest. Cal and Lelani remained standing. Gloria looked around at the group and said, "Please don't hurt my family."

"We're not going to hurt you," Cal said in the calmest tone he could muster. It came off creepy. Cal was too wound up, too serious to come off nonthreatening even with an effort.

"Take anything you want," Gloria begged.

Cat put her hand gently on Gloria's arm. "Gloria, we need your help. People are in danger—*you* are in danger. A boy's life is at stake."

"It's that couple, isn't it . . . from that night long ago," Gloria said. "I knew there was something off about them. Why didn't I just mind my own bee's wax?" she sobbed.

"There was an infant with them," Cal cut in.

"He was in the car," Gloria admitted. She looked defeated, like a woman confessing her greatest sin.

"There was no death certificate, no mention of him in the article," Cat said.

Gloria bordered on despondent—a bad day turning worse. Catherine wanted to comfort her, but could see the answers they needed behind the woman's misery. The secrets spanned more than a decade and no doubt touched lives beyond this room. Gloria could upturn the life of an unsuspecting family, a young boy who may not know he was not his parents' natural child. Worse, Gloria could go to jail as an accessory. Cal was eerily silent, trying not to spook the lady—Cat was concerned about the lengths Cal would go to pry this information from her. She put her hands on Gloria's.

"Please, we're not interested in prosecuting you," Cat said. "We may owe you a debt of gratitude."

"As you owe us for rescuing your family," Lelani said brusquely.

Gloria looked toward the living room where her husband rested.

"He's just asleep," Cal said. "He'll wake up in an hour or so, and we'll be gone."

Gloria told her daughters to tend to their father. As soon as they left the dining room, she began to cry.

"I did it for a friend—for love," she said, in low tones. "It's the only illegal thing I've ever done."

No one said a word while Gloria stared off, collecting her thoughts from over a decade ago. She took a deep breath and plunged in.

"Rita was one of my best friends. She was married to my husband's cousin, John Hauer. Bill and I had just gotten engaged at that time. We had all been friends in high school along with Nathan Dumont and John's younger brother Steve. John had some health issues—testicular cancer—and as a result, he couldn't have children. They tried to adopt, but it was taking forever, lots of snags and bureaucracy. They were a wonderful couple, John the sweetest, most patient man you'd ever meet. We all felt for them. The night of that storm . . . well, I believed at the time that fate had put me there for a reason.

"Bill, Nathan, and I were driving back from a concert in the city. A harsh nor'easter poured down on us, visibility was terrible. Even through the wind and rain, though, we saw the flash of the impact a mile ahead. By the time we arrived, the truck driver had put out the car's engine fire with an extinguisher. No one else was out there; the weather kept people at home that night. The driver of the semi sat on the step of his cab in shock over the Ashes' deaths. It was clear their car veered into his lane and hit the truck head-on. Mr. Ashe's face was crushed by the steering wheel. The woman, however, clung to life by a nail. 'Daniel, Daniel,' she kept saying while choking on her own blood. Somehow, over the thunder and driving rain, I heard the baby cry in the backseat. He was wrapped tight in swaddling and lay in a pillow basket on the floor. He had a bruise on his forehead, but was otherwise okay. I told the woman her son was alive. She said 'Find his guardians,' but her voice got weaker until finally she stopped breathing. She seemed foreign, somehow; I had the impression they had come from far away—that they were refugees. It was just a feeling—you know?

"I put the baby in our car. I don't know why, I just did. It just seemed the thing to do . . . to get it out of that wreck . . . that metal coffin. Bill and Nathan began going through the deceased's effects to find out who they were. In a sack in the trunk, they found a sword, a crossbow, daggers, robes, and other strange items. Nathan guessed that they must have been going to the Renaissance fair in the Catskills; that is until he came across the gold. Nathan was a serious collector, and he could tell real gold from fake. And again, I had my suspicion that these strangers were in trouble and had come from very far away. We used the truck's two-way to call the sheriff, who was Bill's uncle. The truck driver was still in shock—he didn't even realize there was a baby. I told Bill and Nathan that I was taking the child to my place to get it out of the weather. They were hesitant to let me go, but I was hearing nothing of it, and left with our car and the boy.

"Bill's uncle was mad as hell that I didn't take that baby to the hospital. I should have, but I didn't. When the Ashes turned out to have no history, that's when I knew I could get away with it. I worked in the clerk's office and forged some papers, allowing John and Rita to become the child's foster parents. Bill, Nathan, and the sheriff were worried about the game I was playing. That little pink baby would've been put in foster care anyway and eventually adopted by strangers on the state list. But we had our very own family who needed a child. Where was the sin in giving an orphan a good home with a loving couple? They accepted the responsibility, and John even said he'd keep the name Daniel out of respect for the parents who'd lost him. Nathan thought it was risky, but John insisted. At least the boy would have one thing his real parents gave him. Slowly I won Bill and his uncle over to my thinking. Nathan asked for some of the things we found in the Ashes' car. He said if he was going to risk going to prison, he was entitled to some compensation. My reward was seeing John and Rita as parents."

Gloria began to cry. Cal handed her some tissues. Cat could sense the weight on her husband's shoulders lighten a little. The prince was alive, and living in a good home.

"Gloria," Cat started gently, "we're the boy's family. We're the guardians."

"Daniel is my fourth cousin," Cal interjected.

This came as a surprise to Cat. She filed it away for another conversation. "Please, where do the Hauers live?" she asked. "It's important. Their family is in danger."

Gloria descended into a deeper sadness. Her head slumped and she stared at the table. "Well . . . John had a relapse of his cancer and moved back to his childhood home in Baltimore. An old friend of his worked in an aggressive cancer program at Johns Hopkins medical. But it didn't do any good. He passed away several years ago. He was a great father. Rita didn't handle John's death very well. She and I had a falling out. She started taking prescription pills. That led to the drinking, and then she met Clyde."

"Who's Clyde?" Cal asked.

"Rita remarried," Gloria continued. "I think his last name is Kniffer or Knoppler, or something like that; spelled with a K but starts with an N sound. We didn't like him. He was insecure, controlling, and a bit angry. Nathan would have nothing at all to do with them—he never spoke to Rita again.

"You have to understand . . . Rita was vulnerable after John's passing. Clyde moved in and insulated her from the family. I haven't spoken to her in years. I have her number and address in my book, though. If your interests are that boy's health and well-being, getting him away from Clyde couldn't hurt."

Gloria Hauer broke down again. It was clear she had been carrying that secret for many years. "There was nothing I could do once John died," she said. "I was culpable. I couldn't save Rita or Daniel from that horrible drunk of a man. I had to keep the secret . . . for my family's sake."

"Thank you," Cat said, getting up. She gestured to Seth to do the same.

"We're not the only ones looking for him," Cal said. "The others . . . they killed your friends. They sent these thugs tonight. We'll keep your part in this a secret, Mrs. Hauer, but you have to do the same for us. No cops. I think we're all working for the same benefit."

"Is my family safe?" Gloria asked.

"I don't know," Cal said. "The reason they tried to eliminate you was to keep the truth from us. But now that we know, there's no point. I advise getting out of town for a few days just to be safe. Canada, or relatives in another part of the country if you have them."

Lelani wrapped the felidae in a bedsheet and carried it and a shovel out into the woods.

"May we call you if we have any further questions?" Cat asked Gloria.

Gloria nodded politely, but she was clearly glad to be getting rid of intruders.

Cat hooked her arm in Cal's as they walked back to the car. His tension dissipated, but only a little. There was only so much a wife could do with a touch. They had learned much this day.

"These assassins are not the ones that did in Sweeny and Dumont," Cal said. "The MOs are different. Someone more skillful, someone who enjoys killing, did them in."

"The detective?" Cat asked.

"Perhaps. Maybe he followed another lead and left the rest of the clean up for the B team."

Cat shuddered, thinking what would happen if Dorn's people got their hands on that young prince first.

CHAPTER 10

INNER PEACE

1

Theo drove toward Uwharrie National Forest; Allyn sat next to him with the fetish bowl, holding a Tupperware cover against the top to minimize splashing. They had taken Theo's SUV in case it became necessary to drive off road. The finder spell was not specific enough to tell them how far the children were. But the spells worked! Even in this universe, which had never heard of the Quorum—the pantheon of gods that ushered in life and dealt death—who gave the praetors, prelates, druids, and clerics of Aandor their license to do divine work in their names. Jesus, Yahweh, Mithras, Jehovah, Odin, Zeus, Allah, Buddha, Earth Mother, Brahma . . . Pelitos—the universes were brimming with deities. Were they all collectively wrong? Did this world have its own dysfunctional pantheon? Allyn wondered. Or did the wizards with their secular lust for power and knowledge have the right of it? Was the universe just a conglomeration of physical laws with no intelligence behind it?

Allyn had been sure of his convictions for most of his life—faith was his gift, concrete and unwavering, like car racing was to the Earnhardts. He was a pagan with little more than a decade in this Christian world. Despite recalling his true identity, he found that his Christian beliefs had not diminished. For the most part, he preferred them. Even if one doubted the divinity of Christ, his philosophies were revolutionary. He was the cornerstone to one-quarter of the world's believers. The standards of living in the Christian world were not a coincidence, nor were they accidental. They sprang from the ideals of men like Thomas Aquinas, who wrote of natural law, which was the basis of moral and ethical advances in government and society—utilized by men such as Thomas Jefferson and Martin Luther King Jr. How could Allyn abandon his beliefs of brotherhood, forgiveness, and charity? What world couldn't benefit from more of this?

Allyn was happy serving the Lord in a way that had never satisfied him in Aandor. With Michelle and Rosemarie by his side, he was complete. North Carolina was more of a home than Aandor had been. Only a brother and sister remained for him back there. They could never replace his wife and child, and Michelle would never agree to leave this reality to live in a place that was a version of fourteenth-century Europe, teeming with strange gods. And it all came down to family, didn't it?

Darnell Taylor, the missing children's father, was family; he was Allyn's close friend and an asset to the community. Darnell owned the town barbershop where he guided many young clients onto the righteous path of work, God, and education. And if a young man resisted all three, he guided them toward the army, where he was certain six weeks of boot camp would drive all foolishness from their brains. Darnell was the reason gangs never got a foothold in the county. He was a sensible sounding board when Allyn was unsure about a course of action. As much a leader in the community as Allyn was its spiritual center. Darnell was Allyn's rock—he would not let his brother down, even in the midst of his own personal crisis.

"We're here," Theo said. The forest lined the side of the road they traveled.

"Pull off by that opening," instructed Allyn.

"But the meeting place is a mile ahead."

"How would I explain the bowl and fetish to the others?" Allyn explained.

"Moses done parted the Red Sea with his staff," Theo said. "Magic's in the Bible. I love five loaves for the five thousand."

Allyn smiled and said, "I think a low-key approach would be wiser."

He recalled Prelate Soohn's gift for such blessings back in Aandor. Soohn had a knack for feeding hundreds out of a handful of loaves, sardines, and berries he'd carry in his sack. He was proficient at many types of blessings, but Soohn never cared for the heights to which his abilities could bring him within the order. He wore the same worn-out sandals day after day and was happy in his oldest, faded, moth-eaten robe. A jolly man with a shiny tanned head, round belly, and perpetual smile framed by a purple goatee that came to a point under the tip of his chin, Soohn was completely apolitical and never happier than when among the children in the Aavanteen slums of Aandor City. His humor was infectious. Allyn became nostalgic for his friend.

They entered the forest in hiking gear with backpacks full of food, water, and medical kits. Each man carried a hunting knife and Theo carried a Louisville slugger. One of the robbers had eluded police and was most likely still in the forest as well. Allyn hoped there was enough decency in the man to have kept the children safe overnight if they were in his custody. These were hard economic times that sometimes drove good men to do bad things.

The thinning brown and orange canopy of the forest swayed and rustled with the wind. Leaves came off the trees easily and swirled in the air. Allyn enjoyed nature as much as the next man, but never developed a passion for it. Early in his vocation, a friend of his father tried to convince him to join the druid order because he'd shown some natural affinity for druid blessings. It was not for him; one needed fervor for trees and nature to become a druid, and Allyn enjoyed the comforts and pace of city life too much. Magic, however, flowed strongly through forests, and druids were known for the power and purity of their blessings. Allyn sensed the lay line running through the Uwharrie. He wondered if that magic protected the forest from the developing world around it. Some forests seemed to have a knack for self-preservation. Did the Uwharrie influence people to protect itself?

Allyn knew a few things about druid blessings, just as a Christian theologian might know tenets of Judaism or Buddhism. He carefully handed Theo the bowl. "Do not drop this—do not disturb me for the next few minutes," he said.

Allyn crouched, and laid his palms flat on the ground, listening for the forest's song. He closed his eyes and concentrated. It was faint, and he was not fluent in the green's language. Perhaps forests on earth sang in a different dialect. The forest, aware of his attempt to commune with it, sought him out; the song grew stronger with each second. His heartbeat slowed to the rhythm of the forest's life pulse. He was suddenly aware of the warm-blooded creatures within a hundred-yard radius of his position. A family of birds in the tree to the north of him, raccoons under a bush just south, and a deer at the periphery of his senses to his east.

Unlike temple dwellers, druids were finely attuned with the green. They could sense even the smallest glimmer of life . . . insects, flora, and some could even discern the single-celled creatures in ponds and streams. Allyn was not that sensitive. Fortunately, his targets were large and warm blooded enough to fit within the range of his abilities. He pushed his radius out to two hundred yards, then five hundred. Foxes, beavers, mice, badgers—he knew where every warm-blooded creature was—an ethereal map formed in his mind, as though all living creatures were tagged by a spiritual global positioning system. At the tip of his range, he sensed the men of the search parties penetrating the forest from their starting point. Allyn pushed his radius out farther but hit a figurative wall at about two thousand yards. Try as he might, he could not push farther; he hadn't the training. He withdrew himself from the forest and stood up.

"Well?" asked Theo.

"Well . . . they aren't within two thousand yards of us."

"That's amazing," Theo said.

"It really isn't, Theo. I knew a druid who had successfully learned to communicate with deer and moose. He could have reached into the entire forest and simply asked the animals if they had seen the children."

"So what's the plan?" Theo asked.

"The compass points toward Zachary," he said, referring to the bowl. "We walk until we find them."

2

The search had taken Allyn and Theo into a densely overgrown section of the woods, far from any established trails. They would never have gotten the SUV through here. They'd been walking uphill, away from the other search parties, with Allyn checking their surroundings every few thousand yards. About an hour into the search, he picked up two small warm-blooded creatures—about the size of a six-year-old and a four-year-old.

"Got you," Allyn said. His heart thumped triumphantly. "This way."

They found the children huddled together for warmth in a dry brook beneath a tangle of thick roots belonging to a very old tree. Allyn praised God that it did not rain last night; the children may have been swept away. Zach mostly covered his sister, Ruth, beneath him, with his Sunday jacket over them like a blanket. Wind-blown autumn leaves covered the children, blending them into the forest.

"Zachary?" the reverend said. The boy was asleep and cold to the touch. His lips were cracked and colored an unhealthy shade of deep purple. "Zach, wake up."

Ruth woke up first. She let out a high-pitched scream and began crying.

"Ruth, hush. It's Reverend Grey from Church. Your daddy is my friend, remember?"

Whether she remembered the reverend, or just realized he was not the bad man who kidnapped them, Ruth settled down. He handed her an open bottle of water and watched her drink. Zach, however, would not wake up. His hands were cold, his pulse weak.

"Theo, grab the boy's other hand and rub them quickly," Allyn said. They worked the boy's hands as though trying to start a fire.

Allyn opened Zach's shirt and pressed his hands to the boy's chest.

"You going to shout 'clear' or something?" Theo asked.

Allyn closed his eyes and sought out the life energy coursing through the forest. He had trouble pulling it toward him; like taffy that had been sitting out too long. He placed one hand on a thick tree root beside him, and a spigot creeped open, letting the energy trickle into him. He pumped life into the boy's chest, and felt it spread throughout the lad, warming his extremities.

"Dang," Theo said as the energy reached the boy's hands and coursed into his brother-in-law. Zach's eyes opened. Allyn put a bottle of water to his lips and Zach drank greedily without prompting. They were too distracted with joy to hear the rustle behind them.

"Y'all just stand up slow," a voice behind them said.

A gaunt young man with long, greasy blond hair in blue jeans and a ratty oversized Panthers jersey pointed a shaky .32 caliber snub-nosed pistol at them. His face had fresh scratches. There was a tattoo of a flaming cross in blue ink running up his forearm from the wrist.

"Son, put the gun down," Allyn said, positioning himself between the weapon and the children. Theo closed ranks, too, blocking the robber's view of the kids.

"Shut up! I give the orders here. Throw me them bottles of water," he said. "And, whatever food you got."

Allyn threw the robber his backpack. The man was strung out. He had not had a fun time in the forest.

"There's water and protein bars in the pack," Allyn said. "Leave us be. We have no quarrel with you."

"Fuck that! And fuck you! Them stupid kids had to run into the forest. I been cut and banged up, almost sprained my ankle all thanks to them."

"They ain't kidnapped *you*," Theo said.

The robber pointed the gun at Theo—then back to Allyn, then Theo again. "Shut up. You wanna get shot?"

"No one needs to get shot," Allyn said, calmly. "We're sorry for your—inconvenience."

"Gimme the girl!"

"The girl?" Allyn said. "Son, these children have to go to a hospital. If the child dies in your custody, it will go bad for you at trial." Allyn spoke as though the thief's capture was inevitable, trying to get him to do the right thing and leave. "They'll put you away for life."

"There ain't gonna be no trial! I ain't going to jail. They lay off me, I'll leave the girl at the border."

"The border?" asked Theo. "What border? Tennessee?"

"Mexico, you dumb coon."

"You ain't gonna get to Mexico, you stupid . . . !" Theo snarled. "The whole state's looking for you."

Allyn grasped Theo's shoulder to calm him down. Flared tempers would not get them out of this. "Let's all calm down," he said.

"Can't you blast him or something?" Theo whispered through clenched teeth.

"Priests don't *blast*," Allyn whispered back.

"Stop talkin'! Give me that little bitch," the robber said, agitated.

"Look, son—"

"Do I look like a coon?" the thief said, waving the gun at Allyn.

"You'll travel much farther without the girl. I'm a preacher. I'll be your hostage."

"Uh-uh. No. I can't be watchin' out for you tryin' something the first chance you get."

"My word to god," Allyn said. "I will not try anything. Theo will tell the cops that I am with you to keep them from charging in. Let the children go with Theo and I will be your shield."

The man considered Allyn's offer, stupidly scratching his chin with the tip of his gun for an unreasonably long time.

"Okay," he finally said.

Theo resisted at first, but Allyn convinced him to go. Theo handed Allyn his backpack and put a child on each shoulder. Allyn steered him toward a party of searchers about two thousand yards to the south. Once Theo cleared the trees and was out of sight, Allyn turned his attention on the robber.

"What now?" he asked his captor. The two of them faced each other in the empty forest. Even the animals seemed to have cleared out.

The thief lacked a coherent plan. He had been turned around and didn't know where he was anymore, or how to get out of the forest.

"May I sit, while you contemplate our next move?" Allyn asked as he took a seat on a massive root. "I'm Reverend Allyn Grey."

"Friends call me Skieve," the robber said.

If that was what friends called him, what did his enemies . . . ? "Well, Skieve, do you know how to handle that weapon? I don't want it going off by accident."

"I was in the army. Ain't going off 'les I want to put a round in your black ass." Skieve put down his arm, pistol toward the ground. Allyn felt a little better. "You gonna preach to me now, Rev? Tell me what a sinner I am, how my life would be better with Jesus?" He pronounced it *Jay-zus*.

"I'll start with Jesus—but if that doesn't work for you, maybe Buddha or Allah will . . . there are many paths to improvement from where you stand now . . . lots of upward potential."

"What the hell kinda preachin' is that?" Skieve looked incredulous. "You want me to pray like them filthy rag heads that done took out the towers?"

"You're a proud American?"

"Damn straight!"

"But you perpetrated violence against your fellow countrymen."

Skieve scratched the side of his head with the tip of the gun barrel. "Times are tough."

"There are programs for veterans—college aid or skills training."

"That might be a problem seeing as how I'm AWOL. Thing is, I'd go back if they didn't put me in the clink. Took me a wrong turn or two gettin' from there to here. Now I'm stuck. Gonna do time for being absent without leave, and then gonna do time for the robbery and kidnapping. Looking at the next twenty years in the jug if I get caught."

"Skieve, you took an oath. Going AWOL can't sit well with you."

"You don't know how I'm feelin'. You a preacher—you don't break promises."

Allyn thought about his own oath to Aandor, to protect the prince, and how he'd already broken it unwillingly and was about to break it again consciously. His shame hit him like an angry bull. *Who am I to pass judgment on this man?* he thought.

"You quiet all a sudden, preacher."

"I did break a covenant . . . made long ago. What right have I to counsel you when I'm avoiding my own commitments? I came looking for the Taylor children as much as a distraction as to help that family. But I'm lying . . . delaying a decision that is wrong either way I turn."

"Sounds like you got yourself a whole world o' trouble worse than being stuck in the woods with me. Don't go gettin' no ideas, though. You made a promise. Swore to God."

"Actually I swore to *god*. But, I won't do a thing. It's the forest you have to worry about."

"Huh? You ain't makin' any sense."

"The forest is angry at you."

"What kinda crazy talk is that?"

"You brought a lot of negative energy into these woods. The trees can feel it. So can the animals."

Skieve laughed, his voice echoing through the trees. "You tellin' me the critters got it out for me 'cause I went and robbed the Pig?" Skieve doubled over laughing and had to rest his hands, and gun, on his knees. "I ain't never heard such bullshit in all the sermons I been to. What the hell kinda preacher are you?"

A loud crack boomed above them. A thick branch that had seen too many storms clipped Skieve on the head on its way down. The robber fell over, dropping his gun. Reverend Grey kicked the pistol down a ravine. Skieve was struggling to stay conscious, no doubt experiencing bright spots of light at the moment. Allyn took the man's face in his both hands. "Hold still for a moment. This won't hurt."

"You promised," Skieve complained groggily through puckered lips, as Allyn put pressure on his face.

Allyn could feel the anger in the boy's heart—the result of many experiences that shaped his pitiful life, fed his fears, and birthed the turmoil in his soul. Drawing on the forest, praying, Allyn administered a soothe. He felt the magic chip away at the anger and replace it with peace. As the blessing calmed the robber, his protestations lost their intensity. A calm that Skieve had never known in his life filtered through him.

"Wha' kinda preach, are you?" he said, as he slowly slipped into a peaceful unconscious state. "You swore ta Gah . . ."

"Yes," Allyn answered. "But in Aandor, liars have their own god, too."

CHAPTER 11

LIFE INTERRUPTED

1

Brianna MacDonnell jumped into her father's powerful arms the minute her parents walked through the door. Cal's guilt at having left Bree with her grandmother nipped at his joy even as she pressed into him. He had suggested they skip Vivian's place altogether and head directly to their own home. It wasn't that he didn't want to see Bree; he simply had an unfathomable number of tasks to perform, especially with the pending roadtrip to find the prince. There were other guardians to locate, a safe house to set up, assassins to track down . . . the list was endless. Cal didn't think it was the right environment for Bree to be around—too early to bring his daughter back into the mix. Cat insisted they retrieve her; as usual, she won the argument.

Cal relished her nearly weightless body in his arms—her tiny arms wrapped around his neck and the smell of Johnson's baby shampoo. Forty pounds of innocence, she hit his heart with the force of a rhino. The moment saddened him; his own parents never got to know the pure joy that was Bree. It also brought to bear the injustice of his archduke and duchess never having had this simple pleasure with their son. By the time they saw the prince again, if ever, he would be well on his way to becoming a man . . . but what kind of man?

It was Callum's duty to raise the boy with knowledge of his heritage. To raise him straight and proper, teach him right from wrong, and ensure that he was the kind of person that could rule an empire justly.

"We're going to the museum," Bree said.

"We are?" asked Cal.

"No, not *we, Daddy*. My class."

Cat's mother, Vivian Hill, waved a school permission slip. Bree's school trip was the last thing on Vivian's mind if Cal knew the old woman, and he did. She had a plethora of questions for them, each one a brick in the wall of worry she'd erected since they had mysteriously dropped off Bree and headed north to find the wizard Rosencrantz and disappeared for two days. Now was no time for school trips, though. Cal didn't want Bree out of sight or away from family. Heck, he didn't want her more than a foot away from Lelani. Hostages were par for the course in war, especially in Aandor.

"We'll talk about it, sweetie," he said, and put her down.

Vivian came over, the look on her face expressing what she did not convey in words: *Why is someone trying to kill you? Are you safe? Will you go into witness protection? Is Cal still employed?*

Vivian actually asked, "Who are these people?" For simplicity's sake, Cal introduced Seth and Lelani as his protection detail, assigned to him and Catherine since the attack on him in the Bronx.

"Why do you need protection?" Vivian said, her brows knitted with worry. "Is the mafia trying to kill you? Is it that don who got indicted a few days ago—the one that dresses like pimp?"

"Mom, why would Dominic Tagliatore want to kill Cal?" Catherine asked.

"I don't know, you tell me," Vivian said. "I told you to marry a lawyer or doctor, but you had to find a policeman who works in the South Bronx . . ."

Cal wasn't a drinker, but after Cat decided they would spend the night at Vivian's, he wished for two fingers of Jameson's whiskey to get through the evening.

The two-bedroom apartment was in a building on the edge of

Spuyten Duyvil Creek, just overlooking the northernmost tip of Manhattan. It was tastefully decorated with cherrywood furniture, antiques, lace doilies, and smelled of lavender.

Seth made himself comfortable on the couch he would most likely be sleeping on tonight. Lelani staked a corner in the dining room for her needs, but had to push the table out a bit to accommodate her hidden mass. Lelani would still be cramped back there . . . this world was not made for centaurs. Vivian inquired why she was moving her furniture and Cal chalked it up to stakeout tactics.

Viv launched into hostess mode with drinks and snacks and entertained her new guests with stories about how she moved to Riverdale from Rahway after Cat's father passed away so that she could be equally distant between her two daughters and her grandchildren. Cal wondered where "equally distant" would be if Cat returned to Aandor with him—a universe between this one and Aandor perhaps? Would his wife really leave her family forever?

Vivian slid into an accusatory tone, implying to her new guests that Cat and Brianna were in danger because of her son-in-law's choice of vocation. Lelani kept her usual stoic façade, and to his credit, Seth also maintained a neutral mask against the old woman's criticisms even though the cop had been riding him hard the entire trip north. *Viv never wanted Cat to marry a cop. It was beneath her. Vivian and her husband had groomed Catherine for an educated man—someone who worked in an office, as opposed to being a member of a union and on the streets. They certainly didn't expect her to fall for someone who didn't have a family of his own.* Callum maintained a calm indifference against the old woman's opinions. Her nagging came out of love for her daughter. He could at this point explain that he was a lord of the Order of Aandor, that his family had eight hundred acres, thirty servants, their own regiment, and their own town. Vivian had conveyed her love for Cal on many occasions in better times. He recognized her blithering as nerves—an honest case of the jitters when loved ones were in trouble, so Cal let the old woman burn it off without responding.

Brianna, now in SpongeBob jammers, plopped herself next to Seth on the couch. "Hi," she said. "Remember me?"

"I never forget a pretty face," Seth answered. "But do you remember me?"

"You have the star cat," Brianna answered.

Seth made a face like he swallowed something sour.

"Is something wrong?" Lelani asked him.

Seth said, "I forgot about my cat."

Vivian tired herself out nattering. She wished everyone a good night, and took Brianna with her to her bedroom. Cal checked his voice mail and cursed softly after the first message. His bosses wanted to see him the next day. The authorities upstate had sent some follow-up forensics to the precinct in care of him, and the brass wanted to know about this independent investigation he was running when he was supposedly on leave for bereavement (and other psychological reasons). Internal Affairs also had further questions for him concerning his partner's murder. Cal had not been forthcoming on the details. He could claim ignorance because he was not there when it happened, but he knew it was Kraten, the Verakhoon noble who was a childhood friend of Dorn's. But he couldn't tell the brass Erin was decapitated by a knight from another universe taking orders from a homicidal sorcerer out to kill a young boy and all his guardians. They'd lock Cal up for his own protection, and the prince would be good as dead. The last message was from his PBA representative asking to see him in the morning before that meeting with the top brass.

"You have to go," Cat told him.

"I need to get to Maryland," Cal insisted. "We don't know what Dretch discovered upstate. He could be in Baltimore at this moment."

"How can you even think of blowing off IAB?" Cat said. "If you lose your job, your freedom, where will that poor kid be then? Instead of being delayed by a day, you might find yourself tied up for weeks. That badge and gun has been pretty handy so far, but it comes with strings. If you blow them off, you'll be suspended and they'll start digging deeper into our business."

Cat was right, of course, as usual. As long as he was a cop, it would be easier to search for the prince with the goodwill of his superiors. He could access resources from the brotherhood of law enforcement around the country.

"Erin's funeral is also tomorrow," Cat added. "Her partner left a dozen message on our home voice mail. I'm surprised she's even still talking to us. We never sent our condolences."

"I have to get to Maryland," he said to Cat.

"After the funeral."

"Cat . . . I don't know how close Dretch is to finding the prince," he said, stressing each word.

"Damn it, Cal! That woman died because your past caught up with you. Don't make me go alone. What would I tell Erin's family?"

Cal did not know what to say. What could he say? Cat put on that disappointed look she always got when Cal missed a fundamental law of etiquette—the one all wives are issued with their marriage licenses to toe the lines of civility and cow their men when confronted with their inner Neanderthal. He hated when they didn't see eye to eye . . . she was a force to be reckoned with and often got her way. Cal always told his police buddies they were lucky Cat hadn't killed anyone yet—mostly him—with her famous temper.

He looked over at Seth on the couch cutting the knots down on his new staff and tossing the wood chips into a two-gallon ziplock bag. Seth was the cause of this entire mess. Thirteen years ago, Seth bungled a vital spell that would have helped the guardians acclimate to this new world. Instead he gave everyone amnesia. Seth caught Callum's glare and suddenly looked trapped—like a rat.

"Stop blaming Seth," Cat said, reading Cal's mind. "He should never have been there in the first place."

"Life expectancy is forty where we come from," Cal said. "At fifteen, you can own property, marry, have children, joust in tourneys, and join an army. Youth is not his excuse."

Seth excused himself to use the bathroom. Lelani moved to the kitchen. Cat picked up the dishes, cups, and utensils around the apartment and followed the centaur into the kitchen. Lelani was forced against the range to make room for her, and Cat still had to squeeze in. Lelani was trapped in the line of fire between the spouses, which motivated her moving to the kitchen in the first place. Cat seemed oblivious to that fact.

"We've all lost something because of *his* incompetence," Cal said.

Cat threw the dishes into the sink, hard. Cal and Lelani winced at the clash. "You don't even know the half of it, Cal," his wife said. "Before all this craziness, I had finally decided to get my MBA. I already picked up the applications. Then I realized I might be pregnant, again—and I was going to ask you if we could work out a schedule that would let me still go to grad school. If you said that you wanted me to stay home and raise the baby again, I was *willing* to do that, too, because I love you. How sad is that? I find the one worthy alpha male on earth to share my life with, and I'm willing to sacrifice my own ambitions for him. But it was *my* choice to do it.

"All this shit going on now . . . where are *my* options, Cal? I'm stuck with your mission to save the damned prince. Your former life has been crammed down my throat! It's taken over everything! And the way you go at it . . . to hell with our present life! To hell with our friends, our family, your job! *You're* going to do it *anyway*! Where's *my* choice regarding our future?" Cat left the dishes where she dropped them, stormed into the spare bedroom, and shut the door hard.

Seth reentered the room, but had the good sense to keep his yap shut.

Cal was speechless. Catherine's entire life had been co-opted by his mission—turned upside down worse than if a tornado had blasted through their house. Cal was exhausted trying to hold three families together—he only had two arms. Which would he fumble? The archduke and the prince? His parents and betrothed? His wife and child?

"You must give her time to absorb all this," Lelani said. She fixed three cups of chamomile tea for them.

"Time is a luxury in short supply right now," Cal said.

"Catherine is an intelligent woman. She understands the life-or-death ramifications of your task. It is the unknown that frightens her—the secrets. She suspects you are holding back something important." Lelani shot him an understanding look to imply Chryslantha. "She is frustrated, but still with you."

"I'm frustrated, too. Why did Galen and Linnea have to die? If they had made it to safety, they would have raised the prince as their own. You never met a more levelheaded man than Galen—and Linnea, the warmest woman on the palace staff. She had her father's nurturing gift with plants and flowers. Danel would have been safe and happy. How could Galen have driven into a truck with a baby in the car?"

"It may not have been his fault," Lelani said. "Magnus Proust warned me that some, a small minority, that venture between realities might be susceptible to vibrational changes between universes. A malady of the mind might come over such a person before they succumb to death. It's similar to pressure changes suffered by the pearl divers of Karakos."

"I wish Proust would have told me this. Not that it would have made a difference," he finished, looking accusingly at Seth.

"How many times do I have to say I'm sorry?" Seth said.

"My whole life is upside down . . . ," Cal began, but gave up and excused himself to Lelani to join his wife.

"He never cuts me a break," he heard Seth comment as he shut the bedroom door.

2

Callum tossed and turned throughout the night. His wife slept soundly, having taken one of her mother's Ambiens. Cal's mind raced with too many thoughts about the past, present, and future—the possibilities about the mission ahead—strategies, tactics, pitfalls, trying to guess what Dorn and his minions were up to. Would any of the other guardians rise to their responsibilities? Or were they even now gazing at their sleeping spouses and children, choosing to sacrifice the prince and Aandor for the new lives they had built? What if he were alone with only Lelani and the idiot.

After some fleeting bouts of fitful sleep, the sun snuck up like a thief. Callum slid from the bed, with the energy and clarity of a man that had just run a marathon. Cat was still out. He shuffled into the living area to prepare for a day full of bureaucratic headaches. It was quiet. Lelani slept in the corner, but the couch was empty with the blanket neatly folded on top of the pillow. A note was taped to the staff leaning against the couch. A bad feeling crept into Cal's gut. The note, in Seth's handwriting, read:

> *Have loose ends to take care of in the city. Have the new cell phone you gave me. Will meet you later tonight. Seth.*

Cal crumpled the note and flung it at the dining room wall with deep growl. Lelani jolted awake, dagger in hand. She looked around, groggily, and then at Cal for an explanation.

"The idiot has gone AWOL," Cal said.

CHAPTER 12

WALKABOUT

1

Seth waited for the Fidelity Investments branch at 61 Broadway to open for business. His watch read eight thirty—it was his first appointment in what he hoped would be a productive day. His life before Lelani's arrival dominated Seth's thoughts—a life like a moth-eaten tapestry, all holes and frayed fringes in need of darning. He had to account for his hurtful actions or he would be stuck in this point in his life forever; no moving forward, no evolution, just weighed down by the past. He was finally in a position to make amends and set up a brighter future—assuming he survived the present.

New Yorkers rushed around, oblivious to the agents from an alternate reality that threatened to infringe on their cynical, hardened, and exhaustive existence. They were a strange lot, all living within a foot and a half of each other at one time or another, according to one gifted writer. They prided themselves on being able to blend the gift of privacy with the excitation of participation. The city was like poetry—compressing life, races, and breeds into music for the greatest human concentrate on earth and for whom the full meaning of the city would always be elusive. A city designed to absorb anything that comes along without inflicting the event on its inhabitants. Despite the incredible pressures of living here, New Yorkers seem to escape hysteria by some tiny margin every time. Seth prayed this would continue . . . that the rushing masses would stay ignorant of today's happenings, for their own sake.

Seth needed a shave and change of clothes, but thanks to the likes of Russell Brand and Dave Grohl, investment bankers were wary of turning away the slovenly, lest they be secretly filthy rich. A Fidelity coordinator placed him in a waiting area until a representative became available. The décor was green, white, and shades of tan. Balanced on Seth's lap was a large plastic envelope that he had purchased at a drugstore upstate. Cat had given him the money for nicotine patches, but the deals he would make today were worth jonesing for. It was typical of Seth's luck to get saddled with a group of nonsmokers just as his entire life was turning inside out.

He studied the cuts on his hands earned from whittling his staff. It took him a while to get the hang of slicing off the brown and green bark. He found the knots especially difficult to work around. The staff now lay in Vivian's apartment under an enchantment Lelani cast to dry it out quickly so that the inner bark, which still needed to be shaved off, would reveal itself by changing color.

Seth's cell phone rang. Not being familiar with the ring tone, it took a moment before he realized it was his—one of the disposables Cal had purchased for the group. The cop was tracking down his wayward soldier. Seth didn't feel like a soldier, though. Herr MacDonnell thought he was the center of the universe and the boss of everyone. *Fuck him,* Seth thought and muted the call.

He had responsibilities, also—and the adventure upstate had presented him with a unique opportunity; Seth believed it was time he looked after his own interests. MacDonnell should be grateful he at least left a note. *Let Cat deal with Captain Rage.*

Cat! He had forgotten his pet, yet again. Hoshi would soon run out of food and water in Lelani's rented room. Seth didn't have time to retrieve her, not if he wanted to get everything done before relinquishing his freedom to the cause again. But to neglect her would only add to the list he was trying to work through. He tried to remember Earl's number as he punched it into his new phone.

"Hello?" answered a sleepy voice.

"Earl, it's Seth."

"Seth? Seth! We thought you were . . . Where've you been, man?"

"It's a crazy story . . ."

"Hey, why didn't you tell me Joe was dead?"

Seth didn't want to start the conversation on the defensive. "Why didn't you let me stay with you when I told you my house blew up?" he responded.

"You didn't say your house blew up, asshole. You said you had a fire . . . made it seem like an inconvenience. My girlfriend hates you . . . What was I supposed to do?"

"Look, I need someone to get Hoshi out of a boarding room on Twenty-third. I'll text you the address. She's out of food and water."

"Why can't you—"

"'Cause I'm tied up with *stuff*, Earl. Please just do this for me. I know I'm a jerk, but you're the only friend I have left and I need you to do this."

"Yeah. Well—Marge likes the cat . . . and I'm holding kitty hostage until you pay up for the bags I fronted you." Seth breathed a sigh of relief. Hoshi would be okay. After a short pause, Earl asked, *"Are you coming tonight?"*

"Mr. Raincrest?" a Fidelity agent motioned he was available. Seth put his index finger up—the universal signal asking for one more minute on the phone, and followed the man to his cubicle.

"What's tonight?" he asked Earl.

"Joe's service. His mom flies him back to Cali tomorrow. The guy's been your friend for years . . . Are you going to miss this, too? Is this Mindy's abortion all over again?"

"Thanks for getting the cat. Room three-thirteen." Seth ended the call. Earl was one of his oldest friends; it became apparent how daunting getting out of the hole he'd dug himself into over the years would be. He really was a first-rate asshole. If it weren't for Lelani, Cat, and even Cal, he'd truly be alone.

"What can I help you with?" asked the rep. He was a young black kid, thin, just out of college, and probably wearing the first suit in his life his mama didn't buy for him.

"I need a trust . . . mutual funds—something that doesn't need a lot of hands-on care."

"How much are you investing?" the representative asked.

"A lot."

"Can you be specific . . ."

"No. Lots of zeros," Seth said. "The money's coming later, but I need to open the account now."

The representative went through several funds, throwing terms at him like "Lipper" and "Morningstar." Seth opted for a slightly aggressive four-star fund with a consistent track record. He linked his new investment account to his bank and thanked the rep for his time. Seth headed to his bank next to make POD provisions in the event of his untimely demise. With that set up, it was time for the real business. But Seth couldn't walk into the next establishment looking and smelling the way he did. He had to go home first. *Home.* He dreaded this moment.

2

The door had been replaced with a temporary slab of plywood and sealed with police tape. More plywood covered the big holes in the wall separating the hallway and the apartment. A second piece of board across the hall covered his neighbors' wall where debris had blown through. Seth ripped through the police tape and made his way into his home gingerly, avoiding gaps in the floor. The apartment gave off a distinct vibe that he could not define. He chalked it up to the ash dust and the gloomy grayness it gave everything. These charred remains of his old apartment were symbolic of his life. Seth tried to see something positive in the destruction. These items represented the years he lived in selfishness and anger. The fire wiped away that past. It meant renewal—purification. Wasn't *his* prince's sigil the phoenix, after all—a bird that dies by combustion and reinvents itself continuously? On second viewing, a lot more stuff had survived the explosion than Seth had realized the last time he was there with Lelani.

The brunt of the explosion had been in the living room/kitchen area. Unfortunately, the bathroom behind the kitchen was a jumble of ash, twisted metal, and shattered porcelain. No showering would be done in there. The bedroom walls were blackened skeletons of their former selves, but the bedrooms suffered the least damage. In the closet hung his favorite wool peacoat, a deep navy blue with double-breasted black buttons and a wide lapel that flipped up and made him feel like a Merchant Marine officer. It smelled of smoke like everything else in the apartment, but with cold weather coming in, it would be better than the jacket he'd been using. Seth located his backpack under the charred remains of his bed. It was covered in ash, but was relatively intact. Inside, was an unopened pack of Camel cigarettes. Seth thanked the god of small things and stuffed any surviving documents and bank papers into the backpack along with the new paperwork and plastic folder he'd been carrying. His credit cards were slag, and he had tapped out all his remaining cash the day of the fire. Behind the stove, he retrieved two hundred dollars wrapped in tinfoil that had belonged to his roommate, Joe. He'd forgotten about it the day of the fire. Joe certainly didn't need it anymore. He rummaged through more of Joe's property and found some white T-shirts and boxers still in their plastic wrapping. Seth welled up with tears and suddenly had to sit on the floor. The underwear was from Joe's mother—she often sent her son care packages from California. Joe freely shared their contents with Seth—homemade biscuits and jam and an overabundance of clothing. It was Seth's good fortune that he was about the same size as his ex-roommate; more so to have had a friend with the patience and goodwill of a saint like Joe.

Seth let out an emotional barrage the likes of which he couldn't remember ever having done before. It built up out of nowhere and took him over. He had lost his brother. Seth's behavior after Joe's death was abominable. Even with the mission, it would not have taken much effort to make a few phone calls—to tell friends what had happened and to offer condolences to Joe's family. Who better than Seth knew what it was like to lose a family member to a fire? The lost, senseless, hopeless feeling that nothing in the universe makes any sense.

The vibe in the apartment continued to nag at Seth—in fact, it bugged him more now, yet was still just beyond reach of recognition. As Seth grasped at what it was, his neighbor Ramone, a portly five-foot-two South East Asian type with short black hair, ran into the living room wielding an iron skillet raised over his head.

"Rahhhh . . . !" Ramone growled.

He may have looked fearsome if not for the large flowery red and yellow Hawaiian shirt, white hot pants, and white Dolce & Gabbana flipflops. "Oh my God. Seth? You scared me," Ramone said, with a trace of his Filipino accent. He was holding his chest and panting.

"I scared you?" Seth retorted. "You're the one wielding a deadly weapon."

"The homeless keep trying to squat in here. Chad and I shoo them away."

"Thanks . . . I owe you," Seth said.

"You look like hell, sweetie."

"I've had a rough few days. Your apartment pretty much survived?" Seth asked.

Ramone nodded. "Everything still smells like smoke," he said like a man that had spent a lot of effort scrubbing everything down.

Holding fresh underwear, Seth remembered what he had come back for. "Can I use your shower?" he asked.

"Of course. Let me tell Chad we're having a guest first. My little magic monkey walks around naked," Ramone whispered in a hand-to-cheek side note, as he flipflopped out of the room.

The "magic monkey" was too much information for Seth. He tried to keep the image of a hanging Chad out of his head.

Magic, he suddenly realized. *That's the vibe in this apartment.* A sensation at the periphery of awareness—it's what he felt around Rosencrantz. It was the residual magic used when Symian blew up the apartment—perhaps even the spell from Lelani's brass compact. Seth closed his eyes in an attempt to feel it out around him. It was like the smell of the ocean from a mile away, barely there and yet so. The more he concentrated, the harder it was to pinpoint; as though he were repelling the energy with the effort.

Seth decided on another tack. One of his nude models, a yogini that had always tried to get him to meditate, was obsessed with clearing Seth's mind, opening his chakras, and expounding the virtue of nothingness. Seth had put up with it because he was obsessed with opening up her other parts for his own pleasure. He sat in the lotus position and calmed his breathing. He cleared his mind by first thinking of snow on a serene mountaintop. Nothing happened. He was too on edge. He needed something to calm his nerves before he could calm his thoughts. Seth cracked opened the Camel cigarettes and lit up. It tasted better than sweet salted butter on a croissant. He rested his arms against his folded legs, cig between his fingers and again tried to clear his mind. The energy around him grew stronger—more opaque. It drifted out of the walls, the charred remains of furniture, but he remained receptive, open, wanting nothing. Seth didn't know how long he would need to sit there before something noticeably obvious happened. Should he acknowledge the energy when it reached him? He heard a gasp and opened his eyes. Ramone stared, bewildered. *The cigarette?* Seth thought.

"I just needed something to calm . . ." As Seth raised his hand with the cigarette, he noticed a faint silvery glow flickering about his hand like burning gas. He quickly realized the aura covered him.

"You're on fire," Ramone said.

Seth lost focus, and the light dissipated.

"Yeah," Seth agreed. "Can we keep that between us? I've got a lot on my plate these days as it is."

Ramone nodded and said, "It's okay to come over now." He rushed out of the room.

Seth wished Lelani had been there to explain what had happened. Obviously he was sensitive to the magic . . . he just didn't know what it was good for. If the energy left every time he concentrated on it, how would he ever use it to cast a spell? Seth went to take that shower quickly, before Ramone changed his mind.

3

Seth walked into the York Avenue lobby of Sotheby's auction house showered, shaved, and freshly changed, feeling like a new man. His friend Mitch, who served on the board of directors for the Museum of Comic and Cartoon Art, gave him a contact for the rare books specialist at Sotheby's. Mitch also cautioned that appointments were usually done weeks in advance. Seth had an idea this would be the case. Fortunately, he had "borrowed" Lelani's silver flower pin with the credibility enchantment, which was now pinned to the collar of his peacoat.

"Seth Raincrest to see Alistair St. Cloud," he said to a very serious man in a jacket and tie at the front desk.

"Is Mr. St. Cloud expecting you?"

"Absolutely," Seth said confidently. He brandished his cell phone. "In fact, I just spoke to him. Alistair said I should just come up because his secretary would be out to lunch at this time."

The security man's brow clenched like he needed an Advil, but handed Seth a visitor's pass anyway and pointed him to the right elevator bank. As Seth walked off the elevator, yet another receptionist greeted Seth. This company had more layers than Fort Knox. He gave the girl on this floor the same spiel, and she called St. Cloud's assistant to come get him. The assistant was an older woman with short white hair, impeccably dressed, with a string of white pearls and sensible shoes. Seth told her he was there to see Mr. St. Cloud.

"Mr. St. Cloud is very busy at the moment. What is this in reference to?" she asked skeptically.

Seth noted a degree of resistance coming from the woman. He didn't know if the silver pin was losing its mojo or if the woman's age or intelligence had something to do with it. Perhaps she did believe him, but it was the nature of her job to hold people off regardless. Seth pulled the plastic folder out of his backpack. He opened it and gingerly pulled out a copy of *Action Comics* number one with the iconic image of the Man of Steel holding a car over his head. She took it carefully and examined it. Seth suspected the woman's reaction had more to do with the last reported sale of this issue being well over a million dollars than her being a comic book fan.

"You have more?" she asked.

"Yep."

"May I see?"

"I'll show St. Cloud," he said.

"Wait here," she said, handing the magazine back.

A few minutes later, the assistant escorted Seth into a posh office of mahogany and brass décor. A trace of pipe smoke lingered. The bookcases were filled with moldy old texts, protected behind airtight glass doors. There was a black-and-white photo of St. Cloud in a black suit. He wore a short-cropped dark Brylcreemed haircut and thick black square-framed glasses standing behind a huge old tome on a pedestal. The brass plaque on the frame said *Gutenberg Bible 1969*.

"Are these stolen items?" asked a deep velvety British voice behind him. It exuded snobbery.

Seth turned to find the man from the photo, aged several decades, in a tweed jacket. His hair was still full, but white. His jowls wobbled as he talked.

"Excuse me?" Seth asked.

"The items you have brought . . . Are they stolen? Do you have any way to authenticate your ownership?"

Seth thought of Ben and Helen Reyes, the original owners of the magazines. The nexus to their home in Puerto Rico was filled with periodicals from the past hundred years. That was until they needed to build pyres in the meadow to fight nocturnal dog-men. When Seth saved these comic books from the flames he wasn't even sure why he did it. At the time, he was certain he wouldn't survive to cash them in. Ben and Helen had lived on top of a fortune for years, but couldn't have cared less about the money. Ben was the caretaker of the world's last sorcerer, a sentient tree named Rosencrantz. And that charge had cost Ben his life when Seth's group brought violence to their home. Still, Ben was a proponent of Seth turning his life around; the money these few books would bring were the cornerstone of that plan.

"I bought them at a yard sale in a small town in Ohio a year ago," Seth lied. "The people selling them had no idea what they were really worth. There's no receipt." Seth didn't think he'd need the enchanted pin to push this one over on St. Cloud. Things like this happened all the time. It helped that there were no police alerts for stolen rare comic books, and possession was still nine-tenths under the law.

"Can I see them?" St. Cloud asked, putting on his reading glasses.

Seth opened the envelope and placed *Action Comics* number one on the desk. He gingerly pulled out *Detective Comics* number twenty-seven, the first appearance of Batman, and laid it next to the first one. St. Cloud's passion for rare and expensive things was etched on his face. A naked, drunk, and horny Scarlett Johansson couldn't pry St. Cloud's attention away from the desk at that moment.

"What else have you got?" St. Cloud asked. He eyed the folder and tried to contain his excitement.

Seth pulled out the remaining books with equal care and laid them next to each other: *Amazing Fantasy* number fifteen , *WHIZ Comics* number two, and *All Star Comics* number three. They were all in good condition. Rosencrantz's proximity must have preserved the paper. The only scuffs and creases were from Seth's handling them.

St. Cloud puckered his lips and let out an approving whoosh. "If these are real, there is at least two million dollars on this desk right now," he said. "If I can get monsieurs Tarantino, Spielberg, and Lucas in the same room, maybe five million."

St. Cloud checked each one under a large magnifying glass. His assistant snipped a piece out of each magazine that was no bigger than the head of a pin and placed them in individual test tubes. She went through a mahogany door disguised as a wall into a modern brightly lit room with glass cabinets and metal tables.

"If the chemical analysis of the paper and ink comes back authentic, we're in business," St. Cloud said.

Seth knew they would and said, "I'd like a small cash advance of a few thousand against the sale. I'll leave the items here with you. My only request is that we fill out the paperwork now. I'll sign everything in advance."

"We don't know what the final sale will be," St. Cloud said, surprised.

"I'll sign blank applications that you can fill in later and leave deposit slips for where I want the money to go. Take an extra percent on your end if this is unorthodox. Assume that after today, you might never see me again. But I want the money to go to those accounts."

St. Cloud agreed to the terms. The man looked honest enough; Seth didn't have a choice—he could be running for his life, in another universe, or dead, in the coming days. But at least he'll never be poor again. St. Cloud might take a healthy cut of the action, but it'll get done right. Seth filled out the paperwork and presigned the necessary papers for Sotheby's and his financial institutions. St. Cloud handed him six thousand dollars out of petty cash.

As he walked out of the building, a great burden lifted from Seth's shoulders. He had accomplished the most important task. *What is good?* Ben's voice echoed as though the old man were there beside him—guiding him.

It was 6:00 P.M. Joe's memorial service would start soon. He hailed a cab and aimed it for the East Village.

4

Seth stood under a tree across the street from the East Village funeral home where Joe's service commenced, smoking a cigarette, watching everyone arrive. They were all in there, his once and former friends. He tapped the butt into the sidewalk with the tip of his shoe and crossed the street.

It was bright inside, a welcome contrast to the cold darkness that had fallen on the city. The walls were freshly painted, faded yellow with patterns of gold leafing, bordered by intricate white ceiling moldings and an inoffensively colored carpet that could have been either gray or beige. The mood was tranquil with bland organ music spilling out of camouflaged speakers. A few days earlier, he would have found such a serene place contrived and hokey. A sign pointed to Joe's service. Some friends of Joe's whom Seth did not know were chatting at the entrance.

At the far end of the room was Joe's casket. True to Catholic tradition it was open. This was Seth's first view of Joe since their last conversation a few days earlier. He'd blown off his friend to buy some pot. Lelani was hot on his tail with fantastic stories about life in another universe. Seth thought she was crazy, but humored her in hopes of getting her to pose nude in a photo shoot. He genuinely thought she was disturbed—a total nutjob, and still he had intended to exploit her. Seth couldn't believe the type of man he used to be. By the time they'd returned to his apartment, Joe was dead and Seth was again homeless. That was a lifetime ago.

Seth took a single step into the room and observed from the back. His friends hadn't yet realized he was there. He studied the crowd. Earl and his old lady Marge were on the left in the third row next to Mitch and his spouse, what's-her-name. Mindy, her straight brown hair cut in a short-cropped flapper's do and wearing a black sleeveless above-the-knee dress, was standing against the wall on the right talking to one of Joe's colleagues from work. She was one of a small number of Seth's models who made it out of the porn business relatively unscathed by drugs or humiliation . . . except for her personal relationship with Seth. Aware of his arrival, a growing ensemble of whispers pulled Seth from his observations. He wondered how many wished it was him in that coffin and not Joe. As he walked up the center aisle toward the casket, he heard murmurings of "nerve," "asshole," "can't believe . . . ," and other musings regarding his presence. If he hadn't showed up, the talk would be about his no-show. There was no way he could win. Seth hoped no one would challenge his right to be there. He was not looking for trouble, and would not leave until his business was done.

For a dead man, Joe looked great. Except for some minor changes in bone structure where the mortician reconstructed his face, it was Joe pre-fire blast. His burns were covered with a healthy coating of makeup. His usual wispy three-day growth had been shaved, his wavy black hair trimmed and combed, and he was in a sharp black suit that Seth knew his friend had never owned. Joe looked ready to sit up and chastise him over missing the rent or the innumerable other offenses Seth imposed on their friendship. The room behind him was an odd combination of silence and diminished rumbling. Apparently even friends of Joe he'd never met knew who he was. He put his hand on the side of the casket and bowed his head. It occurred to Seth that he didn't know any prayers, the last time having set foot in a church being for a two-girl photo shoot involving wayward nuns called "Lickity-Split Confessionals." No one else in the room knew that, of course, so Seth simply stated his regret in plain language for his part of Joe's death and hoped that his friend would forgive him, wherever he was. A righteous anger arose in Seth for the first time in his tragic life. Those who murdered his friend, who intended to murder him, had no right to make decisions about who lived and who died. Joe was never part of their war. These monsters callously shucked aside anyone who got in their way—a trail of collateral damage with complete disregard for the web of lives surrounding each individual. The family and friends who are affected each time are left trying to pick up the pieces to make sense of the vacuum created by the loss. These assassins had a thing or two coming to them. Finding the prince and stopping Dorn was beginning to feel like Seth's own mission instead of someone else's agenda.

There was nothing else Seth could do for Joe. He turned and approached Earl in the second row.

"Hey," Earl said. Marge sat beside her man indignantly and refused to look at Seth.

"Hoshi?" Seth asked.

"Scarfing down a can of Friskies in our kitchen."

"Thanks." One more check on Seth's karma list.

Seth reached into his pocket and pulled out an envelope, which he handed to Earl. Earl cracked it to find several fifty- and hundred-dollar bills—more than the amount Seth initially owed him for the pot he'd purchased on credit.

"Here?" Earl whispered angrily. "You're doing this here." He looked around the room, paranoid.

"I may never see you again. I wanted to square things."

While Earl tried to absorb this statement, his girlfriend cut in, "I'm keeping that cat!"

Seth nodded. "Yes, you are."

Marge gave him a dubious look, running through several interpretations of what that might imply. "I'm serious," she emphasized. "Thing's scrawny as a scarecrow."

"Not going to argue."

Seth pulled out another envelope filled with more money and this one he handed to Marge. She wouldn't take it, looking at Seth suspiciously. "This is to cover Joe's transportation to California and burial," Seth said. "Can you give it to his mom when she arrives?" Marge, still unsure whether she was making a deal with the devil, took the envelope and tucked it in her purse.

Seth made his rounds around the room, apologizing for acts of selfishness, and in some cases, even acts of apathy. He returned money he owed to people, with generous interest. Most politely took the cash, but wouldn't give him more than a minute of their time.

"What kind of twelve-step bullshit is this?" Martin Lipsinki had asked. Seth had wrecked his car a year ago on the way to a photo shoot and left Martin hanging when the insurance wouldn't cover the loss. Martin opened a thick envelope with enough cash for a decent down payment on a sedan. He was dumbstruck. "You selling dope now?" he finally said. Seth smiled, patted him on the shoulder, and continued through the room.

"I hope you don't think there's any amount that can make up for what you put me through," a raspy voice said behind him.

Mindy Dietz was as beautiful as the first time Seth met her. She had been a fresh arrival from Iowa who quickly made her rounds in Alphabet City's party scene. During their four-month-long relationship, one of Seth's longest, she trusted him enough to get her the centerfold in a reputable publication like *Playboy*, *Maxim*, or at least *Penthouse*. Instead, all she got was a tasteless back-issue spread at a second-rate rag called *Likely Legal*. And she got pregnant. Seth never showed up for their appointment at the clinic and virtually ignored the girl after her D&C procedure. Left scrambling for someone to take her home after the operation, Marge had to leave work early and pay for the abortion on her credit card. Mindy eventually paid Marge back with no help from Seth, who even cheated Mindy out of her fee for the photo shoots. This one was high on his list of haunts, but still not the worst. It was difficult to look her in the eye.

"There isn't," Seth admitted, answering her greeting. "I should have at least paid for the abortion." He pulled out another envelope and waited for her to take it. "I'm sorry I was such an asshole," he added. Mindy was always strapped for cash. The joke was that if you paid Mindy at 11:55 P.M., she'd find a way to spend it before the clock struck midnight. She looked at his offering for several seconds, considering whether to take it from him.

"Go to hell," she eventually said, and walked away. Seth was sure his reservation was in already.

Whatever his friends thought of him, Seth knew this was the right first step. *What is good?* It's doing the right thing even when it's hard and causes you pain. His task at the funeral home was done. A few former friends forced smiles as he parted, likely wondering among themselves how long this Robin Hood act would last before the real Seth returned. Seth let them think his behavior was due to Joe's death; he wasn't in a position to share the other life-altering events that had been thrust upon him the past three days.

As he walked out onto the brisk dark street, a large hand grabbed his shoulder from behind and thrust him against the wall.

"You have got to be the stupidest man I've ever met!" Callum MacDonnell growled inches from his face. Seth thought it was a pretty decent impression of Batman—Christian Bale, not Adam West. Cal wore a light-brown suede jacket over a blue, yellow, and green plaid flannel shirt; a pair of dark blue jeans; and brown Timberland boots with thick soles—a big, blond bully of a lumberjack, whose remarks made many heads turn.

"We're supposed to be heading to Maryland," Cal said.

"Uh—maybe there's a better place to discuss this than here,

dude?" Seth immediately regretted saying "dude." Typical of his vernacular, which was forged from avoidance of accountability, it came off cavalier—too informal for the self-important Captain Rage's current mood.

Cal gripped him by his jacket collar and dragged Seth along the funeral home wall.

"You think this is a game?" the cop asked.

"I had a life before all this, too," Seth said. He sounded more defensive than he intended. "Don't I have a right to put my affairs in order before you send me up against a sorcerer that's probably going to clean my clock?"

"Your affairs are not your concern anymore," Callum said. "We're in this predicament because of your actions, you incompetent asshole. Do you have any idea how complicated you've made my life? How many people have been hurt and will still be hurt because of you? I want you where I can see you—where you can't do any more harm." Cal shook him some more and the envelope with Mindy's rejected money fell out. Cal picked it up.

"What the hell is this?" he asked. He counted through the bills quickly. "Where'd you get two thousand dollars?"

"Somebody gave it to me," Seth said.

"Okay," Cal responded, and put the money back in Seth's jacket pocket. "Wait . . ."

Cal noticed the silver flower on Seth's lapel and yanked it off. He punched Seth in the gut and the photographer crumpled to the ground holding his middle.

"Lie to me again," Cal said. "Do you know what I went through today? I needed this enchanted pin to deal with IAB, the police brass, and my union. Instead, you take it and leave me floundering for my life, looking like an asshole trying to mask a truth I can't possibly tell them." Cal pulled him up by the scruff and dragged him away from the funeral home entrance. When they were around the corner he threw Seth against the wall in an alley. "Are you still determined to tank this mission?"

Seth was never determined to sabotage the mission—this much he knew was true. Rosencrantz's spell let them witness the night they came through to this plane of existence; Seth saw a scared thirteen-year-old, out of his depth, trying to cast a complex spell in the middle of a thunderstorm that was bleeding away the ink on his scrolls. Callum saw the events as well—his suspicions were unfounded, and Seth resented the way MacDonnell treated him.

Cal raised his fist again to strike. Much as he disliked the cop, he deserved a smack for putting MacDonnell in a bind with his superiors, but he didn't deserve to be a punching bag. Seth closed his eyes and wished the cop wouldn't hit him. A second went by, then another, without a strike, Seth cracked one eye open to see the fist still hovering in front of him, shaking.

"Are you going to hit me, or not?" Seth asked.

"I'd really like to hit you," Cal said. "But I can't move my fist."

"You can't . . ." Seth looked around in a panic. "Are we under attack?" Seth didn't want to die frozen like a pair of Popsicles in an alley. He scanned the alley and the street for the goons that had been on their tail but saw only the normal bustle of a city street. Callum let go of his scruff and looked around as well. Neither of them was frozen, only Cal's arm hanging in the air in striking position.

Seth had a thought. "Try opening your hand," he said. Cal did this easily, and his arm released the tension.

"What the heck . . . Did you do that?" Cal asked, shaking his hand.

"I don't know," Seth said, sounding pleased. "I really didn't want to be hit."

"Can you do it again?" Cal asked.

"I don't know."

Cal sucker punched him in the jaw with a right hook. The

photographer lost his legs and crashed on his butt. White spots circled his head.

"Apparently not," Cal said, as though it were a harmless experiment. "My car is around the corner."

"Where are the girls?" asked Seth, rubbing his jaw.

"Bree's staying with Cat. I left Lelani behind to protect them. It's just us heading south."

"Wait, I have one more thing I need to do up here," Seth said.

Callum MacDonnell's glare made it abundantly clear Seth's excursion was over. Any protest from him would lead to more beatings.

Great, Seth thought. Without Cat to calm her husband on this trip, Seth was likely to be the short, tubby half of an Abbot and Costello routine all the way to Maryland. He moved his jaw back and forth trying to regain its normal feeling.

"Did Lelani track me?" he asked, as they walked toward the Ford Explorer.

The cop shook his head. "Any active cell phone, even disposables, can be triangulated," he said. Seth noticed his staff and the bag of shavings was in the backseat. Also a lacrosse bag that Seth suspected held Callum's recovered sword. "Worry less about that and work on that defensive magic," Cal continued. "It'll be handy if we run into Dorn's goons."

"They're not the only ones," Seth murmured, stroking his jaw.

CHAPTER 13
THE KINDHEARTED KILLER

1

Callum and Seth pulled up to the Glen Burnie, Maryland, home of Clyde and Rita Knoffler in time to greet the sun as it emerged from the horizon. They had driven through the night at Cal's insistence, stopping only for a vital nap in a rest stop parking lot as exhaustion finally overpowered the cop. Cal nudged Seth, who sat in the passenger seat, and thankfully had slept for most of the ride down.

A liberal helping of police tape cordoned the house declaring it a crime scene. Cal's hopes dissolved into his gut with a discomforting slosh.

"I'm tired of seeing that tape everywhere we go," Seth declared.

Cal thought that for once, he and the idiot were in total agreement. Seth opened the door and got out, but Cal remained in his seat staring at the sealed dwelling. Dread had rooted him in that spot. The boy was dead—this was the end.

"Are you coming?" Seth asked.

Cal couldn't move. For all his courage and ability to face an army wielding swords and axes, he just couldn't bear to discover what had happened in this place. He was stuck to his seat like a raw recruit, as if a spell had pinned him there. Everything he loved back home in Aandor, everything he suffered for, could be over in an instant . . . as dead as the young boy he failed to protect. Seth walked over to the driver's side and tapped the window. Cal did not acknowledge him.

"It could be anything," Seth said, through the glass, displaying some nascent intuition for the first time. Cal looked at the photographer—he had guessed what was going through the cop's mind. The idiot was not as oblivious as when they'd found him a few days earlier.

"Maybe they got robbed," Seth added. "Maybe someone else got killed." Seth spotted a paperboy making rounds and ran over. They talked for several minutes with Seth pointing to the house. The paperboy was animated about what had happened, making wide gestures with his hands as though this was the most important thing to have happened in his neighborhood in his lifetime. He handed Seth a newspaper from his bag. Seth trotted back to the car. This time, Cal cracked his window.

"Clyde's dead," Seth explained. "The boy's still alive."

Cal let out a long breath he didn't even realize he'd been holding in. He inhaled, and the air was crisp and sweet.

"But . . . ," continued Seth.

No buts . . . the kid's alive, that's all that matters.

". . . it was the kid that killed Clyde. He ran away and is hiding from the cops." Seth handed Cal the local paper.

TEEN KILLER
STILL AT LARGE!

FATHER SLAYER DANIEL HAUER
ELUDES POLICE

Cal stared at the headline in disbelief. *The kid's alive, that's what matters,* he repeated to himself over and over.

A Glen Burnie police cruiser sidled up to them driver side to driver side. "Can I help you folks?" he asked. "There's no trespassing on these premises."

Cal flashed his NYPD badge. "I'm working a case," he said as professionally and detached as he could. "It led me to this house. Looking for a kid named Daniel, about thirteen. Can you tell me what happened?"

"Killed his old man is what happened," the deputy said, thumbing toward the property. "Sheriff had him in the station a few days ago on an A&B. Beat up his classmates with a two-by-four and sent them to the hospital."

"Did he fight a lot?" Cal asked, trying to get some sense of who his prince had become.

"Don't know if he got into a lot of fights growing up," the deputy said. "But I heard he tore up all his desks at school—costing the city hundreds to replace them."

Cal wondered how it came to this. Daniel was his ward to raise into manhood. He and the guardians were to bring the kid up in a safe environment and imbue him with an understanding of his role and responsibilities to his kingdom, to be a good, civilized person. How could he have ended up a juvenile delinquent . . . patricidal? If he and Seth had arrived just a few days earlier . . .

The kid's alive, that's what matters.

"Can you clear me to go in there?" Cal asked the officer.

"Let me call it in, make sure forensics has everything they need. It's a pristine scene. The wife OD'd on some pills shortly after and had to be taken to the hospital. No one's been in there since the incident. We didn't get a jump on the case early enough, though. Neighbors only realized there was a problem when the little girl wandered bawling into the street. We think the boy's left the county."

Always a step behind. But the delinquent is still alive, and that's all that matters.

2

It was a typical middle-class American home. The furniture had been of good quality once; nicks in the wood, worn threads, and frayed edges told a story of neglect. The dining room hutch was scuffed, the plates within it did not match, and the varnish had lost its luster a while ago. In the center lay a broken dining room table and bloodstains on the carpet beneath it. Cal walked gingerly through the home, careful not to disturb the scene. He studied the broken table and the stains.

My prince did this.

Cal had mixed feelings about the incident. In Aandor, new recruits were kept at arm's length by experienced troops until after their first battle. It was claimed to be a hazing tradition, but in truth, no grunt knew whether an untested soldier would be able to take another's life in battle when the time came. It was one thing for a young recruit to do well in training, or to boast of his bravery over drinks at a tavern surrounded by friends and buxom wenches, another to find oneself opposite a man you are expected to hack to death with iron and steel. Noncombatants assume when you put on a uniform and act the soldier that you are capable of dealing death. It's not that easy.

Sometimes the most obvious warriors falter and bring shame on themselves, or if they're lucky, a quick death. No veteran soldier wanted to bond prematurely with a coward—to develop feelings of brotherhood and camaraderie with a man unable to do his job and defend his regiment and country. Sometimes the least obvious soldier—a tailor's son or a musician; the weasely, good humored, or immature—surprised you, and turned out to be the man you most wanted at your side in a trench.

Often, the troops discussed whether their king or prince, seldom in battle themselves, was made of the same stern stuff as their most fervent soldiers. *Daniel's answered that question at least,* Callum thought. The boy had taken a life. He had true grit. At least that could be said for him. But was he someone you wanted leading your kingdom?

Something was missing, though, and Cal searched his mind hard looking around the living area of this home. There were no family photos displayed in this house. The few pictures there were, were of a little girl. But where was Daniel? Where was his presence in this family?

From the empty beer cans and other bottles in the pantry—enough to shame even the worst college fraternity—Cal took a measure of the man Daniel had killed: a sad waste of a human being. The mom was no better. Prescriptions for Valium, Xanax, Percocet lined the kitchen counter and her nightstand—it was not that needing these types of prescription made one a bad person . . . but she was clearly incapable of defending her adopted son from this man.

Cal walked into Daniel's room. He had expected posters of sultry women, heavy metal gods, an Xbox with Grand Theft Auto and other violent games stacked beside it . . . perhaps the smell of cigarettes or a hidden bong. What he found instead was a small collapsible drafting table and an extensive collection of books, mostly fiction. He didn't know who Philip K. Dick, Isaac Asimov, or Roger Zelazny were, but recognized J. K. Rowling and Stephen King. On the floor was a long white cardboard box brimming with comic books in plastic sleeves. On the dresser rested a photo of two boys at some type of convention, one very fat, the other thin, posing with SpongeBob SquarePants. Cal knew the thin boy was Daniel right away. He had his mother's coloring and her eyes. They were not the eyes of a delinquent . . . a killer. He looked intelligent—a normal kid who liked to read comics and draw.

Cal removed the photo from its frame and sat on the bed, studying the boy. He tried to see the room from Daniel's perspective. What did the boy think of his life? Did he wish for a better home, a better father? What were his hopes and aspirations? Seth walked in and took stock of the scene from the doorway.

"Not exactly what I thought a prince's room would look like," he said. "Or a murderer's," he added. He picked up a copy of Joseph Campbell's *The Power of Myth* that lay at the top of a stack on the nightstand. "My ex-girlfriend tried to get me to read this once. Only made it through ten pages. Kid's smart, huh?"

He was smart, Cal silently agreed. Not just book smart, either . . . he'd eluded the police for two days already, and they didn't have a clue as to how to find him. They were doing the usual, canvassing the places he's been known to associate and checking at friends' houses. But this boy was creative—he thought outside the box. He was gone—out of state, and probably out of country soon enough. In one regard, Cal was grateful—Daniel had eluded Dorn's agents as well. This was the break he had prayed for. Being lost was the best protection for the prince until Cal could catch up with Dretch.

As they exited the home, signs of life began to emerge on the block. Kids with backpacks full of books shuffled their way to school. A sheriff's car pulled up to the curb. He wore mirrored aviator sunglasses under a cowboy hat with a star on the front. Cal didn't know if they were far enough south to justify a sheriff looking like he stepped out of *Smokey and the Bandit*.

"I'm Sheriff Ed Maher," he said. "You the folks looking for the Hauer boy?" he asked, knowing full well that they were.

"That would be us," Seth said.

Cal put a hand on Seth's shoulder and squeezed to indicate *Let me do the talking*.

The sheriff filled them in on the details of the past few days: the fight with the Grundy boys, the conversation he had with Daniel's mother about her abusive husband and his feelings that he was being lied to by the both of them about Clyde Knoffler's abusive behavior.

Cal asked the sheriff about the school desks Daniel supposedly destroyed. The sheriff laughed.

"I don't know if 'destroyed' is the right word," the sheriff said. "Boy liked to draw on his desks. The principal's a bit of an asshole; I can say that because he's my cousin. But I don't think he would have put the boy in that position with his pa if he knew the whole situation at home though.

"I think the kid was acting out," Maher continued. "Can't grow up in a home where a drunk ex-Marine is pounding on you and not pick up a few bad habits. I mean them Grundy kids he beat up were no angels; they been terrorizing the school district for better part of the decade. It's possible things went down like Hauer said. Got a doctor that'll swear on a stack of Bibles Danny's bruises came from a grown man's fist, not them other boys."

"Have you talked to his friends about where he might have gone?" Cal asked.

"Didn't do any good. His best friend ratted him out and his girlfriend stepped out on him with the captain of the baseball team. She ain't said much of anything. Doesn't stop them coming by this house every day to see if anyone's home. I guess if they knew anything, they wouldn't be bugging me every six seconds, like they are now, standing over there waiting for me to finish talking to you."

Cal looked at the corner. The chubby boy from the photo and a dour-looking girl in a wrist cast, thin with dark puffy eyes and auburn hair, stood in front of a bus stop bench. Neither waited for the bus.

The sheriff got a call on his radio about a domestic disturbance. He and Cal exchanged business cards as he got into his cruiser.

"Girl's Katie Millar," Maher said. "The chubby kid's Adrian Lutz. Hope you have more luck with them than I did." He clicked on his roof lights and drove off.

Cal and Seth walked over to the kids, trying not to appear eager. The kids looked distrustful of them.

"We're searching for Daniel Hauer," Cal said.

"What do you want him for?" Adrian asked.

"We don't want to arrest him or anything like that," Seth added.

"I'm family," Cal said. "Daniel was stolen as an infant. The family's put some time and effort into finding him."

The kids looked at each other incredulously.

"Danny would've have loved to know his real ma and pa," Adrian said. "The ones he had were crap. And now he's run off for his life two days before y'all show up with this great news." Adrian shook his head. "He can't catch a break."

"Do you know where he might have gone?" Cal asked.

"No," the girl said softly. "We'd tell you if we knew, mister." She seemed to be looking elsewhere, not at them when she softly whispered, "I'd do anything for Danny."

"Me, too," Adrian said.

"Didn't you rat him out?" Seth asked. "And didn't you cheat on him?" he said to Katie.

Cal wanted to smack Seth in the head. They didn't have time to stumble and bumble through the interview and alienate a possible lead.

Adrian's lip began to quiver. "I regret that I didn't do the right thing," he said. "Them Grundy boys were waiting on the street to beat me up, and Daniel defended me. He put them both in the hospital." Adrian started to cry.

"Them Grundys threaten to set fire to our house and beat up my ma and pa if I didn't tell the sheriff we were just joking around that night, and that Danny went rogue." The quivering gave way to full-fledged sobs. "He deserved a better friend than me."

Katie, who had been mostly quiet and detached, struggled to get her thoughts out. She looked like she hadn't slept in a while. Cal had seen his share of abuse victims in his years on the NYPD, and this girl displayed signs of trauma. She was only a few years older than Bree, not quite a child, but not yet a woman, and she bore a heavy burden of which even her portly friend was unaware. Cal gently put his hands on her shoulders. She flinched, but fought the urge to shake him off and instead started to cry.

"Seth, why don't you take Adrian to the car and get the rest of his stories?" Cal said. "Learn anything you can about Daniel, his hobbies, likes, dislikes, anything that might help us discover where he went."

When the two of them were out of earshot, Cal asked, "Who's abusing you? Someone at home . . . your father?"

"Oh, God no," Katie said. "My dad is awesome. They suspect

something. They're worried it's drugs. I don't know how to tell them."

Cal motioned to the bench and sat alongside the girl. "I'm a policeman in New York," he told her. "I hear a lot of stories, see a lot of things." He took out a picture of his family. "I'm also the dad of a little girl. If you'd like to tell me something, I'll keep it between us—unless you want me to help you."

"I . . ."

The words stuck in her throat. She choked on them. Cal had seen this before on calls for domestic disturbance. Katie seemed caught between telling a complete stranger about the most painful and humiliating event of her life, and keeping it bottled in, where he knew it would fester and grow like a living poison, ready to suffocate the last vestiges of her sanity. Callum could only guess what happened, but she *needed* to say it. Katie, no doubt, believed it was something she could move on from, like burying a beloved pet. But it wasn't. Katie was in jeopardy of becoming withdrawn and following a negative track in her life, driven by a sense of worthlessness and powerlessness. Cal had seen this too often.

"I was—I was—he forced me," she finally got out.

Cal put his arm around her. She collapsed into his arms and cried. Cal dreaded his next question. He knew nothing of his prince. The boy looked innocent enough in the photos, but many people hid their anger issues in public.

"Was it Daniel? Did he hurt you?"

Katie pulled away like Cal had just shouted a string of obscenities. She was angry.

"Daniel is the most decent person I've ever met in my life," she said. "He's the truest friend anybody . . . If I hadn't been so . . . to have an older boy . . ." The oxygen had run out and Katie was trying to adjust. She took a second to compose her thoughts.

"Josh came looking for me after he attacked me. He wanted to rewrite history—convince me that what happened didn't really happen. That it was a 'misunderstanding.' I was afraid. But Daniel found me first, and I knew—I just knew I'd be okay.

"Danny stood between Josh and me even though Josh outweighed him by twenty pounds. And he took Josh's punches for me and he just punched back and he never begged him to stop or ask for mercy. He took it all for me even after I hurt him by taking up with that asshole. And then his father . . ."

"Daniel's father? You mean Clyde?"

"Yeah. He was there at the fight. Making out in his pickup with some floozy. He was so mad that Daniel caught him cheating."

Katie began to cry again. "I can just imagine Clyde going home drunk and angry. Daniel was only at that baseball field because of me. And now he's gone and the police want to arrest him." Katie began to hyperventilate. Cal rubbed her back gently. Her panic attack subsided after a moment.

"It's my fault that he had to kill his dad," she continued. "Adrian's right . . . Daniel deserved better."

"I don't think he'd agree," Cal said. The girl's intensity stunned him. She was too young to have so many adult problems. He waited a moment until she was calm and said, "You should tell your parents."

Katie panicked and shook her head. "NO!"

"Then what?" Cal asked calmly. "Are you better off than you were a few days ago? Is time helping? You look like you haven't slept. Keeping this secret will change the person you are; the person that Daniel loved. And think about this . . . your story would help Daniel's case in the eyes of the law."

"It would?"

"Self-defense is the only legitimate reason to kill someone. He wouldn't do jail time. Katie, there are professionals who will help you work through the pain and help you get back to the person you were. If it were my daughter, I would want to know. I would still love her, and I would not blame her. It's harder than you think for a daughter to disappoint her father. I hope there's some part of you that realizes this."

She sat stiffly for a while. Eventually she nodded.

They walked to the car and joined Seth and Adrian.

"Adrian, you go on to school," Cal said. "We're going to drive Katie home. She isn't feeling well."

They headed for the Millar residence several blocks away.

Hearing Daniel's friends speak so loyally of the boy lifted Callum's spirit. These were the people who knew the prince best. For Danel to overcome such obstacles as his adopted parents, and still turn out honorable, brave, and loyal to his friends filled Callum with a new hope and a reenergized vigor to save him. This was the kind of leader Aandor had been waiting for—the type of prince who could unite the old empire. He had to find Daniel. Cal would not let his prince down, just as he was sure his prince would not let him down if the roles were reversed. For the first time, Cal allowed himself a glimmer of optimism that things may not be as bad as they could be.

They dropped Katie off and headed toward the school to speak to the principal. Callum's cell phone rang—his permanent phone, not the disposable. He didn't recognize the number, and didn't have his Bluetooth set up, so he handed the phone to Seth. "See who it is."

Seth began with a simple "hello." He turned eerily quiet and the blood drained from his face. Shaken, he handed the phone back to Callum. "You really ought to take this."

"Who is it?" Callum asked.

"He has the kid."

"Who does? Who's on the phone?" Cal repeated.

"The detective. It's Colby Dretch."

CHAPTER 14

TARDS ON A PORCH

1

Daniel opened his eyes to the morning sun creeping through Luanne's venetian blinds. She was missing from the bed; he wondered if last night had been just a dream. He sat up and pulled the covers back—his lover's lingering scent, and the crusted stains on the sheets, confirmed their deed. Parts of the bed were still damp. His health education teacher never mentioned how messy sex was.

In all the ways Daniel imagined losing his virginity, if it ever was going to happen, seduction by a hot, older trailer park sex kitten never crossed his mind. What was Luanne thinking? All those movies where parents freak out because their teens are left alone overnight finally made perfect sense. The only restraint is the will not to do it, and that's as effective as a paper roof in a hailstorm.

Daniel shuffled out of bed. The room was warm, the vent grate hot to the touch. Slipping into his jeans, he padded out into the kitchen to scrounge a bite. There was leftover corn bread on the counter.

Daniel heard giggling on the back porch. He peeked out the kitchen window to find a cool, sunny day, with wind rippling along the lake. Tiny waves crashed along the shore.

Luanne was on the vinyl loveseat, dressed in a red blouse and jeans that looked spray-painted on. She sat flirtatiously close to a heavily tattooed man who was wearing a white T-shirt, worn denim vest, and camouflage pants. His size-twelve construction boots were planted on the cable spool table and Luanne had her hand on his lap.

An old black Cadillac DeVille convertible the size of a boat was parked on the grass behind the porch.

Daniel was so distracted by Luanne's proximity to the wannabe cracker, he almost didn't notice the fat girl with the spiderweb tattoo on the side of her neck sitting to the side. Plastered with black mascara, she had metal piercings in her nose, ears, and eyebrows, and was dressed in loose-fitting black polyester clothes. Her dyed jet-black hair made her skin look almost as pasty white as Colby Dretch.

The phone rang. No one attempted to pick up, so Daniel answered. "Bev's place," he said.

"You working as Bev's secretary, now?"

Daniel was pleased to hear Colby's gruff tenor. How sad that this washed-up old transient constituted his only friend right now.

"Where are you?" Daniel asked. The fat chick cackled at something funny. He saw Luanne laughing, too, but the guy was stone-faced.

"Up north," Colby said. *"My past is nipping at my heels, Dan. Bev fronted me a loan and I'm doing proactive damage control with the people I worked for."*

Colby was always sketchy about his work. Dan had no clue about the man's profession. "When'll you be back?" he asked. The girls were looking at something Daniel couldn't see. The guy smoked a cigarette, and looked off in the other direction.

"Tomorrow night—day after at the latest. You sound distracted."

For a homeless alcoholic, Colby was oddly astute. It wasn't the first time Daniel noticed the man's honed instincts. On the bus ride down from Baltimore, Colby came off as one of the most introspective men Daniel had ever met. He shared a lifetime of experience freely with the boy. Daniel, in need of more wisdom than he possessed at the time, was drawn to the man.

"I'm good," Daniel said, leaving the window area for the living room. "Bev bought barbecue last night."

"Good for her. Is Luanne treating you okay? She can be a ball buster."

"Uh—she's nice enough. We watched TV last night." Daniel looked around for his other sketch pad, which he was sure he'd left on the couch last night.

"Good to hear," Colby said. *"You hang tight. I'll only be another day or so. Once the heat on you dies down, I'll help you get your life straightened out. Just promise me a couch to crash on if ever I need it."*

"I'll have a guest room just for you, Colby."

They ended the call with an awkward exchange of niceties, and Daniel went back to observing Luanne and her friends. Daniel realized he was having a stupid reaction to Luanne's fawning over this guy. Last night had been a one-time deal—there was no heat in the trailer and they made some together to keep warm, but that was it . . . no more fun with Luanne. He couldn't risk it. Against his better judgment, Daniel walked out to the back porch with his corn bread.

The man ignored Daniel's entrance onto the scene and lit another cigarette. His left arm was covered in tats of devil heads, skulls, and hot naked women with demon tails and horns mostly rendered in red, white, and black. Around his throat was inked a line of barbed wire and on his right inner forearm, a detailed rendering of a .357 Magnum with skeletal fingers around the grip and smoke emanating from the muzzle, trailing up behind the elbow. He guessed the guy was in his early twenties, but something about him looked older than that. His teeth were stained and he was muscularly cut, with three days of dark blond stubble and a nascent mullet.

"Danny! Come meet my beau, Cody," Luanne said. "And this is his cousin Eljay." The girl had an unwashed look about her, and must have known it because she was doused with enough cheap perfume that dogs in Baltimore could probably smell her. "This is Mama's houseguest I told you about," she explained to them.

Daniel wished for a relationship that just once didn't involve triangles or the potential to get one's ass kicked. Cody stared at him like he was a bug. Dan could hardly blame Cody for not being pleased—a strange teenage boy suddenly moves into his teen nympho girlfriend's trailer out of the blue—had to be a nightmare for the guy. Heck, Luanne had liked Daniel for barely half a day, and he was already jealous of Cody for being her "beau." No way Cody knew that something went down last night—he'd already be stomping on Daniel face with his boot. Or did he know . . . ? Did Luanne and Cody have an open arrangement? Was Luanne that detached from reality?

Cody's stare had gone beyond rude and was bordering on creepy. There was something primal in the glare—as though he could subconsciously smell Luanne's scent on him.

"Is there something you want to say?" Daniel asked.

Cody reached toward Eljay and snatched Daniel's sketch pad from her. With a quick snap, he flung it at Daniel. Daniel caught it awkwardly, dropping his corn bread. To his relief, it was his old pad, not the one with the nude. That one was still in Luanne's bedroom where he'd been working on it the previous night. This pad had the drawings of Luanne fully clothed—well, relatively fully clothed for her—watching television.

Cody took another drag on his cigarette—his eyes said, *Stop staring at my girlfriend.*

"Cody, don't be a jerk," Luanne scolded. "I only showed you 'cause he made me so pretty. Why don't you buy it and hang it in your bedroom?"

"I don't have to buy somethin' tha's already mine," Cody said. He blew smoke at Daniel.

That tiny molecule of reason in Daniel's brain was back, telling him to shut up and walk back into the house. Instead, he said, "Renderings belong to the artist." Daniel intended to keep all the drawings of his first lover . . . no matter how dumb she was.

Cody stood. He was taller than Daniel realized—at least six foot two. He yanked the pad from Daniel's hands and thumbed through sloppily, ripping out the drawings of Luanne.

Daniel wanted to take a bat to Cody's head but couldn't risk it. Worse than getting thrown out of the mobile home park would be cops asking questions. He maintained a neutral expression, drawing on the memory of his lovemaking with the douche bag's girlfriend just hours earlier. Would that be considered retroactive revenge? he wondered. The glint of defiance in his stare must have unsettled the thug—Cody pulled up his T-shirt to reveal a pistol stuck in his waistband.

"Cody . . . ," said Luanne.

"What?" he said, eyes locked on Daniel.

"Customers."

A man and a woman, both emaciated, in unwashed parkas and worn-out sneakers shuffled toward the porch. Their teeth had rotted from neglect, hers more than his. Daniel couldn't fathom their age . . . they looked to be in their twenties and their fifties at the same time. Both desperately needed a bath.

Cody covered the pistol. He pulled a tiny ziplock bag filled with white crystals out of a planter beside the loveseat and waved it before the newcomers. The sun glinting off the tiny rocks mesmerized the couple.

"Money?" Cody asked.

The man handed him a crumpled ball of bills. Cody pulled them apart. "You're short," he said. The two became agitated and began hopping side to side, like they needed to use the bathroom. Cody and Eljay shot each other shit-eating grins, like kids torturing ants with a magnifying glass.

"Tell you what," Cody said. "You take missy here over to Kooter's, and she can 'work off' the difference in the back. You catch my drift?"

Both meth drones nodded excitedly. Cody tossed them the bag, which slipped through their fingers and landed on the grass. They scrambled for it like hungry dogs and then slunk off.

Cody turned his attention back to Daniel. "You ever draw another picture of Luanne, I will blow your fuckin' head off."

Luanne looked up at the sky swallowing a chuckle, innocent as the day she was born.

2

Daniel should have been scared. But after living with Clyde for much of his life, he just couldn't get worked up by Cody. Nevertheless, he hid the pad with Luanne's nude under the bed and adjusted the comforter so that it covered the space. No reason to risk leaving something like that lying around.

Daniel washed up in the bathroom, studying his face in the mirror for signs of facial hair. It was well known back at school that once a guy got laid, his facial hair would start to grow in. He was aware how stupid most of his friends were when it came to biology and relationships, and had to smile at his own gullibility and wishful thinking. Still, a beard or 'stache at the moment would go a long way to hiding his identity on the road. And if he did end up in South America, facial hair was almost a cultural necessity.

Daniel didn't recognize his eyes anymore. Even though they were the same shape and color, he'd become someone else. His short-cropped hair gave his forehead more altitude. Was that it? He gazed at his own reflection in the mirror, trying to pinpoint exactly what was different. Cody noticed something too when Daniel stood his ground. It scared the cracker enough to make him brandish his weapon. *I've got artillery to deal with you mo' fo'*, it said. Eyes are the windows to the soul, some long-dead writer claimed. Daniel's soul, if he had one, was sullied. Is that what looked back . . . having lived thirty years in just thirteen? Was there a stain upon his soul for killing his stepfather—for making love to someone else's girl? Murder and sex in the space of three days had put some depth into Daniel's stare. His fourteenth birthday was just a couple months away, but he had already stopped seeing himself as a thirteen-year-old. His eyes had lost their innocence. That's what Daniel imagined Cody saw . . . he didn't expect to find an old soul in a boy's eyes.

Cody's Cadillac tried to gain traction on the wet grass with its bald tires. The cracker burned a gallon of gas just trying to get the car to the hard dirt road in front of the trailer. He'd probably do a lot better if his fat cousin got out of the car. What was really stupid was that his hangout was by the general store near the trailer park entrance, and it was only a ten-minute walk. Luanne trotted into the kitchen carrying the remains of Daniel's abused sketch pad. She was obliviously cheery—an adrenaline junkie that just swallowed a tasty snack.

"You want to sketch me again?" she asked.

"Didn't you hear Methy McTats?" Daniel said.

"Cody's just cranky 'cause some kids in the next town started cookin'. He don't handle competition so good."

"Just a businessman . . ." Daniel played along. "He projects that Donald Trump charisma."

"Funny," she said sarcastically, handing the pad to him. "That's what I get for fuckin' a *little boy*."

Daniel looked around in a panic.

"Mama's not here," she reassured him. "Spent the night at her beau's."

"Who fixed the heat?"

"Turns out, the thermostat just needed to be reset." A devilish grin took over, complete with twinkle.

"Did you . . . just to . . . ," Daniel said. His ego just inflated.

Her smile evaporated, replaced by a not-too-pleased-look. "Dang it . . . I was neked in front of you and all you did was draw me!" she said. "I knew you wasn't queer! I saw you hidin' your thing behind the counter. You din' even try anythin' while we watched TV . . . like somethin's wrong with me!"

"I don't want to get *thrown out*!" he said through gritted teeth.

"You're supposed to at least *try*!" she said, like it was the most obvious rule in the universe. "Made me feel like I was ugly or had cooties." Her expression softened a little and the twinkle came back to her eye. "Ain't many around here see me or talk to me the way you do, Danny. I came in to tease you last night—get you back for makin' me feel like shit after I posed. Didn't plan to . . ."

Luanne didn't have the rest of that sentence formed. She gave up on it and shot him her usual suspicious smile.

"Well . . . I don't regret it," she whispered. "Good thing you poked me, too. If you ain't done nothin' after I started on you, left me hangin' on a limb, I woulda told Mama you came onto me anyway. Can't make a girl feel ugly in her own bed, Danny."

Luanne's colloquial vocabulary and one-dimensional pursuits had hidden some of the depth Daniel was seeing in the girl now. She was devious and capable of thinking a step or two ahead. It wasn't book smarts—it was the intelligence of desperation—the eking out of position among dirt and rocks and people born into the same lot in life. If she'd grown up in a wealthy neighborhood, she might have been the mean girl terrorizing a school of well-groomed boys. She was suddenly more attractive, and no one was more surprised than Daniel. She was worth talking to for more than just a safe place to hide, some meals . . . or other things.

"You ain't . . . uh—*aren't* ugly," Daniel said.

"Oh, like, I'm just borderline pretty?" she teased, sidling uncomfortably close to him. "I *just* made your cut."

"Really, *really* pretty," he said. She could go far in life—strip club headliner, B movies, Fox News commentator.

"You like my body?"

His armpits were damp—Daniel felt flushed. "I—I *love* your body." He was in the top 2 percent of his class . . . How did this simple girl have him stammering?

She walked to her bedroom door and took off her blouse. The

vision of her bra straining to contain her bosom shot straight to Daniel's loins. "I'll be in our bed—come draw me again."

Our bed?

Cody's warning bounced inside Daniel's head like one of those superballs chucked in an empty tin water tower. God help him if Cody ever found out the full extent of his involvement with Luanne. God help him if Beverly or Colby found out. Essentially, everyone in the world that still liked him would be furious and turn his life into a world of crap. He'd be tossed into the street so fast . . .

Daniel was mad at Luanne—really mad. Half the problem wouldn't even exist if she hadn't shown Cody the damn sketchbook. Then she could have played with him all she wanted. Why would she do that? The right thing to do at that moment was go for a walk in the brisk country air—get Luanne's scent out of his head. That's one of the advantages of being in the top two percentile of his class—lots of smarts and an abundance of common sense. Except, his shoes were by the bed. *Their* bed.

"I can still have you thrown you out, queer boy!" Luanne sang from her bedroom, scorning his dawdling.

His loins stirred again at her voice. He walked toward the bedroom, determined to get his sneakers and leave. *How did men ever survive precivilization with everything in the jungle trying to kill them and their penises constantly goading them into stupid decisions?* he thought.

Statistically, husbands died before their wives. That was making more and more sense to Daniel. *Why bother with marriage? Men can live longer without women.*

His sneakers jutted out from the corner just under the box spring. On the bed, Luanne lay on her side, head propped up on one arm, completely naked. With her other hand, she drew him with a seductively oscillating finger. Her lips pleaded to be kissed. He walked toward her. In that second, Daniel completely understood why men were willing to die.

CHAPTER 15

RELUCTANT HERO

1

Allyn sat in his study under a reading lamp, turning the scrap of paper with Callum MacDonnell's number over in his hands. His daughter had found the captain living in New York, the city closest to where they had come into this universe. A news photo of MacDonnell's NYPD headshot confirmed that it was the right man. Allyn had delayed calling for over a day, unsure of what to say, unsure of his own mind as to what he would do next. The news media wasn't making things any easier for him, distracting him with many requests for interviews, calling him at all hours, as though their desire to increase their audience to sell more ads for laundry soap and Chevys trumped all other concerns.

The morning's headline read—

SHEPHERD FINDS LOST LAMBS

This time, he thought. Prince Danel deserved to be found as well.

Allyn's desire to serve the prince teetered between his oath to the archduke and his duties to his church and family here. He prayed for guidance, though not exactly sure who to, but hoped the universe would sort it out and get the message to the right deity. Allyn wasn't sure of what he was afraid of more . . . that he'd find the boy alive and well or that he wouldn't. If the boy were already dead, the burden of Allyn's failure would haunt him to his grave—but he would be free from his pledge and could continue his life and ministry in North Carolina. The wars of far-off places would stay exactly that—far off. Away from his family and the community he loved. Allyn could spread peace and love beyond his small church. With his rediscovered ability to heal, he could do wonders. If the prince were alive, though . . . well—that was an entirely different matter. He should call MacDonnell either way. Better to know for certain.

Rosemarie had done excellent research. Callum MacDonnell had been in the news recently. His partner had been killed on a call in the South Bronx just a few days ago. Decapitated. It had the earmarks of an Aandor-centered event. *Either that, or criminals in New York have swapped their guns for long swords.* Allyn's reemergence from the long sleep was no coincidence. They were calling up the reinforcements. Everyone was in danger, not just the prince.

In his gut, Allyn knew the situation could not be simple—the prince raised peacefully in some quiet suburb. Something went wrong. They had all succumbed to the apprentice wizard's botched magic. Everyone in the party had fallen to their knees in pain, grasping their craniums like balloons filling with too much water. What happened was not meant to be. Their brains were scrambled.

"Wizards," Allyn whispered to himself in disgust.

He dialed the number slowly. It rang twice before the answering machine picked up—a woman's voice: *"Hi, you've reached Cat, Cal, Bree, and Maggie—we can't come to the phone right now; you know what to—"*

Allyn hung up without leaving a message.

So MacDonnell himself had married and had children. This supported Allyn's suspicions: everyone's minds had been affected; the captain would never have consciously betrayed Chryslantha Godwynn. And now, his family here was in danger. This was reason enough to stay out of this conflict. If the captain called to convince him otherwise, Allyn would appeal to the man's concern for his own family and insist that he was acting in Michelle and Rosemarie's best interests. A man protected his own first.

The decision to abandon his old life left him with a heavy heart. Allyn loved Aandor. He loved the archduke and duchess almost as much as his own family. Sophia was especially kind and graceful, and her family a generous contributor to the temples of Pelitos. The temple in Aandor City would not have been completed as quickly if not for her patronage. How could he abandon her son? The obligation ran deep in Allyn—he drummed the armrest of his chair unconsciously, struggling with the urge to take Danel into his home and hide him from all his enemies. How silly a notion was that? It was unlikely child services would allow a white child to be placed with a black family. He could never explain where the boy came from.

Allyn's mind was a pendulum swinging between two worlds. *Get involved—don't get involved.* He crushed the scrap of paper in his hand.

"It would bring wizards to my house," he grumbled. "And other undesirables." Allyn tossed the scrap, but in midswing altered his aim for the desk instead of the trash. A conclusion to his internal debate still eluded him when the front doorbell rang. The murmurings of greetings came through the study door.

Allyn joined Michelle in the foyer and greeted his guests, members of his church's board—Miles, Fred, a rejuvenated Maurice, Shirley Johnston, and Sheriff Kevin Martin. Michelle welcomed them into the foyer and instructed Rosemarie to put on some coffee.

"Wanted to see how you was holding up, Al," Miles said with a smirk. "We all knows how much you love the press."

A cadre of trucks with large white dishes on their roof had stationed themselves on the block. Allyn had become the latest obsession for bookers of the network news shows. Reporters fluttered along the sidewalk; Allyn was a flame to a moth in this hero-starved world. The sheriff had posted tape along the perimeter of the lawn and told the reporters if anyone crossed the line he'd arrest them for trespassing.

"How're the Taylors doing?" he asked Maurice.

"Coming along. Darnell sends his apologies for not stopping by—they're releasing the kids from the hospital about now."

Allyn dismissed the need for an apology and showed everyone into the living room. Michelle went into the kitchen to fix snacks. They made small talk about the Panthers' chances for getting into the Super Bowl until Michelle and Rosemarie emerged with trays filled with biscuits and coffee.

Miles turned serious and leaned toward Allyn across the table, resting his arms on his legs. "We came by tell you that we unanimously granted your request for a temporary leave from your duties as minister," he said.

"With full pay, of course," Shirley cut in.

The group laughed.

"Thank you, my friends," Allyn, said. "I am so blessed to have you in my life. I never doubted I could count on your support." He looked around the living room at the faces of his congregation . . . his family. Miles had coached high school football for the past fifteen years; Fred retired from fishing the Outer Banks for twenty years; Shirley was the third generation Johnston to run the Happy Ochre diner in town; and Kevin, who served as an even-keeled sheriff after twenty years in the Army Rangers . . . these were his people now, with ties that bound more tightly than anything he had in that other universe.

"I have decided not to take the leave," Allyn told them. Michelle shot him a look. He smiled back at her, confident about his decision. He would ride out the war at home.

The group enjoyed its coffee and biscuits, relating the progress of the Taylor kids and each offering their opinion on the fate of the man that had chased them into the forest. The phone rang and Rosemarie answered.

"Dad, some man's asking to speak to you," she said.

"I am not doing interviews."

"He's not a reporter," she said. "Says he met you a few years back. Someplace called 'And Door.'"

2

Allyn locked the study door behind him and listened for a moment to his colleagues and friends chatting away in the living room. To Michelle's credit, she barely reacted to the news that someone from Aandor was on the phone for him—she recovered quickly, averting a near disaster of spilled coffee all over Shirley's lemon-yellow skirt.

Allyn carefully picked up the receiver. A moment passed, and when he heard the click of the other extension, he cleared his voice and said, "Captain MacDonnell?"

"Not quite," came the response.

The voice was familiar, but not Callum MacDonnell's. It was higher than the captain's confident baritone.

"Malcolm Robbe," the voice said.

Allyn flipped through the Rolodex of his brain to remember thirteen years back, in the pantry with a group of people he had only just met. The centaur was Fronik, the lieutenant was Tristan, Malcolm was . . . "Ah, yes . . . the sergeant at arms."

"Very good, Prelate Grey."

There was something in the man's tone—a confidence. He sounded rich.

"Did MacDonnell task you to find me?" Allyn asked.

"I have not yet met with the captain, nor spoken with him," Malcolm said. *"He's currently unavailable, so I've tasked myself with finding the*

prince's party independently. I have—resources." The word "resources" resonated with an understated air. The word did not match the entirety of Malcolm's tone.

"I see," Allyn said. "I do not have—resources. What I have is a wife and daughter—responsibilities to a community. I have a life."

"As do we all that still live," Malcolm answered.

"Who's died?"

"I've yet to track down Galen and Linnea, but the Raincrests died many years ago of causes unrelated to the mission. Tristan was murdered a few days ago. Like you, he had a family. Now there's only a widow and two boys, halfway to being orphans. The home of Proust's apprentice was recently torched. No sign of the lad—he may be dead. MacDonnell himself was attacked a few days ago, as were his wife and daughter. I believe he's taken off with his family. No idea whether he's engaged in this search. Perhaps like you, he's forsaken his oath."

The dig did not sit well with Allyn. This was Malcolm's attempt to light a fire under him. Pride was listed as a deadly sin for a reason. Allyn fought the urge to defend his decision. Instead he asked, "If the captain was not engaged in the mission, who returned our memories to us? Someone is obviously working for our cause. We would have been sitting ducks otherwise."

"Our cause?" Malcolm stressed the first word.

Allyn could almost hear him smiling on the other end, like a cat with its paw on a mouse's tail. *Yes, damn you!* he thought.

"I wish no harm to befall the prince," Allyn said. "I pray for his health and that he will be reunited with his family soon and placed on his rightful throne. I just—I can't involve my family in this conflict. They need me. My church needs me. I am invested in this community. My roots run deep."

The line remained silent for a while as both men mentally pivoted for the next round.

"I have a life, too," Malcolm said. *"A damn good one; much better than*

my lot in Aandor. Things are more—complicated—for me than I care to divulge."

"We're each responsible for our own decisions."

"I won't begrudge your choice. I am just a sergeant, after all. But can you do one thing for me? One thing for which I will be extremely grateful and will not bother you further."

Allyn tensed. He was wary of any commitment. Even small obligations had the potential to suck you into larger matters of which you'd rather not be a part. "What is it?" he asked warily.

"Locate the prince. Use your abilities the way you found those children in the forest. I will retrieve the boy myself; you need not be involved in any effort to extract him. Do this, and I will make it worth your while. I will even set matters straight with the captain regarding your choice to remain with your family."

That was a fair request. Allyn's anxiety had been over leaving his loved ones. Malcolm Robbe had offered to carry the burden of collecting and protecting the boy. If he'd advocate on Allyn's behalf with MacDonnell . . .

The reverend wanted to help the young prince. Now he could do his part in the safety of North Carolina, without leaving his home—the family . . . without heading toward the mayhem up north.

"Do you have anything that might have the prince's blood, hair, or skin on it?" Allyn asked. "A rattle, a blanket?"

"I have as many items as you do, Reverend. That might change the more we dig up; I have leads on other guardians."

"It will be very difficult to find him without some personal effect. Even something with only an emotional attachment would do."

"I'm sorry, I have no such items. Will you try anyway?"

Allyn wracked his brain for a solution. He was long out of practice in the clerical arts.

"I don't have anything at the moment, but yes—I will try."

CHAPTER 16

HIS BROTHER'S KEEPER

The sensation of speeding through a black tunnel backward, away from the light, had inverted itself. As Oulfsan came out of the darkness, the scene around him sharpened into focus. The whole exchange took less than five seconds, but the pain and exhaustion lingered as though it were an hour-long exertion. Though he and his brother had swapped consciousness thousands of times, he would never get used to the switch—each time he wondered if death would finally drag them to the bowels of hell.

If it were pleasant, it wouldn't qualify as a curse, he thought.

The frequency and randomness of the swaps had accelerated since coming to this plane of existence. In Aandor, they could go days before switching, but here it was almost daily, sometimes as short as several hours.

Oulfsan took note of his surroundings; he was in the Baltimore motor lodge rental they used as a base to spy on Colby Dretch. Hesz was already on his way down with Hommar and Todgarten, and it was odd that they were not already there. Oulfsan took stock of his surroundings; everything looked the same as the last time he was here, except for the bloodied leg—foot to knee—hanging on the far edge of the bed. Oulfsan walked around the bed to find that the leg belonged to a dead naked woman facing up on the floor. Her eyes were open and rolled back, her throat had a large gash across it, and she had a knife wedged in her gut. Her legs were spread, one lay bent on the floor slightly under the bed and the other went up the side of the bed, hip and butt braced against the mattress—like she'd fallen out in her sleep. She smelled like sex and blood. What Oulfsan would find upon arrival after a switch was always a mystery; Krebe was most unpredictable and every bit chaotic.

His brother's striped boxer shorts, which were the only things he had on, were greasy from lack of washing. Krebe was shorter, stockier, and fatter, with coarse black ringlets of hair over his torso, arms, and legs. As for the man's hygiene, if the switch wasn't jarring enough, the assault on Oulfsan's nose each time he returned was enough to wrench his gut. Krebe enjoyed torturing his brother from afar to see how long he could go before Oulfsan bathed for him. To Krebe it was all a game—the young woman dangling off the bed was just another play.

The brunette was in her twenties, with fair skin, freckles, and a delicate upturned nose most boys seemed to favor. She'd be missed. Her blood seeped into the rose-colored carpet from the wounds, fueling spongy brown stains that tried to join each other beneath her. It was Krebe's third kill since arriving to this reality. If Dorn found out, he would kill Krebe for jeopardizing the mission. Oulfsan doubted if Dorn would even care which body his brother inhabited at that moment—he could end up losing his true vessel. And then what . . . ? What happens if his brother ceases to live? If they knew for certain that the death of one of them would end the switch, Krebe would have killed Oulfsan years ago. Uncertainty was the only thing that kept that psychopath at bay.

Oulfsan had some bittersweet gratitude toward his brother for providing a plastic tarp to dispose of the body. It was his duty to clean up the dirty mess because Krebe was too thick minded to handle the details. And, if Krebe went to prison, Oulfsan would also live half his life rotting behind bars. This untenable existence is what led Oulfsan to seek out Lord Dorn in the first place. His part of the agreement to serve Dorn included the wizard's help in breaking the curse.

He sold the idea to his brother by playing up the fortune they'd both earn in pay and plunder—after all, in a world with no telephones, their trick was useful in relaying information quickly between whatever distant points they occupied. One brother could scout miles ahead while the other stayed with the master, so that when they switched, information would be relayed instantaneously. Oulfsan convinced Krebe he'd have ample opportunity to engage his murderous hobbies across the continent and be protected under Dorn's patronage. In Farrenheil, Dorn's word was second only to his uncle, the archduke. Should Krebe's habits be discovered, he would have been protected; Dorn and his uncle couldn't care less about dead peasant girls. But here in this world, a serial murder investigation could jeopardize everything. Dorn was barely hanging on to sanity as it was. Oulfsan had to work quickly . . . the others would arrive eventually.

He wrapped the girl's body in the tarp and used duct tape to seal her in. He placed her in the bathtub gently and tried not to think of her life or the family that will miss her. He filled a large trash bag with ice from the lodge's three machines, enough to pack the tub. The landing outside their room had a wide view of the parking lot; he hated the exposure. They should have gone to a traditional motel. The Baltimore area was still a mystery, but resided next to a bay with a large crab population. They were excellent scavengers and would make short work of the girl in no time. He would do it right after he located Colby.

Oulfsan checked the iPad on the nightstand. The device was a late adaptation to this new reality due to Dorn and Kraten's insistence early on that their group would not be in this universe for very long. Therefore they did not need to waste time with its alien distractions. As soon as it became clear they were not on the heels of the prince's guardians, that in fact, some years might have passed since they arrived to this reality, Dorn relented. Kraten still clung to his archaic ways, but then that was the character of desert dwellers . . . they resisted change and resented progressives.

The one device Oulfsan cherished and wished he could bring back to Aandor was the cellular phone. Assuming Krebe was willing to utilize it, the days of popping into his brother's body, ignorant of his whereabouts or situation, would be a thing of the past. It was the most disconcerting thing—he'd once relocated to find himself in the middle of a tavern brawl that Krebe had instigated. Oulfsan could hold his own in a fight, but lacked his brother's ruthlessness, and suffered for it often. Another time he found himself in the middle of having sex with a homely peasant girl who noted with dissatisfaction that he wasn't nearly as rough toward the end as he had been when they started. She had no idea how close she'd come to having her throat cut that night, saved only by the switch. Oulfsan instructed her to change her appearance, gave her ten pieces of silver, and the most serious threat on her life he could muster to ensure she'd flee the village while she could. Krebe was furious at him for weeks as evidenced by the painful cuts on his arms and chest each time Oulfsan returned to his body.

In Aandor, they wrote notes for each other on parchment, which they kept in specific pockets since they could never tell when they'd switch—but here they used the iPad. His brother's recent log said:

> *No sighting of Dretch. Car still at Days Inn on Governor Ritchie Highway where he checked in. No signal from his cell phone.*

When did Krebe find time to monitor the detective between luring and killing the girls? thought Oulfsan. There was a digital photo of the car, a tan 1995 Chrysler LeBaron, time-stamped four hours earlier. To add insult to injury, the last entry said:

> *Clean the room before I return.*

Oulfsan launched the GPS application linked to the transmitter hidden in Colby's trunk. Did Colby suspect they were tracking him? The car still sat in the Days Inn parking lot a few blocks away. Another app traced Colby's cell phone, but that program worked sporadically. Oulfsan did not know enough about this technology to determine whether the program was malfunctioning or experiencing typical problems. It was as alien to him as magic. He found Krebe's mobile phone in his brother's coat and called Colby's number. It went straight to voice mail.

"Damn," he whispered.

Dorn had decided to reveal to the detective that he had been followed to Maryland and to inform Dretch he was no longer permitted to disappear for long periods. The master was shortening his leash, despite the age-old wisdom that the best hounds did not hunt tethered. There was no reason to doubt the detective; he'd been brilliant in picking up a trail from the fumes of thirteen years past. Dorn and crew had stumbled about with no success for weeks before Dretch. Nevertheless, his lordship was piling on the deterrents against any insubordination . . . anything to avoid eliminating the detective before they had the prince.

Krebe's cell rang. He didn't recognize the number.

"Hello," Oulfsan said. His crisp annunciation clashed with his brother's deep guttural rasp of a voice.

"You rang?" came Dretch's gruff Brooklyn accent. The sound of wind and cars in the background buffeted the phone.

"Why are you not answering your mobile?" said Oulfsan.

There was a moment's pause. Oulfsan would have thought the connection cut if not for the car horns. *"I'm in legal trouble in New York,"* Colby said. *"They trace cell phones. Can't have the law realizing I've left the state. I check voice mail on a public landline, when I can find one, and call back from there."*

There were a couple seconds of silence and ambient street noise before Oulfsan realized the detective was waiting for him to speak.

"You're not to be out of contact with us for more than a few hours going forward," Oulfsan said. "Call any of our numbers with updates, but call someone."

"You know . . . ," Colby said, *"if you'd hired me a day earlier, the kid'd be in your hands already. He's on the run from the law. Lousy timing."* A few more seconds of near silence—cars and wind scraping through the earpiece. *"Sure bet he's out of state. I'll do my best to stay in touch, but if he's in the boonies hiding under a coal mine, I may not even get cell reception."*

"Twelve hours, max," Oulfsan said, grateful that his brother's murderous voice gave weight to his threat—the same voice that saved that peasant girl.

A blaring ambulance sped past the motor lodge.

"Which one are you?" Dretch asked unexpectedly.

"Krebe," Oulfsan lied. "We met outside the diner in upstate New York."

"The tall butler?"

Oulfsan hesitated—he was, in fact, the tall neatly dressed man, but explaining the switch would only confuse Dretch. "The other one," he said, instead. Wind and car sounds danced through the receiver joined by a siren getting louder—even as the siren outside the motor lodge faded. *He's close,* Oulfsan realized.

"I want to meet," said Oulfsan, trying to not sound desperate. The detective had no idea how much danger he was in with Dorn. Oulfsan wanted to protect him for all their sakes. The whole mission rested on Dretch's abilities. "I can be in Baltimore in . . . huh . . . four hours."

A few seconds later Colby added, *"I'll have some leads by end of day tomorrow."* The ambulance siren had nearly vanished on Colby's end. *"We'll meet up before I go on the road."*

That would work . . . give Oulfsan time to dispose of the girl's body and figure out what to tell Hesz. "Very well," he told Dretch. The detective hung up first.

Oulfsan was about to call Hesz to inquire about the delay when someone pounded on the door. He froze, looked at the bloodstained carpet and then toward the bathroom. A second impatient thump followed. Oulfsan shut the bathroom door and threw a towel over the stain. He pulled one of Krebe's daggers out of his brother's jacket and silently made his way to the window facing the landing. The hulking figure of Hesz; the manly Hommar; and the smaller quadroon giant, Todgarten, nervously surveyed the parking lot under the indigo dusk sky. Oulfsan let them in.

"Good journey?" asked Oulfsan.

Hesz, who had no receptor for sardonic humor, scowled. "MacDonnell's all-points bulletin for me forced us onto the small roads to avoid highway cameras."

"We were lost in New Jersey," said Hommar. "In New Jersey, one turns right to go left, and the roads are littered with infernal circles that defy all rules of directional sense."

"A most infernal place, this New Jersey," confirmed Todgarten.

"What news of the detective?" Hesz asked.

"I've spoken to Dretch today. He is again on the trail of the prince, who has run off to avoid the law. We meet with him tomorrow."

"Dorn is troubled by his continual disappearance," Hesz noted.

Aristocrats regularly took "lesser" men for granted, as though it were part of their highborn DNA, even when their servants' abilities contributed to their advantage. All those not of noble birth were dispensable, which left 99 percent of the population in a very bad position.

"Colby's success is no doubt derived from his unorthodox methods," Oulfsan said. "They might seem alien, even insubordinate to a lord of Farrenheil, but they have served us well. Was it not you who found this detective, Hesz?"

The giant's deep-throated grunt of affirmation confirmed for Oulfsan Hesz's pride in accomplishing something Dorn and Kraten could not. Dorn's temper and impatience were already legendary before he began to go mad. Dretch was poking a hornet's nest with his mysterious tactics. He prayed the detective did not suspect they had no way of reverting him to normal, but given Dretch's high intelligence and the ability to sniff out information from the smallest threads, Oulfsan had to consider that very possibility.

"Colby is our greatest asset at the moment," Oulfsan continued. "Even Dorn's alternative plan for capturing the boy depends on the detective's accomplishments so far. Let us not allow Lord Dorn to forget the man's value to our cause."

For the sake of the mission, Oulfsan had to protect Dretch, and he needed allies. If Lord Dorn died a failure on this world, Oulfsan may never again find someone powerful enough to break the curse that bound him to his brother. Too many fragile links connected the steps of Oulfsan's plan to rid himself of his brother and his bane. But, if they captured the prince and returned to Aandor in time to save Dorn from his malady—well, there were worse things than the gratitude of a powerful sorcerer.

Hesz grunted again, cementing his reputation as a man of few words. Oulfsan wagered the frost giant wanted to see Dretch succeed as well. He seemed to have his own agenda independent of the mission to find the prince and, like Oulfsan, had to get past this point to achieve it. He would help cover for the detective—at least until there was evidence that Dretch plotted to betray them.

Hesz caught the scent of something in the room and pulled the towel back from the blood spot on the carpet. He looked in the bathroom. "What is this?"

"My brother's habit," said Oulfsan.

"This can undo us." Hesz grimaced. "Does Dorn know?"

"No. Please . . . do not tell. I will take care of the girl before we meet with Dretch."

"This mission hangs by a thread," Hesz said. "We lose men even as our enemy gains allies. And Lord Dorn still suffers the head pains. We cannot afford mistakes."

"I cannot control Krebe any more than you can control Dorn," Oulfsan said. "I can only clean up after him."

Hesz grunted again. Oulfsan was beginning to pick up the distinctions in his grunts, like they were a language unto themselves. "Show me the prince's home on a map," Hesz ordered.

Oulfsan opened a map of the greater Baltimore area and pointed out the boy's home and their relation to it. Hesz let out a deep moan as he scratched his chin. "Dorn's alternative plan requires the prince's personal effects. I will steal into the boy's home and retrieve them, and then I will head back north. You will accompany the detective on his quest from this point onward." Though Hesz said this calmly, Oulfsan detected the whiff of a command.

"He claims he is more efficient unencumbered," Oulfsan said. "He will decline my company."

"He is no longer to be left alone," Hesz said more strongly. The giant removed the small thumping velvet sack holding Colby's heart and handed it to Oulfsan. It fidgeted on his hand like a scared rat. "If he truly cannot find the prince again, destroy him. If you discover he has played us false, Todgarten will dismantle him, and throw his still-living parts into the sea. Bring only his head to Dorn."

CHAPTER 17

TEA WITH MUSSOLINI

1

Cat, Lelani, and Bree pulled up to the MacDonnells' building in the Bronx in a rented van just as the sun hit its noon apex. Though they'd only been away three days, to Cat it felt longer. A police cruiser sat across the street, watching the house. Cat didn't recognize the officer on watch—a young one, barely out of the academy. The kid tipped his hat to her.

Catherine balked at the glimmering shards on the curb below Bree's bedroom window, a reminder of how close they'd come to being kidnapped, or worse. The glass had been swept into a pile against the building—no doubt a neighbor's effort. Cat loved her block. The people looked out for one another. Seth's shoddily repaired front door still held up. Cat hoped it wouldn't fall off its hinges when she entered. Bree unclipped her seatbelt and reached for the passenger side door handle.

"Wait," Lelani said from the back of the van. She exited through the rear doors and came onto the sidewalk with her ornate brass compact in hand. "Clear," she said. That meant spells and enchantments, not henchmen in the shadows.

Cat felt for the Colt .32 caliber in her coat pocket. "Come out this way," she told Bree, and the girl hopped over the driver's seat to stand beside her mother.

"Catherine?" Mrs. Sullivan emerged from her front door a few yards away and approached gingerly in her housecoat and walking sneakers. "Good Lord, we thought the worst had happened."

"We're fine Mrs. S. The police are looking for the thugs who attacked us." Cat looked her building over again and a wave of apprehension came over her. Despite the police presence, she wondered if it might be a good idea to check it out first.

"Mrs. S . . . Would you mind watching Bree for a moment?"

Mrs. Sullivan took Bree into her home with the promise of fresh biscuits.

Lelani led the way. Bits of splintered wood from where Hesz had smashed through the door still littered the hallway.

"You want to take out that bow?" asked Cat.

"Bows are not for close quarters," the centaur answered. "No one is in your apartment. I have a hunter's sense of such things."

Cat gave Lelani a *pretty please* smile. Lelani indulged her. She mumbled softly, igniting specks of intense white light hovering above her palms. They grew into balls of crackling white energy—mini white suns that lit the hallway like a movie set. When they reached the size of softballs, Lelani kicked the door open and entered.

The living room to their left faced the street. It was empty, as was the dining room to their right, which faced the backyard, and the adjoining open kitchen at two o'clock. Lelani swiftly moved into the back bedrooms and declared the house free of hostiles. The wizard's phosphor balls disappeared with a pop and stream of wafting white smoke.

Cat sighed in relief. She desperately wanted her home back—but more than that, peace of mind within it—to know that she and her family were not being hunted. Cat threw her coat on the living room couch and crossed over to the kitchen. "I could use some tea," she said.

Lelani concurred, and situated herself on the dining room side of the stone island that separated the kitchen from the eating area.

Cat set the kettle, then cried out, "Shit!" as a bug scurried in the corner where the stove met the wall. She pulled a large can of insect spray from under the sink and zapped the spot, but too late. It disappeared into a crevice.

"When we started renovating upstairs, they moved down here," Cat said, wondering if centaurs cared about bugs in their . . . What exactly did centaurs live in?

"Cat . . . ," Lelani said quizzically. She came around the island staring at a spot to Cat's left on the stove. "That red light . . ."

Cat thought she might have set the oven timer by accident, until she saw the lens flare on her kitchen window and realized the red dot Lelani pointed to glided along the stove, the wall, and toward her.

Cat lunged at Lelani. Trying to push the redhead back was like pushing a confused horse. The kitchen window behind Cat exploded, as did the spice rack on the counter and the wall behind it. Several more shots in quick succession, eerily quiet on the firing end, blew holes through the wall next to the window as the gunman attempted to recover his target. Cat's kitchen exploded into shards of shrapnel. The centaur, finally realizing they were under attack, backed up, pulling Cat with her into the dining room.

"He's on the roof next door!" Cat shouted.

Mrs. Sullivan's building was a floor higher than hers and jutted out farther in back, giving the gunman a perfect vantage point into her apartment. The dinner table blocked their way to the front door—but before either woman could make a dash for it, the dining room window crashed inward, spraying them with glass. A man dressed in black rappelling gear and a ski mask swung in on a line and landed loudly between them.

The invader's momentum had pushed Cat back toward the kitchen. He turned toward her just as she hit the ground and smashed into her stove. Cat couldn't help notice how awful the man smelled, like he'd just crawled out of the sewer.

Lelani attacked the invader from behind. He was swift, grabbing her wrist and twisting her arm until Cat thought it would break. The move was intended to throw Lelani off her balance, but it didn't work. He didn't know there was four hundred pounds of invisible horse attached to the redhead. Lelani put her free palm up toward his face and sparked a phosphorus ball. She grew it rapidly and fired at his head. He twisted to avoid it, and the shot flew wildly into the wall and curtain, setting it ablaze.

Cat grabbed the kettle off its burner and doused the flames.

Lelani started another phosphorus ball, but the man whipped out a canister of mace and sprayed her point-blank. The centaur shrieked. He let her go and she jolted backward, slamming into the far wall and collapsed to the ground, hands pressed against her burning eyes.

The assassin pulled out a hunting knife and turned toward Cat. She banged her head into the oven handle trying to getting up, jostling the can of bug spray on the counter. As the assassin came toward her, she grabbed the can, pressed the nozzle, and ran the spray past the burner, igniting a jet of fire that she swept around toward the killer.

His mask and turtleneck caught immediately. He dropped the knife, pulled off his mask and vigorously patted out the flames on his shirt. The man had a Middle Eastern look about him—black hair in a military crew cut, unruly eyebrows, and deep-set brown eyes.

Cat ran toward the Colt .32 in her coat on the sofa. The assassin grabbed Cat from behind. Lelani barreled into him with the force of a freight train and he pulled Cat along, refusing to relinquish his grip. Lelani's eyes were closed and tearing, but she didn't need to see him to know where to stick her dagger. She stabbed him repeatedly on the side of his torso. He finally let go of Cat.

She retrieved her gun, clicked the safety and waited for Lelani to finish. The killer head-butted Lelani harder than should have been humanly possible. The centaur staggered and fell over. He squirmed his way out from under her, seemingly unaffected by Lelani's vicious stabbings. Cat fired three shots point-blank into his chest. The force drove him back, but didn't stop him. He continued to move toward her. She fired a shot into his temple, clearing out bone and gray matter. Again it drove him back, but he righted himself and came again.

Oh shit, Cat realized. *He's one of those.*

The assassin was almost upon her. Cat was about to let fly her remaining bullets, when her front door smashed open.

Two men dressed like Secret Service agents burst in and fired indiscriminately at the attacker. Their silencer-tipped guns drove the killer back down the hallway toward the bedroom until their clips were empty. He started toward them again.

"Hold him!" came an order from a third man—about five feet two, of stocky build, wearing an expensive business suit with thinning coppery red hair and a thick neatly trimmed beard to match. He was carrying the big fire ax Cal kept in the stairway by the fire alarm.

The Secret Service guys grabbed the assassin's arms and held him.

"Do you see, Tom . . . what I mean about magic now?" said the shorter man. "You can't kill him by normal means. He feels no pain and is a thrall of a greater power."

"Okay," said the older of the two men, looking a few years short of retirement age. "I'm a believer, Mr. Robbe. What now?" They struggled to hold the killer.

Mr. Robbe approached the killer, reared back with the ax, and as his men ducked, swung for the assassin's neck.

2

A well-groomed man in his thirties, with hazel eyes, brown hair, and tanned complexion brewed four cups of tea in Cat's kitchen. He wore an olive cardigan sweater over a pink dress shirt with the sleeves folded up one turn, pleated brown trousers, gold Rolex watch, oxblood loafers, and stood perhaps two inches taller than his boss, the man that had come in the nick of time.

The Secret Service guys had left with the still-moving dismembered remains of the attacker rolled up in a carpet that had yet to be laid in the apartment upstairs.

Mal had arrived in a limo with a black security van trailing him. Cat didn't feel right about lying to the rookie cop who wondered about all this activity. The kid's inexperience helped cover their story that the men in suits were the carpet store owners personally picking up a return because of a shortage of laborers and that what he thought were gunshots were actually a nail gun's misfires. It was a thin story, but Cat sold it and would never again complain about the deficiencies of a public education.

Robbe's people identified the assassin as a world-level terrorist suspected of dozens of killings throughout the Mideast and Europe, including children and families. Mal sent the killer to his research facility, where he'd be put to a final rest in one of his industrial ovens. The diminutive boss was unfazed by his role in making this man "disappear."

Lelani finished flushing out her eyes in the kitchen sink. They were bloodshot to the nth degree. She had a nasty welt just above the bridge of her nose where she'd been butted. A few inches lower and he would have broken her nose. She joined Cat in the living room.

"This is Sergeant Robbe," Lelani said, formally introducing the man.

"Sergeant Malcolm Robbe of the Dukesguarde, at your service," he said. He held out his hand palm up. Cat accepted it and Malcolm bowed. "Lady MacDonnell," he said.

Cat made an awkward curtsy.

"No," Lelani said, shaking her head.

"Huh?"

"You're his superior."

Malcolm straightened and smiled. "She means you are not required to curtsy. I actually work for a living."

"Oh," Cat said, cursing the stupid rules of aristocracy under her breath.

"This is my partner and man Friday, Scott Wilcock," said Malcolm.

Scott approached with the tray and placed it on the coffee table. He shook in the traditional manner—his hand and his grip were soft. The term "partner" took on a new dimension.

Scott greeted Lelani more cautiously.

"You'll have to excuse Scott," said Malcolm. "Aandor and magic are new to him."

"Join the club," said Cat.

"I'm creating a twelve-step program for spouses and partners," Scott said mischievously. "Meetings twice a month, and be prepared to sing 'Kumbaya.'"

"I'm in," Cat said. She liked him immediately. Scott had been thrust into the same boat as she; it was nice to have another oarsman.

Lelani claimed a spot on the floor in the space between the loveseat and couch. She swallowed one of her purple allergy pills with her first sip of tea.

"I'll have some men come in to repair your apartment," Malcolm said.

"That's very nice of you," Cat said, "but—"

"Least I can do after all you've been through. Finding you wasn't hard; I have friends in the authorities that clued me into what had happened the past few days. I'm a man of some means in this reality. Had I never been reminded of my origins, I would not have died unhappy."

"Damn straight," Scott mumbled.

"The memory spell was our doing," said Lelani. "I know that it was not a pleasant experience, but Lord Dorn was systematically hunting down the guardians."

Lelani looked glumly into her tea. Cat understood that the centaur felt responsible for not rousing the prince's guardians from their long sleep sooner. She barely managed to save Seth and Cal. For all her competence, Lelani was still young—hardly a woman. The pressure she was under would have broken most folks, but high stakes for her people in the Blue Forest spurred the centaur on.

Cat placed a gentle hand on her shoulder. "Tristan was not your fault," she told the girl. Dorn had murdered Cal's lieutenant.

"A shame," Mal said solemnly. "I was just reading about his death. My security service has been searching for all the guardians. I'm gathering everyone at my suite in the Waldorf-Astoria as we speak. Has anyone heard from Fronik? Where would a centaur hide in this world?"

Lelani's sullenness took on an angry tinge. Cat could feel her muscles tense under her hand. The handle of her teacup cracked, and the tea spilled on the carpet.

There goes that set.

"We haven't yet been able to locate Galen, Linnea, or Tilcook, either," Mal continued. "Is it possible they changed their names and are raising the prince somewhere safe?"

Cat and Lelani glanced at each other, realizing Malcolm had only half the story. "Galen and Linnea were killed in a car accident thirteen years ago," Lelani said. "The prince has been lost since infancy. He is unaware of his identity."

The tight line of Malcolm's mouth betrayed his disapproval. "But he knows, now," Mal said. "The spell . . ."

"The memory spell undid Seth's damage from thirteen years ago," Lelani explained. "But the prince was only an infant then. What memories could he have? A stormy night under a tree for which he'd have no frame of reference?"

"Then the prince is completely unaware . . ." Mal broke off and again studied the view outside, his face painted with concern.

"Not much longer, hopefully. The captain and Seth arrived at the prince's home in Maryland this morning."

"See," said Scott, rubbing the tension from Mal's shoulders.

"What is MacDonnell's plan once we have Danel back?" Mal asked more cautiously than his previous tone.

Cat wasn't comfortable with Malcolm's casual reference to her husband. Her husband, it seemed, had several titles, including "mister," and his sergeant ought to be using one of them.

"Captain MacDonnell will adopt the boy," Lelani said.

"What?" Cat blurted out.

"Apologies, my lady—I thought the captain had discussed it with you."

Cal had brought the matter up, but they had not made any final decisions. At least Catherine hadn't.

"After that . . . ," Malcolm said. "What about Aandor?"

"We haven't thought that far ahead," Cat said, though she wondered if Cal had, and simply hadn't clued her in. Her husband was a different man—more buttoned up and secretive.

"Is there something specific you had in mind, Sergeant Robbe?" asked Lelani.

Malcolm took another sip and let the question hang for a moment. He stretched out the pause, studied them, and seemed to conclude they did not have the answer he was looking for.

"Never mind," he said. "It's a moot point while the boy is in danger." He looked out the window again, lost in his ponderings.

"He told me about his village . . . ," Scott said. "Back there." Scott jabbed at the wall behind him with a thumb, but Cat understood it to mean much farther away.

"His village?"

"Malcolm's people are in a similar situation as mine," Lelani said.

"He's a centaur?" Cat asked.

"What's a centaur?" Scott asked.

"He's a dwarv."

"A dwarf?" Cat repeated.

"That's not very nice," Scott insisted.

"Dwarvs," she repeated, emphasizing the V, "are highland dwellers. Farrenheil drove them from the eastern kingdoms. They are craftsmen—armor, shields, weapons, jewels . . ."

Mal emerged from his ponderings to explain. "Dwarvs and men share common ancestors, but like Neanderthals and Cro-Magnons we diverged at some point long ago. Farrenheil does not consider us 'pure.'"

"Farrenheil gets worse the more I learn about them," Cat said.

"The only laws their ruling family enforce are the brutal ones that serve them," Mal said. "Prince Danel was our best hope at keeping those jackals in their place. That's what this universe hop was for. If Danel dies, Farrenheil will soon have the next closest claim to the regency of the empire. All these breeding races—crazy way to run a society, wouldn't you agree?

"Here's the craziest part . . . there are several girls who would qualify for princess regent of the empire—except, we don't count girls. One of them will be paired up with the prince to produce the next emperor."

Cat was frustrated with all the rules and accords that had turned her life upside down. "Why do the people put up with this crap?"

"People?" said Mal, disgusted. "Wars burn down their farms and homes. But they could give two bits about politics or law even though it's in their best interest to care. They care only enough to know what the highborn ladies are wearing to the balls, who ranks at the top of the jousting lists, or the latest scandal or gossip."

Cat felt a headache coming on. Cal's family was neck deep in this ass-backward method of running a society. It went against everything she believed in, everything she struggled for in her youth to bring about a more inclusive society. She followed Lelani's example and stayed quiet, something she imagined she'd have to learn to be better at if she ever met her in-laws. Cat would present a united front with Cal in public, and take these issues up with her husband in private. If he really expected her to go back to Aandor with him, and part of her hoped that wasn't inevitable, some commitment to change was forthcoming. Some agreements on how they would raise their children.

Mal stood up. "It would be safer if you came to the Waldorf. It's unknown to Dorn. My workmen will finish repairs here and keep the rats out. Hopefully, Callum will have the prince by nightfall and we can discuss the next stage together."

Lelani left to retrieve Bree. Mal excused himself to use the facilities.

"Confident," Cat said to Scott.

Scott smiled and rolled his eyes. "He runs a twelve-billion-dollar corporation. Anything the Pentagon wants to make bulletproof, they send to him. He's brilliant."

"And are you okay with all these revelations?" Cat was hoping for an answer that would make her feel less guilty about her doubts regarding Cal.

Scott thought about what he would divulge before finally confessing, "I trust Mal with my life . . . but I have the strangest feeling he's keeping something from me."

So it wasn't just her. Cat wanted to meet the other guardians more than ever now—to fill her in on what she didn't know. Cat had some major decisions to make, the easiest of which was the adoption of a thirteen-year-old boy into her family. She knew nothing about the kid. What if he was troubled? How would his presence affect Bree and the new baby? The only bright side was at least Cal was human.

"You're handling your partner's dwarv lineage very well," she said.

"Honey, please . . . I grew up gay in the backwoods of Virginia with the name Wilcock. This is nothing. I'd love that man if he sprouted goat legs." He took a sip and suddenly his eyes opened wide. "Oh!" he exclaimed. "Centaurs! Greek independence bacchanal in the West Village, 2004—the boys dressed as one. She's a horse!"

Cat cringed.

"Did I say something wrong?" Scott asked.

Mal emerged from the bathroom. "Scott, whatever you do, don't compare centaurs to horses. They're sensitive. It would take days to work out."

"We just dodged that bullet," Cat said.

Cat packed her large suitcase with a few days' worth of items for herself, Cal, and Bree. How long would they be away? At least until Dorn and all his henchmen were gone. And then what?

Cat sat on the bed. A vein of sadness opened within her as she prepared to abandon her home—wondering if she would ever feel safe here again. It was more than that . . . leaving now was a temporary reprieve from the possibility of going to another universe and leaving home for good. It was a lot to ask of someone. After all the work they put into their dream home, it bothered her deeply. The building wasn't a castle, but it was theirs. They picked it up for a song when it was in shambles, and created a place worth living in.

Cat thought about Malcolm Robbe, a natural leader, and wondered if Cal could leave the *going back to Aandor* part to him and just stay in this reality to finish the life they'd started together. Cat knew her husband too well, though. If she didn't go to Aandor, he would anyway, with every intention of coming back for her. But she would be a much older woman by then—assuming Cal survived.

Mal was alone when Cat emerged from the bedroom. "You didn't need to wait," she said.

"Not leaving you alone . . . you've been lucky up 'til now, but luck eventually runs out."

"I have a request," Cat said. "Let's not tell my husband about the attack here today. Cal's been under a lot of pressure. I want him focused on his trip, not worried about my safety."

"Cal no longer has reason to worry, Catherine. You're under my protection now."

Mal had a take-charge personality, similar to her husband, except Cal wasn't as pushy. Maybe it was a height thing like Napoleon or Mussolini. She wondered how much of that he had when he served under Cal in Aandor, and how much came about as the executive of his own multibillion-dollar corporation. *What happens when he and Cal have a difference of opinion? How many leaders can a company have?*

"Mal—with Tristan dead, does that make you second in command of the group?"

Malcolm paused. He thought about it, put on a strained smile, and said, "Something like that."

Whatever Mal had edited during that hesitation raised Cat's hackles. Still, it was a matter to be taken up later. Extra bodies for the cause meant a more liberal distribution of the burden. That had to be a step in the right direction.

CHAPTER 18

CHESS IN THE PARK

Sawmill Creek Park off Dorsey Road consisted of four baseball fields that were empty at this time of year. Dretch asked to meet there, but wasn't specific as to where in the park. He only said the open area. Cal pulled the Explorer into the parking lot and he and Seth surveyed their surroundings. A young man played Frisbee with his golden retriever in one of the outfields, in the far distance. He looked too carefree to be part of this conflict. Seth tugged Cal's sleeve and pointed to a man in a trench coat, sitting serenely with a steaming cup of coffee, thirty yards away at a picnic table under a tree.

Cal's disposable cell rang to the tune of Liza Minnelli's "New York, New York"—Cat's tone. He tensed, imagining his wife was in danger and would require him to return immediately.

"Hey," he said.

"Surprise," she answered in a cheery tone. Cal didn't realize he'd been clenching his jaw until he released. *"Guess what?"*

"I'm about to meet Dretch," he said, throwing a wet blanket on her exuberance.

"Are you in danger?"

"I don't think so. We're in a park. Not too many places to hide."

"Well, I have some good news . . . Say hello to an old friend . . ."

"Good afternoon, Captain MacDonnell." Cal's heart lifted at the sound of Malcolm Robbe's velvety tenor.

"Malcolm!"

Catherine reclaimed the phone and brought her husband up to date. She was in Malcolm's limousine heading to his suite at the Waldorf Astoria in Midtown. Malcolm's business partner drove Lelani in the rented van. Robbe had apparently become filthy, stinking rich while in this reality. Cal wasn't a jealous person by nature, nor was he motivated by money—so why did he feel a tinge of regret at the discovery of Malcolm's success on this side of the pond? Cal didn't want to spook Colby and promised to call back soon with details.

When he ended the call, Seth said, "Liza?"

"Huh?"

"'New York, New York'—you picked Liza over Frank for your ring tone?"

"Catherine's in New York—she's a woman, Liza's a woman."

Seth stared at him frozen with disbelief. "That's some pretty fucked-up linear thinking, man."

"They play Liza at Yankee Stadium," Cal argued.

"When they lose!" Seth pointed out.

Cal mentally kicked himself for wasting time with Seth's nonsense. Was he hesitating—nervous about meeting Dretch. This was it . . . the first substantial contact with the enemy.

"Stay here until I figure out what's going on," Cal said.

"What should I do?"

"Whittle. At least you'll be holding a big stick and a knife if things go south."

Cal reached into his jacket and released the safeties on his Glock 9 mm. The clip was loaded with Speer Gold Dots, and there was one in the chamber. He took a deep breath and marched toward the dick.

Dretch was fifty-two, but looked older. He divorced eight years back and had a twelve-year-old quadriplegic son. He'd been a beat cop at the 79th Precinct in Brooklyn before earning a Medal of Valor and a promotion to homicide detective in Manhattan. Five citations for exceptional duty later, he took early retirement to go private. The gumshoe was under indictment in New York for extortion, tax evasion, illegal wiretapping, and failure to report abuse of minors by very wealthy clients. Dretch had fallen far because of greed; now he'd graduated to kidnapping and murder. He was looking for the lost prince so that Dorn could kill that innocent boy. Cal wasn't sure what the next step was as he approached the picnic table. Dretch couldn't possibly think Cal would help him in any way.

Dretch's bare hands were folded on the table next to the coffee. A cell phone with the battery removed lay next to them—a sign that the detective didn't want anyone to know his location. Cal took a whiff of something not entirely fresh—almost foul—and on top of it, the smell of aftershave as though to conceal it. Colby looked like he hadn't shaved in a few days, but there was no one else around from whom the smell could have come. Maybe the guy couldn't find time to shower.

"Hello," Dretch said politely. They could have been friends meeting for a beer.

Cal nodded, but made no sound.

"I've been looking forward this," the old dick added.

"I find that hard to believe," Cal said. He surveyed the park for signs of an ambush. The table was at a good vantage to spy the area around them.

"We're quite alone," Colby confirmed. "Please sit." He offered the bench opposite him. The table beckoned for a chessboard, though their game had far more serious ramifications.

"Where's the prince?" Cal asked.

"Someplace safe. Neither you nor Dorn will find him." It came out: *Neetha you noahr Doan will find 'im.* Dretch was a Brooklyn boy to the core.

Cal raised an eyebrow. "Dorn hired you to kill him," he said.

"He hired me to find him . . . I'm not a killer."

Cal let loose a sardonic snort.

"What's with the attitude?" Colby asked.

"A trail of corpses all over upstate New York everywhere you've been."

"I didn't kill anyone," Dretch insisted.

"Sweeny. Nathan Dumont. Erin Ramos." Cal threw his partner's name on the list, though Dretch wasn't even in the Bronx when she was killed.

Dretch was genuinely put off by the news. "Sweeny and Dumont were alive when I left them. I never even heard of this Ramos."

"How can I believe someone who helped a Hollywood producer secretly diddle young boys for years and swept the evidence under the rug, strong armed the parents, then blackmailed his client?"

Colby shifted in his seat, then leaned forward looking genuinely disturbed. "I've got a lot to answer for," he admitted. "But what I did, I had good reasons for. My boy has special needs that insurance don't cover. But I swear, with God as my witness, as far as Sweeny and Dumont, the last thing I wanted was to bring the law down on top of me. They were both alive when I last saw them. I wanted *you* on my tail."

Colby held his cup with both hands without taking a sip. "Dorn's been sanitizing the trail," he realized. "How did you find me?"

Cal ignored the question. Gloria Hauer had suffered enough without killers coming after her family. "Why would you want me to find your trail?" Cal asked. "There's no payday if the prince survives."

Dretch took a sip of coffee and looked off toward the man playing with his dog. "Looks like a fucking Cialis commercial," he said pointing at the scene.

"Answer the question."

"I agreed to the job before I knew what I was signing on to," Colby confessed. "I thought it was a rich mob father trying to find his son in witness protection. The money they were offering . . . it was obscenely generous. All my lifelong instincts that warn me when something's too good to be true got trounced by the answer to all my prayers. My kid . . . he needs . . . but . . ." Colby paused, gazing again into the distance, looking to all the world like a man that wanted to switch places with that boy and his dog.

"They took my heart," Dretch said in one raspy breath. He waited for it to sink in.

"Sucks for you," Cal said evenly.

"I'm pretty sure they're lying about putting it back."

"When you sleep with dogs . . ." Cal struggled to remain civil, but he really didn't like the guy; and besides, there was little he could threaten a walking corpse with anyway. "What do you want from me, Dretch? How do I get my prince back?"

"You got a magic guy?" the dick asked.

"Of course," Cal exaggerated, like this was par for the course. As far as Colby knew, Cal had a platoon of wizards at his disposal. Dretch didn't need to know it consisted of a student and an idiot.

"Here's how I see things," Dretch continued. "Either I can't be fixed, in which case, nuts to all you fuckers; or I can be made normal again and I want to hear your best offer."

Dretch looked vulnerable, desperate. The dick had one foot out the door toward abandoning his master. Dretch broadcasted too much—he was probably better at negotiating when the stakes weren't so personal. Something didn't jibe here . . . why would it be *nuts to all you fuckers* if no one was able to fix him? There was still the payday . . . he could hand over the prince and get his money and at least his heart back? Cal suspected more than just self-preservation prompted Dretch's shift in loyalties.

Cal played a hunch.

"I'm not sure he's worth the effort or the risk," Cal said. "The prince is a delinquent: assault and battery, destruction of property—patricide. His having been raised away from his guardians has tainted him. I'm having a hard time imagining him running an empire."

"You believe everything you read?" Dretch said.

"He must be a handful. Aren't you worried he'll lift your wallet and cut your throat while you sleep? I know you wouldn't die, but he doesn't know that and it could get pretty annoying walking around with your head in your arms."

"About as annoying as it is for you to walk around with your head up your ass," Dretch said. "I trust that kid more than half the priests in Brooklyn."

"That a fact?"

Dretch was about to respond when the realization that Cal had outmaneuvered him filtered into his expression. MacDonnell smiled and wondered if he should have gone down the homicide track instead of ESU.

Dretch wore the grin of the defeated. "Danny's smarter and tougher than either of us," he said. "Staked out that kid for twenty-four hours after I came down here, trying to figure out my options." Dretch talked at length about the profile he scraped together. The gumshoe had seen his share of deadbeat drunken dads and mentally short mothers in his line of work over the years, but Clyde and Rita were real pieces of work. "No one gave him any breaks," the detective said. "But he stands up for what he believes. The kid has heart.

"Daniel stood up for his friends and never cared about the odds . . . yet most of the adults in his life, especially the ones that were supposed to be looking out for him, were MIA. That sheriff tried to help, but it was too little too late. Total system failure. I didn't expect Danny to kill his old man, though. The crazy sot made it hard for him not to."

The detective stopped talking. Cal looked up to find a victorious Cheshire grin on the man. It was Cal's face that now betrayed him, revealing his thoughts to the detective, beaming with pride and even some moisture around his eyes. Danel—Daniel's character had been tested through hardship and tragedy and came through intact.

"He's a lot better off with us," Cal said.

"Bunk. He's better off with *neither* of you," Dretch insisted. "If Dorn doesn't kill him, his reward is to become the bull's-eye in a political battle back in never-never land. The other side will never stop trying to kill him. His own people will prop him up and try to control him—tell him what to eat and who to fuck. They won't even let him pick his own wife. Who in their right mind would ever want to inherit a throne? The only king who ever has fun on a throne is the one who earned it—by sword or cunning. The hand-me-downs are just grief for the heirs."

"His parents would be touched by your concern," Cal said.

Dretch was right, though. Daniel's life would not be his own. Still, he was the only prince Aandor had, and it needed to be the boy's choice. If the detective had formed a fondness for the boy, then Daniel meeting his true parents was something Dretch couldn't deny him. Not after the life he's had.

"I have to look out for myself," Colby said, getting back to basics. "Just meeting with you can get me killed. Look," he said, pointing to his disassembled phone, "I have no idea what tricks these wizards can pull. I only risked this because my guys seem off balance at the moment, and they've left me a long leash. Who knows when that could change? I'm meeting with them tonight—I have to tell them something. Do you have what I need?"

Cal looked toward Seth, who was whittling intently. *The witless whittler—so much for a lookout,* he thought. He whistled to get Seth's attention. Cal met him halfway, out of Dretch's hearing range.

"S'up," Seth said, failing to be cool.

"They took Dretch's heart," Cal said.

Seth looked at Colby in the distance and then to Cal. "He's one of *those* guys?"

"Yeah. Wants to know if we can put it back?"

"How should I know?" Seth said.

"Call her, idiot."

Seth dialed Lelani and explained the situation. He listened to her response and hung up. "A wizard can't undead somebody," he said.

God! Cal thought. *How do I leverage a desperate pissed-off dead man?* He fingered the butt of his pistol more as a nervous habit than a call to action.

"But . . . ," Seth continued, "in theory, a wizard working with someone called a prelate or an augur can do it. What the heck's an augur?"

"You could have started with that information," Cal said, irritated.

"That's how they talk on *CSI*."

Cal returned to Dretch.

"Does Dorn have a cleric with him?" he asked.

"Not following . . ."

"A priest. A druid, a prelate, an auger?"

"There's no one remotely priestly in that lot."

"Then Dorn's bullshitting you. He can't reverse your condition. Any wizard can take away your life, but only a wizard working with a cleric can put you back together."

Dretch looked forlorn, very much as Cal imagined he would at the news.

"Do you have a priest?" Dretch asked, desperately.

"Yes," Cal lied, though it was only a half lie. They just hadn't seen him in thirteen years. "On that list Dorn gave you to track us down . . . Allyn Grey is Prelate Grey of the temple of Pelitos."

"You're not lying, are you?" Cal didn't feel the need to work too hard trying to convince the man. Dretch had suspected this all along or he wouldn't be in this park talking to them.

"What do you think?" was Cal's only response.

Looking into Colby's cold dead eyes, he knew the detective believed him. Now, if they could only confirm that Allyn was still alive.

CHAPTER 19

OFF THE PONDEROSA . . .

Jeb's general store at the entrance of the trailer park was the only one within walking distance of Bev's home. They were in the middle of farmland, miles from the closest town. Daniel intended to make dinner that night as a way to thank Beverly for her kindness—and in a sick, guilty way, for the affections of her daughter, though Bev hadn't a clue. He left the safety of his "home" and took a long route winding through the park to stretch his legs, the coolness of the weather tempered by the late afternoon sun. Seeing the different nooks and circles in the park gave him a good sense of who his neighbors were. More importantly, it got him away from Luanne for a spell. His brain was still floating from her scent—she was the living embodiment of nitrous oxide. He was so stupidly happy around her, breathing in everything and ogling her bumps and curves that he was grateful he was not going to school down here for fear of ending up in remedial classes from lack of focus.

Making dinner served a second purpose . . . it also ensured their meal would be palatable. On this last thought, Daniel realized his actions were self-serving on every level. Was that what drove everyone?

Clyde, Rita, Principal Conklin, Katie Millar, Luanne—everyone's first impulse was to do for him- or herself. Satisfaction was the product of selfish acts. So was safety; the tribe demanded it. An unselfish act on behalf of his friend is what caused him more trouble than he ever imagined. Fighting Adrian's battles for him cost him his freedom and future. Arrested at thirteen for battery and sued by the Grundy boys' trashy parents. That mess, combined with discovering his stepfather's affair because he went to help Katie Millar, despite her rejection of him, escalated into Clyde wanting to beat the crap out of Daniel when he got home—and that incident led to Clyde's death. It was a simplified account of events, but his thoughts looped over those last few days, wondering what might have been if he'd just minded his own damn business.

Maybe Clyde was right to get upset at the way Daniel poked his nose into everything. Adults seemed to know that self-interest and minding your own business were the cornerstones of cohabitation and self-preservation. It made Daniel suspicious of Colby's motivations for helping him. *Friendship* was becoming a thinner excuse the more time passed. They'd only met a few days ago . . . How could they possibly be friends? Why would Colby risk jail to help Daniel avoid capture? What was in it for him, if not a way to use Daniel at some future point?

Jeb's was a ramshackle, hastily slapped together structure of wood and aluminum sheets, about as big as a double-wide, just inside the gate of the park. The park's fence only extended about fifty yards in each direction, backed by some sorry-looking bushes that ran along the inside of it. All someone had to do to get into the park was walk toward the farm next door and around the end of the fence. The blacktop from the state road ended at the gate—the trailer park roads were dirt and gravel, lined with weeds. The more industrious residents had gardens around their homes.

A dusty police cruiser sat parked in front of the store. Daniel hovered back behind a trailer waiting for the cop to leave. Colby assured him being two states away and in the middle of butt-fuck nowhere was relatively safe, but there was no point in taking chances. All he needed to ruin his life was one ambitious country cop looking for a promotion. He studied the trailers on this side of "town" while he waited, kicking the occasional large pebble from its bed. Some took pride in their dwelling—decorating their home with curtains, gardens, fresh paint; they lived beside folks for whom a pigpen would be a step up. These were mostly single trailers around the park entrance—*where the po' folks lived,* as Luanne would say. Daniel had forty dollars left to his name, so he must be one of the "po'." These were his people.

The sky was the color of bluebird eggs, crisp with a late autumn's cold. There was a lot of sky around these parts. The land was flat in all four directions, with only the occasional silo or barn to break the monotony. The park was *tornado bait*—something a classmate had once said about their proximity to natural disasters. The cop came out of Jeb's with a doughnut stuffed in his mouth and a bottle of Coke in one hand and a white paper bag in the other hand. He got into the cruiser, pulled out onto the state road, and peeled off like a man saturated with processed sugar. Daniel climbed creaky steps and entered.

Daniel's senses were assaulted by the schizophrenic nature of Jeb's wares. The pungent, mingled odors of beef jerky, laundry soap, dairy goods (not all fresh), women's hygiene products, colas, candy, beer, tobacco, and sawdust merged like a dysfunctional symphony, baked into the wooden shelves and particle floorboards by years of Carolina heat. Daniel picked up some Kraft Mac & Cheese boxes, hotdogs, buns, relish, two liters of Coke, and some cans of peas for color. As he laid the items on the glass counter, he spotted a condom display underneath the glass. It just occurred to him that Luanne might be crazy enough to not be on birth control. That's all he needed. He couldn't even support himself. Daniel pointed to a box of Trojans to be thrown on the pile.

The steps creaked louder as he exited, under the extra weight of the bags. Daniel's foot just touched the dirt when he noticed Cody and two other guys leaning on the Caddy DeVille at Jeb's corner. One of the toadies was thin with long greasy blond hair and wearing a black Slayer tee under his denim jacket. He seemed especially jittery. The other was tall and solid, with close-cropped nappy red hair and shoulders that drooped from a lifetime of hunching. They loitered between Daniel and Bev's trailer. Daniel hoped these grassroots capitalists would be too preoccupied with their ventures to notice him, but since when had his luck ever run that good?

"Hey," Cody said, as Daniel walked by.

Daniel stopped beside the hoods and turned casually to face them. Cody leaned against the passenger door, lighting a cigarette.

"Hey," Daniel said back matter-of-factly.

"Interested in some rock?"

Daniel wasn't sure of the subtext. It might be a straightforward offer. "Not particularly," he said. "Thanks, though." Politeness was always a plus in the South, even with death-metal, gun-toting meth dealers.

"Where you from?"

"Up north."

"I know you're from up north. Where?"

Daniel weighed the risk of telling the guy to go fuck himself and ending up in a fight that might bring cops to the park or send him to the emergency room. He wasn't a good enough liar to make up a story. Who knows where Cody's business ventures have taken him? "Baltimore," he said. It was mostly true. Glen Burnie was a suburb.

"Yeah?" Cody said. "What's the best crab place?"

"Obrycki's," Daniel said. At least that's the one his mom liked best, so they went there.

Cody took a drag and blew smoke. Daniel got the sense that he'd passed the first test.

"Why you stayin' with Luanne?"

"I'm not staying with Luanne," Daniel said. "I'm staying with Bev. She's my friend's sister and is putting us up for a few days. Luanne also lives with Bev."

Cody's expression didn't change, but Daniel sensed annoyance at the way he successfully skirted the question. "Why you drawin' pictures of her?" he asked. Another drag. More smoke.

"Bored. She doesn't have any books, no videogames in the house; nothing to do around here. Did you happen to see the twelve other drawings in that pad you tore up that had nothing to do with Luanne? Why'd I draw the lake? Why'd I sketch a tree?"

Cody took a drag, blew it out, and spit really close to Daniel's sneaker.

"You hangin' out with a fifty-year-old bum and his sister . . . no mom, no dad. Seems shady."

Daniel was tired of playing twenty questions. "Why you hanging out in front of the store with your car?" he asked back.

"None of your business," the greasy blond kid said.

"Exactly," Daniel responded.

The three of them came off the car slowly in unison. This was their turf—no one was going to tell them to mind their own business in their corner of the trailerverse. Cody did his best to give Daniel the cold dead-eye stare. Daniel ignored the other two and locked onto Cody's stare. Daniel refused to budge or blink in the face of this pretender. After all, Cody had never killed anyone and Daniel had. The meth head blinked first, looking down into the shopping bag. He shot his arm into the bag and pulled out the box of Trojans.

"What the fuck is this?!" he asked.

Shit.

"They're for Bev," Daniel lied, thinking fast on his feet.

"That old cow's dried up," Cody said. This time his stare had an edge to it. "You hopin' to get lucky with someone?"

"Maybe Bev's beau has VD," Daniel said, trying to act like he didn't care. "Or maybe she's giving them to Luanne. What do I know? She asks, I buy."

A black Cadillac Escalade pulled into the trailer park with music blaring loudly. Four young men poured out. Cody's attention switched to them swiftly, as though danger had arrived. The leader of the other crew, a tall, blocky lad with pink ears and pink neck approached. He wore a black leather vest over a striped flannel shirt, boot-cut jeans, and a huge silver buckle. The other two looked like off-the-shelf southern white guys, the type you'd forget two minutes after they left; the fourth guy was a skinny geek type with a Bluetooth in his ear and an open laptop computer that he cradled with one hand and typed into with the other. Daniel was caught between the crews.

Daniel tried to slink away and allow the men to talk business. Cody grabbed his arm and held him firm. "We ain't done," he grumbled.

"That's no way to treat a customer, Cody," said big belt buckle.

"This our park, McCoy," Cody's greasy blond lackey stressed.

"Don't get your panties in an uproar, Weasel. We going into Jeb's to get some smokes is all." The geek was talking into his Bluetooth, confirming a delivery for that night.

"'Sides, we don't need to come here to sell. Yo' folk come to us to get product. Walk five miles to buy rock from me." McCoy jerked his thumb toward Bluetooth guy, and added, "We doin' business the modern way—on the interweb."

McCoy and his cronies guffawed stupidly, like fifth-graders giving heck to third graders. Daniel wished he were miles away from what was obviously a turf war. *Cody doesn't do well with competition,* he remembered Luanne saying. An insecure idiot with a gun, under pressure.

Daniel looked up and down the state road, hoping the police cruiser would return. At this point, jail might be preferable to being shot or stabbed. Daniel decided he couldn't wait for the law to save the day and took a chance that just the threat of police would work.

"Cops," Daniel said.

Both groups craned their necks searching nervously up the road. Cody shifted his body; Daniel slipped free and strolled off at a calm pace. By the time Cody realized, it was too late; he couldn't turn his back on McCoy or walk away from his homies on his own turf.

"Why don't you finish your business with the nice gentlemen?" Daniel said, continuing his streak of southern politeness. "Keep the rubbers. But if Bev catches the clap, you'll hear hell from her."

Cody looked like he was chewing on rusty nails. Once out of view, Daniel doubled his pace back to the trailer. He shouldn't have rubbed it in as he walked away. Daniel wondered if the trailer park was still a safe place for him and whether he should start thinking of leaving before he ended up with a bullet in his back.

How do I get myself into these messes?

CHAPTER 20

WHY WE HATE GROUPIES

The Waldorf Astoria was the most opulent hotel Catherine had ever been in. Even Lelani, sporting Bree on her back, craned her neck, impressed at the beautifully decorated lobby. The art deco remnant of the Great Depression had a three-story ceiling supported by large columns—the lobby floor was marble with a decorative circle-of-life mosaic underneath a grand chandelier. Above the entrance canopy resided an art deco grill, and inside a luxurious lounge with a grand piano. The lobby's palette was creams, gold, deep rust, and black pillars, accented by warm lighting. Even the sound of the hall was a subdued echo granting airs and privacy at the same time. The many guests had an international flavor; Cat suspected a few of them owned horses, which they learned to ride as children, and had nicknames like Biff, Buffy, and Mitt. And here, Malcolm Robbe entertained guests and business associates from around the world in his own private suite.

Lelani had ridden over with Scott in the van, leaving Cat and Bree time alone with Malcolm. In the limousine, Mal regaled Cat with stories of his exploits both in Aandor and in this reality. Malcolm Robbe hailed from a distinguished line of mine owners. His grandfather, Fengus Robbe, fled from his hillside home with the family during one of Farrenheil's infamous purges—a thinly disguised land grab draped in the cover of threat to racial purity. Their mines had the richest deposits of rubies and diamonds in Farrenheil, not to mention good quality iron ore and silver. They had been stewards of those mines for seventeen generations. The Robbes relocated to the northern part of Aandor, far from the madness of Farrenheil, but never reclaimed the status they'd once held in the old kingdom. Malcolm's three brothers could barely stay employed as miners—the villages were saturated with refugees. It was impossible to buy a decent hill or mountainside to start anew—Aandor had its own dwarven hierarchy, and those old families, dubbed the Longtooths, protected their lands and power against the arriving waves. Malcolm left his family in the north for Aandor City to find his fortune in other vocations. Thanks in part to the MacDonnells, whose family seat was also in the north, and for whom Mal's family built irrigation canals for their crops, he found a position in the palace guard. The day of the invasion, good fortune placed him near the pantry, defending the infant prince.

Among refugees, there was great affection for Archduke Athelstan, who exhibited high tolerance for émigrés. Everyone had looked forward to the young prince's naming day celebration . . . fealty to the archduke's family went to the core of each subject, and Mal would have died for the boy if necessary back then.

Like the others in the guardians' party, Seth's botching of the identity spell left Malcolm with no memory of who he was or where he'd come from. He stumbled, starved and drenched, into the Presbyterian Church in Smithfield, New York. The pastor took pity on him and hired Mal as a handyman. Malcolm, it turned out, had a natural affinity with tools and construction.

He found work as a welder and discovered he had a talent for handling metal as well. Soon, Malcolm began to moonlight as a repairman, fixing farm equipment, and even constructing his own attachments for Caterpillar and John Deere tractors that were better than the manufacturers' designs. His boss and friends at the shop convinced him to do more with his talents than remain in Smithfield. Mal applied to several engineering schools. With no history of prior education, it was tough getting the acceptance boards to take him seriously, but he managed to convince the folks at Stevens Institute in Hoboken, New Jersey, to give him a probationary period. Malcolm graduated three years later at the top of his class with dual degrees in mechanical and chemical engineering. Today, he was CEO and chairman of Hartschell Corp., one of the country's top weapons' manufacturers. His specialty was armor.

As she walked through the opulent lobby, Cat wondered about the eddies and currents in life that led two lost soldiers to different fates. Wealthy, landed, and tutored Callum ended up in the NYPD and a three-story walk-up in the Bronx, while penniless uneducated Mal ended up at the top of his social hierarchy and on an estate on the eastern shore of Long Island. More importantly, Cat suspected Malcolm was also very aware of the irony. Mal was at ease giving orders. It had been a long time since he last took one from her husband. Could the mission handle a power struggle among the guardians?

Outside Malcolm's grand suite near the top of the building stood an NFL-sized African-American in his forties wearing a black suit, sunglasses, and an earpiece. He whispered something into his shirt cuff and opened the door for them. The room inside was a buzz of activity. It continued the lobby's opulent motif with dark-gold carpet, cream-colored drapes, and off-white walls. The lines on the molded tray ceiling were crisp and the furniture was restored vintage; Cat suspected no two suites of this caliber were decorated alike at the Waldorf. The living room had a working gas fireplace and plush couches facing each other divided by a large red-stained oak coffee table in the middle. A plush loveseat crowned the set, facing the fireplace at the other end of the table. The tables in the room were a mixture of fine wood antiques and ones with marble tops, like the coffee table between the couches. French doors on opposite sides of the room separated three bedrooms from the common area. A breakfast counter marked the border of a kitchenette with microwave, sink, and a fridge.

Cat was grateful to have Lelani with her because she hated meeting strangers in large groups, and this room was filled with people. Too many names, purposes, interests to remember all at once—and in this case, doubly so because some had a second life in Aandor that she would have to remember as well. Malcolm's security detail stood out because they looked as though they'd been recruited from a Secret Service catalog—black suits and wired earpieces. Malcolm likely paid better than the government. Of the detail, a woman in her thirties with short-cropped red hair was wearing a telephone headset and sitting at an antique desk in the corner in front of three large computer monitors. The older man, Tom Dunning, who led the charge at her apartment in the Bronx was on his cell phone in the kitchenette. Despite the snow on Tom's roof, he still looked fit enough to lead a squad of marines through hell and back.

Sitting comfortably on the plush couches, knocking back drinks, were three who were definitely not part of the usual entourage—a young man in his twenties, thin, with tattoos on his arm and shoulder-length brown hair, wearing skinny jeans, Converse sneakers, and a tight black knit sweater with brown leather patches sewn into the shoulders. He looked unhappy and also slightly familiar. Next to him was a beautiful young woman with long, straight dirty-blond hair wearing designer jeans, black calf-high leather boots, and a pink blouse buttoned only to the point of her cleavage. On the other side of the coffee table from them sat a preppy man in his fifties, messy salt-and-pepper hair with a receding hairline, wearing a tweed jacket with elbow patches, a bow tie, tan corduroy trousers, and brown leather wing-tipped shoes. He had an unlit pipe in his mouth.

Malcolm stood beside Cat and announced to the people on the couch, "The Lady MacDonnell and her daughter Brianna."

The men on the couch looked at each other with confused expressions. After a slight delay, Malcolm cleared his throat loudly, and the men stood and introduced themselves.

"Balzac Cruz, at your service," said the older man. His affect gave the subtle hint of an English accent without actually having one. He smelled of gin, and his pinkish face had a bit of that bulldog droop that would eventually lead to jowls. There was a slick manner about him beneath the preppy veneer.

"Clarisse," said the blonde. She had a bubbly manner, a stark contrast to her partner's dour look. "This is Tim. Some crazy shit, huh?"

Cat covered Bree's ears. "Yeah."

"Sorry," Clarisse said.

Clarisse was too flippant for Cat's liking. People were dying around them and the blonde looked ready to go clubbing.

The white-haired man in the kitchenette got off the phone and approached Mal. "This is my head of my security, Tom Dunning."

Dunning made his salutations and turned to Malcolm. "Copter's still in Toronto with the financial team. They're back in the morning. I've cleared its schedule the rest of the week."

"Oh, do we get to fly around in copters?" Clarisse asked excitedly.

"Uh . . . no," Malcolm said. "But from this point on, one of the suits goes with you everywhere. They're all linked through GPS."

"Is he going to follow me to the urinal?" Tim asked in a snarky tone. "Take a satellite picture of my winkie?"

Scott excused himself to take a call in the master bedroom.

"I was hoping we might discuss protective measures from—uh—their *special* abilities," Dunning said to Lelani.

Lelani gave Malcolm a quizzical glance. Cat, too, wondered how much Dunning knew.

Lelani waited, and it took Cat a second to realize the centaur was waiting for permission to take her leave. "By all means," Cat said, waving toward the command center.

"Want some wine?" Clarisse asked, and left to fetch it before Cat's answer.

Bree tugged at her mother's skirt looking tired and bored. "I need to put her down for a nap," Cat said. Mal pointed to the second bedroom.

"I think we get Nickelodeon," he said.

Cat steered her toward the room, tiredly carrying their coats, and hoped Bree would nod off.

"I've rented the suite next door as well," Mal said. "I'm hoping to get every guardian here in the next few days."

"What if someone doesn't want to come?" asked Cat.

Tim snorted. "He's not giving them a choice," he said, and took another sip of his drink.

"You gave an oath," Malcolm said.

"Right, an oath . . . a decade ago when I was sixteen and scared for my life."

Scott called Malcolm to their bedroom. He motioned animatedly at the phone in his hand and mouthed *Pentagon*, with a harried look.

"Please excuse me," Mal said. "Generals and congressmen are as demanding as children."

Cat glimpsed several computer monitors through the open bedroom door, one of them playing CNBC. *More work and less play with those two*, she thought. The LGBT rights marches in college were filled with artists, musicians, and humanities majors, but not many from the business school. Or maybe they were there? Regardless, this couple was aptly suited to each other.

Balzac and Clarisse conversed by the wetbar mixing fresh drinks. Balzac glanced over, leading Cat to believe he was discussing her. Tim sat on the couch with a small guitar, plucking away and writing on a music sheet.

"You're a musician?" Cat asked.

"Rock star," he said. "Funny, huh?"

"In what way?"

"I was a lute player in Aandor. I completely forgot that I was a lute player until two days ago. My quartet played for the archduke at the naming day ceremony. Talk about bad timing."

"And they brought *you* along, to another universe?"

Tim smiled. He began to sing to the tune of "Every Rose Has Its Thorn," by Poison.

Ev-ery prince needs his court
Just like ev-ery duke needs his wars
Gods forbid, that he should carry his own gourd
Or be at risk of being bored.

Tim laughed at his own cleverness and took another swig.

"Or need to cook his own food or fetch his own horse," he continued. "It's a feudal thing. They whipped a royal court up on the spot. Can't have the prince being out of touch . . . not know all the popular songs like 'The Knight and the Centaur.' It would be a public relations disaster. We even drafted a cook, still holding his bloody cleaver. Anyone they could swear in."

Tim stared into what was left of his whiskey and swirled it around in the glass. "My bandmates were killed before my eyes. I ran into a kid from my hometown working as a palace guard . . . he told me there was sanctuary in the pantry. The wizard put up some sort of magic screen that stopped the enemy from popping in the way they did everywhere else. Everyone in that pantry was glad to hear of a plan to get out of town. No one asked the details. All we knew is that we'd live." Tim swallowed the last of his whiskey, then swirled the last bits of ice around in the glass.

"You hear a lot about wizards in Aandor. Folks go their whole lives without ever seeing a spell cast. Those magic types travel in their own circles. If one did stop at a sleepy hamlet on the way to wherever, they'd never reveal who they were. They never show off."

Tim was losing his train of thought. It was not his first whiskey of the day—but it didn't mean he was lying. She watched Lelani talking to the security team. The centaur never cast a spell she didn't need to. She had tremendous respect for the magic and treated it as the dangerous thing it was. Cat was not comfortable about magic being used around Bree. It was more than just an alien thing to her . . . she felt the sorcerers were playing around with a primal force that even they did not fully comprehend—like sixteenth-century men suddenly finding themselves in a nuclear power plant control room filled with shiny buttons.

"Do you have family?" Cat asked the musician.

"Father's a thatcher. In fact, he's a tenant of Lord Godwynn's—you know—Chrysla—" Tim stopped midsentence. He looked at Cat with sad eyes, then back down at his glass, burped, and suddenly stood.

"These drinks are going right through me," he said. "Hey, Red!" he shouted toward the command center. "Fire up that eye in the sky cause I'm about to take a whiz! A wide-angle lens is recommended." He excused himself. Cat had that feeling again . . . that there was something everyone else knew that she didn't.

Clarisse returned with Balzac and handed Cat a glass of pinot grigio.

"Tim's not usually like that," Clarisse said. "It's that bastard Malcolm."

"What did Malcolm do?"

"Everything. Tim's band was on the tour of their career. Then this whole thing happened. We got a call the next night inviting us to Lord Shorty's suite. They hugged and said how happy they were that they were both alive and successful. Then they started talking about the prince. Tim was very up front about the tour, the band, and how he wasn't going back to Aandor. I mean can you blame him? Where would he plug in the amp? They argued. Mal really laid into him about duty, honor, all that crap. So we left."

"But you came back?"

"Heeeee . . ."—indicating Mal with a finger aimed at the bedroom—"BOUGHT THE FREAKIN' RECORD LABEL!" she yelled. "And then, he sold the band's contract to another label for a ridiculously low fee, under the condition that Tim not be associated with the band in any way, and then he paid off the other band members—THOSE DOUCHE BAGS—to not reform with Tim under any circumstance! And those assholes took the money!"

Clarisse was red and breathing heavy. Clearly, they'd been drinking for quite a while. "It don't matter what universe you're from . . . ," Clarisse continued. "The rich and powerful always fuck the small guy. It's like nature or something."

"Ah nature . . . ," said Balzac, who had remained quietly amused during Clarisse's tirade. "Found in every corner of creation. Nurture, not so much. Lady MacDonnell, don't you find it fascinating how our inborn natures manifested themselves in this reality? How the different realities reward the same talents?"

This guy is a mind reader, Cat thought. Her guard went up when Balzac spoke—something about the quality of his words, or the way he said them, belied his genteel appearance.

"Tell me, were you not glad to learn that Callum was a high-ranking officer from back there, instead of a foot soldier with parents cramped into a thatch-roofed hovel?"

Balzac's abrasive querying would never win him friends. The man was itching for the kind of debate Tim or Clarisse were not capable of having and that Malcolm would have no patience for. *Why do I get stuck?* she thought.

"He didn't have two coppers to rub together in this reality, much less a family, and I married him anyway," Cat said.

Balzac showed his big white grin. "Tim was an excellent minstrel in Aandor," he said. "He packed them in at the Phoenix Nest, the largest tavern in Aandor City. But he could never have achieved the success he had here. Universe hopping is the best thing that happened to Tim."

"It's true," Clarisse confirmed. "Babies Ate My Dingo have the number nine video on MTV."

That's where I know him . . ., Cat thought. The band's ads were everywhere.

"Malcolm comes from a long line of smiths and miners," Balzac continued. "He could have pounded his anvil for a thousand years in Aandor, and never have attained the power and wealth he acquired here in just thirteen years."

"Mr. Cruz, I'm not sure where you're going with this," Cat said. "You'll get no argument from me about the drawbacks of feudal economics."

"I'm speculating. It's just interesting that Callum has essentially the same vocation here as he had there, but here, force is subordinate to intelligence—political maneuvering and people skills, and he did not attain a similar status to the one he had in Aandor."

"My husband wasn't a cop in Aandor."

"He is a knight," Balzac affirmed. "He uses force on behalf of his rulers to maintain the order. Same difference."

"He protects *everyone* here," Cat said, resenting Balzac's tone.

Balzac laughed. "My, you *have* sipped the Kool-Aid. Fine—it's not crucial to my point."

"It being . . . ?" Cat asked. This guy made her skin crawl. Where the heck was Malcolm?

"Tim and Malcolm are creators, and once freed from the limitations of despotism, they prospered. Callum's role in both universes is to protect and serve the established ruling class—a glorified bodyguard to maintain the status quo. Only here, MacDonnell was not born into his status. And force, not being equally as rewarding, he did not have the capacity to work his way to the comparable level in this world that he enjoyed in Aandor."

The pompous ass was dancing on Cat's last nerve. She took a sip of wine and counted to ten in her head. "What were you back there, if you don't mind me asking?" Cat said to change the subject.

"He was a clown," said Clarisse, amused.

Balzac threw the girl a wicked glare. *You don't want to get on his bad side, honey,* thought Cat.

"I was the court jester," Balzac corrected. "More George Carlin, less Bozo. Before that, a scholar of nonmagical studies."

"And here?" Cat asked.

"Tenured professor of literature."

"So educators are poor and taken for granted in all universes," Cat said.

Clarisse giggled.

Balzac's smile was a thin red line. "Men of *science* are held in a different regard in Aandor. But I wouldn't call myself poor. Working in a royal court, one comes across opportunities. It's like Congress."

Cat was tired of Balzac. Red faced, he probably downed as many drinks as Tim. She looked toward Mal's bedroom, wishing he'd return.

"Your husband is nothing more than a commoner in this reality," Balzac spat out. "That's all I was trying to point out."

"We're all commoners in America, Mr. Cruz," Cat said. "My husband's title is 'mister,' same as the president."

Balzac acceded to Cat with a raised glass and a nod. "True. But the ramifications of this excursion to another reality are greater for some than for others. For example, you don't think Malcolm is actually gay, do you?"

"Why should I care?" Cat shot back with venom in her voice.

Balzac put up his hands in a mock form of surrender—thick, hairy fingers . . . the fingers of a juggler. All that was missing was a twirled mustachio. He had initiated some sort of game, and they were the pieces. Why was she putting up with this when she could go lie down with Bree?

Because Balzac had information. And he was willing to parcel it out, as long as his game was in play. Cat took another sip and dug in.

"My dear," Balzac said. "Malcolm is a great victim of Proust's folly."

Balzac's volume had increased—the exchange garnered attention. Lelani gingerly navigated her way to Cat.

Cat said, "What makes you the expert of other people's affections?" Her ire was up.

"Balzac is alluding to the nature of dwarven women," Lelani said.

"What about them?"

"Physically, they are almost identical to the men," Balzac said with an almost gleeful twinkle in his eye. The man was made for gossip. "They have thick muscular limbs, are squat like the men, and sport facial and body hair and have high testosterone levels. They smell manly. Malcolm could not have found women in this reality as attractive—they're biologically wrong for what excites him. He tried—married and divorced within a year, which works out fine for his wife back in Aandor."

Cat was stunned. If this was true . . . Did Scott know? For some reason, this track of the conversation made Cat sick to her stomach. A pit rubbed against her innards. Too many secrets . . .

Balzac excused himself to find the lavatory. *What a besotted little group of losers,* Cat thought. Bree called for Cat from the bedroom. Lelani offered to check on the girl.

"He's a little full of himself," Clarisse said.

"Are you from Aandor, too?" Cat asked.

"God no. California."

"And Tim's made his decision about not going back."

"Definitely not going. I'd go back if he did, though. I love Renaissance fairs. At least I'm lucky—Tim didn't have someone back there, like Mal or this captain guy they talk about."

Cat froze. She felt like a fish that had just been hooked and yanked out of its nice safe ocean. She didn't realize she'd spilled her wine until she felt the liquid soak into her stocking.

"Does one of the other guardians have someone back home?" Cat asked in a soft, breathy tone.

"The captain, whoever he is. He and this girl . . ." She snapped her fingers repeatedly trying to come up with the name, and failing. She waved her hand, dismissing her unfinished thought. "Well anyway . . . They're engaged, and supposedly are like the Brad and Angelina of Aandor. Everyone wants to be them."

The pit in Cat's gut morphed into a thick snake, sliding its way up her abdomen.

"Clarisse," said Tim, who had quietly reentered the scene. He stood behind his girl—his face, a tense, haunted mask resolved to make her shut up.

"Who has a fiancée?" Cat repeated. Her pulse quickened; it was harder to breathe.

"I told you—the captain!"

"Clarisse!" Tim forced her name through gritted teeth.

"What! Don't make faces . . . Can't you see I'm talking?"

Cat's blood turned to ice.

"Shut the fuck up," Tim said.

"What is the matter with you?" Clarisse said.

"The captain? Really?" he said. "Captain MacDonnell. Lady MacDonnell's husband."

Clarisse's eyes became saucers—her delicate mouth shaped into a perfect black O.

"Oh, God," she whispered, looking at Cat. The horror poured into her drunken face. Her hand began to quiver. She splashed her drink down on the table and turned to Tim. "But you called him lord. How can a lord be a captain?"

"One is a hereditary political title," said the redhead at the command station. "The other's a military rank. You can be both."

Clarisse was crimson and on the verge of crying. "Balzac just told me this while we were making drinks. He never . . . I—I thought . . ."

Cat stood quickly, and immediately realized her legs were giving way and that her vision was getting dark around the edges. She heard Clarisse yelp and a rush of footsteps run to her side.

Shit, I'm actually fucking fainting, she thought. Strong hands grabbed her before she reached the floor and guided her back to the couch. *They're going revoke my feminist membership.*

A cool towel brushed her forehead and Cat began to come to. She had blanked out for only a few seconds, but bigger problems were coming up. Cat bolted for the bathroom, knocking Balzac against the door frame as he came out of it. She made it in time to pour her stomach into the porcelain bowl. People crowded around the door with concern. She kicked it shut behind her with a slam and retched again. She was vaguely aware of the Kohler stamp on the white porcelain as her mind raced through the last few days. Tears soon followed the retching. *Lots of women marry men with past wives and girlfriends,* she thought. *It's not a big deal. Why am I crying?*

The stab of pain in Cat's chest didn't come because of Callum's past . . . it was his present that hurt her. His choice not to tell her of the woman he left behind. Cal had kept this from her . . . this very important item that should have been the first thing he shared. It was *his* responsibility, not some airheaded groupie from California blurting it out over cocktails.

Why keep it secret? Unless he still had feelings for her. That was it. The spell that awoke all his memories also returned his love for this woman, fresh and clear, as though it was just yesterday. He'd never fallen out of love with her; never had a fight, an argument—a change of heart over spending his life with her. He still loved her.

Cat thought she had a choice about whether to go to Aandor or not, to wait for him until the war was over and the prince secure on the throne. But now, there was another woman still waiting for his return, to pick up the life they had started together.

Cat threw up again. She wanted to wail with all her might, but choked back the scream and pounded the sides of the bowl with her fists until they ached. If only Cal had told her. It was the first time she felt truly alone since this escapade started. If only Cal had told her . . . if only he'd trusted her enough to share this news. Then Cat would believe she'd truly won his heart from this other woman.

She flushed the toilet and wiped down the bowl with paper towels. She splashed her face and rinsed out her mouth with a complimentary bottle of Scope until the taste of puke was gone. Only Lelani, Bree, and Malcolm remained in the suite when she came out.

"Are you okay?" asked Malcolm.

Seeing Bree put things in perspective. He would never abandon her. The other woman deserved Cat's pity, not fear. *Then why am I still shaking?* she thought.

"I'm okay," she said hoarsely. She shot Lelani a fierce look: *You knew.* Lelani met the glare and to her credit did not flinch. The affairs of noblemen and their many loves took a backseat to her race's survival. This was probably not the first triangle she'd encountered . . . it was the way of her world. A clearly marked pecking order placed Cat's need to know subordinate to Cal's ability to finish the mission.

"I need to erect a protective web around the hotel," Lelani said.

The girl talked of magic webs while Cat bled emotionally.

"I have to go to Central Park to acquire the energies to accomplish this. I should not be long."

"I'm coming," said Cat. "I can't sit here doing nothing, or worse listening to Balzac. I'm already stir crazy."

"I'll send Collins with you," Malcolm said.

"Great," said Cat. "Which one is he?"

"Big scary black man; wears sunglasses indoors."

"Perfect."

Cat helped Bree with her coat. She hesitated, then turned to Malcolm. "You need to tell Scott," she said.

"Tell him what?" Malcolm asked.

"The truth."

Malcolm scratched his beard. "My situation's not the same, Cat. I recently discovered I'm a dwarv and I'm straight. But I can't tell Scott I don't love him, because that would be a lie. I can't say I don't look forward to his company because I still do. My father arranged my marriage in Aandor. She's a good wife. Scott was *my* choice. It's not really that complicated. I've been living under the notion that I was gay for years now . . . ever since I left my wife in this reality for Scott. Call it what you will. . . . my feelings are real."

"He should hear that from you," Cat said. "Tell him, before someone takes that choice away."

They left for the park.

CHAPTER 21
CALLANTHA

Cat, Bree, Lelani, and Collins approached the Seventy-ninth Street entrance to Central Park. Cat couldn't remember the thirty-block walk from the Waldorf. Her brain was numb, floating in the never-never realm beyond reality, trying to wrap her mind around the thought of her husband's fiancée. Collins had insisted on using the car, but Cat refused; the whole point of getting out of the hotel was to get fresh air to clear the fog from her brain—at least what passed for fresh air in Manhattan.

She was struck by the irony of her fairy-tale life being turned on its head by the intrusion of an actual fairy-tale life. It was the reverse of what a Disney princess had to endure . . . she'd had the perfect life, the mysterious knight—strong, protective, truthful, loving, putting her needs above all others, and it was being chipped away bit by bit. Her life had been almost too good to be true—no ex-girlfriends to contend with or live up to, no nagging mother-in-law, no awkward holiday dinners haggling over whose house to go to and where to spend Christmas or where to put the uncle that made inappropriate jokes, which invariably every family has one of. Cat never thought she'd been a good enough person to deserve the life the universe picked for her. And pick it did, since it was Callum that chose her from among an entire room of scantily clad dancing nymphs that he could have virtually chose from at will. Her husband's blank past had been a secret blessing neither of them knew about; turns out it was really a hidden charge that she was now paying for in spades.

Cat was livid that after everything they had been through, Lelani had never mentioned Callum's engagement. The centaur could have made better time on foot without her, but she remained at Cat's side as they walked. Whether this was to fulfill her pledge to protect Cal's family or out of sympathy, Cat didn't know. The girl was all business, but had warmed up to their ensemble like an au pair who eventually becomes part of a family. Every time Cat thought she had Lelani figured out, the centaur surprised her. This was probably the way of wizards.

The view before them as they entered Central Park was timeless . . . it could have been any era. The light dusting of snow was as if a sieve of sugar had been rapped over nature—a mad confectioner's masterpiece. The sun dipped toward the tree line, painting a kaleidoscope streak of pink mauves and yellow purples across the western sky. The bare branches were dark lines under white crowns, streams of wet black ink on a hanging page—a street drawing from a gilded age.

Catherine and Lelani were solemn, so Bree walked with the more chatty Collins several feet back. He took her hand with no complaint, clearly a man that was comfortable with children. Collins scanned the area constantly and spoke softly on his Bluetooth, leading Cat to believe the redhead at the suite was monitoring them by satellite. Malcolm had certainly done well for himself in this reality. From what Cal had said of Aandor, the best luxury his wealth could provide—provided she went back with him—was indoor plumbing, as 90 percent of the populace still used outhouses. Her sister's blue-collar Jersey-boy husband could provide that in his sleep. On this world, Malcolm ran a corporation and had his own helicopter and satellite.

The conversation with Balzac had infected her brain. His observations were turning out to be like poison poured in her ear. Was that how a jester exerts power? Cat tried to shut out the conversation, but a seed had taken root. What kind of society was she thinking of joining? Cal's family was part of the 1 percent that ruled his violent world. They stayed there through brute force and marriage beds. Was that really a life that she wanted for herself and Bree?

The path to the left of Turtle Pond led to Belvedere Castle.

"Up ahead where the base of the castle meets the pond is where I entered this universe," Lelani said.

"That's the lay line?" Cat asked.

"Yes. Usually they run like a fifth-dimensional river, dipping and surfacing in and out of realities. This one is unusually stable—I discovered an obelisk several hundred yards northeast of this position that anchors it to this point. You can just make it out through those trees."

They looked across the pond, through the skeletal trees. "That's Cleopatra's Needle," Collins said. "Gift from Egypt. Very ancient."

"Who knew it was magical?" Cat said.

"It is not necessarily magical," Lelani said. "Lay lines can be drawn, repelled, or pooled into reservoirs using a henge. The pattern and composition of the stones is crucial, but they are often normal stones. Clerics have a natural instinct for henge building."

"Clerics?" Cat said.

"Priests with a sensitivity to magical energies, which they call mana. They believe the lay lines are connected to divinity. They call their spells blessings and their studies are limited to what dogma claims are moral magicks. My uncle was a druid and preached often to have me take up the calling. Hidden among the trees and myriad objects of this park is a massive henge pattern that uses the obelisk as its anchor stone. Whoever constructed this henge is likely long dead. It is a mystery."

Cat's husband was the only mystery she was interested in. The revelation of his fiancée had eroded Catherine's trust. How many other secrets had he kept from her? Executing innocent men? Bastard children? Ever since Cal's old memories came back, Cat had suppressed the notion that her husband had become an alternate version of the man she married. But now it was glaring. The Callum she knew would never have kept this fiancée a secret. How could she go to another universe with this imposter? And yet, looking at Bree and feeling the possible new life within her, how could she not? They resumed walking.

"What's her name?" Cat asked, out of the blue.

Lelani stopped and blew out a strong gust as though she'd been holding her breath. "My lady—it is not my place to—"

"I'm not *your* lady," Cat interrupted. She held Lelani's gaze—gray eyes subjugating green—anger dominating uncertainty. "I'm trying to hold my life together after a mysterious redhead came out of nowhere and blew it up."

That broke Lelani's resolve. She frowned and turned her head away to study the path they'd just come up. Cat couldn't muster any sympathy for the girl's discomfort at the moment.

"Look at me when I talk to you," Cat said.

Lelani turned, misery etched in her eyes.

"Did I deserve to have my life blown up?" Cat asked.

Lelani waited a moment before answering a simple, "No."

"Damn straight. We had—have—a good marriage. Do you know how hard that is even under the best circumstances? Do you have any idea how many women would love to have my husband? He's a good man . . . strong. He's the shield between every bad thing in the world and us," she said, gesturing at Bree. "I had to bat girls away with a stick before we got married. He's such a yokel . . . too decent to see what those girls were really after. They said I have a temper. They said I'm a bitch . . ." A tear on Cat's cheek scouted ahead for the deluge behind it. Cat took the lapels of Lelani's coat in her hands gently and brought the centaur close. "Well, I never cared what anyone called me because I had him. Because I knew if I lost him, I'd spend my whole life trying to find him again . . . and that person doesn't exist. I had to claim a man from a whole other universe to have my prince charming. And now, I have to fight for him all over again."

Lelani stayed silent. Most women would launch into a litany of comforting statements and outright lies of comfort. The centaur was stoic and seldom uttered a word that didn't have a purpose. Cat wondered if this was the way of centaurs, or if Lelani was unique—awkward even among her own people. She was truthful and loyal, so Cat believed her silence spoke volumes.

"Does he still love her?" Cat asked, point blank.

Lelani shook her head and turned away. "I do not know what lies in Captain MacDonnell's heart, my lady. We were never friends in Aandor. He does not confide such things in me."

Bree squealed with delight as Collins swung her by her arms. Cat was grateful for his distractions. Lelani resumed walking toward Belvedere Castle.

"He is tortured by this predicament, that much is clear," the centaur said. "He cannot win either way. This is a man who has never broken a pledge in his life—and now, he *must* break an oath to one of the women that he loves. Most men could recover from such a thing, but Captain MacDonnell is not like most men—the decision will haunt him either way. For what it's worth, I do not believe the captain will leave you for Chryslantha."

What a stupid name, Cat thought. "Have you met her?" Cat asked.

"Once," Lelani said. "Her father is a benefactor of Proust's Academy. We held a banquet in his honor."

"Well—dish . . ."

"My lady, this is truly a conversation you should have with the captain—"

Cat stopped her again. "Lelani, do you respect me?"

"Absolutely," she said, with no hesitation. Lelani looked hurt that Catherine would even consider otherwise.

"Are we friends?"

"I—I would be honored if you considered me your friend, Catherine."

"Please . . . if I'm going to fight for my marriage, I need to know. Just tell me the truth. I'm on my last nerve with all the secrets."

Cat could see her own pain reflected in Lelani's eyes . . . or perhaps she was subliminally picking up her own reflection in Lelani's large pupils. Whichever it was, Cat felt she'd broken through the girl's defenses. Lelani exhaled and spilled.

"She's the oldest child of Lord Godwynn, one of the wealthiest and most powerful nobles in Aandor after Archduke Athelstan, and one of Archduchess Sophia's ladies-in-waiting."

Rich brat. Paris Hilton wannabe.

"The MacDonnell and Godwynn estates are north of Aandor City and border each other. The captain and Chryslantha have known each other since they were children. They were betrothed a year before the invasion that sent us here, and though I don't usually follow gossip, I know this because it was all the scullery maids at Proust's talked of for a week. Callum's family are minor nobles and not particularly wealthy, though they are held in high regard because of their loyalty to the archduke and their skills on the battlefield. Lord Godwynn could've married her off to someone politically more advantageous to his interests, but Chryslantha is his favorite, and he's allowing her to marry for love."

Great, thought Cat. *In a society where fathers pawn their kids off for money and power, Cal finds the one girl to marry for love.* "How sure of this are you?" Cat asked. "I thought you didn't know Cal back there."

"Catherine, we don't have movies, television, or radio. What we do have are tourneys and jousts. Our knights are what every lad wants to become and whom every lass wants to marry. Callum ranks high in the lists. He's won a number of tourneys. So people know of him and talk of his adventures, both on and off the field. The scullery maids, shopkeepers, servants, town guards, and even the baser denizens of our kingdom follow the knights' exploits, even who they are—uh . . . courting."

"Okay," Cat said, satisfied. "Tell me she's stupid, short, and ugly."

"Dumb as a sack of rocks, a bowlegged dwarv practically, and has the nose of a pig," Lelani said, very seriously.

"Really?" Cat said. It was the most cheerful she'd been all day.

"No."

Cat punched her *friend* in the arm. "That's not funny."

A hint of a smile crossed Lelani's lips. Cat realized she had been overreacting. Her husband hadn't left her and he'd given her no indication that he intended to. Perhaps some levity wasn't a bad thing.

"Thanks for trying," Cat said. "So . . . dish."

"Blond hair, green eyes, tall, thin. I spied a mummer that looks similar to Chryslantha in this reality."

"Mumm . . . ? An actress?" Cat guessed.

"I do not know her name," Lelani added. "It was a—movie—on the television. I only saw a small portion of it . . . the lead player was a tall man with great abilities. He wore a tight costume, more exciting than peasant dress, and searched for his purpose as he stumbled through life drunk."

"Superhero?" Cat asked.

Lelani scratched her head. "The character's name eludes me. He wrecked a train simply by standing before it. The mumm—uh, 'actress'—played his long-lost lover."

"Train?" Cat remembered a train in *Superman,* but not a wreck. "More about the hero."

"Dark of skin, tall, somewhat handsome . . . if you like the look of a jokester."

A black superhero searching for his purpose . . . "Hancock?" Cat said excitedly.

"Yes!" Lelani confirmed.

Cat never thought her Netflix subscription would turn out to be this useful. "Will Smith and . . ." Cat's heart sank into her gut and lodged into her colon like a sharp stone. The revelation slowly seeped into conscious thought. "You're shitting me?" she said. "Tell me you're joking again . . . please."

"No," Lelani said. "This woman is the image of Chryslantha."

"She looks like Charlize Theron?!"

"Yes, although, Lord Godwynn's daughter is seventeen," Lelani said, as though this detail was somehow important.

Cat stopped walking and sank down onto a large rock beside the path. She muttered to no one in particular, "My husband's childhood sweetheart-slash-fiancée is a filthy rich debutante who looks like a seventeen-year-old Charlize Theron."

Lelani, who had gone on a bit before realizing Catherine had stopped, walked back to her friend and confirmed her statement with a soft, "Yes."

Cat arched back facing the sky, shook her fists to the heavens and screamed, "ARE YOU FUCKING KIDDING ME?"

Park dwellers stopped and glared at them. Bree tugged on Cat's coat to get her attention and with her finger in the shush position against her lips, she told her mother, "Bad word."

Lelani helped Cat off the rock. Her arm was strong, solid. The centaur could probably make a Pilates instructor weep with her work-out regimen.

They were silent until they reached the castle wall. Cat grumbled, "You could have lied a little."

Lelani rolled her eyes while pulling out four white polished stone tablets from her satchel. Catherine sat by the bank breaking reeds. The wizard placed the tablets against the castle's stone wall to let them soak magical energy. They were about the size of an iPad, with runes etched across them. Lelani said they could power wards, a type of magical shield, around the Waldorf, just in case Dorn discovered their location.

Cat looked at the edge of the park, studying the few buildings that cleared the tree line, and wondered where her husband's enemy resided. Lelani said Dorn's aristocratic tastes probably led him to take up residence in Manhattan, in a townhouse near the park, or possibly in a luxury hotel suite of his own. If this sociopathic sorcerer from a feudal world could just blend in with the Upper East Side crowd, what did this say about Manhattan's residents?

Their previous conversation did not help her mood. Cal's fiancée was young, rich, smart, and beautiful. They were Aandor's Brad and Angelina. They were "Callantha." His childhood sweetheart was waiting for him in Aandor, still looking forward to her wedding day because the time differential between their two universes meant that only a few hours had gone by, while thirteen years had passed here. Lelani had the truth of it—there could be no winning solution for Cal. If he stayed with her, the thought of how it would destroy that poor innocent girl made Cat sick to her stomach. She tried to see Chryslantha as the competition, but all she could think of was a young girl, still a teen, dreaming of the life she would have with the man she loved. Dreaming of their children together. The thought churned Catherine's stomach; Chryslantha had done nothing to deserve having her dreams shattered. She was guilty only of loving an incredibly good man. Cat was pinned by forces beyond her scope.

She watched Bree chase ducks along the bank and realized the reason she could empathize with Chryslantha's plight was because she already knew Cal's decision in this matter. The higher commitment was to his daughter. Brianna had been his lifeline in a world where he had no blood relatives. He loved her more than he loved himself. He would never abandon her or the child that grew within Cat. Cat suddenly had a selfish thought. Staying because of the kids wasn't enough. She needed to know how he felt about her. Was Chryslantha still first and foremost in his mind? Was Cat only the runner-up by default?

But what if that wasn't all? In feudal times, marriage contracts were business arrangements. They had more to do with the parents' machinations than the bride and groom's. Cal's sense of honor would also not allow him to skirt the issue by staying behind when the prince returned to Aandor. If there were consequences to his broken oath, he would meet them head-on and honestly. He would be truthful regardless of who it hurt.

"Lelani, Cal broke his oath to Chryslantha. Are there consequences?" asked Cat.

"It would go better for the MacDonnells if Lord Godwynn or his daughter were killed during the invasion," Lelani answered.

What a gruesome wish—can it get any worse? Cat thought.

Cat had not seen Collins for a while. Perhaps he needed to relieve himself. His absence emphasized how grateful Cat was to have someone watching her back. She looked around for him. It would be dark soon—Cat wanted to get out of the park as soon as possible. She regretted not taking the car, as Collins suggested. "Are you almost done?" she asked Lelani.

Lelani didn't respond. Her hands hung in the air before her as though she were about to conduct an orchestra—she stood perfectly still.

"What are you doing?" said Cat. The centaur did not move.

Cat tensed. Something was wrong. She approached the centaur slowly. Lelani was still as a statue. Something hit the tree behind her with a loud thud. Collins's bloody body lay in a heap at the base of the trunk. Cat heard crunching in the woods. Three men stepped onto the path—she recognized the swarthy one with a sword right away from the attack in her apartment—Kraten! With him was a slight, gray man with yellowish eyes wearing a hoodie, and a third man as large and blond as Cal was behind them.

Cat's hands began to shake. Her voice was trapped in her throat. As Kraten crossed the path toward her, she found its release.

"Bree! RUUUUNNN!"

CHAPTER 22

A LEAGUE OF HER OWN

1

Lelani realized a second too late that someone had targeted her with a spell. She stood frozen in place, unable to help herself or her friends. Catherine continued to speak, unaware that anything had occurred; her voice came through muffled, as though her head were within a tin pot covered by a blanket. This stasis spell was a very costly lesson; Lelani failed to implement Proust's third rule of engagement: Act first.

Three men approached them from the woods: Symian and Kraten from the tenement fight in the Bronx and a third conspicuous man as big and pink as Captain MacDonnell. At the tenement, Lelani had implemented the third rule and took out the enemy sorcerer with the first blow. Now the roles were reversed. This spell was a little more advanced than she thought Symian capable of. She was embarrassed to have let a first-year washout get the drop on her.

Cat had realized something was wrong and slowly approached Lelani. Collins's body flew through the air and hit a tree just at the edge of the centaur's field of vision. Cat screamed; Lelani saw it more in her friend's strained, reddened face than heard it because of the muffled nature of sound in stasis. Bree ran crying up the path toward the castle. She fell and skinned her knee, but picked herself up and ran out of Lelani's view. None of the men went after her.

Cat pulled a pistol from her coat pocket just as Kraten came upon her. He swung his sword at Cat's hand, and Lelani's heart jumped, expecting to see her friend's hand lying on the ground severed. But Kraten tilted the blade and struck her with the flat of the sword, knocking the gun from Cat's still intact appendage. Cat lunged at him like her namesake, claws ready to tear. The swordsman grabbed her wrist with his free hand and punched Cat in the face with the sword still in his grip. She dropped like a brick.

Symian approached, sporting a big troll grin bookended by his canine incisors. He gloated before Lelani, waxing poetic on a multitude of points she could not distinguish through the muffled hum of the stasis spell. As he spoke, he relieved her of her satchel and the mana tablets. Lelani was fairly certain he called her a witch several times, or at least something similar sounding. She was certain about the "itch" part. Symian had not cast a perfect spell; Lelani should not still be able to think in real time. She was grateful that the second of Lord Dorn's sorcerers set against her was no better than the polyester leisuresuit–wearing fool upstate had been.

K'ttan Dhourobi of Aht Humaydah had been a sloppy, lazy wizard. In fact most wizards were flawed wizards, and were really only skilled sorcerers undeserving of the title *wizard*. Proficient wizards have described wielding magic as the art of herding cats. It was far different than science, more chaotic because it included qualitative elements in addition to quantitative ones. The mood of a wizard could affect a spell beyond the components used to cast it. So could the position of the moon, the distance from a lay line, and many other archaic factors. Perfect magic did not exist. How could it? Magic wielders did not create the energy they employed in their art. It came to them from a far-off place. No one knew if it was a by-product of some pan-dimensional equivalent of a star, or was in fact the blood of the gods as many clerics proselytized.

Lelani began to construct the counter spell in her mind, shutting out Symian's raging soliloquy at having been nearly burned to death at her hands a few days earlier. He launched into hyperbolic detail about his painful recovery. If he ever finished his rant, she was to "experience pain beyond her imagining," et cetera, and so on.

Symian pulled a silver knife from his coat and began to wave it in front of her face. The knife had strange writings on the blade and a pearl handle that was luminescent against the gray of Symian's skin. Lelani needed another minute to call up the final components of the counter spell from her memory. Every component had to be placed in order just as if she were laying them out on a table, but all in her mind's eye. The last swish of Symian's knife nearly scratched her nose; Lelani was acutely aware that his boasting was coming to an end and her time grew short. But the counter spell was extremely difficult, and she didn't dare rush it. It is normally accompanied by certain phrases and hand gestures with fingers in specific positions for focus. She would need to run through those gestures and say those words in her mind as she released the components of the spell organized in her thoughts. She had to coordinate three independent actions simultaneously, all in her head. She'd only succeeded at this once in Aandor out of five attempts. This was advanced spell casting, the type that made experts appear omnipotent because they could cause actions to occur with but a thought. It's what separated those with sensitivity to magical energy from those with the capacity to become great wizards.

Kraten approached Symian from behind with Cat trussed up over his left shoulder. He wore that oily smile he always had, the kind that only those born into entitlement are issued at birth. They were discussing the most horrible ways to demean and kill her. Centaur parts were in high demand to some conjurers: centaur tail, a hundred Krakens; centaur nipples, five hundred Gryphons . . . Kraten waved the point of his sword at her—beside Symian's knife, it looked like a contest of manhood, with Kraten the clear winner.

The henchman behind Kraten was less enthused by the murder game. *He is not going to go far under Dorn,* Lelani thought. She needed several more seconds, but when Symian raised his arm for the killing blow, she knew it was time she would never have. Lelani couldn't even close her eyes.

The left side of the big pink henchman's head exploded.

Whatever did that was outside Lelani's field of view. Symian put up a shield. Bullets ricocheted off, lodging into the ground and chipping pieces of tree about them. The hail of bullets grew intense, Symian and Kraten backed away until they were into the brush. Lelani cast the counter spell. Normal sounds returned. She dropped her arms as the stasis spell peeled away.

Malcolm approached with his team. Tom Dunning checked the brush where the attackers fled. Kara, the redheaded security woman from the hotel suite, leaned over Collins checking for a pulse.

"Are you okay?" Malcolm asked.

"Yes, thanks to you."

"Collins alerted us just before they got him."

"Is he . . . ?"

"We'll get him to a hospital. Where's Cat and the girl?"

"Bree fled up the path toward the castle entrance. Cat is a prisoner. I must reach them before they leave this park. I can track well through woods. You find Brianna!" she entreated, pointing at the castle and bolting into the brush after Catherine.

"Wait!" she heard Malcolm yell behind her—but Lelani was already through. She had, at best, ten minutes before they hit the streets of this city and disappeared without a trace.

The area just south of Belvedere Castle is known as the Ramble—a lush forest in the middle of a sprawling metropolis. When Lelani first arrived to this world, she lived in the Ramble until she could get her bearings, procure money, and confidently mingle with the inhabitants of this reality. When she was anxious, at her lowest energy, she would always think of this woodland as her oasis on this strange and alien world . . . she praised the people who preserved such beauty against the encroaching city in her daily prayers.

Kraten and Symian were in a mad dash to get away with their prize, and as such left a stumbling, bumbling mess of a trail that even a child centaur could follow. It was a desperate move for them, but a strategically sound one—with Cat as their prisoner, Captain MacDonnell was effectively neutralized. If Cal found the prince first, they would offer an exchange. There was no doubt Dorn would kill her without a moment's hesitation. The problem was . . . would Cal trade the prince for his wife? Was his fealty to his prince, his family back home, greater than the one to Catherine? Lelani realized the irony of her doubts . . . they were the very same ones Catherine had been feeling since she'd entered their lives—doubts made even more uncertain since learning of Chryslantha.

It was near dusk; soon it would be hard to differentiate people as they turned to silhouettes. Lelani had crested the summit of the Ramble and now headed downhill through brush and trees toward the lake. She spotted them at a steady trot ahead of her on a path that would take them to that old bowed bridge that reminded her of Valentino's Crossing in Aandor. Lelani hit the lakeside path and ran toward the bridge at a centaur's speed, preparing the same stasis spell that had been used on her. The bridge was a popular spot for people to take wedding photos, and it was crowded with Asian people in tuxedos and gowns this evening. One of the bridesmaids, alarmed at Lelani's inhumanly swift approach, cried out, alerting Symian to the centaur's charge. She cast the spell at him, but Symian deflected it with a show of colorful sparks that ruffled the lake's surface. The wedding parties panicked and scattered off the bridge.

Symian stood sentry with Lelani's stolen satchel hanging across his shoulder. Kraten crossed over the bridge with Cat and ran to the left toward Bethesda Terrace. Cat was the centaur's primary goal, but to sidestep Symian would leave her vulnerable from behind. She had to keep the troll in front of her and give him her undivided attention. She knew of Symian during his time at the academy in Aandor—how could you not notice a troll in your midst. He was half the sorcerer she was then. Studying with Dorn had bolstered his confidence. He showed no fear and looked eager to demonstrate his prowess. She couldn't conceive of Dorn as a patient teacher. Much of what wizards studied required repetition and refinement. If the stasis spell he cast on her was any indication of Symian's skill level, then the troll was overconfident.

"Why do you align yourself with Farrenheil?" she asked. "They despise your very existence."

"Everyone despises my existence!" he shouted. "Was I treated any better at the academy? Dropped after one year. At least Farrenheil pays."

"You lacked proficiency and focus," she said.

"The instructors withheld their knowledge from me. What little I learned I did so on my own. Dorn would not suffer a fool of an apprentice."

"Your stasis spell was shoddy. Surrender."

Symian yelled as he launched dozens of sharp, pointed ice crystals at her. Lelani made a splashing motion with her hand and a large surge of water rose from the lake and deluged the troll and his ice barrage, knocking him to his knees. He rose quickly and launched a second attack, this time a column of fire, which Lelani thought was reckless considering the flammable oil that covers his skin. Lelani motioned with her other hand, bringing a second wave from the other direction. Symian dropped his flame attack to deflect the column of water toward the centaur. Lelani stuck her arm out as though to shake hands with the wave and the column of water split down the middle, each side falling over the rail, except instead of returning to the lake, Lelani directed both halves along the side of the bridge back toward the troll and walloped him from both sides as the ends of the columns came together.

"You're all wet," she said.

Symian's rage intensified, made all the more comical by his unorthodox appearance of grayish skin and yellow where the whites of his eyes would be. He was soaking wet and exhausted. To her incredulity, Symian commenced a second attack of the same fire spell, in serious breach of Proust's sixth rule of engagement: Never use the same attack twice in a row if the first time failed. Although the sixth rule did not apply to defensive measures (that was the twelfth rule, and it spurred much debate among those who felt switching a defensive spell that's already proved itself was inviting an uncertain outcome), Lelani was concerned about water getting into her satchel and drenching her scrolls and notes.

She waved her arm, palms toward the flames. They met an invisible barrier a few feet in front of the sorceress. Symian poured it on, perspiring, straining with effort to break through the centaur's shield—steaming the water off the age-old bridge's floorboards and singeing the railings black. Lelani realized he could not break her—he was completely unfocused, using rage and anger as a crutch to propel his sloppy spells. She was fortunate that so far Dorn's minions were middling talents at best. Her placid veneer conveyed her indifference to Symian's rage, despite the effort it took to maintain the shield. She would show no hint of effort or struggle, determined to eradicate his confidence.

Lelani was her old self again: The test of wills she relished back in Aandor, mock battles, war games, conflicts that determined dominance among the students. With the lay line so close, she could cast spells with no fear of depleting her magic. Her confidence surged—and as Symian's began to wane, she redoubled her efforts and pushed her shield back toward him across the bridge. Soon the fire would blow back on him, his own flames licking his clothes and the highly flammable oils on his skin. He ceased his attack and fell back on his haunches.

A curtain of gray smoke and white steam wafted from the floorboards between them. Through the haze, she said, "If you surrender, I promise mercy."

Symian's eyes communicated more panic than rage now. He

hastily pulled two silver daggers from his coat, the one he threatened her with earlier and its twin. Her first instinct was to deflect them, but in the micro second it took Symian to reel his arms back for the throw, it occurred to Lelani that her foe knew what she was capable of. What then was the point? Unless Symian believed the attack would succeed because of something she didn't know.

Proust's twelfth rule nagged at her even if it was overly cautious. In that nanosecond, Lelani decided to cast a dangerously ambitious spell she'd only just read about in Proust's book—after all, she had all the magical power she needed in Central Park, and Symian simply wasn't advanced enough to fathom a countermove this unexpected. Symian released the knives. As they flew toward her, Lelani arched her arms out and channeled a generous amount of magic to tear a small opening in time and space in front of her. The rip generated a thundering boom that bounced off the lake and echoed against the skyline around the park. The lake-lined trees bent away from the epicenter same as they would acquiesce to a gale force wind, the bridge shook, and a towering cloud of thick black brimstone, like animated black yarn, billowed from the spot. Lelani fell through the opening and, causing a second boom and quake upon the overpass, reappeared behind Symian. Symian spun around, abject fear written across his face—the look of a sorcerer that realized he was outclassed. This was a magic user's worst nightmare . . . to find out one was in the midst of a duel with an opponent that far excelled them. Symian could not even begin to counter a spatial displacement spell. Though it took all of Lelani's effort to cast that little jump across only a few feet, and she was exhausted for it, she didn't show it. The move was more psychological than practical. Symian's ignorance had him believing she could drop him into the bottom of the deepest lake or into an active volcano at her whim. Frozen in place, he struggled to think of his next move. *He's brain locked,* she thought.

Lelani called upon a spell the tree wizard, Rosencrantz, recently taught her. From the lake around her, green vines flew at her opponent like bolts from a crossbow, ensnaring Symian's arms, legs, and torso. Lelani moved her hands like a puppeteer, controlling the offshoots. The vines dragged Symian toward her. He'd forgotten spell casting altogether and dug his troll's nails into the wooden planks of the bridge, but to no avail. Eight bloody claw marks in the bridge's singed wood chronicled the drag.

She pulled the vines back to immobilize Symian, spread eagle, before her. Lelani grabbed her satchel and his own bag of tricks with one hand and broke Symian's nose with a jab of her fist. He squealed, and then his head drooped down.

A glint down the bridge showed where one of the knives he'd thrown had landed. She jumped over him to retrieve it. It was as she suspected . . . faerie silver. Not silver really, it was in fact a form of enchanted platinum brought about by a light exposure to certain naturally occurring radiation; the dwarvs who forged it coined the name faerie silver because they thought it had a nicer ring. This was one of the most rare metals in Aandor and its chief property was complete neutrality to magic. It would have ignored any spell or shield she put up. Worse, had the knife broken skin, minute traces of the metal in her blood would have rendered her magically inert until they had worked their way out of her system. She would have been unable to cast spells and been completely at the troll's mercy. The other dagger was out of view—she should search for it, but Kraten was getting away with Cat. The fight had eaten precious minutes, and dusk had set in. If only she had a sample of Catherine's blood, skin, or hair.

Symian had passed out. Lelani nicked him on the wrist with the knife, rendering him magically inert for the better part of a day. She took the dagger's sheath from his coat and secured her new weapon. Kraten's course took him toward Bethesda Terrace. She made it as far as the fountain, still exhausted and light-headed from that teleportation spell. There was no trail to pick up upon the bricks and concrete of the square. The terrace reminded Lelani of Aandor's many piazzas. Even in the chill of the evening it was crowded—street performers on the stairs and pickpockets pilfering the tourists' wallets. No sign of Kraten lurking among them; Cat was gone.

2

Lelani returned to Bow Bridge. Symian had slipped his restraints. The coward had faked unconsciousness. Her pursuit was a complete failure. She fingered the sheath of her new dagger and thought, *Maybe not a complete loss.* As she trotted back to Belvedere Castle, the inevitable battle pushed its way into her thoughts. So far, she'd been lucky that Lord Dorn was only able to recruit lesser talents. Perhaps his ego was too brittle to feel secure around other proficient wizards. One thing was certain—if Lelani went up against Dorn, she would likely lose. She would be in the similar position Symian and K'ttan Dhourobi had found themselves in against her.

Malcolm waited alone at the base of Belvedere Castle. Even the body of Dorn's henchman was gone; it looked like nothing had happened.

"Lady MacDonnell?" Mal asked.

Lelani shook her head. She thought about whether Malcolm could be trusted with a conclusion she'd arrived at on her trek back. "They knew," she said anyway.

"I'm sorry . . . Knew what?" he asked.

"That we'd be in the park."

"Not possible," he said. "Just bad timing. They use the same watering hole you do."

"I had not told anyone of this lay line's location, not even Catherine. Dorn's people likely discovered it shortly after I left the Ramble in search of Seth Raincrest. I don't deny we share this source of power in New York. But they knew exactly what time we'd be here. I do not believe in coincidences."

Lelani remembered Symian's pack and opened it. She shook her head in frustration.

"What now?" asked Malcolm.

"This is Symian's satchel. Their mana batteries are not here. And I cannot figure out what spells he is collecting for based on these components. They had stolen irradiated material from Indian Point when we battled them in the woods. The only spells that accelerate magic using radiation are forbidden ones. Can Dorn really mean to use such magic? Radiation affects magical energy the way catnip affects cats—makes it erratic, wild . . . unpredictable. The spells react at volatile speeds. Once activated, it's hard to shut down and the spell could expand exponentially and move beyond the caster's control. Something bad is coming."

"You can't know for sure."

"I feel it in my bones," she said, shaking. She shook Symian's bag before Malcolm. "Nothing good can come of radiation-fueled spells."

Malcolm looked doubly troubled. "There's another problem—a less epic one," he said softly. "We haven't been able to locate the little girl."

"Gods!" Lelani said, exasperated. "And you wait until now to tell me?"

Lelani's failure to protect Brianna's mother would not extend to the girl. She walked to spot where Bree skinned her knee running away and carefully scraped blood and skin off the blacktop with her pocketknife. She pulled out a tube and a small wooden kit from her bag, put the scrapings into the tube and poured in liquids and powders from the kit after it. She cut some plants and weeds growing in the area and grinded bits of them into the tube and then put a drop of pond water in as well. She plugged the tube with a stopper and shook until the solution fizzed white. She chanted a finder spell, imbuing the liquid with magic and purpose—the solution fizzed even more and became a luminescent yellow. There were a few people left in the darkening park, but it was Lelani's experience that

New Yorkers were use to oddities in their city and mostly minded their own business.

"Watch out," she told Malcolm. Lelani uncorked the tube. A radiant white mist shot out in an arc over the pond, heading west. A faint white trail, like a white monochromatic rainbow, shined in the air. A few of the park patrons pointed out the effect to their children, possibly attributing it to some type of firework.

Malcolm whistled approvingly. "Can Dorn do that?"

"Yes—and worse," she said. "But he needs something of the prince. Let's pray he does not find it. Head back to the hotel. I am much quicker alone and will join you shortly."

"Wait," he said, grabbing her arm. "One last thing. Do not tell MacDonnell his wife's been captured."

She yanked her arm from his grip defiantly and challenged him with a glare. "You would have me lie to him after I've failed Lord MacDonnell so miserably? I bear this shame . . . I swore to protect his family!"

Malcolm looked at her with the serenity of a professor lecturing an errant student. "One: Lady MacDonnell is not in immediate danger," he pointed out. "She's Dorn's bargaining chip—insurance. Two: MacDonnell has enough on his plate just trying to reach the prince before they do. What do you think will happen to his concentration once he learns his wife is a prisoner? Bad judgment's liable to get him killed. Three: If he abandons his quest to search for Catherine, *they* find the prince first, cut the boy's throat, and kill Catherine anyway because she'll be of little value at that point."

Malcolm's rationale was sound, even if lying to the captain ran against Lelani's instincts. Was there no honor left? This mission poisoned the soul. Were Malcolm, Seth, Balzac, and Timian always this way, even in Aandor? Lelani was greatly nostalgic for her home in the Blue Forest at this moment. The centaurs did not favor guile—did not reward the craftiest liars or the best game players. They exulted the best hunters, the most artful musicians and poets. It was a simpler life.

"We'll tell him when he returns with the prince," Malcolm continued. "I'll take responsibility."

"Yes, you will," Lelani said. She walked away, following the wispy trail, which had begun to dissolve like fairy dust into the lake. The trail took her over the castle and onto Vista Rock overlooking the pond and Great Lawn. The castle and vista made the centaur long for home. The luminescent arc descended into a nearby amphitheater on the other side of the lake.

The Delacorte Theater was closed for winter, but that proved no obstacle for the sorceress. Lelani entered, surveying the grandstand seating. She found Brianna huddled under a seat, the only one in the amphitheater not in the upright position.

"Bree . . . ," Lelani said.

Bree came out from under the seat, her knee skinned with lines of blood dripping down to her shoe. When she realized it was Lelani, her face lit up. She jumped into Lelani's arms and gave the centaur a tight hug. Tears streamed down her cheeks and she shook from crying. "I thought the bad men made you dead like Maggie."

"Almost," said the centaur, and Lelani realized she relished the love emanating from this little girl. MacDonnell's family was becoming her own.

"Where's Mommy?"

"Your mother . . ." Lelani bit her lip and thought carefully about what to say. Lelani wondered if Bree would be safer at her grandmother's. But then, the old woman was likely to call Callum and inquire after Catherine, thus revealing that his wife was gone.

". . . is on a mission, like your daddy," Lelani finished. "She has entrusted you to my care."

"I don't know what 'in-trust-en' means," Bree said.

"You will stay with me—in Uncle Malcolm's hotel room." It was the best plan for Bree. Lelani would defend the girl as though she were her own daughter.

Bree sniffled and wiped her cheeks. Lelani threw Bree on her back. The illusion spell made it look like Bree was riding piggy-style, but she sat quite comfortably on Lelani's equestrian half. They took the path along the Great Lawn heading east. The Metropolitan Museum and Cleopatra's Needle could be seen through the trees on their left.

Lelani contemplated the evening's events. It was hard to tell what she did right and what she did wrong. This lay line had been Lelani's only source of magical energy when she first arrived in New York. But with Dorn's discovery of it, it had become a dangerous watering hole—a place where deer and lions shared their drink. And Dorn had the fissionable material he'd stolen from the nuclear plant. With enough mana, he could power frightening spells—arts that the collective wisdom of all the wizards in Aandor had forbidden from being practiced. She looked at the skyline and guessed where the other lay lines flowed into this reality. She doubted Dorn was aware of the connection between universal and local architecture. Dorn was a man of action not a scholar—more sorcerer than wizard by the academy's standards. What if he didn't understand magic's effect on the material world?

As they went past the monolith known as Cleopatra's Needle, an idea hit Lelani. This was the one known stable spot of magical energy on the island of Manhattan that they knew of. Without the anchor, the rivers of energy would not pool into this area of the park. They would resume their natural courses through this reality. She retrieved a leather-bound book from her satchel, older than she was, older than her great- grandmother. It was a gift from Magnus Proust. She could not make heads or tails of some of the spells, but Rosencrantz had helped her decipher a few during her time upstate. She wished she could have spent more time with the tree wizard—he was soothing to the soul and remarkably knowledgeable. The spell was at the end of the book—an intensification of her phosphorous balls. Her phosphorous spell was a root by which several other sorceries could be created. The concept of root spells was not alien to her—it said there were essentially thirteen spells upon which all other spells were built. Rosencrantz had shown her how to intensify the heat of her phosphorous balls, replicate the balls smaller, rapidly, and continuously, and move them through the air. Practicing, she was able to focus it into a white hot line that stretched several feet beyond her; another first.

"Bree, I'm going to do something pretty stupid, and it's going to be loud and scary." Bree smiled as only a five-year-old could at such a statement.

Lelani raised her arms. She chanted, channeling the power of the lay line around her, underneath her, and focused her will into her hands, converting the power into heat and light. Her hands turned iridescent. An undulating white-hot line of energy traveled between her palms. She drew more and more power into them, building them beyond anything she'd ever handled before. Her hands went beyond white and became translucent. The surrounding park lit up in stark contrast around them. And when she could barely handle one more photon, Lelani released the power at the foot of the needle where it met the granite base, slicing through with a white-hot arc. She scooped out the top of the base like ice cream from a newly opened carton. The obelisk teetered. She called upon powerful gusts to push it along, a close relation to the sentient wind spell, which Rosencrantz also helped her decipher. The tower fell like a great stone tree. Lelani shifted her motions and called up powerful jets of air beneath the monolith to slow the needle's decent. It touched softly upon the grass with a low boom, knocking up dirt and dust around it.

"Whoa!" said Bree.

With that accomplished, the lay line was unhinged. Whatever Dorn was planning with the radioactive material he'd stolen would probably require more mana than he had stored. *Let's see how he manages in a drought,* she thought. Lelani was certain she'd just bought them some precious time. But now she needed to ration her mana—once again, austerity.

Police sirens blared. Some headed their way. All this activity was too much, even for this greatest of cities. She took off at a leisurely trot toward the woods and improvised an exit over the retaining wall onto Fifth Avenue. In no time, they'd lost themselves within the bustle of the Manhattan streets, two other residents of the Upper East Side.

CHAPTER 23
A ROCK AND A HEART PLACE

Colby pulled into the motor lodge parking lot late that evening. It was a short trip from the motel he'd parked his car at while he pretended to be a vagrant steering Daniel safely toward his sister's home. He turned off the engine and sat for a while to compose his thoughts. He rolled a cup of hot coffee in his hands, absorbing its heat thinking of the two tigers he held by their tails—each ready to maul the other, with him in the middle.

On the bright side, the meeting with MacDonnell had gone better than he'd hoped. Years in the NYPD taught him how to spot an honest cop. MacDonnell was a law-and-order type, true to his word. If there was any chance of getting his life back, it lay with MacDonnell's team. *How to pull it off, though, without raising Dorn's suspicions?*

Dorn probably suspected something was up, if only because he was perpetually paranoid. You can't be the type of person who turns people into living-dead servants without fostering a great deal of ill will toward you. Dorn wasn't exactly the most mentally balanced person either. Even his henchmen couldn't predict what would set him off, and those migraines didn't help the situation. Based on how Dorn's people fretted when he came down with the seizures, it must be a recent development. They tiptoed around him like he was a sleeping grizzly between them and the cave entrance. Although Colby couldn't die by normal means, Dorn possessed his heart and could kill him for good, at a whim, from anywhere in the world.

Colby's biggest fear was that at any moment, without warning, he would simply drop dead. And that was no way to live.

MacDonnell was his one hope—not just for him, but also for Daniel. When Colby first took on this assignment, he had expected to find a spoiled suburban brat whining for videogames and skateboard gear to keep up with his friends. Instead, he found a young man, tougher than nails, who took a bigger pounding than anyone his age should ever have had to—and the kid still came out of it a decent human being. He was smart, loyal, and didn't expect anything to come easily. Daniel had a part-time job and a plan to get away from his miserable adoptive parents. As much as Colby hated to admit it, he liked the prince—heck, he even admired him. Who doesn't look back on their life and wish they'd had the wherewithal Daniel had at that age?

Colby wondered if that was why he was leaning toward MacDonnell's side . . . for what it would mean for Daniel's future. Daniel was also about the same age as his son. Colby couldn't help think of Tory when he was around Daniel . . . the vitality his son would still have if not for the freak diving accident that severed Tory's spinal cord. Just some kids horsing around a pool like millions of kids do around the world. He banged a fist on the steering wheel, angry at himself for not being there to protect his son—for seeing Daniel as Tory's surrogate—angry at his own emotional weakness. That kind of sloppy thinking and sentimentality could finish him. He had to be selfish, ruthless if he expected to come out of this sorcerers' war alive.

There was still some heat left in the cup. He rolled it greedily, pulling out every last joule of heat. Colby had Tory on the mind now. He had not been the best of dads—virtually absent from his son's life the past three years. He wished he could blame the accident, but he had been pulling away long before that. The accident was an impetus for severing contact. It was too hard to face Tory while entrenched in blackmail schemes, protecting pedophiles, and profiting from all his other illicit activities. Better to have the boy think he couldn't face him because of the injury than because he was a dirty, lying crook. Colby convinced himself he did it all for Tory, but the piles of money he sent for doctors, tests, and special chairs did little to alleviate the guilt. Only now, since becoming subhuman, did he realize the value of each precious moment. Somewhere in another dimensional plane, Daniel had parents who loved him. Maybe they'd spoil him, like all monarchs did, but if anyone deserved to be pampered, it was Daniel Hauer. After the life he'd been forced to put up with, he'd earned it. And maybe, just maybe, Colby could get his own ass out of the fire and back to his own family to make up for lost time.

What to tell Dorn?

His cohorts were in Room 209. The shades were drawn—*perfect for shady business.* In and out as quickly as possible was the plan. MacDonnell would be waiting for him at a nearby Starbucks for the trip back to North Carolina.

Risky business.

The minute MacDonnell had the boy, Colby would lose all leverage with both sides. But what choice did he have? He knew nothing about sorcery. He doubted any of the gypsies and frauds in this universe could come close to what Dorn could do. He worried at times about hitting a magic dead zone (no pun intended)—like a mobile phone too far from cell towers, he'd lose his bars and shut down, cut off from whatever it was that kept him animated.

If everything went to plan, Daniel was in for a harsh awakening about his true identity. Years spent in error with a drunken abusive dad when he was actually royalty, slated for a life of opulence and ass kissing. The irony was not lost on Dretch. Colby laughed silently. The kid wouldn't believe them—not until Colby asked him to find his heartbeat. *Nothing says all this shit's real like a room-temperature zombie gumshoe.* Colby went to a payphone outside the motel's office and dialed his sister's number. His niece answered.

"It's Uncle Cole," he said. "How's the kid?"

"Well I'm fine. How are you, Uncle Cole?"

Colby let the snarky remark wash over him; too many irons in the fire to let Luanne push his buttons. He still needed her. This might well be the one good contribution the girl ever makes in her life, and she didn't even realize it.

"Uncle Cole?"

"I'm here. Been a long day, sweetie. Is Daniel still with you?"

"'Course."

Colby let out a long breath of relief. Last thing he needed was Daniel on the run.

"He ain't going anywhere. In fact, after last night, he may never leave," she said, giggling.

The comment hit Colby like a brick. "Jeezus, Luanne. Don't tell me you . . ." Colby couldn't finish the sentence.

"Don't what, Uncle Cole? You said to hog-tie him. You said do anything."

"To . . . flirt—make out—let him get to third base."

Silence.

"No one expects heavy petting for seven thousand dollars," she said, in low tones. *"Now you acting all innocent . . ."*

Colby rubbed his face with his free hand in disbelief. Was his instruction to her that ambiguous? Or was he just fooling himself? Was he so desperate and out of control of his life that he left it to Luanne's judgment in the hopes that she would do anything it took to keep that kid from flying off? Colby could equivocate all he wanted about not saying the actual words, but he offered her more cash than she'd ever make in her life and strongly implied she use her feminine wiles to earn it. *I pimped my niece.*

The horror of it slapped Colby like an ornery Catholic school nun.

Desperation. Everyone in this mess of an assignment was up to their neck in desperation. He was glad he didn't have a heart at the moment because the stress would surely kill it. Colby had put himself in this position with the career choices he had made. He'd brought these monsters into his life and given them power over him.

If he'd been an honest man, spent time with his wife and son instead of extorting big bucks from pedophiles and cheats, he never would have been indicted, driven from his profession, a lonely has-been vulnerable to predators like Dorn.

Luanne's anger emanated quietly through the receiver. Now she felt cheap instead of heroic—stupid for selling more of the farm than she needed to. God help him if any of this got back to Bev.

"Honey," he said softly. "You did fine. You helped out your uncle Cole here. You don't know how important you are to me at the moment. My life is on the line here."

"Yeah?" she said, just above a whisper.

"Definitely. When I get back I'm going to make it ten thousand. For giving it a hundred and ten percent on this one."

Colby cringed and pumped his fist quietly into the glazed brick wall, realizing a second too late that throwing more money to alleviate his guilt only elevated Luanne to a higher class of prostitute. What was wrong with him?

"Well . . . ," she said, sounding less upset. *"It was my choice. He's actually not bad . . . Uh, guy that is . . . he's not a bad guy. But you might want to get back here soon. Cody ain't none too happy about Daniel being here."*

"Who's Cody?"

"My boyfriend. He was with his buds by the general store the day you drove into the trailer park with Daniel. The guy with the Cadillac DeVille."

"Jeezus H. Roosevelt Christ, Luanne! The meth heads? Your boyfriend's a dealer?"

"He's a mechanic at the bowling alley, Uncle Cole. He does the other stuff for extra money."

That's all Colby needed—for Daniel to end up captured in a police raid on the trailer park. Or worse, shot in a love triangle over his niece's well-traveled cooch.

"Honey, keep Daniel away from Cody. Don't even let them talk. I'll be back by morning."

Colby hung up the phone before anything his niece could say would make him madder than he already was. He was severely depressed . . . over Luanne, over two-timing Dorn, over the fact that he would have sold out a good kid to get his heart back. He tried to make a joke of it and convince himself he at least got the kid laid, but it fell flat on the brain. Thirteen was too young. Would it leave emotional scars? He had to get back to North Carolina as fast as possible and put Daniel into MacDonnell's hands. There he would be safest. There wasn't any more time for finesse.

He climbed to the second landing of the motor lodge wondering where his life had gone wrong and how much worse it could get. The shades of the room fluttered at his knock. The door opened just enough to admit him and closed quickly behind him. Krebe, Hommar, and a man almost as big and ugly as Hesz with long black hair stood around in the dimly lit room staring at him like he was under a spotlight. Colby had no misunderstanding of what this meeting was . . . an interrogation. The room had the feel of a tomb. The faint smell of something dead slowly crept into his senses.

Colby clamped down on his rising concerns and put up a strong front. "I thought Hesz was coming down," he said coolly.

"He returns to New York with a gift for Dorn," said Krebe.

They stood looking at each other for several seconds.

"You asked to meet," Colby reminded them. "Every moment I'm here is time I'm not searching for the kid."

"How much longer?" Krebe asked him point blank.

"Look . . . I found him once. But it's not my fault he took off to God knows where. Murdering his dad and running off had nothing to do with us. Just bad timing is all. Dorn has to understand . . . these events would have occurred regardless of whether we were looking for him or not. If you'd only come to me a day earlier—"

"Dorn does not believe in coincidence," Krebe interjected.

"Facts are facts. What else can I tell you?"

"Too many coincidences," said Todgarten in a baritone laced with rolling gravel. "At times, you are completely untraceable. Your use of pay phones instead of our generously supplied device is suspect, as is travel by means other than your own vehicle. We will remain with you while you track the prince."

"That's out of the question," said Dretch. His concern was turning to fear, and he stomped down hard and sat on it. "I can't work effectively with the circus tailing me," he explained in his most businesslike voice.

"Do not mistake this for a request." Todgarten swung a thumping velvet sack before Colby's face, taunting him.

His heart was here, with them?

Todgarten meant to intimidate him with the wayward organ, but it had the opposite effect. His heart within reach instead of in New York and with MacDonnell nearby—this was the break Colby had been praying for. Dorn's promises of restoration were empty and as long as he held on to Colby's heart, he could kill the detective at a whim. But if Colby took back possession of it, Dorn's hold over him stopped—or at the very least diminished. Colby wouldn't constantly wonder if each step he took would be his last—if he'd just fall down dead with no warning.

Todgarten removed the heart from its sack and squeezed it with his massive hand. An invisible pressure gripped Colby's chest. Though he hadn't drawn a true breath in days, only now did he feel as though he couldn't breathe. Colby grasped at his chest.

"We will eventually find the prince through other means," Todgarten continued . . . his deep voice rumbling like a coming storm. "Now that we know his name and where he's resided these many years, the era of your usefulness draws to a close. You want to find the boy first, Detective, if you wish to be reacquainted with your organ."

"They—might—never—find . . ." Colby succumbed to the pain and fell to his knees clutching his chest with both hands.

"But they will," Krebe said, crouching down to look him in the eye. "Lord Dorn has anonymously placed sixty thousand dollars at the disposal of the Baltimore area police departments as a cash reward for any information leading to Daniel's capture. We're going viral. The prince's face even now is being uploaded to Web sites, tacked on telephone poles and billboards within a hundred miles of Baltimore. It's sure to garner interest from the mainstream media as well. In these economic times, who would choose friendship with a father killer over money?"

Colby collapsed onto his back like a Raid-zapped roach, suffocating as the three of them hovered over him with only mild interest. He tried to get the word "yes" out of his throat but emitted only an impression of a smoker's hack. He nodded his head vigorously. Todgarten released the pressure on his heart and Colby could "breathe" again, if that was the right description for one of the living dead.

He needed to buy time. There had to be a way to delay this group so that he could get word to MacDonnell. Colby felt better almost immediately, but played his resuscitation down. He sat on the bed hunched over his knees and made a display of drawing breath. He fiddled with his collar and tie and said, "I have a lead. You can come, but the interviews I do alone. You'll only spook the hell out of people."

"You have twenty-four hours to produce a tangible result," said Krebe. His tone implied consequences.

"You're a bunch of sorcerers," Colby pointed out. "If it's so damn easy, why haven't you conjured him up already?"

"Twenty-four hours," Krebe repeated, calmly—methodically.

The detective narrowed his eyes, keenly observing the Jack-the-Ripper impressionist. "You're not Krebe, are you?" he said. "You're the other one."

Krebe/Oulfsan smiled and gave the detective a courteous bow. His cell phone rang. Dorn had called from New York. They spoke for a moment and Krebe held the phone up and shook it at the detective, prompting Colby to get off the bed and take it. What more could they say to him? . . . He got the message: Daniel or die. Dorn spoke to Colby in dulcet tones like a paramour prodding a potential lover. Then a second voice that could not possibly be came on the line. The next sound was the most painful thing Colby ever heard. Colby Dretch dropped to his knees—the phone slipped out of his hand onto the carpet. He pounded the carpet in despair and wept nonexistent tears, cursing his parched dead eyes for all they'd ever seen.

CHAPTER 24
SETH GOES GREEN

1

Seth and Cal sat in the car in an adjacent parking lot to the motor lodge. Colby's car was in view and they watched him enter the room on the second floor. It was the first time since the battle in upstate New York that they had been within fifty yards of the enemy—the real enemy, not some hapless thrall. Some decorative pine bushes that marked the boundaries of the two properties conveniently shielded their SUV. Seth whittled his staff.

The agreed-upon plan was to meet at a nearby coffee shop, but Cal refused to let the detective out of their sight from here on in. The man's ethics were questionable and the stakes were too high. Colby had used the office payphone to make a call before going into the motel room. Seth knew Cal wanted to trace that call, but they were without resources. Cal had been ordered by his bosses not to take any cases in his capacity as a New York police officer. He was on bereavement leave due to the death of his partner. They expected him to go to church or counseling or just stay home with his family.

Seth found whittling to be soothing—a focus for his anxiety and excess energy. But more than that, with each cut and notch, the sense of calm grew within him. His walkabout in New York before they'd left had started the feeling off. He'd made excellent progress atoning for past misdeeds before Cal dragged him off to Maryland (quite literally). Each action of his that he took full responsibility for literally felt like psychic masonry—as though he were bricking up a large black hole at the core of his being. If only he'd had time for the last and most important transgression of all.

Seth had his car seat set back all the way and reclined a bit to make room for the staff. The bottom tip rested on the passenger-side floor and the top barely cleared the car roof just behind him; like holding an exotic orchestra instrument, only instead of playing it, he was creating one. He had started this task in upstate New York the way he did all challenges—resentment toward work, a negative mind-set, and a belief that he could not accomplish this with any proficiency. Seth could not have been more wrong. From the very beginning, a deep urge forced him to assert himself. He rejected the branch Lelani had originally handed him in that parking lot in favor of another one deep in the bundle on the car roof. He didn't know the right word to explain what made him pick that particular branch: Polarity? Resonance? Vibe? Something about that stick felt "righter" than the others. Lelani arched an eyebrow when he made the request, causing him to suspect the whole thing was a made-up task to distract him from his cigarette cravings. But he listened intently to her instruction, and as he progressed, was sure this was something he was meant to do.

Seth had skinned the outer layer of bark from the stick with a short stout blade, cutting down knots and nubs and reducing its thickness to a respectable two inches. Using a modified paint scraper to shave off a second green layer, he then shaved down the flat edges left by the scraper with a Flexcut rounded edge, smoothing out the knots as well. By the time he was down to the white wood, it was six feet long and one and three-quarter inches thick.

There was a slight curve in the middle of the staff, and the wood was heavy with moisture. Branches normally took weeks to dry out, but Lelani used a spell to speed the process. They dipped the tips of the staff in candle wax to protect it from cracking and checking. Seth had sat with a large flat cutting board leaning on his shins and held the staff against it like he would a cello. He'd had an overprotective feeling of the staff and was nervous about cracking or splintering when Lelani infused the wood with a magical dry heat while Seth placed pressure on the curved parts of the stick to straighten it out. A great weight lifted from him when they succeeded, like watching your six-year-old do well in his first ball game. The straightened staff was lighter, having lost its water weight, and gained an inch in height. The white wood was hard and had a beautiful musical resonance when tapped on. Seth used a square of ultrafine grain sandpaper to smooth it out.

To protect the tips from checking, he whittled a series of cuts around the edge of the tips at thirty-degree angles—the slopes of the cuts met at an imaginary apex a few inches above the end of the staff. Then he added another series of cuts above the first ones. Seth repeated this until a makeshift rounding out of the edge emerged. He took the sandpaper to the edges, but was careful not to eliminate all traces of the original facets. The staff was now prepped for its design elements.

Lelani had lent Seth her whittling portfolio—soft calf leather that folded upon itself and was tied closed by a leather strip. When he opened it, the carving tools lay neatly in their own leather pockets. The tools themselves were well maintained, made of iron or steel with bone and wood handles. Seth could tell the set held some sentimental value by Lelani's hesitation to relinquish it. She had written for Seth on a piece of parchment a series of runes that he was to carve into the staff. A second series of runes lay at the bottom; he was to choose four among those options with no guidance from her. They represented wisdom, intelligence, strength, speed, love, power, war, peace, air, earth, fire, water, black, gray, white, life, death, chaos, order, and balance. Any design motifs or illustrations were up to him, provided they did not break the connection between the first set of runes at the top of the page. While he pondered the finality of his choices, he whittled a hand-sized grip of small concentric circles, like a snake's rattle, around the five-foot mark of the staff. He thought of Ben as he whittled, each notch scooping away something black in his soul, like picking clumps of tar off a golden statue.

"What the hell . . . ," Cal said beside him.

Seth looked up to see Colby Dretch and three of Dorn's men leaving the hotel room. They piled into his car with Dretch at the wheel.

"You were right," Seth said. "He's double-crossing us."

"No," Cal said. "Something's wrong." He started the car and followed them out of the lot.

Colby hit Interstate 95 heading south. Cal was quiet with a worried expression.

"You think they're heading for the prince," said Seth. Cal didn't say anything, but glanced at his fuel gauge. They had half a tank—barely enough to make North Carolina. If Colby's car had a full tank, it could outdistance them before they'd have time to refill. Seth dialed Lelani on his cell. He explained the situation. She had no easy solution, but said she'd get back to him. Seth continued to work on his staff well into Virginia.

2

Seth was having bad dreams. All the people he hurt in his life had been turned into the heartless living dead, and they were all after his brains. Half of them were naked girls—girls he'd photographed, strung out on heroin, cocaine, or worse. He wasn't ungrateful when Cal rudely nudged him awake. "You talk in your sleep," he said, and then continued to drive quietly.

The staff rested against his shoulder in the same position as when he dozed off working on it. He had penciled in the runes. The first set of runes from the parchment he ran vertically, two on the north and south sides of the staff above the grip, two on the east and west sides of the staff below it, careful not to break the sentence structure Lelani indicated. He left space just above the handgrip for the four runes of his choice. Those he would place on the same level horizontally in a circle around the staff. He didn't know which rune meant what. Lelani said that was part of the bond between a spell caster and his instrument. The first set of runes represented what he intended for the staff. The second set of symbols were different from the first and traditionally taught to wizards after they'd created their first staff or walking stick. The wizard chose them blindly because it allowed the universe to communicate its purpose for the spell caster—that there was a place for the magic user within the universal architecture. Lelani said the choice would feel random; all the runes would be calling to him, but he would connect with the ones that matched him best. It was a ritual steeped more in tradition than fact, but many swore by it, insisting the universe was never wrong. Seth figured it was like reading horoscopes . . . everyone sees their life in the prediction.

They had switched to Interstate 85 around Petersburg, Virginia. Outside the car it was dark. The world blended into blue and gray uniformity. "Where are we?" Seth asked.

"Near the Carolina border," Cal said. The fuel gauge indicated low. They'd soon be driving on fumes. "Call her."

"Call her," had become Callum's new mantra. Could he be any more clear that he'd rather have had Lelani on this trip? He left her behind to organize the remnants of the prince's guardians, and coincidentally, she was in a position to protect Cat and Bree. As driven as the cop was to find the prince, he had two duties, really—the other being the protection of his family. To Callum, divided loyalties must be as alien as altruism was to the mafia. Seth chuckled at the likelihood of Dominic Tagliatore opening libraries and orphanages with his ill-gotten gains.

Lelani picked up on the third ring. Seth put her on speaker so that Cal could hear.

"I have a theory," she said. *"This would never work in Aandor because of the abundance of magical energies in the environment, but—to remain*

animated, Dretch must be drawing power from the sparse lay lines in this reality. Otherwise he would just be another corpse. The spell that animates him requires a constant stream of mana. He's drawing it to him. In fact, if he should ever stray too far from any lay lines, he would shut down.

"We might be able to make the energy visible. There are virtually no other spells or enchantments in this reality—nothing to compete with the energy flowing toward Dretch. As long as you stayed within twenty miles or so of him, you could use the mana as a beacon. You'll need some items for the spell though—metals sensitive to magic such as iron, silver, and gold; potassium percolate, aluminum powder, blood, and a few other items."

"When will you know if your theory is right?" Cal asked.

Lelani hesitated a moment, then added, *"I can't cast this spell from New York. Seth must do it in the vicinity of Dretch. I told you, about twenty miles."*

"What? I can't even kill salt," Seth insisted. "Is there a spell to fill our gas tank without stopping instead?"

"There is a spell to propel an inanimate vehicle, but that is far more difficult for someone at your skill level."

"Text him the information for the beacon, and be prepared to help him on the phone," Cal ordered. "We'll pull over at the next service area. Is Cat there?" he added.

There was a moment's pause and then Malcolm Robbe's voice. "Cat just managed to put Bree down in the next room, Cal. She's sound asleep next to her. Should I wake them?"

"No—I'll talk to her later," Cal said. "Hopefully I'll have good news in a few hours." He reached over and cut the connection. "Save that phone battery," he told Seth.

Seth wished he were in a Waldorf Astoria bed protected by professional security. Still, there was something odd about the way Malcolm cut in on Lelani. Maybe he'd been the last to check in on Cat and Lelani didn't know she was asleep. *Maybe.*

3

Seth had no idea the popular child's toy Etch A Sketch contained aluminum powder. Nor did he realize that basic sparklers contained potassium percolate. Malcolm's team researched what readily available items at the rest stop's convenience store might contain the ingredients needed for the beacon spell. He bought a steel saucepan to put it all in and headed back to the darkened picnic area where he agreed to meet Cal. MacDonnell was paying the attendant for gas. Serious as he was already, Cal's mood had noticeably changed for the worse when they left the interstate. They watched Dretch's car drive on as they entered the rest area, almost hitting a Prius that had been backing out of its parking spot. They had maybe thirty minutes before Dretch was out of range.

In the picnic area, Seth laid the items on a table. They were fortunate to be in a rural area with nearby campgrounds. The rest stops on the Jersey Turnpike would not have stocked portable propane cooking stands. As he lit the burner, he made a note to ask Lelani why some magic required elaborate ingredients and fire, and others could be cast with just a few words or the wave of a hand.

Magic was fantastic and mysterious, but there were rules and limitations, their own version of the laws of physics. A wizard, Seth discovered, was a learned sorcerer . . . someone who studied both magic and science, honed their skill, and added to his or her natural abilities. Wizards could blend science and magic to create new, hybrid spells and enchantments. Any hag or bum with a natural inclination to magic could hang a shingle on their hovel and call himself a sorcerer. A wizard belonged to a recognized brotherhood. They were the Ph.D.s of the arcane, researching the depths of their power and the multiverse.

"Well?" said Cal, impatiently. Seth didn't even hear him bring the car up. He couldn't remember the last time he concentrated so hard.

"Everything's set except for one ingredient. Gold. They didn't have any real gold in the convenience store."

Cal took off his wedding ring and gazed at it for a precious few seconds. Then he threw it in the pot.

What would he tell his wife?

"If my ring is destroyed over a failed spell," Cal said. "I will beat you to within an inch of your life."

"You really are an abusive fuck," Seth responded.

Before the exchange could go further, Lelani cleared her throat loudly on the speakerphone and asked to begin. Seth pricked his finger with his Swiss Army knife, and dropped blood into the pot. He recited the words she taught him, pictured the result he wanted in his mind, and dropped a match onto the flash powder. The powder ignited, a cloud of smoke rose from the pot. The ingredients—silver earrings, iron nails, wedding ring, and wishbone of a fowl for divining—were all singed. The two men looked around for some effect.

"What's happening?" said Lelani.

"Nothing," said Cal. "Not a damned thing."

"You may simply be too far from a lay line. Look for an area of great historical significance—a grand piece of architecture, the sight of a great battle, or significant cultural event. Magical energy inspires great deeds and draws these things to it."

Cal sat on the picnic bench, both hands balled into fists. He stared down the highway in the direction of Dretch's escape.

"Red, we're in the middle of butt-fuck nowhere," said Seth. "The whole world isn't like New York."

Silence ensued. Seth thought about the phone's battery life. He was about to sign off when Lelani asked, *"Seth, have you finished your staff?"*

"Not the carving. I laid out the runes and am still trying to figure out the design motif. Kind of like picking out a tattoo."

"The runes are on the staff?" she asked excitedly.

"Just penciled in. I didn't get a chance to—"

"Get your staff!"

Seth retrieved it from the backseat. It was warm to the touch, as though he'd never relinquished it. As he reached the picnic table, he rested the bottom tip on the grass. A jolt ran through him—a tingling of energy, strange and yet familiar. Everything changed color. Living things—trees, insects, people, rodents—emitted an aura. The stars burned brighter and the black sky changed hue to the deep ultramarine of dusk. Inanimate objects were a cold sterile gray, their details lost and rendered irrelevant. Even the headlights on the cars and trucks looked drab compared to the aura of living things. Seth raised it off the grass and unplugged the effect. Everything was normal again.

"Whoa," he said.

"What happened?" asked Lelani.

Seth explained.

"Seth, Rosencrantz has been monitoring your progress. He's reached out through the network of lay lines and the green, but until now had no way to connect with you."

"The green?"

"The biosphere. Living things. When you tapped your staff on the grass, you connected with him. The staff is working. Cast the spell again."

Seth knew better than to argue. He could debate her for a day and still come away not understanding any of this. He used the remaining ingredients to pack a final wad of flash powder and placed it in the pot. He tapped the staff to the earth and his vision changed again. This time he listened and looked for signs from Rosencrantz. That familiar sensation grew in him again. It was like the time upstate when he held on to the tree and killed those gnolls and the undead guy. He repeated the steps for the beacon spell, this time more confident. An invisible force guided him, like a parent behind a running toddler. He lit the powder. This time the flash was more like a column of light shooting toward the heavens. He saw tendrils of warm light with golden flecks wafting around trees. They moved like a meandering autumn stream. Seth felt himself rise. He looked down to see his body still standing, eyes closed, staff in hand. Cal was saying something to him, but the sounds Seth now heard were not of the mortal world. He stopped rising when he reached the point of the highest tree. This, too, was Rosencrantz's doing . . . the perspective of the top leaf. He could see for miles—and there, south of him, a bright light moved steadily on Interstate 85, tendrils of meandering light feeding lazily into it from the surrounding hills and forests.

Seth willed himself down. He opened his eyes and unhitched himself from the green. Cal looked at him with a mixture of confusion, wonder, and hope.

"To the Batmobile," Seth said.

CHAPTER 25

CORPORATE AXMAN

Mal went over his business reports with only half a mind. Catherine MacDonnell's kidnapping weighed on his thoughts; it was an embarrassment. He'd promised to protect her—made a great deal about his wealth and resources, and then lost her to Dorn within a day. Then, to cover up his debacle, he lied to her husband. There would be a reckoning with the captain when the truth came out; he did not relish the idea of reuniting with MacDonnell under these circumstances.

The billionaire sat propped against pillows and the headboard scrolling through his laptop, responding to e-mails, delaying meetings, authorizing purchases, hiring new people, and getting rid of some dead weight that all companies accrue after years without a house cleaning. The latest economic difficulties made it easier to justify downsizing, especially those whose wages and benefits exceeded their productivity. The workers complained that the company made more than enough money to support their continued employment—as though the only reason for his company's existence was to provide them work. Mal could never abide by that sort of backward thinking. He created his company from the ground up. Its purpose was to serve him, and the workers were there to serve his vision. When a body armor plant in Ohio threatened to form a union, Malcolm shuttered it and moved the jobs to West Virginia. A bunch of Appalachians could sew ceramic plates into Kevlar as good as anyone in Ohio, and seemed a hell of a lot more appreciative for the chance.

Someone knocked on the bedroom door. Its immediate opening told Mal that Scott had returned, even before his partner came into view. Everyone else would have waited for his permission before entering.

With his great success, Mal had developed some understanding of the rules of nobility. What was he if not a modern aristocrat, after all, even if he didn't have fancy titles. Everyone wants a piece of the man who's in charge. If it wasn't money, it was favors, some boon, some judgment, some advantage—some little piece of the power he held. The rules were there to keep everyone from rushing forward all at once like a pack of wild dogs barking and nipping at his fingers. Scott was different. He was Mal's kennel master, adept at the game and with a personal interest in protecting Malcolm's privacy, since it was also his own.

Scott carried two stacked boxes, one large, one smaller, that he placed on the end of the bed.

"These just arrived from the Forge," he said, rubbing his arms to soothe his sore muscles. "What is it . . . gold bullion?"

The Forge was Malcolm's research center, where his company tested new alloys and designs to build the weapons that supplied America's armed forces. Malcolm wasn't just any run-of-the-mill chief executive—one of those sons of paper pushers from Ivy League frats with cushy corner offices and stock options and golden parachutes and no vested interest in the company's success. Mal had practical skills. Like his hero Soichiro Honda, who could take apart and rebuild his cars' engines by himself, Mal knew how to smelt, blend, and bend metal—he always had, even when he didn't know who he really was. You could make a dwarv forget his name, but you could never get the forge out of his blood.

Mal set aside the laptop on a pillow and stood to examine the boxes. The larger box was five feet long, three feet wide, and two feet thick. He ripped off the brown paper wrapping and pulled off the cardboard top. Resting inside Styrofoam molds were three sections of a beautifully designed two-sided metal ax.

The ax head was one solid piece of forged stainless steel with two gleaming silver curving blades a foot apart on either end. From the razor-sharp ends it thickened to a smooth five-inch bulge in the center and was topped with a six-inch Kaiser spike shooting up from the ax eye. Underneath was the hole for the handle attachment. The silver handle segments were solid inch-and-a-half-wide cylinders forged from aircraft grade 6.6.2 titanium alloy, grooved the long way with intermittent dwarv design motifs that Malcolm had provided. The valleys of the grooves and etchings were tinted black, making the embossed silver parts of the handle shine brighter by comparison. The design was more for grip than decoration, but there was no reason it couldn't look impressive, too. Just past the thinner throat of the handle end it swelled into a spherical knob. A leather loop strap was anchored into the knob end.

Mal pulled out the sections and began assembling with the eagerness of a young boy on Christmas morning. He inserted the first handle segment into the head and twisted to hear a satisfying and sturdy click. Then he attached the second half of the handle and it clicked solidly into place. Mal felt the weight, its reach, and balance before resting the weapon vertically on the floor. From ground to head, it was four feet high with six extra inches for the spike.

Scott whistled. "The boys do good work."

"And fast," Malcolm said. "I only gave them the specs two days ago."

"Why not titanium all the way through?" Scott asked. "That head looks heavy."

"Titanium blade wouldn't last as long as the steel, and you want weight at the head. Helps drive through bone and muscle."

Scott was visibly alarmed by the remark. "Really?" he said. "Exactly whose bones do you plan to drive this monstrosity through?"

Mal opened the second box and it also contained an ax, similar to the first, only half the size and completely solid steel.

"Did you not notice one of our party was kidnapped today?" Mal said. He laid the big ax against the wall by the headboard, pushed the boxes off the bed and resumed his work position with the laptop.

Scott poured himself a glass of lemon water at the wetbar. "Cat's kidnapping is eating everyone up," Scott said. "Lelani is beside herself. And Collins . . . he'd been friends with most of our security team for years."

"You think talking about my feelings will somehow be better than trying to get work done?" Malcolm said, typing away. The monitor's glow tinted him a frosty blue, adding to his coldness.

"I think not beating yourself up for something you could not have predicted would be a good start." Scott sat beside Malcolm on the bed and placed a hand on his lap. Mal looked up; he gazed into the face of the man who'd been his partner in every way for the past several years, a man he knew like the back of his hand. Scott thought he knew Malcolm as well, but that was the old Mal—the one who thought he was of this universe. New Mal was a conglomeration of two lives.

"I sent one security man with them to the only source of magical energy on the entire island of Manhattan," Malcolm said. "How much more stupid could I have been to not anticipate the possibility of an ambush? Even just a random meeting. From the start I should have sent an entire detachment of guards to secure the lay pool and left them there to keep Dorn's cronies away from the very power they need to vex us.

"I'm very good at secular strategies, Scott. But I've been away from Aandor for so long, I had forgotten how to factor wizards into a fight. Dealing with people who can manipulate the laws of nature with a gesture and a wave will put gray hairs on any soldier's head. We need to be smarter, Scott. This is very serious stuff. We need to be smarter if we're to get home alive."

"But I am home," Scott said, quite solemnly.

Malcolm remained quiet, surprised at his own slip of the tongue. He didn't know yet how to address this issue. It had been the elephant in the room for a few days now. The problem was, Malcolm wasn't sure of his own feelings on the subject yet. He had skin in the game in both universes and was torn between staying and going back.

"This is not my home," Malcolm said. "It's a beautiful life and I've accomplished much, but I came here for a specific purpose." Mal put the laptop down again and faced his partner.

"I love my village. I love our culture, our cuisine, our work ethic—the songs we sang, the things we built. I miss my home. When the invasion came, I didn't just run away like half the other members in our party. I knew my purpose was to protect that kid as though my people's very future depended on it. My people are there."

"I'm your people, too," said Scott, trying to keep the pain out of his voice. These revelations had placed a tremendous amount of strain on him. It was hard for Malcolm to hear. Scott really had been his "people" for years, the only friend Mal needed to have a happy life. They had been talking about adopting a child, and perhaps more after that to check off the last remaining requirements of domestic bliss.

Mal knew this conversation was inevitable. Part of being successful in business was the ability to predict events. He already had a sense of the way it might go, and he didn't want to face it.

"I have two children," Mal said. "A son, Axel, who's fourteen, and my daughter Mathilde, nine. Both haven't even realized yet their pa has lived without them for thirteen years."

Scott would understand the burden of that responsibility. He had two daughters from a previous marriage that had been a lie from the start, prompted by his southern roots to fit in. Mal liked Scott's ex very much. She was educated and open-minded and had been a good sport about it all. Scott's coming out had been a relief to her after years of feeling like she wasn't attractive enough to retain his interests. She simply didn't have what turned him on. The girls, Molly and Claire, lived with their mother in Virginia Beach, but Mal and Scott had them up to the Hamptons often for holidays and summer vacation. Scott was a phenomenal father, made possible by his personal happiness in finally living the life he was born to live.

"And where there's children, there is usually a wife," Scott said softly, more for his own realization.

"There is a wife. But she's not as important as you might assume. It was an arranged marriage . . . a normal custom among my people. We like each other, get on very well, but there was never passion, romance—never a connection of the kind we have."

"Have? Do you still have *it,* Malcolm? That old queen Balzac couldn't keep his mouth shut about how much dwarv women look like men. Told the others you were confused about your orientation."

"Cruz doesn't know shit about my feelings!" Mal's ire rose. The complications of the guardians' lives were bad enough without some effete fool mouthing off his toxic gossip. Balzac was the reason Catherine MacDonnell ended up in Central Park . . . because he couldn't keep his hole shut about MacDonnell's betrothed in Aandor.

"Yes, our women are more masculine," Mal said. "When the restoration spell hit, I was afraid . . . worried that knowing my true self again, my feelings for you would wane. I waited and waited for that moment when I would no longer find you—attractive.

"We're four days in now, Scott, and it hasn't happened. I can't make sense of it—I don't know if I'm a gay dwarv, a straight one, or just utterly confused. This much I know . . . I love you. As much today as I did before the spell. You're still the one that turns me on the most in two universes."

Scott's eyes welled, mostly with happiness Malcolm thought. His face turned beet red as it always did when he became emotional.

"But your children . . . ," Scott said.

"Come back with me," Mal offered.

"Your wife will love that," Scott said sarcastically. He produced a handkerchief from his pocket and wiped his eyes. "Does she get the guest room or do I?"

Mal laughed despite the heart-wrenching truth behind the statement, and Scott joined in.

"I can't leave Molly and Claire," Scott said. "They're not even in high school yet. How could I . . . ?"

"See. It's not easy," Malcolm said. "But it's not just my kids. My people have run out of places to live. Aandor was the only kingdom that could stand up to Farrenheil and its coalition. Many kingdoms won't take us in. They think of dwarvs as greedy, dirty, and uncouth. Who wants to take on a burden when, in addition to feeding mouths, it only earns you the animosity of one of the richest, most powerful kingdoms on the continent? If Aandor falls, we'll be pushed out. The dwarvs' backs are against the proverbial sea. This is as much my fight as it is Callum MacDonnell's. If he had died in these past years, I would still be leading the charge to save the prince and return to Aandor."

"What good can one boy do?" Scott said.

Mal arched his eyebrow and considered what he knew. "You'd be surprised," he said. "We're governed by accords that were signed in blood by the heads of all twelve kingdoms over a century ago. We are in effect a confederation . . . a leaderless empire. The heads of the kingdoms are princes, descendants of the emperors of old, but adhering to the accord, none may use the title 'prince.' They go by archduke or grand duke. It is one big family squabble over who gets to be in charge over a new empire. The heads of the wizards and religious orders witnessed the accord signing and countersigned to validate it. The age of ascension is sixteen in Aandor. At sixteen, you are a man, free to leave home, marry, join the army, start a business, or rule a kingdom. If Danel, Blood of Ten Kings, returns home, in three years, he will be the first ruler in over a century with 'prince' as his title. He would be a step away from producing the next emperor and would draw the support of kingdoms that have so far stayed neutral during this aggression, as well as backing from the Wizards' Council and priestly orders. The neutral kingdoms don't like Farrenheil any more than we do, but as long as they stay neutral—don't criticize the cleansings—Farrenheil lets them be."

"Because that works so well," Scott said. "What was it that theologian who lived through World War Two said? '. . . *Then they came for me—and there was no one left to speak out for me.*'"

"Niemöller. Aye," Malcolm agreed. "But we went through decades of bloody torturous war between kingdoms before the accord was signed. People need to know Danel still has a viable claim before they stick their necks out. It would hearten them, rally them, and may even foster enough force to shut Farrenheil down once and for all. Even Farrenheil's greatest ally, Verakhoon, would balk at such a rising. But none of it means anything if we don't get the boy back alive."

Scott sat on the bed, hands on his lap, rubbing his thighs. It was a lot to take in.

Mal sat next to his partner and rubbed his back. He always liked the texture of Scott's sweaters, always of the finest wools. "I know you won't leave the girls," Mal said.

Scott put his head on Mal's shoulder and they sat there in perfect balance, each exerting the right amount of push, like the voussoirs of a Roman arch. There would be no solution to their dilemma today. But Malcolm would hold Scott for a little while longer and pretend that tomorrow was an open book.

CHAPTER 26

CAT IN A GILDED CAGE

As consciousness approached, Catherine MacDonnell was vaguely aware her face rested against something soft and satiny. She awoke to find herself in a luxurious king-sized bed in one of the most elegant bedrooms she'd ever seen. *Edwardian* came to mind, and she was sure the furniture, bold in details, with gracious ornamentation, was in the style of one of the Louises, probably the fifteenth. Her bed's large headboard loomed behind her; what she took for the ceiling at first was really the canopy at the top of a four-poster bed. A diffused yellow light on the nightstand begrudgingly pushed itself through the room leaving the far corners shadowed and mysterious—the heavy drapes, closed, denied her any sense of time of day.

Cat pushed off from the pillow; her vision swirled and she fell back to where she started with a soft poof. The ceiling shifted in a dizzying jig, which even with eyes closed failed to stop. The darkness was as bad as it sloshed like fluid in a shaken jar. Roman candles burst soundlessly on the black screens of her eyelids. Her thoughts were thick, and despite the fog in her memory, the one feeling that came through clear and undiluted was the piercing throb in her temple. Cat was certain she'd been drugged.

Panic grew as the events of Central Park slowly unfurled. She remembered the three men that came out of the woods, especially the one called Kraten—bloody Collins, frozen Lelani, and—*Where's Bree?* She sat up again, too quickly, and immediately suffered for it.

Her senses spun, she again fell back toward the pillow, but made an effort to go off center as though not ending up in the exact same position she started from was somehow less pathetic.

"How many times are you going to do that?" said a voice in a dark corner of the room.

An obscured man sat in the shadows.

She pushed herself up slowly this time. "Who's there?" Cat asked.

The chair moved forward with the sound of a thin mechanical whir. As he came into the nightstand's feeble light, Cat saw that it wasn't a man, but a boy with short spiked brown hair and hazel eyes in a black, padded wheelchair. It was one of those deluxe chairs with a computer monitor and a tube affixed next to his mouth to help him navigate. Velcro straps secured the boy's torso to the chair and his emaciated arms to the armrests. A U-shaped brace around his parietal bone kept his head from bobbing too far in any direction. *Quadriplegic,* Cat realized.

"Who are you?" she asked.

"Tory," the boy answered. His voice trembled . . . he was hoarse as though he'd been screaming and burned out his throat. *And why wouldn't he?* she thought. Being kidnapped by thugs was scary enough when you could move your arms and legs.

"I live in Carroll Gardens with my mom," the boy continued. "I can't get a call out to her . . . there are zero bars on my pad." He glanced at the monitor. "Do you know why I'm here? No one will tell me anything."

You're another victim of Dorn's war. "I don't know," Cat said. She tried to shake the cotton out of her brain.

"I'm going out of my mind," Tory said. "Most of my life's lived through this monitor—I can't get Wi-Fi or any stations. My battery's running down."

She could hear the fear behind the complaint. She'd read about these modern computers that reacted to eye movements, giving some semblance of control to people like Tory who lived vicariously through others. What would it be like for the simplest tasks in life to become herculean efforts? Cat's maternal instincts kicked in. She hated the thought of any frightened child.

A throbbing in Cat's hand soon joined the one in her skull. She massaged it and remembered Kraten's smack with the flat of his sword. The sheets around her were soft, at least six hundred thread count; they implored her to lie back down and close her eyes. She squeezed her injured hand and winced, coming awake.

"At least it's nice," she said to Tory, and feebly gestured to the room.

A cold, sick feeling ran through Cat. She looked around the room. Bree wasn't here. Cat remembered the girl running up the trail. No one went after her. So where was she? Lost on the streets of Manhattan—or worse. Lelani was probably dead. With Cal in Maryland, who would help Brianna? An overwhelming depression came over her tinged with guilt. She wanted to mourn the centaur, but could think only of her daughter.

"It could be Jay-Z's house for all the good it does me," Tory said.

"What?" Cat said, coming back into the moment. She shifted slowly to the edge of the bed.

"The room," he said. "Luxury doesn't do me any good. There are medicines I need to take daily. I have to be moved several times a day to prevent sores. My chair will run out of power soon. I—I can't eat—or use the bathroom—I can't—anything." His eyes were moist, and he struggled to stay calm. "My colostomy bag needs to be emptied . . ."

He truly was helpless, more than even Bree. Bree could at least run. At least there was a chance she'd run into policeman or a good Samaritan. Cat wondered what value this poor kid could have to Lord Dorn. This was no random kidnapping; they'd targeted Tory. She was afraid for the boy.

"I'll take care of your meals and cleaning," Cat said. "I'll get you out of here." The hollowness of those words echoed back at her. It was a knee-jerk statement to make her feel better, and she was already regretting it. Cat just saddled herself with an extra burden. Her number-one responsibility was to escape and get back to her family. How the hell was she supposed to accomplish that dragging Tory along?

The French doors opened and the brightness of the adjoining room flooded into the dark bedroom. A tall, well-built man with long blond hair tied back in a ponytail entered. He had high cheekbones, a strong jaw, and wore an expensive dark gold suit. Cat was reminded of the actor Julian Sands in his youth. This had to be Dorn. He flipped a switch beside the door and the bedroom's chandelier came to life. The brightness made Cat squint.

"Ah—the Lady MacDonnell." His voice had a trace of an accent, similar to Lelani's. It was deep and penetrating; the kind of voice that led men into battle or broke the laws of physics by asking. His intense gaze made Cat grateful to be squinting. "A pleasure to finally meet you. Please, remain seated," he ordered, as though she was expected to stand in his presence.

Cat had a million questions for Dorn but mixed feelings about voicing them. This was the psychopath who'd invaded her home, killed Erin and Ben, invaded Cal's kingdom. Then a thought occurred . . . if Dorn's kingdom hadn't invaded Aandor, she would never have met her husband. It irked Cat to believe she owed this monster any debt of gratitude.

"Please do not entertain thoughts of escape or rescue," he said. "I have wards around this suite that block any messages or sorceries I do not approve of."

"Where's my daughter?" Cat asked.

"She's not here, if that's what you are concerned about," said Dorn. "A mistake on my men's part since she, too, would have been a valuable hedge against your husband's success. Perhaps the centaur found her, or, no doubt one of New York's finest."

Lelani was alive! Cat considered this news a mixed blessing. Bree, alone in the park at night—she was sure Malcolm wouldn't abandon her daughter either.

"Why have you kidnapped this boy?" Cat asked. "What threat can he possibly be?"

"My lady, kidnapping to create leverage over an opponent, or ally, is a time-honored tradition in my reality. Whole battles can be avoided by a simple compromise. The cripple is simply an insurance policy."

Cat winced at Dorn's very un-PC reference to Tory. It was a bad sign that he didn't refer to the boy by his name. It dehumanized the boy—made him expendable.

"This has something to do with my dad," Tory said.

Dorn picked up on Cat's lost expression and added, "The detective."

"Dretch!" she said, realizing. "But he's your man. We saw his trail of bodies upstate."

Dorn poured himself a glass of something smoky brown from a crystal decanter on the bureau. "Colby has not killed a single person in my service," he said. "His heart is not fully committed to the task. I have been sanitizing the trail behind him. Yet, your husband is quite the sleuth in his own right. So here we are, neck and neck at the stretch. My horse just needs a good kick. Brandy?" he offered.

"He's quadriplegic," Cat said. "His life's hard enough already."

"My dad doesn't give a crap about me," Tory said.

"Quite the contrary," Dorn said, ignoring the boy and continuing to speak directly to Cat. "Colby's deal with the devil was to give his cripple a better life than he could ever provide for on a prison salary."

Behind Dorn, in the suite's common area, Kraten walked in with an unconscious blonde over his shoulder. Cat's heart jumped into her throat. The woman was tied and gagged. He unceremoniously dumped her on the couch. Her leather miniskirt rode up her thigh, her fishnet stockings were torn, and she was missing one red shoe with three-inch heels. She looked cheap, not because of her disheveled appearance but because her hair was too bright to be natural and Cat could smell the overbearing perfume from a good twenty feet away. Cat's instinct said something more nefarious was going on than the carnal needs of Dorn's men. Symian walked into the bedroom pushing a cart of covered food plates and blocked her view of the living room. He placed the cart before Cat and removed the silver covers. Chicken Francese with risotto and a side of string beans. Under a towel lay a basket of freshly baked rolls, still steaming, and next to it, cool water in a carafe, dripping with condensation. A crystal tumbler and wineglass sat next to a bottle of Trimbach pinot gris Hommage Á Jeanne 2000. There was nothing on the tray for Tory.

"What about him?" Cat asked, pointing to the boy.

"In my reality, there are two sets of rules," Dorn said. "One for the aristocracy, and another for everyone else."

"I'm a commoner," Cat pointed out.

"You are James MacDonnell's daughter-in-law, the mother of his granddaughter, and therefore are entitled to be treated in the manner with which we treat captured nobles. In a way, we are two of a kind. Please, regard me as your . . . friend."

Dorn just managed to squeak the word "friend" out of his throat, Cat thought, where it was in danger of getting stuck. The gracious bit was an act. He did not consider her equal to him despite the fancy speech.

"Can you eat this?" she asked Tory. A miniscule shake of his head confirmed that he couldn't. He would need something strained. Cat looked at the meal before her. It smelled great and she wanted nothing more than to dig in. Instead, she folded her arms and looked up at Dorn, refusing to touch even a napkin or utensils.

"These are *rules* of etiquette," Dorn said, calmly, "not *laws*. Pray that you do not try my patience, Lady MacDonnell."

Cat looked around the suite, at the crystal chandelier, the oil paintings, mahogany furnishings, and the rest of the opulence. She turned back to Dorn and in a tone designed to underscore his pettiness said, "Would strained beef and carrots really break your bank, Mr. Dorn?"

Dorn gestured with two fingers, and Symian left the room. "It's *Lord Dorn*," he corrected her. "Your bravado shall make our conversations very *interesting*."

And by "interesting," Cat was sure he meant "trying." "I have nothing more to say," she shot back.

"Ah, but there is so much more that you want me to say, my lady." He paced slowly before Cat, studying her, deciding on a tack, no doubt, by which to wheedle his way into her heart and mind. "You think me the villain," he said. "Your husband has filled your head with his version of events about how *we* invaded his kingdom."

"Do you deny it?" she asked.

"The invasion? No. But there are more shades of gray to this story than on a mountain before the storm."

Cat stood up wobbily from the bed and walked stiffly around the room trying to improve her circulation. "You killed his countrymen, tried to murder an infant, wrecked my home, and now you're here to kill an innocent thirteen-year-old boy," Cat said. "How many shades of gray does that cover?"

"That boy is not innocent," Dorn said in a severe tone. "He is a weapon, stained with the blood of his ancestors." Dorn positioned an expensive-looking chair by the bed and motioned to Cat to resume her seat on the edge of the mattress. Whatever he had to tell her, it required her undivided attention. Cat sat reluctantly, more because he wanted it than her being exhausted from standing up.

"Prince Danel's mother, Sophia of Bradaan, was first betrothed to my cousin Johan, son of my uncle, the archduke of Farrenheil. Had they married, it would be their child with the blood of ten kings and the next prince regent of the empire and father of the next emperor." Dorn sipped his brandy patiently, waiting for his words to sink in. He locked eyes with his prisoner and said, "Johan was assassinated before he could pluck that rose. It looked like a hunting accident, but was a bit too coincidental for an experienced hunter. We offered Bradaan Johan's younger brother, a strapping, handsome lad only one year younger than Sophia. But the duke of Bradaan had already sold his prized heifer to Athelstan of Aandor. Not even four days had passed—my cousin's corpse was still warm." Dorn pushed aside the food tray and bent down low to stare her in the eye, blocking her view of everything. Something was not quite right about the man's look, a frenetic shifting, ever so slight as to be unnoticed—the look of pain and the desperation of hiding it. "Tell me, Lady MacDonnell—who do *you* suppose assassinated Johan?"

Cat stayed silent. This was the big league—breeding contests, wars, and assassinations. Thousands of years of human evolution honed to its deadliest arts. She'd never make fun of Republicans and their dirty politics again if she survived this visit. They were downright congenial compared to Dorn.

"So you see," Dorn continued, "we're simply fighting for our rights."

Everything Cat knew of Cal and Lelani said Aandor was a fair kingdom, inclusive of others. She couldn't imagine Callum being part of any nefarious organization. "You wouldn't cease to exist if Aandor ruled the empire," Cat said.

"What a remarkably arrogant and naïve statement from someone who has never been there," said Dorn.

He ignored her for a moment, his thoughts moving beyond this conversation. Even seated, Dorn conveyed a commanding posture—the center of the room always cohabitated his space. He put one leg over the other and leaned back. Placing his arms on the rests he revealed a gold Rolex watch on his left wrist. Despite her revulsion of the man, Cat wanted to hear him speak. There was so much that she wanted to know about the universe her husband had asked her to join him in.

"This earth is a paradise," Dorn began, gesturing at the room, but indicating the world beyond it. "Despite minor annoyances such as freedom and equality, it is fundamentally a human world. There are no other sentient species here. Ten thousand years ago, men were considered little more than a food source for many species in my reality. Even among the races that did not hunt us, we were little more than clothed primates, pitied and taken advantage of as we tried to build safe havens. We were excluded from the forests by centaurs, pushed from the hills by the dwarvs, and so on. We built villages on open river plains and flood zones. Families huddled in the darkness behind wooden walls and thatched hovels, hoping this would not be the night a pack of gnolls burst in or trolls dug through the dirt floors from subterranean caverns. How could a stone wall stop a horde of frost giants, sixteen feet tall with grumbling bellies? How do you stop a twenty-foot ogre with skin so thick and hairy, it calmly leaves your village with its kill while your men throw so many spears at it, you'd mistake it for a giant porcupine in the dark? Man did not have the breathing room to perfect his science, to develop his technology . . . the smartest were killed as easily as the dumbest and knowledge was readily lost. Life was day to day with no safe havens—man was not master of his domain."

Dorn paused—Cat was greedy for the rest, but didn't want to admit it. *He could make the phone book sound interesting.* Symian entered with a second cart. The unconscious blonde in the background was still tied up on the couch. The new tray contained strained carrots, peas, beef, and apricots. She motioned to Tory to come closer to the bed and put a napkin into his collar. Dorn fell into a silent, paternal observation of them—his hands steepled and resting against his lips.

Symian looked to Dorn for further instruction, but Dorn ignored him, so he left quietly and closed the bedroom doors behind him.

Cat heaped a spoon of strained beef and brought it to the boy's lips. Tory could move his head and facial muscles and sucked up the beef and everything else Cat placed at his animated lips. Dorn still would not resume dinner theater for the kidnapped. Was he punishing her for diverting attention to Tory?

From his jacket, Dorn retrieved a pharmacy prescription bottle, and swallowed a pill with a swig of brandy. He squeezed the bridge of his nose and closed his eyes. Cat knew a migraine when she saw one, and if Dorn was anything like Cal, it would have to reach pain level ten before he made any outward acknowledgment of it even being there. Some of the sheen had come off, and Dorn looked vulnerable for the first time. He opened his eyes and caught her staring at him. The look in his eyes ran through her like an icy pole.

"So . . . what changed since ten thousand years ago?" Cat queried, to move things along.

Dorn leaned forward with elbows resting on his lap, rubbing his hands. He struggled with pain. One of his eyelids fluttered, and Cat couldn't tell if he meant to force it closed or open.

"Men moved across the continent to find refuge," Dorn continued. "The journey was dangerous; they crossed other races' territories, blundered into traps. Of the thousands who made such journeys, a handful survived to found villages west of the Dread Marshes and the Spoke, a large inland sea at the center of the continent. A group founded a settlement on the banks of the Sevren River, and named it Aandor. A most fortuitous event, it is the location of one of the biggest lay lines on our world. And there, humans, for the first time, discovered magic."

"Discovered?" Cat said.

"Yes. Everything I explained came from a time before magic. The lay lines had always been there, and some humans were sensitive to it, shamans and witch doctors and spirit people, but no one had fully utilized the power at that point. The first human to cast a true premeditated spell was in Aandor village. That was ten thousand years ago. No one remembers that first sorcerer or what spell he, or she, cast; it was likely the simplest of spells, but the knowledge was built upon and passed on to others with magical sensitivities. Within a few centuries, the tide began to turn. Aandor, protected by wizards, thrived. Its walls had elaborate wards placed on them to repel gnolls, trolls, frost giants, ogres, korgs—many died as they attacked the village, and soon enough they gave it a wide berth. Travelers knew that if they could reach the gates of what was now becoming a large and prosperous town, they were safe.

"Wizards would travel out to surrounding farms and satellite towns to purge predators from that region, and Aandor's scope widened even more. Wizards would accompany merchant trains traveling east and trade between the new world and the old became dependable. As word grew, more people flocked to the west to live under Aandor's umbrella. Aandor, in fact, means 'man's haven' in the old tongue, and it evolved into the first human city with thousands of inhabitants, spurring the creation of libraries, aqueducts, academies, marketplaces, temples, sewers, and technological and cultural advancements.

"Some sorcerers ventured back to the old world to put down roots. Farrenheil, the safest haven before Aandor, built its wizard the finest house in the village; within one generation it became a thriving town, claiming territory in the surrounding hills and forests in the name of mankind. Now it was we who hunted the ogres and pushed the frost giants back into the mountains of Nurvenheim. Magic had changed the balance of power . . . it allowed our population to grow rapidly, it saved our species from extinction."

"Then why did you attack this society? Why are you trying to kill a little boy?" Cat asked.

It was as though a switch had been flicked—Dorn's face transformed to anger. The point was obvious to him and she was too stupid to see it. He lunged out of the chair and hovered above her, forcing Cat to fall back on the bed. Slowly Dorn crouched over, closing the space between them. He placed his hand on the mattress by her head, pinning her down. Cat could smell the brandy on his breath. He was not the man that had walked into the room earlier—his eyes were wild, like a desperate man who'd run out of time.

"Aandor has *forgotten* its origins," he said, in a guttural whisper.

"It's become soft and fat with happiness. It makes *treaties* with centaurs and dwarvs. It allows vermin to live openly within its borders—within ITS CITIES! It has forgotten that NONE of these races gave refuge to man in our time of need! And now, wizards like Magnus Proust invite abominations like Symian and your precious centaur bitch to learn our secrets—to give to *them* the magic that ensures our dominance!"

Dorn backed away from the bed and regained his composure.

"Aandor may have forgotten, but Farrenheil and many others have not. We will not allow the next emperor to come from the house of Athelstan." Dorn literally spat these last words out, projecting saliva like a rabid dog. The force of his conviction amplified his migraine—he stepped back and grabbed his head in pain. He pressed into his temples and struggled with the turmoil within.

Tory backed his chair to move away from them. Cat could see the terror in the boy's eyes. Dorn would frighten the bravest person in his present state and Cat was no exception. Even those who worked for him were not safe. Now it made sense . . . why Cal worked so hard to secure his prince's throne. It was to deny his world's version of Hitler from implementing prejudice and terror as the law of their land.

Dorn grasped at the pharmacy bottle again. His hand shook so violently; he struggled to get the childproof cap off. Dorn threw the bottle at Cat and ordered her to open it. The bottle read Treximet. The daily dosage recommendation was two pills. She popped the cap and handed it back. Dorn swallowed three pills. He was becoming unhinged.

Dorn threw open the bedroom doors and shouted, "Has the detective arrived at the lodge yet?"

The man who was dressed like a butler came in with a cell phone. Something about the way the butler drooped went contrary to his impeccable dress.

"Detective's there," he said in a gruff manner.

Dorn grabbed the phone. In the manner of one polite and one crazy personality talking at the same time asked, "Dretch . . . Where is my prince?" Cat could hear the detailed buzzing of an excuse on the other end. Dorn's forehead was beaded with sweat as he listened, and his eyes were red. When the buzzing stopped, Dorn breathed heavily into the silence. "Detective—I want you to say hello to my new friend," Dorn said. He put the phone against Tory's ear.

"Dad?" Tory asked.

The buzzing on the other end came through loudly—the sound of a man whose child was in jeopardy.

"Dad, what's going on? What do these people want?"

Dorn took away the phone. "Why can no one, not even the police, with all your technology and street cameras find one scared thirteen-year-old boy?" he asked.

The receiver buzzed urgently.

"You know that I am a miracle worker," Dorn responded. "You've seen what I can do. I'd like to pay you for your service so far, Dretch. I intend to perform a miracle—to reward your loyalty and ensure your absolute commitment going forward. Listen closely."

Dorn placed the phone in Tory's lap. The butler joined his master, blocking Cat's view. She stood up, but Symian grabbed her arms and held her firm.

Cat was worried. If Dretch's accomplishments so far were the result of halfhearted efforts, what would he accomplish for a man that made his son whole again? What would Cat be willing to do for her own child? *Anything.*

Dorn and the butler hovered over the lad. The unmistakable ring of a blade being drawn from its sheath echoed off the walls.

"What's going on?" Cat asked.

"No!" she heard Tory exclaim.

The boy's wailing was almost inhuman, "NO! NO! NO! NO!" he cried repeatedly. "AAAHHHHHH!!!"

What kind of spell was this? Cat never heard a human being suffer like that. It was the soul ripped from the flesh and dashed upon a rock. Tory continued to scream, even after Dorn stopped working. Cat struggled against the hands that held her, tears streaming down her face, as much for her inability to shut her ears to the sound of the boy's cries as for her inability to help him.

Dorn picked up the phone. "Dretch, are you there?" Tory's screams made it impossible to hear the other end of the line. Dorn made the cutoff gesture at his neck and the butler stuffed something in the boy's mouth to muffle the cries. "Are you there, Dretch?" Dorn asked again.

Tory's cries transformed to muffled sobs. Cat wanted them to move away so she could see what they had done. Dorn talked about a reward . . . a miracle. Would Tory be able to walk after this? Was that it . . . to incentivize the detective? If so, the pain now might be worth it in the long run.

"I've performed a miracle on your son, Colby," Dorn said. "And I'll gladly continue to fix him one piece at a time because you're so important to me.

"What did I do?" Dorn said. "Your faith in me is appalling, Detective . . ."

The butler dropped two bloody white objects with a splat in an ashtray. He moved away from Tory to clean up in the bathroom.

Cat struggled to keep her stomach down. There were two bloody black gashes where Tory's eyes had been.

Cat had already thrown up earlier that day; she dry heaved spit and stomach acid all over the expensive carpet. Her throat felt scraped. Symian released her to avoid getting any on himself.

"Why . . . similar to Heshua the Healer, as told in *The Book of Moons* . . . I made a lame man blind," Dorn said into the phone, like it should have been perfectly obvious from the start.

"Find the boy, Colby . . .

"Find the boy.

"Find the boy!"

CHAPTER 27
SANDWITCHED

1

Allyn tried for a day and a half, but still could not locate the prince of Aandor. He channeled the sparse magical energies of this earth in one failed attempt after another, and had to admit, he had no clear strategy on how to find the boy.

The reverend sat lotus style at the center of a makeshift henge in his basement, constructed from cinder blocks, stacks of books, and whatever else he could throw together from the contents of his home. A white painted circle demarked the boundaries of the henge. This circle was not big enough to draw power directly from the lay line miles away, but it tapped into the henge behind the church like an extension cord. Still, Allyn wondered if a blessing of this magnitude was possible from a subordinate henge. His objective was hundreds of miles away, possibly thousands. He should be doing this outside in the larger henge behind the church.

Come spring, Allyn would plant bulbs and seeds in the outer henge. The garden would hide the pagan construct sitting in the backyard of the Baptist church, so that when he used it, it would look like a reverend enjoying the fruits of his labors. Just as important, what he planted would eventually be useful in his vocation. He would share his rediscovered ancient abilities with the people of the greater Raleigh area. His last attempt at a garden had failed, but this time it would be successful, aided by his will. Allyn had a newfound respect for druid orders, which supplied many of the herbs, plants, and animal parts most clerics took for granted. In the city, one simply shopped for them. But on a world where magic was relegated to adventures in children's books, spell casters had to procure their own goods.

Allyn wished there was a way to procure an item belonging to the prince of Aandor. With the Taylor children he'd had Zach's drawing to connect him to the child. But the prince had been lost for thirteen years; the trail was ice cold. He racked his brain to come up with alternative methods to pinpoint the boy and nothing came to mind. A blessing of that magnitude required items that he simply didn't have.

Rosemarie came down the stairs with a tray of hot cocoa and biscuits.

"How's Mom doing?" Allyn asked.

"She's cleaning the bathroom again," Rosemarie said. "Third time since you came down here."

Michelle had been adamant against Allyn constructing "pagan temples" and "casting witches' spells" in the house. Allyn explained that casting outdoors in the actual henge would raise too many questions. The logic was lost on Michelle, who insisted he refuse the request to find the prince in the first place. Allyn only agreed to help Malcolm to keep Aandor as far away from his family as possible. Politics were never Michelle's strong suit—Allyn was the people person. She had more of a mind for accounting and derived pleasure from items lined up neatly in columns. A literal thinker, Michelle did not always get the joke, but it's what the reverend loved about his wife.

Allyn understood the interactions between power and authority and how to lever them to achieve results both within and without the church. He and Michelle complemented each other. They built this beautiful church, which helped lower teen mortality and increased black-owned businesses in the greater Raleigh area. The church helped take people off government programs, preached self-sufficiency, and returned dignity to their lives. It was a center of goodwill. Allyn tried to explain that the henge, too, had the power to heal, but Michelle would not hear it. When he began his task, she took to cleaning the house, as though Clorox and Lysol could scrub away the stains of paganism.

"Home's cleaner than I've ever seen," Rosemarie said. "Smells like a chemical lemon garden. I think I prefer the musty rawness of the basement right now."

Allyn pointed to the old recliner, pushed into the corner, for her to sit on. "Lemons grow in orchards," he said. "You have a book to read?"

"Nope. Want to help you."

"Your mother said you're not to have any part of this." He waved his arms around in a showman's gesture at the circle of books and blocks.

"Well, you said the magic isn't evil. This is so exciting. I never met a *real* prince before."

"And God willing, you never will. Rose, I'm doing all this to keep us out of this fray. If I find the prince for Malcolm, we're done with them."

"I'll bet he's handsome," she said, ignoring her dad. "Have you seen him? What does he look like?"

Allyn was mildly annoyed at his daughter's fawning. How could she be over the moon about a boy she hadn't even met? He blamed the Disney movies, elevating princes to ideal objects of desire when in reality, royals were as flawed as any peasant—more so, since peasants were at least self-sufficient.

Prince Danel wasn't to blame for Allyn's irritation; he was annoyed at Rosemarie's interest in boys in general. She was twelve . . . biologically on the cusp of womanhood. It seemed like only yesterday she had started to form complex thoughts—to assert her multifaceted personality upon the world and her parents. He had only just begun to know her as a person and not just his child—more than a responsibility to care for, a person to educate. Now she was giving back, teaching those around her and bringing newly formed thoughts and ideas to the conversation. And she was looking at boys, one of which would soon supplant the reverend as the most important man in her life.

"I only saw him as a babe, a few weeks old," Allyn said. "He had his mother's coloring—a touch of her olive skin, green eyes with a tinge of steely gray mixed in, dark sandy-colored hair, almost light brown like walnut wood depending on the light. It's obvious what he inherited from Archduchess Sophia . . . his father, Athelstan, is blue-eyed, red-haired, and stark white of skin; tall, thin like a basketball player, with sharp bone structure—ears that stick out a bit and somewhat of a long face, but not unattractively so. He had a strong nose, and defined jaw line. Hard to know from a babe if Danel took after his father in this respect—he was pudgy ball of rolling fat when last I saw him."

Allyn's heart was heavy with the thought that men were trying to find and kill that baby at this very moment. He remembered Sophia suckling Danel at her breast, a tradition in Bradaan that caused much controversy among the ruling class in Aandor, where a wet nurse was traditionally used. The people of Bradaan were earthier and less inclined to tolerate the airs of the "high minded." Sophia had a bit of a rebellious streak—she would visit her husband during council meetings with Danel at her teat, just to watch the politicians, businessmen, and battle-hardened generals squirm at the presence of a mere woman feeding an infant. The common folk of Aandor took to her quickly, and soon Sophia was more popular with them than her husband, their rightful liege. The archduke's line needed fresh blood and a new perspective if it was going to survive to reclaim the emperor's throne. It needed Danel.

Allyn shook out the crazy notions forming in his head. With new resolve, he said, "I don't want to get involved with that mess up north, Rose. Don't be too disappointed in me for keeping that violence at arm's length."

"Well . . . you can't blame me for being curious," she said, smiling. "There are so few princes in North Carolina. How close are you?"

Allyn took out his handkerchief and wiped his brow. "I am failing miserably," he said.

"See, you do need help."

"What I *need* is a personal item of Danel's. I've had to resort to less dependable indirect methods."

"Like . . . ?"

"Determining the difference between people from Aandor and this universe. And by different, I don't mean like a tail or horns."

"We have tails?" she said in mock alarm. She looked at her own behind trying to find hers.

His daughter's use of "we," implying her own Aandoran ancestry, and her faux expression of concern, caused Allyn to break into a giggle. "Maybe college is not right for you, Rose. The comedy club circuit, perhaps."

"Didn't I tell you? I'm going to spend all your money to study drama," she said, beaming. "And postmodern poetry."

"Your mother will love that," Allyn chuckled. As would Malcolm Robbe, whose promise to make Allyn's help "worth his while" was the other reason he was in the basement trying to recall blessings he had not cast in thirteen years. Rosemarie's college would be paid for and possibly the education of several other promising students. For the first time, the church could have a scholarship fund. Michelle could bemoan about witchcraft and blasphemy all she wanted; Allyn knew this was the right path to take. If he failed in this task, he'd regret it the rest of his life.

"Kidding aside," she continued, "you know how on those science-fiction shows, like *Star Trek,* whenever people cross from other dimensions, they have a different vibration. Maybe you folks from Aandor are different like that. Like a frequency."

"Except for the fact that I'm not a scientist or own a tricorder, that is the tack I've taken. We all have auras, Rose, the output of our unique specific energies. I've noticed that mine is brighter than, say, your mother or Uncle Theo's. Yours is brighter than theirs, but not as intense as mine. When I reach out into the town, it's the same—no one burns as brightly as I do. I thought this might be the way to distinguish people of Aandor from those here. But as I reach out farther and farther, I encounter others with the brightness as strong as mine."

"There are others here from Aandor?"

"No. There are those here who if they were in Aandor, might have been sorcerers or clerics. They are wired for it, attuned to the gods' energies, which flow through all creation. But here in this reality where science reigns, they never developed these nascent talents. This frustrates me because it underscores our similarities when what I am searching for are differences. There are hundreds of people like this along my search radius."

"Hmmm?" murmured Rosemarie. "Is there anything special about the prince or his family? Are they sorcerers, too? In books, characters usually have special abilities."

Allyn stood, rubbing his creaking knees and arching backward to pop the kinks out of his back. A series of cracks brought relief to some strain in his lower lumbar region. *Too old,* he thought. *No wonder the high clerics left vespers to the young. Those stone temple floors were too hard and cold.* He left the circle, slowly rubbing blood back into his legs, and joined his daughter, taking a seat on a cardboard storage box marked *Tax Documents.* The top of the box crunched under his weight, but he didn't care and settled in. He sipped hot cocoa and took a biscuit.

"The most remarkable thing about the royal families of Aandor is their resistance to magic," he said. "None of the rulers of the twelve kingdoms can wield magic. It does not connect to them. Some sects had made the argument that this means they lack the gods' graces. Those sects were, of course, outlawed and hunted down to near extinction."

"Really?" Rosemarie said, incredulously. "That makes no sense. Can't the wizards beat up on them and take over then?"

"You would think," he answered, and took another sip from his mug. "It's not as though it has never happened—we had sorcerer kings and cleric kings thousands of years ago, but they never worked out; for both the kings and the people." He shifted his weight and settled more comfortably into the box, just now realizing how uncomfortable the floor had been.

"Magic wielders want to study magic . . . the universe, the meaning of life," Allyn continued. "They are scholars and learned people who want to cast spells, not administrate the nation's problems. The mundanity of court life, judging in trials, hearing appeals, making appointments, being diplomats, studying details of treaties, the running of armies—this is not the life a wizard seeks. Most are too smart for that. So the majority of them never seek political dominance.

"There are always a few wizards who are more ambitious than wise. We called them 'gardener kings' because they want to remake society the way a gardener organizes nature . . . using their magic to force everything according to their personal design. This never lasts, as other wizards will join together to abolish a gardener king.

"But the royal families have their own protection from such wizards. They are magic neutral. Most—almost all—spells and blessings will not affect them. A wizard could not magically take over the mind of any of the rulers in Aandor. You can't transmogrify a prince of the realm into a frog or another person. This resistance to magic is a cornerstone to rule. It gives the duke or prince the confidence that he is his own man, and the people, too, are comforted that their rulers are protected from the whims of wizards."

"So they's impossible to kill by magic?" Rosemarie asked.

"Girl, you will ask that question again, properly."

"*Are they* impossible to kill?"

"No one is impossible to kill. A wizard could send a sea monster to sink the king's galley or cause a landslide to bury the prince's entourage while he travels abroad. But then so could dissenters with a precarious boulder and a long stick."

"But how can you be sure he's protected from magic? Or even really the prince?"

"What do you mean?"

"Like on them shows Leticia watches in the afternoon . . . some woman always having the wrong guy's baby . . . don't know who the baby daddy is."

"Have you been watching those shows?"

Rosemarie's expression froze, regret plastered on her face for letting down her guard in this surreptitious moment with her dad.

"Don't change the subject," she said nervously.

Allyn perked up on the box and fixed a hard stare at his daughter. "Girl, I will pick any subject I want when it comes to what you are putting into that stubborn little head of yours. Don't watch that rubbish. There are no baby daddies in your future. First school, then a boy we approve of, marriage, and then children, in that order; and no Jerry Springer or any of those other fools on the TV. You watch that nonsense again . . . see if I don't restrict you to reruns of *Little House on the Prairie* for a year. Understood?"

"Yes sir," she said, swinging her legs impatiently against the chair. "But how do you know he's got this neutral magic thing?"

Allyn was about to lecture her more on the evils of daytime talk shows when he caught himself, realizing that hammering into Rose was a trait he picked up from Michelle. There were times when his wife even made him wince. Rose was not a bad egg; she was remarkably kind and thoughtful, earned straight As, and was choosing to help her dad at this moment instead of going to the mall with her girlfriends. And he needed all the help he could get.

"The royals' resistance to magic is what modern science would call a recessive trait. Less than a quarter of one percent of all people have it and all of them are descended from royalty. When babies are born to the royal families they are given a test for this trait before their naming day celebrations. It doubles as a paternity test. Both parents must have the gene for it.

"The test is administered by both a cleric and a wizard. A protective sheath is placed around the infant's shoulder with a sticky paste underneath to adhere it to the skin. In the middle of the sheath is a design cut out in the shape of the father's sigil, like a stencil leaving that portion of skin bare. The wizard and cleric create a special elixir, infusing it with hair or nail clippings of the father and deadly magical poisons, which they then enchant. A ceremony is performed with some readings and a small degree of pomp to hide what everyone knows is really a very dangerous ritual. The brew is boiled to a sludge, which is then poured over bare skin of the cutout. If the child has the resistance, the skin will burn and bubble, leaving the wailing child with a birthmark of its house sigil and confirmation that he or she is a true royal. The burn will then settle into the banner color of the house to confirm that the father is true, and not possibly another royal who would also have the resistance."

"Wait! If the kid has this protection from magic, why does the liquid burn? Wouldn't it do nothing?"

"The death magic in the potion is extremely powerful. It takes both a cleric and wizard to make it. If the mother were untrue to her lord, the elixir would seep into the child and raze it from within, leaving a smoldering heap of ash where the baby once lay. It's a gruesome and intensely painful death. The mother would then be put to death. Depending on her parents—who would never attend such a ceremony for obvious reasons—there might or might not be a war afterwards."

Rosemarie's eyes were two big saucers under arched black caterpillars and her mouth was round like a doughnut. "That's messed up!" she said.

"That's Aandor. But there are good things about my society, too.

No Jerry Springer or Maury Povich. Someone would run a sword through them inside of a day."

Allyn and Rosemarie laughed until they heard a creaking on the stairs.

"Is that what you're teaching your daughter now?" Michelle said, refusing to take the last step onto the basement floor. "Burning babies and running people through with swords?"

"It's not like that, mama," Rosemarie said.

"I told you not to come down here," Michelle scolded. "Not to be around this sacrilege. Pagan prayers in our house—next to our church."

Michelle aimed that barb at their daughter, but it was meant for Allyn. He wanted to tell his wife that Rose was his daughter, too, and he had every right to her company, but realized it would throw gasoline on a smoldering flame. The sooner he found the prince and got Aandor out of his life for good, the quicker he could heal the rift in his marriage.

"Upstairs, Rose!" Michelle ordered.

Rose went to give her father a hug. While they embraced, she whispered in his ear, "Good luck finding someone that magic bounces off of." She kissed him and went up the stairs. Michelle threw Allyn a disapproving glance and followed her up. Dinner tonight would be interesting.

Allyn stared at his henge and revisited the problem of finding the prince . . . someone whom spells bounce off of. Bounce off . . .

Wait.

He'd been going about the search from the wrong direction. How many people in this world would have a resistance to magic? A resistance to something they'd barely encountered because of its lack of presence in this reality. When Europeans first came to the new world, they decimated the Native American populations with smallpox and influenza because the natives had never encountered strains of the diseases the English and Spanish brought with them. Virtually everyone on this earth should be susceptible to magic . . . except for Prince Danel. Resistance had been built in the child's blood over generations. Allyn looked at the puny circle in his basement and realized—he was going to need a bigger henge.

2

"You're doing what?" Theo asked as he lugged a hundred pounds of iron weights to the henge behind the church.

Something absolutely crazy, Allyn thought, as he struggled with a pair of cinder blocks. He'd expanded the circle of the outer henge and brought in bigger stones. The weights were for increasing the iron content in specific areas of the wheel. For as long as he could remember, Allyn always had a gift for constructing circles. It was as though the gods had intended for him to be their superintendent of energy—tightening a nut here, putting a screw there to keep the engine of the universe running smoothly. The flow of energy to this henge increased threefold. He hoped it would be enough.

"I intend to pinpoint every living person within fifteen hundred miles of this epicenter," Allyn said. "Like radar."

"Uh-huh," said Theo, pretending to understand.

"Then I will send out a tiny magical current, running it through every person within that radius. No one will be aware of it. It's like the X-ray at the dentist's. But in that one brief flash, that current will be rejected by one individual—it will bounce off or go around him—and in that moment, I will have a location to give Malcolm Robbe. I can repeat the spell, targeting that one area to pinpoint him further once Malcolm is in place to intercept him."

Theo dropped the weights along the edge of the circle with a huge huff. He scratched his head, squeezed his eyelids and said, "But what if he's outside that radius? What if he moved to California? You're only going to cover Maine to Florida to the Mississippi."

The thought hadn't escaped Allyn. He hoped that since so many of the guardians remained relatively close to the transfer point by which they came to this reality, the boy would also be in the neighborhood, so to speak.

"If I build a bigger henge right on the lay line, I can cover all of North America and halfway down to South America," Allyn explained.

"Yeah, but what if—"

"Theo!" Allyn cried in frustration. "Stay positive. Hopefully the boy is not in Russia or China."

Theo continued placing the iron weights where Allyn indicated, muttering, "Like to see Principal Harris let you build a giant henge behind the school."

Passersby stopped to watch the reverend and his brother-in-law work on the henge. The going story was that he was planning a garden for the spring, and he was setting up the framework now for exercise.

The party rental truck had come by in the nick of time. Allyn instructed them to set up the large white tent used for outdoor events over the henge, concealing the construct from the sidewalk. Normally, the henge remained open to the stars because it was also a calendar and observatory, but what Allyn needed to do would unsettle many church members. It would be impossible to explain.

A livestock truck was the next to pull up. Gabby Martins approached in his usual coveralls, work boots, and CAT cap over his straight greasy gray hair. He had a goat on a rope.

"What's the goat for?" Theo asked within Gabby's hearing.

"The petting zoo we're planning for the kids," Allyn said in a *keep your mouth* shut tone.

"You sure you want him now, Rev?" asked Gabby. "I can bring

him on by tomorrow early. He gonna eat you out of house and home if he come off that rope. Worse than a nuclear-powered lawn mower, goddamned goats." Gabby realized whom he was talking to and quickly added, "Pardon my French."

"We're fine, Gab. He's an old goat right? Lived a long life—uh, not a danger to kids?"

"Che here's the Methuselah of goats. Going on fourteen years. Got himself twenty kids, no pun intended."

"The goat's name is Che?" Theo said, petting the small animal.

Allyn wished the goat didn't have a name and felt his resolve waver in the presence of the little animal. He'd spent too many years living as a Christian.

"Name all my livestock after commies," Gabby said. "Got a cow named Stalin, a pig named Castro, and a rooster named Franklin Roosevelt."

Allyn waited until Gabby was well on his way back to the proletariat before proceeding. He led the goat into the tent and staked his leash by the altar stone—a discarded granite kitchen counter Theo found at the junk heap.

"Please tell me you ain't gonna kill that goat," Theo said, concerned.

"I can't cast a blessing this wide and this powerful without a lot of blood," Allyn said solemnly. "It breaks my heart, but better this goat dies than I leave my family to fight in a war I was barely part of thirteen years ago. If I find the boy, I'm free of my responsibilities. More importantly, I am free of my guilt for not joining the others."

Allyn shut the flap to the tent. He had all the elements necessary for the blessing. Who was he kidding, though? This was no blessing. This was a spell on par with what the wizards did. It irked Allyn that the sphere of wizardry and the sphere of clerics overlapped at their edges. He wanted no brotherhood with those types.

He placed althaea root, angelica root, bloodroot, caraway seeds, and star anise in a steel bowl with a large tumble of alfalfa sprouts and doused various oils over the mixture. He struck a match and set it all to flame. He placed the goat on the altar. It was skittish because of the fire, bleating nervously, and Allyn motioned to Theo to hold the animal. Allyn shaved away a patch of hair at the animal's neck with a straight razor. Theo's expression was grim as a hangman.

"After I bleed the goat, take it to that corner. There's a first-aid kit. Wash its wound, and bandage it. Give it some orange juice and spinach."

"You ain't killing it?"

"I need more than a pint of blood, Theo. The goat may die, but I don't need for it to die for the spell to work. Back in Aandor, we'd simply cut the animal's throat and then we'd roast the flesh for dinner. But I'm only going to make a small incision in its neck."

Allyn had not realized how much the boy's faith in him had wavered until he saw Theo tear up and smile a wide row of teeth. Through his smile, Theo's faith in one of his personal heroes was affirmed. How such a mountain of a man who delivered brutal punishment on the gridiron could have so tender a heart was a mystery.

"I am a minister, you know," he said to Theo, defensively. "Do unto others and all that."

Allyn punctured the goat's artery with a long surgical needle. The goat bleated in distress, but remained in place under Theo's massive arms. Allyn placed a funnel with a rubber tube running under it by the hole and placed the tube end over the bowl. A stream of blood gushed into the flame. Allyn instructed Theo to take the goat away when he had what he needed. He closed his eyes and began to chant, pushing out his will and drawing in the energy of the circle, letting the current of power hasten from a lazy river into a roaring rapid. It filled reservoirs within him that had been empty for the better part of a decade. He spread the energy out through his consciousness, like a tablecloth whipped out and billowing over a large dinner party. He let the energy fall on the land and saw the light of millions in all directions from his epicenter. He saw the glow that represented Theo in the tent, the lights of his wife and daughter in the house, the cluster of intense lights in the cities as people massed together in concrete domiciles—living souls in an unbroken web of magical connection. Once he'd reached the limit of his range, he put his hands up, palms out and pushed out a second wave of energy to piggyback the first one, meant to penetrate these beings with streams of magic less than a molecule thick. He pushed it out in a flash and felt the current connect with millions of beings—except for . . . *two?*

Two beings rejected the stream, forcing it around them. *But that was not possible,* thought Allyn. *Danel should be the only one with resistance.* And stranger yet, the two entities were both in the south . . . one near the Virginia border . . . and the other, only a few miles north of his present location.

"Only a few miles north?" Allyn mumbled to himself.

"Did it work?" Theo asked.

"No. I don't think so," Allyn said, defeated. "I must have missed something—forgotten an ingredient." And yet, everything seemed to have worked exactly as he expected.

Rosemarie's shout came moments before she ran into the tent excited and out of breath. She was holding the cordless phone up at him as she tried to catch her breath. The goat in the corner surprised her. She gave her dad a quizzical expression. He pointed to the phone and mouthed *Who?*

"Malcolm Robbe is on the phone from New York," Rosemarie said. "That MacDonnell guy believes the prince is in North Carolina. And he's in a lot of danger!"

"Lord have mercy," Allyn whispered.

CHAPTER 28

PINKIE SWEAR

1

Daniel returned from the store to find the house dark and quiet as a crypt. A note from Bev on the counter said she was doing another double shift at the bar. She left a twenty-dollar bill clipped to the note for food.

Daniel could see why Luanne turned out skinny and wild with so little parental guidance and little to eat. He wasn't one to talk since his own alcoholic stepfather was barely in his life except to beat on him, but at least his mother had been home and tried to keep food on the table between dosing up on tranquilizers. Maybe Rita felt she owed her first husband, John Hauer, that much.

The cold weather was settling in, as was dusk, and opportunities to sketch outside would diminish. He decided to do one last sketch—the waning sun would make for great shadows in the forest—a great setting for werewolf stories. Walking into Luanne's bedroom, Daniel froze when he saw his sketch pad on the bed open to the nude he'd done the previous night. This was the pad he hid so that Cody wouldn't find out what was really going on in Luanne's house. He smelled the remnants of cigarette smoke and cheap perfume.

A wave of dread shot through him. *She wouldn't,* he thought. *Luanne can't be that dumb.*

Daniel thought long and hard about what to do next. He appreciated Bev and needed Colby's advice, but staying put in that trailer even for one more day might be the most dangerous thing he'd ever done.

But just because the pad was out and opened to a naked drawing of Luanne doesn't mean anything, he rationalized. As these thoughts crisscrossed his brain, he realized he'd subconsciously been collecting his items from around the house and packing them in his bag. While his conscious mind had been rationalizing about staying there, his subconscious clearly knew what he had to do.

The thought of heading out into the cold night, in the middle of nowhere, was none too appealing. Raleigh was nearby, several miles away, but there were no taxis or buses. The front door slammed.

He peeked out of the bedroom to see Luanne, alone, with several shopping bags. She was decked out in brand-new formfitting clothes, with open-toed leather pumps that showed off manicured toenails, and a new hairstyle. Gone was the wild bramble of wavy blond hair—she'd straightened and combed it and cut it down to just below shoulder length. Her fingernails were long and manicured as well, a bright lacquered red with tiny black Asian characters along the edge. She looked beautiful. From the window, he spied Eljay driving off in a VW Beetle with several store bags in her backseat.

"Danny!" Luanne shouted excitedly. "Come see what I bought!"

Luanne placed the bags on the living room couch. They were from fine stores—Nordstrom, Macy's, and the like. There had to be hundreds of dollars worth of swag here. No way that this was Cody's doing; that cracker was about to have a serious cash flow problem due to an aggressive competitor. And Luanne was broke. So was Eljay for that matter.

"Where'd you get all this?" he asked her.

"The names is right on the bag. Can't you read?"

"How can you afford this?"

"Oooh—look at this sweater!" she said, extracting something pink and as fuzzy as a cat extricated from a clothes dryer.

She was elusive about the source of her newfound wealth. It was her business after all. He didn't know why he was so mad at her for buying all that stuff—Daniel was just a guest and could push only so hard. Something about the shopping spree bugged him though. Luanne had only one asset, her looks, and his suspicions led him down a dark path of the only way he believed she could earn this much money in so short a time span. The thought disgusted him and made him angry as well. He didn't know why he was angry . . . she didn't belong to him.

"Hey, uh . . . I noticed that my drawing pad was on your bed," he said, changing the subject of one source of aggravation to another.

She continued pulling out new clothes and folding them in a pile on the couch arm.

"Yeah. I wanted to show Eljay," she said a little too bubbly. "That neked picture is the best one. Why'd you hide the pad under my bed?"

It was as though someone poured liquid nitrogen into the base of Daniel's brain and down his spine. Was he frozen with fear or anger? Both emotions fought for dominance right now.

"Weren't you right there when your boyfriend threatened to kill me because I drew you with clothes *on*?" The stress on the word "on" was to indicate how much more Cody would want to kill him when he found a picture with her clothes "off." It did not have the desired effect on Luanne—educating her to a serious breach of trust and common sense of . . . well, biblical proportions.

"Don't fret," she said, swatting her hand down like giving a slap on the wrist. "I made her pinkie swear first that she'd keep it secret."

"Oh! You pinkie swore. Well there you have it. I was worried for nothing."

At moments, Luanne dropped her guard and revealed she was not as clueless as most people thought. Yes, she was capable of bad judgment and reckless behavior, but there were times he recognized in her the con of fostering a ditzy persona for the intentional sake of having others underestimate her. Luanne did not make love the way

Daniel imagined stupid people would engage in sex. Not that he'd had a lot of experience, but he'd seen his share of dirty movies, and there was just something about her that didn't add up.

Their intimacy let him see through her spell. This was one of those moments where he picked up a degree of complexity coming from her that belied the obvious—her eyes conveyed a full recognition of his sarcasm, a detailed understanding about his concern, even the seriousness of Cody discovering their affair, capped by a body language that said she did not care to worry about it.

"I didn't tell her nothin' else, Danny," Luanne said in a *you think I'm stupid?* tone of voice.

"Cody *already* suspects something, Luanne. Now there's a picture showing you were sitting naked five feet in front of me for, like, half an hour . . ." He broke off and brushed back his absent hair. Daniel usually forgot he had cut it all off to avoid recognition. He no longer looked or felt like himself anymore. He'd become someone else.

He turned back to face her, then toward the bedroom, then back again to her, unsure of which direction he wanted. Should he just head out the front door or confront her until she saw some common sense. He had a rational argument worked out in his brain, but when he open his mouth, all that came out was, "A damned pinkie swear . . . really?"

Luanne stomped her new shoe on the carpet hard. "Don't get snarky with me, Danny Hauer!" Her southern drawl had intensified. "I bought you new stuff, too."

She jabbed a bag into his chest with a thwap.

"You might want to say 'Thank you, Luanne, for buyin' me nice stuff. Thank you, Luanne, for bein' a friend.'" Her volume increased. "'Thank you, Luanne, for sharin' your sweet cherry pie with me for my first time in my pathetic, lonely, little life!'"

Daniel's temper rose to match hers. She just didn't get it. The girl never thought more than an hour ahead.

"There hasn't been a cherry in your pie for years," he threw back at her. He regretted the insult immediately.

"EEEEEEGH!" she screamed, and threw a shopping bag at his head. She picked up a shoebox and threw that, too, then anything that was close at hand. Nothing she hurled had any aerodynamic quality—Daniel easily sidestepped the items. She closed in on him until she could do him in with her own hands.

Luanne lunged, newly manicured claws out, shining brightly the color of fresh blood. Daniel grabbed her wrists to protect his face, and they weaved back and forth in some sort of primeval puppet dance. He had her arms over her shoulder and began pushing her back. She launched a knee at his crotch, but he instinctively turned his hip and blocked it with his leg. They ran out of room and he slammed her against the trailer wall, pinning her arms back. She was ferociously strong and wailed like an angry wombat. Her feral beauty aroused him, and again the familiar stirring in his loins betrayed his need for clarity at this time. Daniel's eyes must have conveyed his admiration; when she looked into his eyes, something clicked, simultaneously aligning their minds. He leaned into her, his face barely an inch from hers, waiting to see if he read her true. She made to bite him and he pulled away quick, but he knew she would have had him if she was serious. He put his lips on hers, pressing passionately. She kissed back just as fiercely, tasting him. Any thoughts about open window blinds and unlocked doors melted away as they embraced. They slid to the shag carpet locked around each other and commenced their mating dance.

2

It was completely dark when Daniel awoke. He and Luanne lay on the carpet beside the couch, she curled up slightly on top of him with one naked leg wrapped around his and her arm on his chest. The living room was in shambles. Shopping bags and clothes strewn everywhere, seat cushions piled against each other—they had gone at it like animals in heat.

As rational thinking reasserted itself, Daniel realized he couldn't stay. Whether it was a matter of minutes, hours, or days, this thing with Luanne was going to blow up—it was inevitable. Bev's reaction to his having sex with her daughter may not be any less violent than Cody's . . . she kept a loaded twelve-gauge shotgun in the living room closet.

A drizzle began outside, spattering the windows with cold streaks of dew. *Great,* thought Daniel. *Leave tonight and catch pneumonia.*

The TV remote was on the coffee table beside him, so he clicked on the newscast with the volume off to spy the weather forecast. As the meteorologist spoke of cold fronts, rain, and possible snow, something streaming across the news feed banner at the bottom of the screen perked his attention. It had gone by quickly, and he thought it must have been a trick of the light. Bev ran her cable through a DVR that always recorded the channel it was on; he hit the rewind button on the remote and backed up a few seconds. It was not his imagination; he saw his name in the news feed: *$60,000 reward put up by mysterious benefactor for the capture of, or information leading to, father killer Daniel Hauer of Glen Burnie, Maryland.* The station was a local NBC affiliate, so you could be sure other stations were running it as well.

Colby was wrong. Interest in him wasn't going to die on the vine. This money was going to supercharge the search for him. This news would hit an even bigger cycle the next day, maybe even go national. He should have followed his instincts and fled the country while the going was still good. Now every cop and yahoo up to his neck in bills will be gunning for him.

"Shit!" he whispered. Who the heck would put up sixty thousand for him? No one could be that angry Clyde was dead. His stepfather was a loser squared.

Daniel got dressed and finished packing in the dark. He'd already lingered too long. Luanne awoke when he came back into the living room. She sat up, resting her arm on a couch cushion.

"Why are the lights off?" she asked.

"I have to go," Daniel said.

"What?" she said, coming awake. "Wait . . ." She stood up, her beautiful, naked body a study in shadows as the neighbor's porch light across the street cast itself upon her through droplets on the windowpane.

"I have to go," Daniel repeated.

"You can't just leave . . . I mean—it's cold and rainy outside." Luanne sounded dejected, her expression a mix of sad, scared, and pissed off. Daniel couldn't remember the last time someone wanted him to stay around as much as she wanted him to at this moment. He was flattered.

"I don't have a choice," he said. "On the TV just now . . . I'm in danger, and now I'm putting your family in danger."

"So you just fuck me and take off?"

This she cares about? Daniel thought incredulously. Not Cody's finding out about them, not schoolwork or college, or even about next month. *This?*

"I thought you were different," she said. "One of those smart sensitive types. But you're like all the rest . . . you get what you want and you leave."

That stung. And it couldn't be farther from the truth. Daniel was enamored with her. Imperfect as Luanne was, he cared about her. She was etched in his memory for life, no matter where his journeys took him.

"That's not true," he said.

He wanted to tell her what she meant to him, but there wasn't time. He was only going on fourteen but it felt like twenty, and there wasn't enough time to relay two decades worth of hardship. He'd spent so much of his life holding in disappointments and other things—expressing positive emotions didn't come easily. He stuck to his guns. "My life—my life is over. Yours is just starting."

"You're not makin' any sense," she said. He noted her reining in her anger when he said his life was over. It affected her—worried her. She was having one of those rare moments of absolute clarity. Did Luanne actually feel the same way about him? He was two years younger than her—light-years apart in teen hierarchy. He was a toy for her amusement—some passive-aggressive fun to scratch her itch and get back at her asshole boyfriend.

Luanne was on the cusp of tears—a look Daniel recognized because he'd seen it in his own mirror before. It was the look one had when a person was powerless to stop a person of value from leaving their life, prompting views of one's own worthlessness in the scheme of life. Daniel always resented his private pity parties. He'd never been the object of such a response in anyone else. He didn't like it any better from this side.

Luanne needed the truth . . . if only to help her understand how little she had to do with his need to leave.

"The authorities are after me," he explained. "I did something awful in Baltimore . . . that's why Colby hid me here. I thought I was safe, but that's not the case anymore. If the cops find me here, you and your mom would be in big trouble."

"Cops? Danny, what did you do?" she asked, genuinely concerned—sounding like a girlfriend.

The words wouldn't come out. He'd suffered through Katie Millar's rejection of him when he was as clean and wholesome as kids came—now he was dirty . . . a murderer. Luanne's rejection of him inside of the same week would crush whatever there was left of him that kept him going. He realized just that moment, faced with the need to flee, how much Luanne meant to him. Love had been absent through much of his life. His parents didn't care for him, his teachers didn't love him, his best friend betrayed him, and the one girl he would have moved heaven and earth to make happy said she would never feel the same way about him. There was a vast deficit of this elusive emotion in his life, an epic drought of affection. He wasn't a bad person—as human beings went, Daniel thought he was fairly decent compared with others. And yet, no one thought of him the way he wanted to be thought of . . . until Luanne.

Daniel had been smitten with her since before she came into his bed, something he never tried for or imagined could happen. She was completely wrong for him, yet somehow they filled a need in each other. Danny wanted to tell her anything else but the truth . . . make up something less horrendous. He couldn't stand to experience her revulsion over what he'd done. But he couldn't lie to her either.

"I—I killed my stepfather," he said.

She sucked in her breath. "Oh, my God."

"He was abusing me—tried to kill me. I fought back—and now he's dead."

Luanne's eyes widened, reflecting the trickle of light in the dark room. *What is she thinking?* he wondered. *Fear? That she took a murderer into her bed?*

Luanne was stuck, her pouty mouth opened, probing her thoughts as she gazed into him to confirm his confession. He fought back tears, but his eyes welled up anyway, confessing his shame—revealing his burden. Luanne approached and placed her hand on his chest. His heart pulsed against her warm palm and perfectly manicured nails. Luanne put her arms around Daniel, pressed her naked flesh against him, and gave him a powerful hug. She kissed him tenderly on the cheek and neck. His tears fell, streaking his cheek before landing on his lover's shoulders. And he knew that against all the odds in the world, Luanne cared about him.

"I wasn't supposed to have feelin's for you," she said. "It was just a job. I don't know how it happened."

"Huh?"

"You need to run," she told him, wiping tears from her eyes. "Away from here . . . from Uncle Cole, too."

"Huh?"

"He paid mama to take you in. He paid me to keep an eye on you." She looked at her shopping bags, finally answering his question about the money. She found her purse in the mess and pulled a roll of money out. She stuffed it into Daniel's jean pocket.

"Colby's broke," Daniel said, confused. "A transient I ran into in the Baltimore bus station . . . randomly."

"He's a private detective in New York," Luanne corrected. "Smart as the devil, too. Mama said he had a run of bad luck with the law up north. Can't be broke, though, 'cause he gave me three thousand dollars to make you stay put. Said you were in trouble—that people after you were worse than the police. He might be on your side or workin' a reward angle to get in good with someone. Who knows with Uncle Cole? Danny, you can't trust *anyone*."

Daniel tried to process this new information, but had trouble getting it down. He wasn't anyone of note before killing Clyde—just a regular school kid. Why would he be on anyone's hit list? No one had even heard of Clyde's death when he was at the bus station in Maryland. Why was he on some New York detective's radar?

Headlights momentarily illuminated the room as a car turned the corner. It came to a halt outside Luanne's front door, horn blaring. Cody, his lackeys, and Eljay spilled out of the DeVille like clowns from a circus car.

"LUANNE!" bellowed Cody from outside. "Send that piece of shit artist out now and get your white trash ass out here, too!"

"Jig's up," Daniel said.

"I can't believe she told!" Luanne said. "We pinkie swore!"

"Water under the bridge," Daniel said, zipping up his jacket and throwing his pack on. He wanted to ask her to come with him, but she was already in enough trouble. Once the authorities realized he'd stayed there, they'd drag her and Bev to the station for questioning. Before tonight, Luanne and Bev could claim they didn't know. Going forward, though, it's aiding and abetting.

"Is Cody going to hurt you?" Daniel asked.

"Cody? If that meathead ever tried, my mother would rip his nuts out. Brooklyn Bev don't put up with that shit. Go out the back. I'll hold him off in front with mama's shotgun—make him think you're hidin' under the bed for a while."

That was not the kind of image Daniel wanted to leave people with, but beggars couldn't be choosers. She kissed him one last time; his hand brushed her nipple softly and he felt it stiffen. She smiled. He mustered his last remaining will to pull away, and exited by the rear deck.

CHAPTER 29

I'LL TAKE CRAZY-ASS MESSENGER OF GOD FOR $300

Daniel shut the sliding door behind him softly. A cold, light rain fell intermittently. The backyard was pitch black, unlike the front, which had porch lights. He quietly maneuvered the slick creaky wooden steps and stopped at the edge of the trailer. Cody continued shouting out front. Footsteps approached his position from around the corner. Daniel guessed he had about a second before the person's eyes adjusted to the total darkness in the back. He crouched low below the sight line and hoped it wasn't the really big redhead or Eljay because he wasn't comfortable hitting giants and or girls.

Luck was with him . . . it was greasy Weasel. Weasel turned the corner, and walked past Daniel, but then stopped, just making him out in the darkness. He was about to shout to his crew, but Daniel used the surprise advantage to launch his fist into Weasel's larynx before the kid could even get his hands up in defense. Weasel made a gasping sound, like someone choking on a chicken bone. He gasped, unable to draw air or shout for help, staggered a bit, and fell to his knees near the deck. Daniel drove Weasel's head into the deck with a straight kick to his temple. The toady slumped to the ground motionless. Out front, Luanne was screaming at Cody to go to hell or she'd blow his nut sack off.

Was it just him, or did Luanne channel a lot of her anger toward testicles?

Neighbors came out onto their porches, turning on extra lights in front. Daniel crossed the alley between Luanne's trailer and their neighbor, and kept a steady pace along the dark backyards until he could get back on the street and head for the general store. He needed beef jerky, a poncho, water, and a flashlight. Five minutes tops and then he'd hoof it all the way to Raleigh if he couldn't pick up a hitch. Probably better to walk anyway with the reward on him.

He was making good time on the graveled lane and about to turn left to head for the store when he heard familiar voices around the corner. He scooted behind the nearest home on the left and then made a right behind it in an L-shaped approach to the voices under cover of darkness. Some bushes on the side of the next house provided good cover. It was McCoy and his crew lit by the laptop light of the computer geek working on the hood of the truck.

"Hurry up," McCoy said.

"It would help if we knew the bitch's last name," the geek said.

"You sure it's him," said one of the other guys.

"Positive," said the computer geek. "Picture's all over the Internet. Payin' sixty grand for information leadin' to his capture. And he's in Cody's girlfriend's house."

"Hell with information," said McCoy. "Too easy for other folk to get in on the action, probably have to fight it out with the cop that drags him in. We sack the little fucker ourselves, walk into the station, we don't split the money with no one. No debate that it's our reward."

In the midst of the entire world ganging up on him, Daniel took most umbrage over being called "little." Sure, he was wiry—but five foot five was actually respectable for someone about to turn fourteen. He still had a few more years to grow . . . assuming a coalition of North Carolina's meth dealers didn't gun him down. A shotgun blast went off in the direction of Bev's home.

Luanne! Daniel wanted to go back and check on her.

Luanne's voice echoed across the trailer park. "You try to come in again, Cody, and I will blow you off the porch!"

No mention of testicles this time. She was growing as a person. More people were coming out of their homes now to check on the hubbub. In the cities, people ran away from gunfire; here they were all curious and in everyone else's business. McCoy's crew anxiously piled into the Escalade and took off like a shot past all the other people, heading toward the commotion. If he ever saw Luanne again, Daniel would plant the biggest kiss he could muster on his feral southern belle. One thing he was glad to have done while here was breaking up her and that meth dealer. Hopefully, she'll find a decent guy on the next round.

Daniel headed up the street toward Jeb's. The counter guy came out and asked if he heard a gunshot.

"Yep. There's some crazy business going on back at Bev's place," Daniel said.

The counter guy called it in to the police on his two-way radio and then asked Daniel if he'd watch the store for a sec because he was also the security guard for the park and had to run out to see what the problem was. Daniel agreed and stocked up on jerky, processed cold cuts, bread, bottles of water, a dark green poncho, and extra batteries for the flashlight. It was about thirty bucks worth of stuff. He pulled the roll Luanne had given him and found fifties and hundreds.

"Jeezus," he whispered. "Colby must be stacked." He put the money on the counter and left.

The rain graduated from a drizzle and came down more consistently. The front gate, only twenty yards away, was open. Right or left? he wondered. Which way was Raleigh?

A station wagon pulled up on the main road by the entrance and stopped. It made a right into the trailer park's driveway and rolled past him and about thirty feet, then stopped. It waited there for a moment, idling, then made a U-turn. Daniel moved over to the right to let the car through, thinking the man was probably lost, when it stopped beside him.

The guy probably just wanted directions, in which case Daniel would finagle a ride, but he balanced on the front balls of his feet ready to run just in case. The steamy passenger-side window rolled down. Daniel bent down to look in.

The driver was alone—a wiry black man with short-cropped salt-and-pepper hair, probably in his forties, wearing a dark blue shirt with a clerical collar under a raincoat. He held a small wooden salad bowl in his hand filled with water. The driver looked at something floating in the bowl, then back at Daniel. He had deep soulful eyes, like a bloodhound. He stared at Daniel with an incredulous expression like he knew the boy.

What a weird day, thought Daniel.

"Excuse me, son," the man said in a soothing baritone. "Where am I?"

"Trailer park on Country Road Five-eighty-one, near State Road Sixty-four."

"I see." The man looked Daniel up and down, saw the backpack and asked, "Do you need a ride?"

Daniel did need a ride, but it was odd how quickly this guy was willing to offer one without knowing a thing about him. For all the padre knew, Daniel could be a murderer on the lam from the police. After the situation with Colby, Daniel was more wary of coincidences. Something about this guy seemed too eager. If he didn't know any better, Daniel would swear that the guy had come looking for him.

"Thanks, mister, but I'm good," Daniel lied.

"It's Reverend . . . Reverend Grey." He put the bowl down between the two front seats and placed a Tupperware cover on it. "Catch your death walking in this cold drizzle."

Catch my death getting in the wrong car, the boy thought. "Look, Rev, I appreciate the offer, but you don't want to get involved with me. Really, I'm doing you a favor."

"I see," the man said.

The minister looked ahead as if to drive off, but not seeming to have a destination. He looked down at his hands the way one does when something important is stolen from you and you're wondering if you can rebuild or replace it. The car didn't move—Daniel wasn't the betting kind, but he'd put money on it mattering to the reverend whether he got into the station wagon or not. Maybe the man was legit and had a thing about helping runaways. But those types always worked closely with the police.

The reverend got out of the car, leaving it running, and put up a big black umbrella. He walked around the front and stopped before Daniel. The umbrella was large enough for both of them but Reverend Grey respected Daniel's personal space and left him just outside its shelter. The minister looked up and down the street, as though one of the trailers in the park had his next words painted on their sides. He pursed his lips and turned to look right at Daniel.

"I've been a man of God here for thirteen years," he began. He let that statement sink into the boy. "And I don't think in all that time He's given me a clearer sign of His intention than the one that led me to you, Daniel."

Daniel took a step back. "How'd you know my name?"

"That is not your name," the reverend said confidently. "Your parents named you Danel, after your paternal great-grandfather; your real parents, not the adopted ones."

"My . . . my what . . . ?"

Weird took a huge lunge into *The Twilight Zone*.

"There are some very bad people in the world, son. And they're after you. And there are some very good people in the world as well . . . and they are looking for you. You think you've been on the run since you fled Baltimore—but it's been much longer than that. You've been on the run your entire life, under assault and constant threat for years. It started far, far away from here, farther than you could ever imagine. The most important decisions you have to make in your entire life will take place in the next few hours . . . maybe sooner. And it boils down to whether you can tell friend from foe. There will be no second chances."

"Who the heck are you, mister?"

Every instinct told Daniel to run, but he was cemented to that spot by this man's crazy talk. He was sincere, that much Daniel believed, but also a crackpot. Escapee from a mental ward.

"God brought me to you. He brought you to where I could save you. What other reason can there be that in all the world you would come to my doorstep—my little corner of the world. I tried to deny my debt to you . . . to stay out of the fight for the sake of my wife and daughter, but I could not turn my back on this sign.

"Were I in your position, I would not believe me either. I'm telling you this anyway, even though you'll think I am a crazy old fool—a stranger talking nonsense. But I have told you the truth Daniel Hauer. My life is also in danger now, and I am putting my faith in God. You are a lost lamb in need of shelter and I am His Shepherd. I am trusting in His purpose for us . . . that by some miracle you will believe me, and let me protect you."

The rain must have been flying sideways around the reverend's umbrella; his cheeks were dripping. Daniel was cold and getting wetter by the moment. The heat coming out the passenger window appealed to him, but he couldn't possibly go off with this crazy person. People he'd never met kept coming out of nowhere with their own agendas for him. Why was a skinny kid from Baltimore on so many adult peoples' radars? What the hell was going on?

"How do you even know I'm the right person?" Daniel asked. "I'm walking in the rain in the middle of nowhere."

The reverend smiled. "You have a birthmark in the shape of a bird on your shoulder."

Daniel's mouth dropped. But then he thought . . . that might be on the police blotter from his examination at the hospital a few days ago. He was utterly confused and wished for one of the reverend's handy dandy signs for himself.

"I know your mother, Sophia," Reverend Grey said. "You have her eyes."

No way. No way, no way, no way! This is crazy. Even John and Rita Hauer didn't know Daniel's birth mother.

"I can see you're of two minds, Daniel. I will not force you. I will stand by you, whatever your decision, whatever the danger to me." He pulled out a business card and handed it to Daniel. "Should we become separated, that is my church. My home is next door. My daughter would be very excited to meet you." He smiled when he said that as though in on a private joke.

"If at some point you decide to trust me, I will give you shelter. I can put you in touch with those who want to protect you." The reverend returned to his car and got behind the wheel. He looked as uncertain of leaving Daniel as the boy felt about going with the man. The man had no intention of forcing Daniel to do anything.

From the back of the trailer park came gunfire and hollering in the night air. Revved-up engines and churned gravel grew louder as the vehicles came back toward the store. Down the county road, a pair of headlights with flashers approached. Daniel had to make a decision. The hoodlums and the cops were all heading right to the spot he stood on. But this preacher was nuts. Daniel could be jumping into the proverbial fire. Maybe the cops could detain the meth dealers while he hoofed it through a lettuce field.

A sheriff's car pulled in and stopped in front of Jeb's store across from them. The deputy talked to someone on his radio, and then got out with his walkie-talkie.

"The commotions all the way in the back of the park," Daniel told the cop, pointing in the direction of Bev's house.

The deputy said into his walkie-talkie, "Confirmed. Send backup." He pulled his weapon from its holster and pointed it at Daniel. "Sir, stay in your vehicle!" he told Reverend Grey, never taking his eyes off the boy. "Daniel Hauer, you are under arrest! Hands on the hood! Now!"

The jig was up. He should have hid when he had the chance . . . he should have run. Daniel underestimated the speed with which the reward on him would spread. Someone in the park had ratted him out. Once he was on the news, he knew it would only be a matter of time. Daniel placed his hands on the reverend's car. The heat from the engine felt good. A second car with New York plates pulled into the driveway, but with the cop in the middle of the street, there wasn't room to pass. It parked behind the cruiser. Three men emerged. The driver was tall, like a stockbroker on holiday with close-cropped quaff, square jaw, and wearing a Land's End jacket and slacks. On the passenger side surfaced a shorter, stocky man in an ill-fitting tux, black with gray pinstripe pants and a bowler hat on a nest of black hair. His teeth were yellow and mangled and he wore cloth gloves with the tips cut off revealing the thick fingertips of a lifelong smoker. Out of the rear driver's side appeared a giant—like a reject from a *Heavy Metal* story—seven feet tall with long, black rocker hair, arms like tree trunks that seemed too long for his body, a flat nose and fat bottom lip that protruded farther than the top one. He wore only a white T-shirt and jeans, unperturbed by the cold and rain.

"Boy," the bowler man called out, ignoring the cop between them. "You Daniel Hauer?"

Something in the man's tone sent shivers through Daniel. Juxtaposing this crew and the preacher, Daniel suddenly found his ability to tell friend from foe.

"This is a police matter!" the cop shouted to the new arrivals. "Stay back!"

Around the corner spun McCoy's Escalade and Cody's DeVille and both screeched to a stop before the scene. The rain was coming down harder now. All the vehicles' headlights lit up the makeshift ring before them like a movie set. The usual suspects as well as the guy running Jeb's store poured out of the new arrivals. Luanne was nowhere in sight, thank God. A fourth man that only Daniel noticed quietly emerged from the rear passenger side of the New York sedan.

Colby!

The giant moved toward the deputy, who was too distracted by the arrival of Cody and McCoy's gangs to notice.

"I want everybody to move back from this area NOW!" the deputy yelled at the top of his lungs.

Colby was silently mouthing something at Daniel. *Rug? Rut? Rum . . . ?*

The deputy realized too late . . . the giant placed one hand on his head and the other on his shoulder and twisted like a bottle top until his neck cracked. The cop fell into the mud.

Oh, Daniel realized . . . Colby was saying *RUN!*

"I think I'd like to meet your daughter now," Daniel said, throwing his bag through the open passenger-side window and diving in after it faster than he could say *buh-bye*.

Reverend Grey didn't miss a beat. He threw the car into gear and peeled out of the trailer park, leaving barely an inch between his door and the cruiser, with Daniel's feet still dangling out the window. Gunshots hit the old station wagon as they turned onto the country road.

Daniel managed to right himself and get his seatbelt on. The reverend flew down the road like a bat out of hell. The minister wore a wild, fearful expression customary for a man who probably spent most of his day writing sermons and whose most excitement came from bingo night. Behind them, Daniel heard the screeching of tires as three sets of headlights peeled out of the trailer park and pursued them.

"Really can't wait to meet your girl, padre," the boy repeated shakily. "Please drive really fast."

CHAPTER 30

FOOL'S ERRAND

The bandages around Tory's eyes were soaked through with blood. Catherine unwrapped them gingerly. Not that it would have made any difference—Tory wasn't all there anymore—he'd checked out right after Dorn's horrendous act, when the fuel for his screams exhausted itself and he realized no quantity of crying would ever bring the light back. At least they provided Cat with a bucket of ice from the wetbar, which she put to good use. She even gave the boy a few shots of Macallan 12 to deal with the pain—both physical and otherwise.

Tory slept in short restless fits, whimpering every time he awoke. Cat's heart broke for him each time as Tory's anguish confirmed that the new darkness was not a horrible dream—a nightmare to be washed away by the dawn. Paralyzed and *blind* was the new normal. Tory slept constantly because reality had become unbearable. Cat spoke to him softly and often, exercising the one major sense he had left with which to connect to the world. The communication was one-way; Tory hadn't uttered a comprehensible word in hours, and Cat was worried he may have had a stroke, but there was no way to tell.

She encouraged him to sleep. The loss of sight would be a life-altering tragedy for any full-bodied person. To a quadriplegic, someone who lived vicariously through his visual senses, experienced the world through the acts of others—the only recourse left in blindness was the cinema of his mind. This boy only had his dreams left to live through. Cat could not imagine the depths of Tory's despair.

Dorn had threatened to next make the boy deaf if there was no progress on finding the prince. What would that drive Dretch to do? She was worried for her husband in a way she hadn't been before. Cat knew, as only a fellow parent could, to what lengths a person would go to save their child. Her capture also put Cal in an impossible position. Dorn would leverage her to get the prince if Cal claimed him first.

Her husband was at a terrible disadvantage. Cat wasn't confident that Cal could swap the boy for her. He'd been obsessed with the prince since his memories returned. The prince had displaced Cat and Bree as Callum's topmost priority. But Cat couldn't really blame him—if Daniel were not a prince, just a regular kid, Cal would not trade his life for Cat's anyway . . . and she would never want to be responsible for a child's death. But she resented the situation nevertheless. She was mad at Cal for events not of his doing. Her husband was a top agent in an alternate universe's Secret Service, willing to throw himself on an assassin's bomb to save a stranger instead of living to take care of his own family . . . and then there was the other woman.

If Cat was unreasonably angry with Callum for events not of his doing, she was doubly so for the events he had full control of, namely, not revealing that he had been betrothed in his other life. What was the difference between an engagement and a betrothal? she asked herself. The latter sounded a lot more serious—something permanent that involved serious penalties.

For the first time in her marriage, Cat felt vulnerable. Until a few days ago, she had been secure in Cal's loyalty to her regardless of what the world threw at them. Cal was as emotionally solid and mature as men came. His mission to raise the prince was about duty and honor—she understood that part of him—she accepted it when they exchanged vows. Now there was this "betrothal" to a woman Cal could not even bring himself to mention. He never would have abandoned Chryslantha had he not lost his memory. Catherine Hill had been an accident—a sidebar to his picture-perfect Brad and Angelina existence in a magical far-off land where people curtsied to him and called him "lord." Cat hated that tiny voice in her head telling her Cal's life would be easier now if she ceased to exist. This situation had to be a nightmare for her loyal, truthful, honorable man. She loved him so much that it hurt Cat to know her existence in his life caused him any pain or complication. Between the prince, his duties, and his betrothal to Chryslantha, Cat felt expendable. And that was unfair to her . . . she'd done everything right.

She had to get out. As much for basic survival and the desire not to be used as leverage against her husband as to satisfy the nagging urge to punch Cal in the nose—and that wasn't going to happen from this sorry room. She finished wrapping Tory's new bandages and looked around, wishing for some secret door into existence. If she could just get to the street, get to a cop, she could return for Tory and the other woman on the couch. They were in an opulent hotel in the middle of the city. The phone had been removed from the room. Above and below her were other patrons of the Plaza. There wasn't anything to start a fire with, and truly, such a thing did not guarantee her survival. Dorn might just let her and the hotel burn. She thought of screaming out the window, but they were high up and facing north toward the park. She'd only succeed in getting gagged. She could smash the window, but it occurred to Cat she might only succeed in getting whoever came to rescue her killed. Dorn was a sorcerer.

Maybe . . .

Cat went into the bathroom and plugged the bathtub drain. She shoved a hand towel into the overflow hole and ran both the hot and cold water full blast. If she could flood the room the water would drip into the units below, they'd send maintenance and security to Dorn's suite. Maybe she could get a message out to them or create an opening for herself. Cat didn't know how effective that would be, but any disruption might offer an opportunity to run. She heard the bedroom door creak open. Footsteps approached the bathroom and Oulfsan walked in and joined her.

"I thought I'd take a bath to calm my nerves," Cat said. She silently cursed herself for sounding guilty. The tub was past its halfway point, and she needed him to leave before it topped off.

Oulfsan looked at the tub and back at Cat. Despite his formal dress, his manner was seamy, sordid. He hunched, as though uncomfortable with his height, and moved uncomfortably, as though he wore an ill-fitting suit. Cat waited for his exit.

Oulfsan put down the toilet's lid and sat.

"I'd like some privacy," she insisted, eyeing the water level.

He leered at her. He went so far as to smack his lips. She felt naked before him, fully dressed. Oulfsan jerked his head toward the tub as if to say, *go ahead*—but remained on the toilet. Cat turned the water off, lest her true intentions come to light.

"I'm not going to bathe with an audience," she told him.

"In Aandor, the common folk bathe once a week," he said. His voice was a smooth pleasant tenor, but his speech was guttural, his vernacular lowbrow compared with the other times she'd heard him speak. "Rich folk can have their flowery maidens. I like me a greasy wench . . . musky snatch, the salty tang of their—"

"Please," Cat said, holding up her hand. "Why stay then if you like the dirt? I'll only end up clean in the end."

"I'm studying me canvas," he answered.

Paint with your blood, is what Cat heard in his subtext. His tone was cold, demented—he reeked of ultraviolence. "Does Dorn know you're in here?" Cat asked.

"His lordship's in a pleasant mood. Our suspicions about the detective have borne fruit. He's hidden the boy, and our men now descend upon the prince as we speak. Hesz's return from Baltimore with the prince's personal effects is now irrelevant. You see the justice in our having blinded Dretch's brat now."

"Justice? You mutilated an innocent boy!" Cat shouted. "What does he have to do with your war?"

"In Farrenheil the sins of the father are visited upon the sons. The hunt will soon be over—Captain MacDonnell will have nothing of value to bargain for your return."

Cat stormed out of the bathroom afraid that Oulfsan would grab her as she passed. She caught a different fright once in the bedroom, a familiar voice in conversation through the partly open French doors. She marched up to them and threw them open.

"YOU!" she said.

A mildly surprised Balzac Cruz gave her a courteous nod.

"Lady MacDonnell. I hope you are well."

Catherine let fly the right hook she had cocked for her husband, catching the side of Balzac's ample nose. Balzac stumbled but recovered before falling down entirely. His nose was a red splatter. She immediately regretted the punch, shaking her hand to diffuse the pain. He whipped a handkerchief from his jacket and pressed it to his injury. Oulfsan standing behind her laughed, as did Kraten, Lhars, and the recently returned Hesz in the common room. It was a stupid act, but Catherine was satisfied at having wiped the smug look off Balzac's traitorous face. Balzac pushed Catherine back into her gilded cell, joining Oulfsan, and shut the French doors behind him.

"A peasant's reaction from an overly common woman," he said, trying to regain his pride.

"This coming from a clown." Cat spat back. She checked on Tory. He was asleep again.

"Jester," Balzac corrected. "A clown works in circuses and birthday parties. A jester performs for the benefit of a ruler at court. He's witty and knowledgeable, makes the politically incorrect quips his king cannot say in public—and he is plugged in to *everything* at court."

"You sold out your kingdom for a sack of gold," Cat said. "How original."

Balzac looked genuinely offended.

"Ball Sack is the richest man in Aandor," Oulfsan interjected through a seedy grin.

Balzac conveyed his displeasure at Oulfsan by ignoring him. But was it the play on his name or the revelation of his wealth that the jester objected to?

"Farrenheil would have attacked eventually," Balzac said. "It would have taken them a few more years to muster the coin for twenty thousand soldiers, and they would have squandered it in pointless battles along the fringes of their kingdoms. I supplied the coin for ships, food, and siege weapons, for spies and alliances to force other kingdoms' neutralities. It was simply a push out the door."

"How can you work with these people . . . murderers, sadists . . . ?"

"Spare me," he said in dramatic fashion. Balzac checked the flow from his nose, and satisfied with its progress, dumped the handkerchief in the trash bin. He turned back to Cat. "By the tender age of twenty-one, Callum MacDonnell—as his men boasted, for we know the virtuous captain would never do such a thing—had killed over a hundred adversaries in battle. Did *his* victims not have mothers, fathers, wives, sons . . . pets, who would miss them? Aandor is the Middle Ages . . . death is arbitrary, political; your husband, noble and good as he professes to be, is a virtual killing machine with sword in hand. The status quo's instrument of power retention."

Cat was shocked to hear anyone speak of her husband in that way. Cal had never killed anyone while on the force. He was truthful and lawful and the only time he'd bent a rule was to preserve life, shooting someone in the leg instead of the chest, which is where the academy trains you to aim.

"He—he . . . plays by . . ."

"The rules? But that, my dear, is the point. Does society make the man or the man the society? Your husband is no less a murderer for the people he killed in an alternate universe. It's just that his skills are not as appreciated here. Not unless Mayor Bloomberg sends him to Hoboken to cut the mayor's throat over a bridge-and-tunnel dispute."

"Just a fucking comedian," Cat said.

Balzac laughed until the sharp pain in his nose stifled him. He went to the wetbar and plunked some ice into a doily that he wrapped up and placed on his nose.

"Why? What's it all for?" she asked.

"All revolutionaries are fools," Balzac said. "And all fools revolutionary. Reunification is a step backwards. I originally hail from Teulada, a small kingdom of modest means and great passions. We had, on occasion, experimented with the idea of the republic as the means by which to govern ourselves, but each time it failed against the pressure from the other kingdoms that would ply men and gold against our success and place on the throne yet another despot with the right lineage. It's one bloody family running the whole continent after all, you see, and if a nation showed that it did not need kings and aristocracy to be prosperous, it would inspire revolutionaries across the continent to get rid of this family. All of this posturing to get the prince back . . . the wealth spent, the wars, the bickering, the destruction, the lives ruined . . . it's all bad for business. How can you build an enterprise when it could all be coopted or burned to the ground over the whims of an inbred egomaniac?"

"Heh," grunted Oulfsan, seeing the humor. "He set a continent to the torch to save it from being burned to the ground. And he did it with bells jingling on his head." It came out of Oulfsan's mouth *En' 'eee di' i' wit' belz jinglin' owoo o' 'iz 'ed.*

"No one ever suspects the fool," Balzac said. "How do you think I came to be in this party of guardians? I have access to the inner sanctums . . . I attend meetings, yet no one notices me. No one suspects that my mind is as sharp as any general's or as ruthless as any king's. I'm the perfect shadow in a lighted room. I know when there's about to be war, peace, scandal, treaties, colonization, annexing, power marriages, coups. All my businesses have royal warrants, which is to say I pay protection money to the royal mafia and I get the top contracts. I own taverns, brothels, ships, warehouses, and shops throughout the twelve kingdoms. I run a protection service for trade routes. I am the triple agent who navigates his interests safely through the rocky waters of these mewling despots and their breeding programs."

"Does Dorn know?" Cat said.

"Dorn could not care less. His family has myopic vision. They're happy to end a rival's claim to the emperor's throne and perpetuate their power base for another generation. The war was inevitable . . . I simply accelerated it. I'm a means to an end."

"I don't believe you. I don't think you're here on purpose. I think you were running for your life in the castle just like the rest of them."

"There's risk in everything," Balzac said somberly.

Cat had hit it on the head. Balzac had misjudged the situation—he hadn't anticipated the attack on the prince's naming day . . . that they would reach the capital. She let out a contemptible snort.

"Ball Sack Cruz, super genius," she said.

"I was out of my depth, but I made it here," he said, throwing his arms out to take in the room and the world beyond it. "All's well that ends well."

"Get me out of here," Cat pleaded. "You want to be a revolutionary . . . show some compassion for me, for my family. You've met my daughter . . . she needs her mother."

"We're all pawns, Lady MacDonnell. I have nothing personal against your family. You certainly did not deserve this. You are no gold-digging aristocratic tart breeding her way to the throne. You married a policeman. It mattered little to me whether you and your daughter returned to Aandor with your husband. You'd probably have been killed there within a fortnight. The whole kingdom is overrun with enemy soldiers."

"I'll take my chances," she said.

"But you've seen too much . . . connected too many of the dots. No, it's better that you remain here. Better that you never speak to your husband again."

Catherine's blood turned to ice. "I'm—under Dorn's protection," she said.

"The prince is in his grasp. You no longer matter."

She struggled for words, for the argument that would save her. In desperation she found the leverage to move words that had wedged in her throat since this entire escapade began. "I'm a . . . I'm a noble."

"Exactly," he said.

"But—codes of conduct . . ."

"Are merely guidelines until someone decides they don't need you anymore."

"Oulfsan," she pleaded, turning to him. "You can't . . ."

"This is not Oulfsan, my dear," explained Balzac. "He and Krebe are soul swappers. Unbeknownst to his brother or Dorn, Krebe has been looking after my interests for years. I throw him a little morsel now and then to practice his art on—the price of retaining good help in troubled times."

"Dorn won't like it."

"He'll just say you tried to escape."

"She tried floodin' the bath before you showed," Oulfsan/Krebe said. "We'll start there."

Balzac left with no farewells, conveying his distaste for Krebe's methods. *Effete little asshole,* Cat thought.

Oulfsan/Krebe grabbed Cat by her hair and dragged her into the bathroom. She was in shock. Instinctively, she punched and kicked, but Oulfsan was solid muscle under his tux. He shut the bathroom door. She finally found the wherewithal to scream, but he shoved her head underwater and kept her down until her lungs ached. Then he yanked her out and laughed in her face with wild eyes. He drank in her terror like a sweet wine quenching his long thirst. She sucked several big gulps of air.

"Like to play with water, governess?" he taunted. He shoved her head back into the tub, pushing down until Cat's cheek was pressed against the porcelain bottom. His strength was uncanny, like a rhino lying atop her. She reflexively breathed in water. It burned her lungs. She flailed with her last strength. *This is it,* she thought. He pulled her out again, laughing uncontrollably. She struggled to catch her breath, coughing, trying to convince her lungs she was no longer under the water.

Suddenly, Oulfsan/Krebe made a face as though something with too many legs was crawling under his shirt. A far-off gaze descended on him; he let go of her and slumped back against the toilet.

"The pull," he said, hoarsely. "Spoil the fu . . ."

His gaze went blank; it reset a moment later. Oulfsan looked about, wondering why he was sopping wet and on the bathroom floor.

Cat reached out to him, struggling to find her wind against the weight in her chest, the rawness of throat. "Your brother tried . . ." She fell into a coughing fit.

Oulfsan shot up; ignoring her, he ran from the room toward the suite's common area. "The prince is trapped!" he shouted. "On a farm in North Carolina . . . we have him!"

CHAPTER 31

CAPTAIN AMERICA

1

Callum pushed the Explorer to crazy velocities beyond the speed limit. He was determined to make up the difference since the rest stop, "lest the beacon mysteriously stop working," he told Seth, who knew what the cop really meant was *in case you screw up again and lose it*. The wisps of energy deviated from the highway at Route 64 near Nashville, North Carolina, and then again on a country road that brought them to within a few miles northeast of Raleigh. Seth suspected only a mile separated them from Dorn's car. A mile might as well be a hundred if Dorn's men got to the prince first. It takes less than two seconds to run a knife across a throat.

Malcolm said he'd convinced Allyn Grey to take a ride out to where the boy supposedly was. The prelate was no warrior, but Cal hoped the minister could reach the prince before Dorn's men, and disappear with the kid. Mal tried hard to convince them the pick up would be easy as pie, but something about Mal's emphasis gave away the good cleric's reluctance to become entangled in this affair. Cal didn't believe the preacher was as reliable as they needed him to be.

Cal had become unbearably intense. He refused to talk unless it was to ask Seth whether he could still see the trail. It burned the cop to have to depend on him. Nothing Seth had done so far on the trip swayed Cal from the opinion that he was incompetent, useless, and probably evil. In a way, Seth respected Cal's unfaltering single-mindedness—his ability to know what he knows and the inflexible manner with which he resisted change. That single-mindedness is what got them within arm's reach of the prince.

Eight hazy headlights emerged from the inky blackness ahead of them. They grew brighter quickly and zipped by; the first one, a station wagon, passed them at over eighty miles an hour. *Crazy way to drive in the rain,* Seth thought, ascribing the behavior to the customs of country folk. The second car, clearly in pursuit of the first, glowed brighter, with tendrils of energy dancing upon its roof giving it the appearance of a ghostly jester's cap. It sped past, as did the two vehicles right behind it.

"Turn around," Seth said.

"What?" asked Cal.

"That second car . . . It's Dretch. They're all pursuing that first car. One guess who . . ."

Cal slammed the brakes and in a crazy police-academy maneuver, pulled a bootleg turn on the slick road, switching the direction of the Ford Explorer 180 degrees. He had it back in drive and pedal to the floor before their backward motion even stopped.

This was it—contact with the bad guys. Seth had never been much of a fighter, and with three carloads full of hostiles ahead of them, they were extremely outnumbered. And yet, Cal rushed forward without blinking an eye. He would literally die trying to defend the prince with no thought of his wife and daughter in New York.

The convoy's lights were in sight, headed up a slight grade in the road that allowed Seth full view of the chase. Dretch's car overtook them and smashed into the rear of the station wagon. When that failed, it pulled up beside the wagon and smashed into it from the side. The wagon almost went off the road, but righted itself.

Cal threw all the power of the Explorer's V8 into catching up with the rest. The vehicle they came across first was a black Cadillac SUV.

"I don't suppose you figured out how to shoot lightning from your stick yet?" Cal asked Seth.

"Uh . . . no. Still on training wheels."

"Didn't think so." Cal pulled up beside the SUV, and once lined up with the driver, swerved into the truck. The other car, completely taken by surprise, ended up in a ditch on the edge of a farm.

"One down," whispered Seth.

The repeated attempts to push the station wagon from the road resulted in it suddenly pulling off to the right and onto a service road. Its red taillights blinked and were eventually swallowed up by the darkness as trees and brush hid it from view.

Dretch's LeBaron went several yards past the turnoff, did its own bootleg swing, and followed the wagon up the trail. The next car around that turn was the old Cadillac DeVille followed by Seth and Cal. The dirt road was thin, muddy, and made for a bumpy ride. Not too far ahead, the DeVille, with its rear-wheel drive, had become stuck in the mud. The way past them was a tight squeeze; Cal pulled around them cautiously. Four young locals gave them the finger and shouted obscenities as they drove by.

"It's like a fucking Blake Edwards movie," Seth said. "What the heck did that kid get into down here?"

The road ended at a dairy farm. They saw the headlights of the station wagon and the LeBaron ahead reflecting off the side of a massive red barn. The cars sat abandoned in a large muddy circular yard before the barn, the station wagon's doors were open to the elements. To the right was an open garage with a Jay-Lor feed mixer and other tractor attachments against the wall. To the left was a massive shed connected to the barn by an enclosed passageway. All the buildings were dark. The only sounds were the wind and patter of raindrops on wood, metal, and mud.

"Which way?" asked Seth.

"Don't you know?" asked Cal, pointing to the staff.

Seth tapped it on the ground, but nothing happened. In the excitement of the chase, he'd lost hold of the spell and lost the signal.

"Nothing," Seth said.

"Take the shed on the left. I'll take the garage."

Seth was afraid Cal would say that.

2

Reverend Grey couldn't help wonder how it had come to this. Despite his efforts to stay out of the fray, he was now in possession of the prince of Aandor with half the county's meth dealers and a contingent of Lord Dorn's thugs gunning for them. Allyn was never an athletic man; his heart threatened to burst from his chest with all this activity.

The barn housed over fifty cows. He and Daniel had found a dark niche to hold up in crouched behind a large contingent of Jerseys. The enemy was out there somewhere—at least one carload of pursuers that Allyn knew of. *Why am I here?* he thought. His plan was to completely avoid this conflict. Why was he about to die?

After Rosemarie conveyed the location of the prince back at the henge, Allyn had a revelation of sorts . . . of all the places in the world for the prince of Aandor to end up—that Daniel should be in North Carolina, upon his very doorstep, was a sign from above. This burden was practically handed to him on a platter by biblical standards.

Free will being the Lord's greatest gift to man, it was Allyn's choice to live up to the Almighty's expectations. God did not force issues. He did not teleport the Jews from Egypt and plunk them down safely in the land of milk and honey—homes already built and crops abundantly sprawling. He did not remove the tree of knowledge from Eden where the possibility of its fruit touching Adam's lips might stain his descendants for generations. God set expectations and left men to choose their paths. The harder path did not always guarantee a reward. Even without the prompting from Malcolm in New York, without the guilt of a broken oath, Allyn understood the message—he had little choice but to drive out to retrieve the prince if he hoped to live with himself.

Daniel tugged at his sleeve.

"I just wanted to say thank you," Daniel whispered.

"Thank you?"

"It's obvious from your driving that you're not good at cloak-and-dagger stuff. I appreciate that you tried to help."

Allyn was surprised at how much he relished the compliment despite their predicament. With all his ponderings about God's intentions for him, his oath to House Athelstan, he'd forgotten about the human element. Saving a young life, even if the boy was not royalty, was a noble effort unto itself.

He was strangely proud of the boy, who seemed wise for his years. It was some consolation in the face of death that the object of his demise was at least worthy of the sacrifice.

"We're not done yet," Allyn said in his bravest whisper. "I have a trick up my sleeve . . . If I can come in contact with one of our pursuers, I may be able to convert him."

Daniel scrunched his nose in a way that Allyn read as a *yeah, right* response toward his statement.

"No offense, Reverend, but did you see that seven-foot guy?" Daniel whispered. "He's Mary Shelley's version of Frankenstein. We need superheroes, not sermons."

"We have a superhero," Allyn whispered. MacDonnell was in a car heading south, the source of that second blip Allyn had picked up when he cast his search spell. Malcolm had communicated to the captain that the prince was in the vicinity of the trailer park. The wizard who cast that spell thirteen years ago and wiped their memories was with him. That didn't give Allyn much confidence. Perhaps the boy had learned a thing or two in thirteen years.

"I pray that he finds us in time," Allyn said.

Someone kicked a milk can at the other end of the barn. The two of them held their breath. It rattled loudly, disturbing cows in that section before coming to a halt. A hushed obscenity drifted on the wind accompanied by several cow emissions.

"Which one?" asked Daniel.

"What?"

"Which superhero?"

Though Allyn was being metaphorical, he actually put some thought to the question, as though the exercise were a substitute for having a plan of action. He considered the pantheon of heroes he'd heard about through movies and advertising, and the occasional confiscated comic book from Sunday school, and wondered which mold MacDonnell fit.

"Captain America," Allyn concluded.

"Really?"

"Yes. Muscular, tall, blond, with a good heart, and prone to noble deeds," he explained. *God help his opponent when MacDonnell's holding a sword and shield.*

"We should probably call him Captain Aandor then," said a third whisper behind them.

Allyn lunged between the boy and the intruder and grabbed the man by the shoulders. He cast a blessing for a powerful soothe, only to feel his energy turn back on him, searing him with a terrible black pain. He was stained . . . polluted by the effort.

"What kind of abomination are you?" Allyn asked, half stunned.

"Keep your voice, down. Jeez . . . ," said the man.

"It's okay," said Daniel, putting a hand on the reverend's arm. "Colby tried to warn me about them back at the park. You're in as much trouble as we are, aren't you?" he said to the detective.

"You don't know the half of it, kid. I really was looking out for you . . . tried to string them along. But they got my . . ." Colby lost the rest of his explanation to some far-off painful memory.

Allyn sensed the strain of an impossible quandary on the man. Daniel patted Colby's arm.

"Buck up, Colby," Daniel said. "It's more than my best friend ever did for me."

"Lucky for you, these guys couldn't find a dinosaur in a flock of sheep," the detective said. "There's three of them—Krebe's the stocky one, the giant's Todgarten, Hommar's the normal-looking one. We have to get you out of this build—"

The barn lights came on.

"Who's there?" said someone with a deep southern drawl from the barn door. "Show yourself."

The farmer moved slowly into the barn with a deer rifle. With the lights on, Daniel, Colby, and Allyn's hiding niche had lost its advantage. They moved silently to a corner behind a tool shed.

"Mister, you okay?" they heard the farmer ask someone.

Through the cows' legs, they spied the farmer approach Krebe, who lay motionless on his back. His bowler sat inverted beside his head.

"Oh, no, no . . . ," Colby whispered.

"What's wrong?" said Daniel. "Maybe he got kicked in the head by a cow."

"Why'd they have to switch now?" Colby said to himself, working into a near panic.

"Switch what?" Daniel asked.

"That guy in the butler suit is about to turn a whole lot more psychotic."

The farmer tapped Krebe with his boot. Krebe's arm shot up and grabbed the man's belt. He hoisted himself to the man's belly and shoved a blade in the farmer's gut with the other hand. With his foot, Krebe deflected the rifle barrel as the farmer fired off his dying round into the dirt.

The look of sheer pleasure on Krebe as he sliced across the farmer's abdomen sent a shiver through Allyn. Rapturous glee, normally reserved for welcoming a new child to the world or winning a gold medal, radiated from the killer's face as he disemboweled the farmer. The thief in the forest a few days earlier was a pious soul by comparison. This was real evil.

The farmer fell face-first after his own blood and bowels into the hay. Krebe stood, unhurried, replacing his hat, like a man reborn savoring his first breaths of life. The cows, in distress, mooed and backed away from the scene, causing the group's hiding place to shrink further. They were in danger of being crushed.

Krebe's cohorts, alerted by the rifle shot, came to the center of the barn.

"We must hurry," said Todgarten. "The farmer's woman called the local patrol before I silenced her."

"They're in this barn?" asked Krebe.

He picked up the farmer's rifle and aimed it at the nearest bovine's head and blew its brains out. Then Krebe began firing randomly at the cows, blowing out brains like they were ducks at the county fair. The herd panicked, crushing each other as they struggled to get away. They broke their enclosure and stampeded from the barn. Allyn heard them smashing into objects outside as they escaped. He'd just finished paying off that station wagon, too. Once gone, Allyn and the prince were exposed. Colby was no longer with them.

Todgarten grabbed Allyn, Hommar took the prince, and they dragged them to the barn's center before Krebe. Allyn tried to cast a conversion on his captor, but Todgarten remained unaffected. The hearts of frost giants were cold to the passion of godly devotion.

"Well, well, well . . . ," said Krebe, with the gleam of a starved man sitting before a savory pork chop. Up close he appeared in need of a shave and some grill work for his crooked yellowed teeth. All Krebe lacked was a fat smelly cigar between the thick gritty fingers of his partially gloved hand. "You're what we're all fussin' 'bout 'round here, aye?" He pronounced "here," *ear.* Krebe flipped open a cell phone and informed someone on the other side about their situation.

Krebe clicked the phone shut, beaming with exuberance.

"Thought for sure Dorn would want to cut you himself," Krebe told Daniel. "But his lordship would rather the deed be done as soon as possible. Your head's good 'nough for him." Krebe wiped the blood and guts off his big knife onto his pant leg. "Ain't never cut a prince before," he said. "I'll relish this."

"You have the wrong kid," Daniel said. "I grew up in foster care."

Allyn's heart broke in the face of Daniel's dread. He was innocent, unaware of his importance or the reasons why anyone would want to end his life. Nothing would stay Krebe's hand—asking this child of Satan for mercy would only egg him on. Allyn prayed silently for help. He asked forgiveness for his weakness and implored divine intervention for the sake of the boy. *Take me in his place, Lord. I give my life for the boy.*

Krebe pointed the knife at Daniel's throat with a most lustful smile. A shot put a bullet into the ground before Krebe's next step. Heads snapped toward the barn entrance. Two men entered, a tall blond with a sword on his back and a gun aimed at Krebe, the other, a thin arty type with a staff.

Thank You, Lord, prayed Allyn. Captain America had arrived.

CHAPTER 32

FLOWER POWER

Why Cal only shot a warning before the knife-wielding maniac was beyond Seth's understanding. Perhaps some code of decency prevented him from shooting a man unawares. The two groups faced off with each other, each trying to figure out who had the upper hand. A blocky Nordic-looking man had the prince. His thick arms looked capable of snapping the boy's neck in less time than it took to squeeze a trigger. And Cal would need his entire clip just to take down Todgarten.

Cal had rushed the barn stupidly like a one-man cavalry, and Seth felt pressured by Cal's opinion of him as a coward to follow. They barely avoided the stampeded cows. Seth was scared out of his mind. He looked around for a place to hide should things go south, as they most assuredly will, and spied the long concrete pit of the milking station at the other end of the barn. Extraction hoses hung from racks on either side of the pit designed to accommodate several cows. Typical for Seth when under pressure, his mind wandered, and the farm's operation gave him an idea for a porn set—amply endowed women fixed to the milking hoses: *Deflowered Rebel Milkmaids.*

Cut that out! he admonished himself. His former self still lingered in the dark places, waiting for the chance to pop out. *At least die with clean thoughts.*

"Let the prince go, and I'll let you leave," said Cal, snapping Seth back into the moment. "My word by the Twelve."

"Not very sporting of you, me lordship. Is it?" said Krebe stolidly. He appeared unafraid of death—or more accurately, unbelieving that this was the moment of it. There was a scary cockiness about him. His voice was rusty nails and shards of glass scraped over sandpaper. "You know full well Dorn would 'av us kilt if we return empty-handed. No. I'm afraid we're in a bit of a pickle. Me an' the boys—we end up dead in most of the ways this little drama turns out—we 'ave nothing left to lose—but you . . . you got everything to lose." Krebe looked at the boy. "The rightful prince of Aandor—grand duke of the kingdom, father of the future emperor, lord regent of the realm and all that whatnot—such a tragedy to die so young."

"No one needs die," implored Allyn. "Hunting innocent children is madness. This child has done you no wrong. Walk away . . ."

Krebe ignored the preacher and remained focused on Cal. "I'll make you a deal, me lordship. I take the boy, and spare your wife. You have *my* word."

"My wife?" Cal said.

Seth was as confused as Cal looked.

Suddenly, a group of young people stormed into the barn. Two men with guns and a fat goth girl holding a pitchfork surrounded Daniel, Allyn, and their captors. They were wet and their legs caked with mud. A fourth man snuck up behind Cal with his gun pointed at the cop's head. Cal didn't budge, keeping his gun squarely fixed on Krebe only a few feet in front of him.

"Ya'll just hand Hauer right over," said the man behind MacDonnell. He wore a mullet, so naturally Seth assumed he was their leader. "I got no quarrel with none of you," added mullet head.

"Cody, you're an idiot!" Daniel shouted.

"You think I'm gonna just let you go? After you screw my girl? Specially with sixty thousand dollars on your head?"

Krebe maintained his happy cool. "On second thought, I see a better arrangement," he told MacDonnell.

Krebe addressed the newcomers. "Kill the captain," he said pointing at MacDonnell, "and truly we will have no quarrel."

"Is he a Fed? Shit!" Cody said.

The meth dealers must have been sampling their wares. They were jittery and bloodshot—shaking from more than the cold—too much energy with no clear release.

Another armed foursome of local boys rushed in behind the first group through the entrance, drenched to the bone and caked all over with mud. This was the crew from the SUV Cal had pushed off the road. They took positions around the barn, one with a pistol on Cody, another covering Cal, the third covering Krebe, and the fourth on Daniel, his captors and Cody's people. They too had sampled their wares to give them a boost under stress and pressure. No one in this barn was in his or her right mind. The situation had deteriorated into a scene from a Tarantino movie; everyone shifted pistols nervously from target to target to target. Only Krebe and MacDonnell remained unfazed, with Cal's gun locked squarely on the point between Krebe's eyes. They were one jittery finger away from a melee not seen since bootlegging days.

"Everybody cool it," said the large square pink guy with the big silver belt buckle.

"Hauer's mine, McCoy!" shouted Cody. "This is personal! He—he fucked Luanne."

"Everyone's fucked Luanne," McCoy said in a cruel tone. "Now, put your fuckin' guns down."

Krebe's laugh rose slowly like the sound of a coming train—the intonation of a man who seldom uttered such a sound, who lacked mirth unless it involved the torture and death of another living thing. If fear was infectious, this man was its carrier, seeding the disease among the unwary. A shiver ran down Seth's spine. Everyone was transfixed in the presence of this force, looking at him as though nails were running down a chalkboard.

"Wha's so funny, Fauntleroy?" said McCoy nervously.

"Every one of you with your peasant schemes has failed to aim your weapon at the most dangerous man in the room," Krebe answered, pointing his knife at Seth.

Seth had been happily under the radar until this point. Not a gun aimed at him, barely a notice for the skinny photographer in jeans with dark ruffled hair and a passing resemblance to John Lennon around the eyes. The staff was the least threatening item in a barn filled with meth dealers, cops, assassins, giants, firearms, pitchforks, and knives. Even the fat goth chick looked more dangerous. Now, in the midst of this jittery strung out assembly, Krebe turned the spotlight on him.

"He a ninja?" Cody asked sarcastically. The Carolinians laughed thinly, like graduates of the same school of comedy.

Then it came to Seth like the flicking of a switch . . . Cal was not the reason Krebe's men were frozen in the standoff. Lelani once said, *Only a fool goes into battle undefended against a wizard.* The boys from Aandor thought they were compromised.

"Wizard," Krebe answered McCoy seriously. "We could all be dead at a word. We should be, and yet . . ."

Every successful spell Seth had cast came with the aid of Lelani or the tree wizard Rosencrantz. Neither was present in the barn. Krebe was beginning to wonder why this whole situation wasn't over already. That too much time had passed without a magical resolution. A bead of sweat trickled down the back of Seth's neck, camouflaged by the dripping rain. His stress level, already at DEFCON 2, had crept up another notch. Cal never took his focus off Krebe's glabella. Was the cop waiting for Seth's move? Something to get the prince away from Hommar? That wasn't fair. Seth agreed to do anything Cal asked of him on this trip, but strategies were the cop's domain.

Cody and McCoy had positioned themselves to include Seth in their coverage. Their hands were shaking, their eyes confused. It was apparent that someone tonight was going to die, maybe a few someones . . . maybe everyone in this barn. The tension rose like a symphony playing toward its fourth movement.

"He's the most dangerous man in the world," Krebe said, throwing fuel on the fire.

"We got no beef with them, mister," said McCoy. He wiped the sweat off his brow and fought to stay focused under the drugs. "We just want the reward money for the kid."

"I AM the reward money!" Krebe bellowed, stressing the key points for his mentally deficient audience. "I AM the sixty thousand, and HE'S going to STEAL your money," he said pointing at Seth. "He'll take the boy, and the MONEY will be GONE, and the cop will arrest you and throw you in the dungeon WITHOUT your drugs . . . no more sweet rock to smoke." Krebe turned to Cody. "And the boy will FUCK Luanne until his cock shoots dust and her belly swells with his spawn, and—your—life—will—be—SHIT!"

"I don't wanna go to jail," Cody cried.

Cal whispered to Seth, "You need to do something now."

"Even now they plot to end your existence!" Krebe hammered away. "End them first!

Krebe's motion was both the fastest and slowest move Seth had ever seen in his life. He dropped the farmer's rifle at the same instant that a second smaller dagger dropped from his sleeve.

Relative to everyone, Krebe was a blur compared with the frozen minions around them, but because Seth was the object of his murderous rant, each second of movement seared into his brain, slowing time to where a hummingbird in flight became still. In that next nanosecond, Seth was aware of the following: the knife's trajectory was perfect for Seth's heart; Krebe's attack triggered every itchy finger in the barn; they all opened fire—every gun had been pointed at Cal and Seth; a gaggle of bullets flew at them.

Seth's internal distress exceeded its preestablished parameters. His stomach and shoulders clenched tightly to the point of pain, anticipating the impacts of multiple slugs; he thought he'd squeezed out every drop of juice, every ion of energy in his corporeal form. His staff soaked this tension like a sponge—a spot in the back of his brain erupted in a fiery burst as though a blot of boiling oil had dripped onto his occipital lobe; he believed a hoodlum had shot him in the back of the head, until the sensation exploded throughout his brain and his staff emitted a burst, like radiation from a nova, just as the knife and bullets approached him.

The blade and every single bullet in the air shimmered and transformed into small purple blossoms, flowers with a pungent sticky sweet aroma that bounced forcefully off their jackets and heads. Real time reasserted itself as a final blossom bounced off Krebe's ear while he attempted to avoid Cal's return shot.

Cal tried to fire off another round at Krebe, but the gun jammed. He pulled out his clip, which was completely wedged with purple blossoms. Everyone in the barn was picking flowers out of their guns.

"Really?!" Cal cried. "Every single bullet? You couldn't have left mine?"

With that, Cal pulled Bòid Géard out of its scabbard in one artfully smooth motion that carried it through into an arc behind him to sever Cody's gun hand from his forearm. Cody screamed like a little girl and dropped to his knees, clutching at his newly minted stump. McCoy threw his pistol at Cal, who deflected it with the sword, twisted to avoid McCoy's feeble attempt at a punch, throwing the big guy off balance and exposing his back to the cop. In a swift motion, Cal changed his sword grip to that of holding an ice pick and drove the sword through the back of the man's thigh and out through the quadriceps. Instead of pulling the sword back out the way it went in, he twisted the blade's angle and yanked sideward, cutting the hamstring and anterior cruciate ligament like an Easter ham to free his weapon. The bull of a man went down in agony and bled into the dirt. MacDonnell had done both Cody and McCoy in less than five seconds.

These people are all way too fast for me, Seth thought.

The other meth heads, realizing no amount of money was worth getting hacked to pieces, took off. Each crew collected their respective leader on the way, wrapping belts and T-shirt tourniquets around their wounds, and disappeared into the cold darkness. Krebe's face showed its first sign of distress—Seth wasn't as magically neutered as suspected, and MacDonnell was better armed. Cal was upon Krebe in a beat.

"What about my wife?" Cal said.

Krebe reclaimed the farmer's rifle in time to stave off Cal's raging thrusts, parries, and ripostes with the steel barrel and his ornamental dagger. He lost his bowler as the cop's offensive drove him back into a dimly lit corner of the barn.

Seth had never seen Cal so angry, not even at him. The reverend, the prince, and their captors were the only ones left.

"Back, wizard," ordered Todgarten, holding the reverend like a shield. Seth appreciated the irony of the seven-foot bruiser's fear of him, in lieu of his lack of magical proficiency. He didn't know how he did the flower trick and didn't think he could repeat it unless his life depended on it.

Cal and Krebe continued to go at each other in the darker far corner of the barn. They could barely make out the figures, gray silhouettes against a gray backdrop. Someone was losing badly.

"Why should you die for Dorn?" Allyn Grey posited to the two henchmen. "The captain will not harm you if you spare the boy."

"Krebe's art is death," Todgarten said, trying to convince himself more than the others. "He is a master."

So much for team loyalty . . . Todgarten had no intention of going to help Krebe fight Callum, Seth realized. Dorn's style of management was fear driven; his people's priorities shifted depending on what they feared most at the moment. How did Farrenheil ever get anything done? Dorn's family must be the scariest in the Twelve Kingdoms.

Daniel wheezed under Hommar's forearm lock. He had to get the man off the kid's neck. The lackey believed Daniel's life was the only thing protecting him from Seth at the moment. Seth's incompetence years ago put this boy in danger. Daniel's life was hard and mired in pain instead of love. Hommar was waiting for orders—anyone's orders. He was not a big-picture thinker, but if Hommar realized he could end Aandor's claim with one well-placed snap, all their efforts to save Daniel would be moot.

Colby Dretch snuck up behind Todgarten with a pitchfork. The detective jammed it into the giant's calf. Todgarten yowled in pain and tried to swipe Colby with one arm while holding on to the reverend with the other. Colby retained the pitchfork and jabbed at the giant again, this time sticking him in the ribs. The giant let go of Reverend Grey to extract the farm instrument.

Reverend Grey lunged at Hommar, who was too distracted by Dretch's attack to realize the minister was on him. Grey didn't struggle—he closed his eyes as though in prayer. Hommar tried to pull away, then made a face like he was in shock, like he'd just materialized in the middle of Antarctica in winter. Reverend Grey moved a hand to Hommar's face and touched his own forehead to the man's. Hommar relinquished his grip on Daniel, and Seth pulled the kid away from them. Daniel's neck was red from the pressure. He rubbed it and took several deep breaths.

"Who are you people?" the kid asked. "When did I become the center of the universe?"

"Kid, we need a whole lot more time than we have right now to explain it," Seth told him.

Hommar stopped struggling. "Prelate, how may this sinner serve the gods?" he asked the reverend.

"Stop the giant," said Grey. "Take him down."

Hommar lunged into a football tackle, driving into Todgarten's back. The giant, who'd been focused on the unkillable Colby Dretch, was taken completely by surprise. Hommar jammed a hunting knife through his former cohort's ribs.

"Hommar, you fool," yowled Todgarten. "You allowed the cleric to bless you."

As they struggled, Colby jumped into the fray, helping to weigh the giant down. Todgarten kicked the detective off easily and put his attention toward the more dangerous opponent. Colby shook his head, got up, and calmly joined Seth, Daniel, and the reverend. "Not jumping back in?" Seth asked.

Colby produced a thumping velvet pouch, one that had been on Todgarten's belt moments before. "Nope, got what I wanted."

Todgarten broke Hommar's back on his knee and then snapped the man's neck just as easily. He threw the man aside like a bag of garbage and faced the four.

"Your tricks won't work on me cleric and the wizard is a fraud. I will break your bones as I did—"

The whup-whup-whup sound of the tumbling dagger was only audible for a second before Krebe's ornamental knife lodged into the side of the giant's neck. Blood gushed forth, but not as much as if Todgarten had removed the knife. Miraculously, the giant remained on his feet.

A bloody Cal MacDonnell emerged from the dark corner of the barn. The giant picked up the pitchfork and swung it at Cal, who ducked and then used his sword to trap the pronged end against the ground. Todgarten tried to raise it again, but Cal snapped the handle near the tines with his boot. The giant started to lunge at the knight, but pulled back just in time to avoid a deeper cut across his abdomen as Cal arced the sword across Todgarten's belly. Todgarten backed up and tripped on a hay bale.

"I yield," he said coming to his knees, putting his hands in front of him to ward off the knight. But MacDonnell hacked the creature's hands off in one swipe, adding two more red streams to the giant's tally. Todgarten wheezed and gurgled, his neck wound filling his mouth and throat with blood.

"For Tristan," MacDonnell said. He pulled the dagger out of the giant's neck, unimpinging his carotid artery. Todgarten's blood poured forth like mountain streams in a spring thaw.

"Holy shit!" cried Daniel.

Allyn Grey lightly smacked the back of the boy's head. "That's what my daughter gets when she talks nonsense," he told the prince. To Callum he asked, "Is that the last of them?"

"Not quite. I came to get you."

They followed the knight back to the start of a red trail . . . a mortally wounded Krebe dragged himself along the barn floor, the bloody period on a red-streaked exclamation point he etched into the dirt behind him. His right leg below the knee was gone.

Krebe propped himself up against a bale of hay to face his enemies. They observed him, like roadkill not lucky enough to have died instantly.

"I—I choose who dies," he sputtered. Blood spat out when Krebe talked. A wild, demented stare had set into the eyes. "I am the artist—the warden of death. The bringer of pain."

"Stealing the lives of young girls is a coward's delusion," Cal said. "You are a madman serving a mad master."

Krebe focused for a moment. He looked at his severed leg and smiled. Bloodstained teeth added to his sinister appeal, like hyenas after a kill. "My brother will be so disappointed to play the cripple for half his life," he said, laughing hysterically.

"What did you mean about my wife?" Cal said.

"The master hears voices in his migraines," Krebe said, responding to questions not put to him. He'd lost his train of thought.

"My wife," Cal repeated.

Seth wondered about Cat himself. Something wasn't right. They hadn't heard from her in over a day and Krebe had been entirely certain of his ability to barter Catherine for his life.

"My greatest masterpiece," Krebe laughed mechanically, sputtering blood all over himself.

Cal put a boot on one of Krebe's hands and instructed Colby to secure the other. Then he looked at the reverend. "Prelate, I have to know," Cal pleaded.

Krebe squirmed and writhed in horror at the approaching cleric.

"No! No! No!" he screamed.

Reverend Grey laid hands on him. Fear had converted to sobbing—Krebe had suddenly become burdened by a deep affecting sorrow.

"Oh gods," he wailed, wretchedly. "Oh gods . . . what have you done? My gift! You've taken my gift! My art . . ."

"What did you do?" Daniel asked.

"The darkness within him . . . his inner pain holds it together and gives it shape," Grey said. "I cured the pain and released the bind. He's now reliving his lifetime of evil from a new perspective—without the pain and anger that inspired his actions."

"Ooooooh gods!" Krebe exclaimed, in the midst of intense remorse.

"You're dying," Allyn told him. "Please, my son, make your final act a repentant one—that some god somewhere might take your soul when you leave this mortal coil."

Krebe, burdened by a lifetime of guilt spilled everything: The Plaza hotel base, Cat's capture, Dorn's madness, the headaches, how they got to this world, and how many men they had left. And then he rambled about his murders; the hundreds of maidens he raped and tortured, until the guardians could barely stand to hear any more. Krebe grasped desperately for redemption from a lifetime of evil as his life ran out of him. He wound down still confessing, and then just closed his eyes and stopped.

Seth realized as hard as his personal path to redemption was, it would never compare to Krebe's. Krebe would need several lifetimes to atone for his sins. Seth was glad this monster had left the world.

He believed, finally, that he could accomplish good after all and make amends for the past. Ben had been right. It would be a long road, but not an impossible one.

Cal turned to Daniel and looked at the boy from head to toe, as though he were purchasing a racehorse—as though to affirm his existence. Cal laid his big hands on Daniel's shoulders. If it were not for Cat's kidnapping, Cal would be exuberant at this moment. Instead, the cop was gazing at a nonbarterable treasure—the only thing in this universe Dorn would relinquish Cal's wife for.

The boy smiled, nervously, unaware of the cop's predicament. He was also obviously in awe of Callum.

"Thanks for saving me," he said.

Daniel exuded a humble sincerity infectious enough to make even Cal smile.

"It's my very greatest pleasure to make your acquaintance, Daniel," Cal said. "Has the reverend told you of your origins?"

"There wasn't time," Allyn said.

"Uh . . . am I going to jail?" Daniel asked.

"No," Cal said. "I'm responsible for everything that's happened to you. You should never have had the life you ended up with—to have to defend yourself from a child abuser."

Seth's heart sank. Like a good leader, Cal took full responsibility, but he was not to blame. Seth wanted to confess that Daniel's hardships, his trials and tribulations, were his fault.

"Ever ride in a helicopter?" Cal asked the boy.

Seth noted the dead farmer as they walked to their vehicles. How would Cal square all this with the local cops? Were Malcolm's pockets so deep, he could sweep even this away?

"You did well," Cal said. Seth looked around to make sure the remark was meant for him. Did Cal mean in the fight, or the spell that located Colby?

Seth didn't realize how much he yearned for the cop's approval. "Really?" was all he managed to say.

"No guarantee Lelani could have done better." There was a mark of bitterness in Cal's voice as he said this.

Poor Lelani. Catherine had been her charge. Despite being the superior wizard, she'd failed. Seth had been lucky. He was deaf, dumb, and blind in the ways of magic, a possessor of a complex machine with no instruction manual, but somehow made it through stumbling and bumbling along.

"Flowers?" Cal added as a side note. He pulled a purple blossom out of Seth's hair and handed it to him.

"I—uh—had the word 'deflower' stuck in my brain," Seth said truthfully. "Please don't ask me why." Seth was grateful he hadn't turned the bullets into flying rebel milkmaids.

CHAPTER 33
SANCTUARY

1

Basked in the glow of the new dawn, Daniel Hauer and his protectors flew over New York Harbor toward the island of Manhattan and toward his future as the rightful prince of Aandor. Lady Liberty's torch shimmered gold under the rising sun—a beacon heralding a new era.

Try as he might, Daniel could not fathom how he went from abused foster child on the run for murder to savior of an alternate universe in just a few short hours. The last few days were surreal . . . he'd lost his family, best friend, childhood crush, virginity, and good faith in meth dealers as stalwart pillars of the community. Sneaking around backyards in the rain to avoid Luanne's boyfriend, his biggest concern had been to not end up dead in a ditch on Route 581. Turns of events of these kinds happened only in cheesy movies . . . at best, young adult novels written by English authors on welfare. *These people might, in fact, all be bonkers—completely nuts,* Daniel thought . . . except they had real weapons, resources, and conviction. They had a freaking helicopter.

The story they told him was, quite literally, unbelievable. And yet, he saw the evidence with his own eyes—bullets that turned into flowers, giants, preachers that could convert a man's soul with a touch. Had someone slipped him an acid Mickey at some point during the day? One thing for certain, even the guys trying to kill him believed he was this prince. Enough to die for it.

Someone called Malcolm had "people" cleaning up the mess they left in North Carolina. "People" were driving Cal and Colby's cars back to New York in a covered trailer. "People" had collected Krebe, Todgarten, and their friend and would forensically "sterilize" the farm. The farmer was left for the local police to find and the meth heads had been set up to take the fall for his death and the cop's at the trailer park. The problem with being a drug user is that when you start yammering about swordsmen, giants, and bullets turning into flowers in midair—your credibility goes right out the window.

Cal told Daniel about his encounter with Adrian and Katie Millar, and how they stood vigil on his block, praying for his safety. Katie was finally talking to a counselor about what Josh Lundgren had done to her. Daniel was glad to hear that he was missed and wanted very much to call them and let them know he was okay.

This news from home prompted Daniel to talk about his life. His new best friends listened intently to Daniel's story: the prescription-pill–popping mom, the violent drunken ex-Marine stepdad, the fight with the Grundys in defense of Adrian, defending Katie Millar from her douche of an ex-boyfriend. When Daniel realized Cal and Reverend Grey suffered under each morsel of depressing backstory (conveyed through subtle changes in their mood and body language), he changed the subject to his love of books, art, and science fiction and John Hauer, his first adopted dad. He explained how happy he'd been the first few years of his life.

Daniel was keenly aware of tension between his guardians. Cal tried to project a united front, but now that Daniel was safe, everyone had pressed him to pursue his own agendas.

Reverend Grey insisted on driving home to his family. In Aandor, Grey was some sort of priest with special abilities. He'd done his part for king and country and now had to look to his own life. But Cal pleaded with him, having promised his services to help Colby regain his humanity. Colby also pleaded with the reverend, for the sake of his son as well as himself. Malcolm even offered the reverend more financial help than promised for sticking around until the loose ends were tucked away. Reverend Grey sighed under the verbal onslaught and reluctantly agreed, like a happily married man at a friend's bachelor party, cajoled into a turn with the rented prostitute so he wouldn't ruin the mood for everyone else.

Seth had a private matter in the city to attend to that Cal was reluctant to give him space to address. The wizard was very secretive, resisting Cal's interrogation, saying only that he could find no peace of mind until his personal matter was set right. He blamed Cal for not letting him finish his business before they left for Baltimore. The cop was worried that once out of sight, he'd never see Seth again. There were still bad people in the world looking to kill Daniel. Seth refused to even look at Callum the rest of the trip north. He whittled obsessively instead. By time they'd reached New York Harbor, he'd finished etching in the drawings and symbols that were penciled on the staff.

Colby was a walking dead man who kept his beating heart in a sack, and ultimately the reason Daniel bought into this whole fantastic story. The boy had been extremely skeptical of the group's claims; magic and alternate realities were the stuff of the Syfy channel. Colby let him hold his beating heart. The detective revealed the welts from the spell that had removed the organ and had Daniel place his hand on his cold chest to note the absence of a beat. Daniel wanted to believe Colby had been his friend all along . . . but Luanne's suspicions had been right; the detective was just angling to get his life back. Still, it was hard not to feel something for the guy whose son, Tory, now suffered in his stead. Cal offered Allyn's help for the boy, likely trying to secure the detective's loyalty, but Allyn, who was integral to that plan stayed quiet, neither confirmed nor denied his desire to help, resisting any more commitment to the cause than he absolutely had to give.

And then there was Callum; captain of his palace guard, and self-proclaimed personal protector to Daniel. Six foot five, and solid as an NFL linesman, the reverend called it when he equated the cop to a superhero. Where was Cal all those years Clyde had used him as a punching bag? How does one lose a baby? Cal remained stoic most of the trip. His men avoided talking to him—they all wanted to pursue their own interests at exactly the time Cal had discovered Dorn held his wife prisoner. Who could blame them, though? For thirteen years, they had built their own lives here and now they were being asked to step away from their families to fight old battles. Just like that. The seams of this hero's life were fraying and the strain of keeping it together was evident in his distant stares.

The others talked among themselves.

"So you are the second source of deflected magic?" the reverend asked Seth.

"Probably," Seth responded. "Lelani says I have some sort of sophisticated shield protecting me. It's about the only magical thing about me that works right."

"It is filtering much of the energy around you," Allyn said. "The spell does to you what comes naturally to Daniel through his lineage. You will never reach your potential as a wizard as long as this shield surrounds you. The magic needs to filter through you."

"Great. Like, finding inner peace so I can thread the needle isn't hard enough," Seth said.

"But that is exactly the thing," Allyn said. "I don't know what this 'threading the needle' metaphor means, but being at peace with yourself can alter the harmonics of such a shield. Like the combination to a lock." The reverend looked dissatisfied with his explanation and scratched his head for another perspective. "A wizard may explain it in more technical terms . . . but, being at peace would modify your aura—allow the universal energy to mingle with you. Whoever cast it on you was not only protecting you . . . they were protecting others from you. It's a leash in some ways, forcing you to reach a certain level of maturity to unlock your true potential."

"Padre, that sounds like Eastern spiritual mumbo jumbo," Seth said. "This is real magic. You should see what Lelani can do. It's unreal."

"I'm well aware of the abilities of a wizard, young man. I'm inclined to find out how this blessing was cast so that I can put one over every wizard I meet and stay the tide of destruction they bring to those around them. Unfortunately, at this time, we need your abilities to protect ourselves from Dorn. Is there something in your life preventing you from finding balance?" asked the reverend.

"Definitely," Seth said. He threw an accusatory look at Callum when he said this.

"Then you must address it to move forward. Inner peace, otherwise known as being comfortable with the man you are, is likely the key to this lock. God gives us these tests for a reason. They are like the locks of a canal, each one lifting us to the next elevation."

"Which god?" asked Callum. "Sometimes you talk of 'God' and other times of 'gods.' Your theology is a mishmash of Pelitos and Christianity. Do you know who you are Prelate Grey? Have you picked a side yet?"

Jabbing a wounded rottweiler would have induced a friendlier response than the one Grey gave Callum. The reverend remained glumly quiet the rest of the trip.

So these are my protectors, Daniel thought. *A minister with a crisis of faith, a walking dead man that would have sold me out for a magic trick, a captain no one wants to follow, and a wizard that can't cast any spells. Perfect.*

At the Thirty-fourth Street heliport, Seth made it abundantly clear that he was going to attend to his personal business. Realizing he couldn't stop Seth, short of hog-tying, Cal tried to extract a rendezvous time. Seth said he didn't "do" curfews. He would come to the Waldorf as soon as he was able.

The limousine traveled north on the FDR Drive and got off at the United Nations exit. It was Daniel's first time in New York; the streets were abuzz with activity. Never had he seen so many people in one place, heard so many sounds, smelled so many smells (not all of them pleasant), or felt so many potholes. As crowded as the city was, it also looked like a really good place to be alone.

They entered the Waldorf Astoria through the loading dock on Fiftieth Street. Some way for a prince to arrive—but Daniel remembered that the president of the United States also entered and exited through kitchens and alleyways. Better safe than sorry. A man that looked like a Secret Service agent met them when they exited the elevator—Daniel was whisked into a large, lavishly decorated suite.

"Prince Danel of Aandor," said Cal to the room.

His guardians immediately distinguished themselves from the hired help with bows: a beautiful tall redhead; a short stout man with a coppery red beard; and a guy that looked very much like Tim Mann from Babies Ate My Dingo knelt before him.

Weird, he thought. Daniel was uncomfortable by so much attention. He could never get used to this.

2

Callum and Malcolm squared off silently like gunslingers of a bygone age. Their proximity to each other made the scene almost comical—Cal at six foot five and Malcolm at five foot two. Not all was merry among Daniel's band of guardians. Leave it to him to fall into a fairy tale with no happily ever after, he thought.

"Mal," said Callum.

"Cal," Mal responded.

Everyone was frozen as the greeting unfolded. The tension was so thick, dust motes hung in the air for lack of a current.

"You want to hit me—don't you?" Malcolm said. He smiled harshly, daring the cop to strike.

"She was under your protection," Cal said.

"She was under my protection," Malcolm affirmed. "This is not lost on me."

"Whose decision was it not to tell me?" Cal queried.

The tall redhead approached Cal, her eyes glistening with regret. There was no shortage of guilt in the room—enough to commence a Sunday mass. The redhead put her hand on Cal's arm, but he brushed it off gently and shook his head ever so slightly at her. It wasn't her he held responsible; Cal maintained his glare at Malcolm, who took the full brunt of blame and didn't bat an eye.

Daniel thought that maybe he should intercede; after all, it was for his sake all these people were supposedly in danger. He searched for the right thing to say when suddenly a cry of "Daddy!" came from behind him.

The girl, only slightly older than Daniel's stepsister, Penny, cut through the room like a knife and leaped into Callum's embrace. Cal cried as he breathed in her scent and stroked her hair. The bubble had popped, and everyone relaxed. There was a lesson in this. Among warriors, billionaires, and Secret Service henchmen, the least powerful person wielded the most influence. It was more complex than solely love; Daniel loved Katie Millar but still didn't end up with her. The ties that bound people were a strange force unto themselves, more mysterious than magic. He had to remember this for when (*if*) he ever started writing again.

Daniel's opinions of Callum from the trip up, both the good and bad, transformed in the presence of his daughter's unconditional love. The loss of Cal's wife, this little girl's mother, now weighed on Daniel's mind heavily. The cop wasn't a superhero; he was three-dimensional person—someone who ran the gamut from joy to agony, and experienced pain and loss. Since the barn battle, Daniel felt he could walk away from this . . . that their opinion of him would turn out to be a mistake, or that he could use these people's delusions to his advantage to get away from the authorities. But Aandor was getting realer by the minute as was his role in this group. The jury was still out on what it all meant to him. Surely this was better than moving to Costa Rica to avoid the law; learning a new language, scraping by, struggling to get an education.

People resumed their business—whatever it was they did before he returned. Activity reached the frenetic pace of a ship's bridge on naval maneuvers. The Tim Mann clone and his hot girlfriend seemed not to be part of the enterprise. They drank morning cocktails at a window seat, watching the traffic on Park Avenue. Daniel joined them.

"Anyone ever tell you you look like Tim Mann from Babies Ate My Dingo?" he said.

"He is," said the hot girlfriend. She giggled. "I'm Clarisse . . . nice to meet you, your honor."

Tim cast her a fierce look. "He's not a bloody judge," he said. His speech was well on the way to slur. "Hey," he said to Daniel. "Glad you're alive. No, really. Always liked your mom and dad. Maybe now I can get back to my band and my bloody fucking tour." Tim downed the rest of his cocktail.

"Uh . . . I didn't realize you had to stop touring for me," Daniel said.

"The band didn't stop touring," Tim explained. "Only I did. Thanks to the self-appointed Lord Robbe." From behind him on the sill, he pulled out another ready-made cocktail. "Cheers."

"I didn't realize Malcolm was also a lord," Daniel said.

Tim snorted. "I said 'self-appointed.' He's a fucking sergeant. A soldier. A stinking, ambitious, little dwarv."

"A dwarv?" Daniel said.

"A smelly, stinky, dirty race of muscular midgets who fuck hairy women that never shave and smell like sweaty male goats in heat that piss on themselves. They spend all day mining for jewels because aristocrats love sparkly baubles on their shiny dresses and will hock their husbands' left nut for one." He lifted his glass. "Cheers."

Clarisse slapped Tim a little harder than playfully. "Be nice."

This fairy tale's getting darker by the minute, Daniel thought.

"You don't write the lyrics, do you?" Daniel said sarcastically.

"Nope."

"He's just pissed because things were going really well for us before the magic gave everyone their memories back," Clarisse said.

"Is that what happened?"

"One minute I'm rocking Madison Square Garden," Tim said, "the next I'm back in a thunderstorm from thirteen years ago as my brain reboots ancient history."

Daniel remembered a moment like that, too, at the bus station the night he met Colby. There was less and less deniability as the day went on. Could he actually be their prince?

"You'll have to excuse my friend," said an older gentleman joining in. He had a hint of jowls, salt-and-pepper hair, and a preppy tweed jacket with patches at the elbow. "Balzac Cruz, court jester, at your service, Your Royal Highness."

"Uh—just Daniel is fine," the boy said. "Really? A jester? How many people came across with you guys?"

"Many more than are here," said Balzac. "Sadly, some of our party are no longer with us: Tristan, Callum's lieutenant; Galen and Linnea who were to be your adoptive parents. They died in a horrible car crash when you were but an infant. She was the palace groundskeeper's daughter and much loved among the staff. Her husband was the duke's personal tanner, a man of great skill with leathers and furs and a great generosity of spirit."

"What were you?" he asked, turning back to Tim.

"Minstrel."

"So people here pretty much became what they were already back there to some degree."

"Not exactly," said Balzac. Pointing to Cal and Malcolm, he continued. "A knight is not a policeman. A metal smith is not an industrialist. This dynamic is about to turn interesting. Malcolm has the status and authority in this world. He earned it and is used to being the leader. Callum's authority comes from the old world . . . it was inherited, and he remembers being used to being the leader. They need each other. Who is the legitimate authority?"

"You sound like a professor," said Daniel.

"I am, my dear boy," said Balzac. "I was. Before becoming a jester, I was a young scholar in the kingdom of Teulada."

"Magic?"

"Nothing so gauche . . . philosophy, literature, and history. I would have been your tutor had we not lost our identities. Oh, the pain of all those lost years. I could have taught you so much. A tragedy. Where is the young wizard, Seth, by the way?" he said, looking about.

"The guy with the staff? He had personal business."

"Has a staff now, does he? Well, I hope he does less harm with it than he did with that identity spell thirteen years ago."

Hanging out with a drunk, angry rocker and an old fart professor that reminded him of Dr. Smith from *Lost in Space* was not Daniel's idea of a good time. Outside was Park Avenue, one of the most famous streets in the most exciting city in the world. The suite, despite its size, was taking on the characteristics of an opulent prison.

"Who do I talk to about going out for a walk?" Daniel asked.

Tim snorted. Balzac gave him a forced smile like Daniel should know better. Clarisse pointed to the tall red-headed woman talking with Colby Dretch and Reverend Grey.

Daniel approached them, impressed by red's height and physique—a stunningly beautiful woman, with olive skin and large green-gray eyes. He circumvented a couch to reach them, then realized walking up behind the tall redhead would have been quicker, and wondered why he didn't. He looked at the area behind her.

"No," the redhead said.

It must have looked to all like he was checking out the woman's butt. Flushed with embarrassment, Daniel stammered, "I—uh . . ."

"You cannot go for a walk," she added.

"Oh. I didn't even . . ."

"I have remarkably good hearing, Your Highness. Lord Dorn is still searching for you—perhaps more a threat now than even he himself realizes if what the detective says about his migraines is true."

"Why should I care that the guy trying to kill me has a headache?"

Turning back to Colby and Allyn, Lelani said, "Transversing universes is a dangerous undertaking. There's no long-term knowledge of its effects; but it would seem some people are more vulnerable to the changes between the two realities, like changes in water pressure to some divers. This malady starts with headaches and discomfort and evolves into full-blown madness. I believe Galen succumbed to this malady the night of the accident upstate. The migraines and dementia caused him to drive head on into that truck. Linnea would not have known what to do."

"Good for us, right?" Daniel interjected.

"No, Your Highness," she said, finally addressing him directly. Behind her eyes lay an entire universe . . . he wanted to fall into them. "Lord Dorn has in his possession scrolls with forbidden spells—banned magic from a much darker age in our history. He's been procuring the components to cast such a spell. This magic in the hands of a madman will only lead to death and destruction on a wide scale."

"He doesn't need to threaten on a wide scale," said Callum, joining them. Bree sat in his arms with her head resting on his shoulder. "He has Catherine . . . He has my wife."

CHAPTER 34

POWER PLAY

Callum didn't recall Malcolm ever being this obstinate, and he really didn't care for the change. Their heated disagreement had reached a point of discomfort for all within earshot; the other guardians stayed to the edges of the suite, giving the contenders ample space to quarrel. Mal ordered his security team into another suite entirely to give the guardians more privacy. This was Aandor's affair. Only Colby, Scott, and Clarisse were allowed to remain with the guardians.

"Attack now!" Malcolm insisted.

His cheeks were flushed, and with his coppery hair he appeared ready to burst like an angry volcano. "They can't have many men left. We can wipe them out for good." This was the third round in under an hour with the very same suggestions and tactics. They were arguing in circles.

"Our priority is to set up Daniel in a new life miles away from here," Cal said. "Get him off the same island that Dorn's on." Cal was frustrated to no end. Malcolm had exactly the resources needed to make Daniel disappear, set him up with a new identity in a town of their choosing and give the boy a life worthy of a prince of Aandor. But Cal couldn't sign the man's checkbook for him. Malcolm's wealth was his own—self-earned and of this world. Cal's anger was tempered only by Malcolm's loyalty to their cause. He had not abandoned the prince as Prelate Grey had tried, or successfully ignored the call to arms as Tilcook had (if the man was even still alive).

"Your number-one priority should be your wife," Malcolm insisted.

"If only to alleviate your guilt over the debacle that lost her in the first place, is that what you mean, Mal?" If the billionaire had been standing on a box, Cal was sure Mal would have socked him in the face for that last remark.

"If that's what you choose to believe, Cal . . . if that's what will get us to bring the war right back at these pigs, then yes! Damn you! I'm tired of being on the run. My family's been running for a generation. We have nothing good to show for it! Let's give the warmongers their own medicine and see if they have the stomach for it!"

"We can't turn Midtown into a war zone," Cal said. "We'd be discovered. Even your wealth and connections couldn't hide us from that. We're invaders from an alternate universe—political aliens . . . they'd have us in lockdown and throw away the key. Our best strategy is a stealthy one. Special forces style—surgical strikes."

"You'd be surprised by what I could bury," Mal said. "Don't you know billionaires have carte blanche in post-Bush America? Are you willing to sacrifice Catherine for Midtown?"

"Cat's safer now than she would be if we attacked," Cal said, calmly. He wished he believed his own words as much as he was trying to make Mal believe them. "As long as we have the prince, Dorn won't try . . ."

"Haven't you listened to your own people?" Mal said. "Dorn's going insane. This is Dorn of Farrenheil . . . He never played with a full deck to begin with. You remember the crap he pulled last time he visited Duke Athelstan's palace. The man screws his own aunt for gods' sake! He's not going to care about hostage etiquette or keeping a low profile. Our best strategy is to use overwhelming force—take him out fast and hard."

"Once we have the prince tucked away . . ."

"What! What!" Malcolm challenged. "What next? Daniel becomes an adult, goes to college, gets a job, and grows old? When

Daniel turns sixty, only a few days will have passed by in Aandor since he left. Are we bringing his great-grandkids back to reclaim the throne, because I have news for you, they aren't going to have the concentrated blood of ten kings. What's the point of saving HIM if we don't get his ass back on the throne, running his country? We need to find a corner of the kingdom that's safe and set up a de facto government and resistance movement. We wipe Dorn out NOW so we can get back to the business of getting home, repelling the enemy, and saving the kingdom."

"Daniel needs to be trained," Cal said. "He doesn't know a thing about Aandor . . . about how to rule."

"What's the difference, Cal? It's a monarchy . . . a flawed system of government even under the best ruler. We're restoring the old status quo. The same advisers, council members, generals, and nobility will be running his government, as they did his father's—the same one percent—nothing changes. Daniel's not going to get to pick who he'll marry. He just has to fuck the girl *they* pick for him and make little baby emperors. Maybe, just maybe, that kid will be grateful enough for my efforts to restore the mines stolen from my people. You get to go home to Castle MacDonnell and your eight hundred acres if we win. I still have to lead my race a thousand miles back east to Farrenheil to pick up the pieces of our broken lives. So excuse me for being a little impatient.

"Mark my words: Dorn and his lackeys are not done bringing the war to us. He's not suspending his campaign to kill us all on the possession of your wife."

Cal was tired of this tennis match. He could see that the others were exhausted as well. The more they argued, the more they inched ever closer to an unretractable statement that would threaten the fellowship of the group. To his credit, Mal refrained from acting autonomously. He could have simply launched his own attack with his security people, all experts in the way of combat, except Mal desperately needed Lelani. Only a fool attacked a wizard without one of his own. Even Symian was dangerous enough to make Malcolm hesitate. But the centaur was loyal to Cal and would not follow Mal's orders.

Cal also heard Mal's desire to have him lead the attack between the lines of his argument. Maybe it was respect for Cal's skills, or maybe he needed Cal's blessing to assuage him of responsibility should something happen to Catherine in the battle. Dwarvs were known for their stubborn natures—personalities as immalleable as the granite they hewed to reach their ore. They were also notoriously frugal and practical. With time, though, even water could wear down stone.

"Can we all just take five," Scott suggested.

"I'm getting tired of the sound of my voice, too," Malcolm said, and retired to the wetbar to fix himself a drink.

Cal could use a stiff one himself, but wanted to retain his clarity in the midst of this pressure. He did a survey of the suite—of the people sworn to help him in his cause and their significant companions. Bree conversed animatedly with Clarisse, who appeared to reciprocate his daughter's enthusiasm. Tim was alone in his own corner working on his fifth cocktail of the day. What were they thinking thirteen years ago, bringing a musician along, as though Tim would risk life and limb for the prince instead of saving his own selfish ass? Minstrels were worse than mercenaries—coin grubbers with no combat ability and always ready to bed your servants or someone's wife.

Lelani, Colby, and Allyn Grey were in their own corner consulting about the spells necessary to restore Colby's heart. The reverend kept getting interrupted with calls from home—always from his daughter because his wife had stopped speaking to him. From what Cal could gather, his wife had packed Allyn's belongings and placed them on the curb, but his brother-in-law had retrieved them and hid them in the garage. Grey looked dejected. Cal realized how lucky he was that Catherine had accepted . . . or maybe that was too strong a word . . . *tolerated* the intrusion of his former life. But with Cat in the hands of the enemy, he was able to forgive Allyn's decision to stay out of the fight to protect his family. Cal did not have that luxury.

The reverend was a little stuck-up about working with a wizard. Perhaps it was the strain of being separated from his family, or finding himself back in a war he wanted no part of, but Grey had mentioned that perhaps it was God's intention that Colby go the other direction to a true death.

Scott chimed in with a "What would Jesus do?", which didn't upset the reverend nearly as much as pointing out that Colby was a heck of a lot more alive than Lazarus was when Christ plucked him from his crypt. What ultimately convinced the reverend was the torture of Colby's son. Dorn had gouged out the poor lad's eyes to spur Colby into action. The boy was already quadriplegic. The horror of it touched Cal deeply. He looked at Bree, safe inside these walls and thought *There but for the grace of God . . .* Tory would need his father more than ever.

What a sorry lot, thought Callum. How was he to fight a war with this rabble? His best officer had his own schemes and couldn't agree on tactics; his cleric was lost between two different faiths and depressed over his wife; he had a minstrel and a fool—utterly useless; a private detective who was halfway dead and whose motives Cal could never be sure of; and his best sorcerer, albeit brilliant, was still a student and green in the ways of warfare. And Tilcook, the amiable colossal cook who served in the army for fifteen years before coming to work at the palace, who would have been a great boon to Cal's efforts, was either dead or refusing to show up for duty. Everyone had his or her own agenda—everyone wanted something that Cal couldn't give.

Balzac had Daniel cornered by the window overlooking Park Avenue. He hovered over the prince like a predator. Cal's opinion of jesters was not too much higher than that of musicians. They always made him ill at ease, as though they knew more than he did about everything; a perpetual smirk lay beneath whatever expression they chose to wear like a mask and with Balzac Cruz, doubly so. He was affectionately known among the palace guard as "Ball Sack Cruise," but no one would call him that to his face. Some of the palace guards were indebted to him, having borrowed money to offset gambling debts at the Phoenix Nest. Where a jester found the coin to finance loans to dozens of guards was beyond Cal's understanding. Cal never liked it, but graft and usury were part of the culture. Aandor did not have anticorruption efforts like the NYPD. Half the city guard took bribes from local crime chiefs. Cal wondered what changes he could implement if he returned in one piece . . . if they ever repelled Farrenheil.

Though Cal didn't know why, he didn't like seeing Balzac alone with the prince. He was being possessive, but considering the effort and personal cost in reclaiming the boy, he'd come too far to ignore his instincts now. He joined them with a smile, hiding his own suspicions like a jester. Daniel looked grateful for the interruption.

"Ah, my lord MacDonnell," Balzac said. "Am I correct in understanding that we know the location of our friends from Farrenheil?"

"Perhaps—nothing's been confirmed," Cal said.

"What a marvelous advantage. I hope that your dear wife has not suffered at the hands of those brutal thugs."

"Lord Dorn is an earl and councilor in his uncle's court. He's very familiar with the rules regarding hostages of noble standing."

Balzac threw him a sad smile. It struck Cal as thin, like a single coat of whitewash on a bright red wall.

"Your faith in your fellow nobleman is admirable, my lord," said Balzac. "But hostages in Aandor are given, not taken, and the rules of protection apply to those who voluntarily submit to their hosts. I do hope you are right, though . . . that the whispers of Farrenheil's contempt for etiquette and the laws of the continental concord are . . . exaggerated."

For a fool, Balzac said very little by way of humor to lighten the mood. Cal couldn't find one sincere note in any of this man's utterances. Perhaps they were just never meant to be friends. "Would you mind if I spoke to the prince for a moment?" Cal asked. Balzac bid them a gracious adieu and left to torment Tim, who was too anesthetized by drink to find anyone annoying at that moment.

"Thanks," Daniel said. "He creeps you out, too, right? Like he's always saying one thing, but he's really thinking another."

"Yeah." Cal smiled, admiring the kid's good instincts. "Thanks for not turning out dumb."

"Huh?"

"I'm in a lot of hot water for losing you thirteen years ago," Cal admitted. "It was my responsibility to raise you safe and make sure you understood the world you came from. Your family has a long history. I was supposed to prepare you to run a kingdom. Two kingdoms, in fact . . . your mother has only two younger sisters, and her father is the archduke of Bradaan. Your grandmother died giving birth to your youngest aunt, and the archduke vowed never to remarry. So no trueborn sons means you would inherit that kingdom independent of the continental accord that governs our continent."

"From the way you talk, though, Aandor is the prize," said Daniel.

"We all love our own nations, Daniel."

"What's it like there?" Daniel asked. "I mean, you use a sword, so what's closest with regards to here?"

"Fifteenth-century Europe. Objectively speaking, Aandor is more progressive, the most advanced of the Twelve Kingdoms . . . by the standards of our world, of course. It's no accident that Aandor became the seat of an empire that ruled over eleven other kingdoms many years ago. There was a long peace that helped everyone thrive. A rising tide lifts all boats. In many ways, we are trying to reclaim that golden era, but without war and conquest as it originally had been done. So it became a breeding contest instead, and subsequently a cold war."

"And we were winning?"

"It's not like others haven't come close. I won't lie to you, Daniel . . . Aandor is just as guilty of sabotaging other kingdoms' efforts in the past. Each of the twelve houses is distinct; the families have character traits, and those traits and beliefs would influence the entire empire if a particular family attained dominance. So alliances have been formed between families and kingdoms who are similar enough in their ethical, moral, and economic beliefs. No one wants to be ruled by someone whose beliefs diametrically oppose their own."

"So you guys still have suits of armor and all that?" the boy asked.

"Yes."

"Jousts?"

"Yes."

"Awesome!"

"There's some fine literature and music, too. Our maidens are fair and unspoiled . . . mostly. We also have cholera, plague, death by infections, and we butcher civilians during war. This is not Disney's Magic Kingdom. No real place is perfect."

"Can't we change that? With what we know?"

"Some of it. Aandor is not a place that embraces rapid change. We've been in the 'fifteenth century' for three hundred years. The laws of physics work slightly different there. We never developed gunpowder. We have true magic that, honestly, most people will never experience in their lifetimes. Most who do are scared of it and never want to encounter it again."

"When are we going back?" Daniel asked.

"That's what the argument's about. I don't want you going back too soon. Everyone will be pulling you in a different direction, seeking favors, wanting boons, ingratiating themselves. Even your own parents' agendas may not be in sync. You don't know anything of our history, politics, or culture. You might offend without realizing it and start off on a bad foot. I want to give you a few years to catch up. That's what I meant by 'thanks for not being dumb.' I have faith in you, Daniel. You're not spoiled. You're a survivor, extremely loyal, and you don't back down from bullies. I can actually see that new golden age of peace and prosperity under your rule."

"We don't want to fuck it up," said Malcolm, joining in. He had a scotch on the rocks in hand, but his eyes were all business.

"Are our five minutes up already?" Cal asked.

"I get that he's your charge, Cal. And as role models go, he could do a lot worse than you. But I have a ton of resources I'm ready to commit—I just want assurances of what I will receive for that help."

"You took an oath, Malcolm."

"Aye, I did—to fight for the prince with ax and shield. My oath says nothing of my vast wealth and enterprises. Pull that oath thing on me again, and that's all you'll have—my ax and shield."

"What do you want?" Daniel asked the billionaire.

"My people came into existence in the mountains of Farrenheil near the western border of Nurvenheim and the Unclaimed Lands. We'd been there for generations mining, smelting, crafting—since before dwarv and man branched apart. Those mountains made us who we are today. And because we are different, impure—we were pushed out. I want your commitment to recognize these mountains as belonging to the dwarvs. Aandor is in a full-scale war regardless of whether it's winning or not. So commit your armies to march on Farrenheil at some future point to route them from our mountains. We want our mines back . . . we want to go home."

"Uh, how big is our army?" Daniel asked Cal.

"Exactly," Cal said, as though his point had been made. "Daniel doesn't even know what resources his kingdom has," Cal said to Mal. "Yet you want him to commit to treaties. We know even less about the kingdom after the invasion. The whole army could be wiped out—cities, villages."

"I want a good-faith commitment, Cal. Nothing written in blood."

"You know that's not fair, given—"

"Yes," Daniel said.

Cal and Malcolm looked at the boy, each like they weren't sure what they'd heard.

"What?" asked Mal.

"I said yes," Daniel repeated. "I agree to this commitment. The mountains to the west of Fahrvergnügen . . ."

"Farrenheil."

Daniel nodded and gesticulated in accord. "Whatever . . . they belong to the Dwarfs . . ."

"Dwarvs," Malcolm said, stressing the ah sound and the V. "D-wah-arvzz."

"Sure," Daniel added.

Cal's lips became a thin line of reproach. "Daniel, you can't—"

"Sure I can. I'm a prince, not a candidate. You guys are going around in circles here, driving a lot of people nuts with no results." The others in the room perked up at the change in the conversation.

"Yes, but—"

"Miss . . . ," Daniel called out to Lelani and motioned for her to join them. "Who am I?"

"You're Grand Duke Danel of Aandor, Blood of Ten Kings, Prince of the Realm, and Regent of the Empire of Aandor," Lelani said.

"So either I can make this decision now, and end this squabbling, or I'm really just a glorified hostage in a very nice hotel room."

Malcolm laughed. "I like him!" he bellowed.

"Daniel, the age of ascension is sixteen," Cal said. "Your father the archduke still runs Aandor."

"That's not really the point. I know I'm not in charge, but if we have the resources to help Malcolm's people get their mountain back, we should commit to this to access whatever assets he can bring to bear now. If we don't, we can't very well blame him for not helping.

"Look . . . I'm a geek; I've played enough strategy games to know holding back resources at a crucial time only costs you more in the long run. There's a time to make like a squirrel and store your nuts, and then there's the times you have to commit to the larger plan, take a leap of faith. This situation is a no-brainer. Another kingdom invaded my home, captured my parents, killed my subjects—man it's weird to say that—and tried to kill me. They evicted Malcolm's people from their ancestral home. So are we realistically close to negotiating a peace with them? Or prepared to let them go home and say *No hard feelings*? No, right?

"We *have* to take the fight back to their country, otherwise we're a bunch of wusses and they're just going to try again. So either we lose and it doesn't matter, or we win and one of our conditions of surrender is the dwarvs get their home back. We don't really have anything to lose by giving Mr. Robbe his good faith commitment. There's only upside here."

Cal scratched his head. There was a gaggle of things Daniel had not considered, but overall, it wasn't bad ball-park logic. *Did I just get bamboozled by a kid just shy of fourteen?*

"Mal, you know this doesn't hold water back home," Cal said. "I can't believe you'd leverage this situation to your personal advantage . . ."

"Look around you," Malcolm said, pointing out the opulent suite in the middle of Manhattan. "No one makes it to my station in life without leveraging opportunities that come his or her way. I have competitors cursing my name from Miami to Seattle. I'm the gay billionaire bastard from hell. The kid wants to commit to my conditions. I take him at his word. He gets anything he needs from me. So what are we doing right now . . . Today?"

The two went at it again; this time it was Cal's cheeks that turned crimson with vehement objection. It was about to come to blows, but Scott pulled Malcolm back while Lelani and Colby worked on Callum. When they, too, were at risk of being engulfed by the maelstrom, Reverend Grey interceded and cast a calming blessing over the room. This was the full extent of a cleric's soothe without physical contact. It worked until Mal, a few moments later, threatened to lop Allyn's hands off if he ever manipulated his emotions with magic again. Allyn took umbrage to the accusation of using *magic* like a common wizard, and a new round of bickering ensued.

"Hey, there's some sort of parade going on in the street," Clarisse said, standing at the window. "Is the circus in town?"

Balzac waded through the group to the window. His face turned ashen. It was the first honest emotion Cal had seen on the man since being reintroduced to him. Clarisse opened the window. They heard the increasing honking of horns as gridlock settled in and sirens in the distance. Police flashers came on in several directions—and then . . . screams. Everyone situated him or herself at one window or another to witness the anarchy outside. Cal got a good look at Clarisse's animals. It wasn't the circus. It was Malcolm being right yet again. Cal caught his sergeant's stare—their arguments suspended until further notice.

"My God," Reverend Grey said. "What—what are those?"

"Incoming!" Cal shouted.

CHAPTER 35

THE WAITING GAME

There were no further updates from North Carolina. Cat waited in the common area surrounded by Dorn, Hesz, Lhars, Oulfsan, Tom the minion, and Ilyana, the other female prisoner. Despite Balzac's boasts of his influence with Farrenheil, Dorn was furious that he'd tried to kill Catherine. He wanted to possess Prince Danel's bloody corpse before deciding her fate. She would remain among them until Krebe returned. All communication with the farm ceased after Dorn gave the order to kill the boy.

The tension in the room increased tenfold. Cat had no knowledge of her husband's fate. Perhaps they were deep in the country out of cell tower range—or sunspots were screwing with the satellites.

Ilyana sat gagged on the floor against the couch, her hands and feet tied with rope. Symian had acquired her in the meat packing district on the west side of Manhattan late one night—she was just at the wrong place at the wrong time. That was one of the dangers of living in New York. It was Cat's job to take care of her needs.

Like too many of her countrywomen, Ilyana came to the U.S. illegally from Russia to pursue a pole-dancing career. It was more than cliché—it was epidemic. The cotton rag in American money must slide softer on flesh compared with other currencies, Cat thought. There was something off about the girl Cat couldn't quite put her finger on. Symian had targeted his victim well—her few friends were also here illegally and not inclined to go to the police about her disappearance. God help her Russian handlers if they tried to retrieve her; Hesz and Kraten would cut them to pieces.

Cat felt protective of Ilyana, but was stretched thin because she still had to tend to Tory. His crying became unbearable at one point . . . Hesz simply shut the bedroom door and instructed Cat to ignore him. Dorn declined to mention his plans for Ilyana. Catherine wished she could do magic—she wanted to cast a protective shield over everyone.

The clock ticked by slowly. Hesz read Malcolm Gladwell's *The Tipping Point*, a book Cat had on her own bucket list. Perhaps he'd loan it to her before slitting her throat, she wondered. There was a deep, sharp intelligence behind Hesz's bright blue eyes that belied his size and ugly mug. He was detached, patient, calm in a way none of the others was. The more time Cat spent around him, the more certain she was that he was not a zealot to Dorn's agenda. Some other motive drove that giant brain and for now it was aligned with hurting her friends and family. Dorn was reading some very old parchments over a table stocked with Bunsen burners, a microscope, beakers, flasks, test tubes, powders, liquids, still coils, prongs, and the such. A small lead can with the radiation warning sat among the items.

As he read, Dorn popped back prescription pills like they were M&M's, and his henchmen looked down, away, or at each other whenever their master did this, like a choreographed routine. Dorn's health waned. His puffy eyes were glassy; his golden hair had lost its luster and thinned, sallow skin gave him a malnourished sheen. Cat wondered if the pills caused his decline or were holding him together.

Symian and Kraten returned with bags full of items to replace the ones they lost to Lelani in Central Park. Daniel had been seconds from death as of the last update, and all hoped Dorn would not need to use one of his special spells. It said something about the risk when Dorn's own people were hoping against it.

"The lay pool is gone," said Symian. His voice, soft yet stern, was like that of a father telling his wife their child had died.

"Gone?" repeated Dorn.

He clearly had trouble understanding "gone" as a concept. Dorn put fingers to his temple and tried to rub away a migraine. Cat was familiar with the pain—more than a headache, migraines fogged the thoughts, and light and sound bludgeoned you like solid objects.

"The witch," Symian continued. He looked to Cat when he said this, as though it were her doing—like Lelani belonged to her. Symian was the most otherworldly of the rogue's gallery: yellow where the whites of his eyes should have been with ink black pupils, grayish skin, and canine incisors. His hair was jet black and rough, like printer cartridge toner that had clumped together. How he moved through New York masked by only a ball cap, hoodie, and scarf was beyond understanding. He would never get away with it in another city. New York was still the best place on earth to be utterly alone.

"The lay line was gone when we returned," he explained. "The pool all but dried out. We took what was left, but that spot will not replenish."

"Where pray tell is there another source in this gods-forsaken city?" asked Dorn.

"It took us days to find that one, my lord. If we had a cleric . . ."

"Curse us for not including one when we went to kill, pillage, and rape people," said Dorn sarcastically.

"There is a theory that magic can inspire laymen to accomplish great feats in its vicinity. I can search . . ."

So the all-powerful Lord Dorn was out of gas with no station in sight. Desperation would only make him more dangerous. Cat wanted—no needed—a break in the news from North Carolina. She was as antsy as her captors.

Oulfsan stood—that familiar preswitch look came upon him.

"My lord . . . ," he cried.

All in the room watched, like the man was about to explode. The switch that was normally instantaneous was drawn out this time. His face started the tiniest of expressions, an unfinished movement that looked to Catherine like the beginnings of terror. Then the man went blank. Oulfsan teetered forward like a chopped tree and hit the carpet hard. They turned him over—he breathed shallowly, his nose was a swollen broken mess, and his stare was hollow—no one was home.

"What happened?" asked Hesz.

"Was Krebe unconscious in North Carolina?" Symian queried.

"Even unconscious, he would have awoken alert on this end of the switch," said Dorn. "Such was the nature of their curse."

"Then Krebe is . . . ," said Kraten.

"Krebe is dead," Dorn confirmed. He popped another pill and pounded on his temples.

CHAPTER 36

WE USED TO BE FRIENDS

1

Dorn looked over the last of his men on this world. His migraine had escalated—only two Treximets remained. If he did not get home soon, he would die a failure, forgotten in a foreign land. *How did it come to this?*

No matter what, the Kingdom of Aandor could not be allowed to reclaim its rule over the other nations of the old empire. Farrenheil had worked assiduously for centuries to create a paradise free of the lesser races—those creatures that at one time or another had hunted men, or worse, in their disdain, failed to help when it had been in their power to do so; to allow the ogres, trolls, gnolls, frost giants, goblins, kobolds, and myriad of other races prey on men. The elevation of inferior races, a sharing of man's knowledge, their power, their magic, was an invitation to doom the purity and dominance of mankind on his world. This could not be allowed. If Dorn had to die, he would not go alone. Prince Danel would accompany him into the afterlife—a fair price for ripping Dorn from his beloved Farrenheil . . . from Lara.

Strategizing through his migraine was like swimming against a strong current in icy waters. Dorn pointed at Ilyana and barked, "Prepare her!"

Dorn put on a full-length apron and long surgical gloves. He began mixing components for the compound. In a large five-hundred-milliliter beaker he put in water for oxygen and hydrogen, graphite dust for carbon, liquid nitrogen, calcium tablets, red phosphorus powder, potassium, sulfur, sodium, and all the remaining minor elements of life. Small bits of plants, weeds, tubers, fungi went in next—beside the beaker he set one of his mana stones and then lit the burner. The concoction soon boiled into a dark muddy green. Dorn opened two wrappings of sealed wax paper. In one, long white hair strands from a polar bear in Central Park, in the other the shorter gray strands of a wolf. The spell called for the hair of a single beast with follicles still attached. One beast. Dorn dumped both sets into the boiling mixture. In the reflection on a beaker he saw Symian wince.

"No mistake," he told the half-troll. "The ancients kept the creature lines pure because they sought to preserve some capacity for reason. Our creations will be given but one single unyielding directive with no restraint in ferocity. We are returning to Aandor *without* these creations. Let this wretched world deal with them after we're gone."

What made this spell different was the nature of its accelerant. Radioactive isotopes as a catalyst would supercharge cell mitosis. Dorn whispered a spell to create a bubble of hyper-dense air around the lead container. It would protect him from the radiation. Opening the container, he removed a few small bits of fissionable material with some lead tongs and plopped them into the beaker. He quickly shut the container.

"The girl," Dorn said. Hesz lifted Ilyana with one hand and lay her on her back with her lumbar region across the arm of the couch. With his powerful arms, Hesz held her legs and chest down. Dorn ripped off her micro skirt, exposing her midsection, and she screamed. He ripped her underwear off next and stuffed it into Ilyana's mouth. Symian cranked the stereo to drown her muffled screams. Cat jumped up to confront Dorn, but Lhars grabbed her.

"Please, Lady MacDonnell . . . now is not the time for hysterics," Dorn said. "You are about to witness my endgame . . . my final solution."

Dorn sliced a line across Ilyana's lower abdomen from right to left between her belly button and mons veneris.

"Sadist!" Cat screamed, struggling and kicking. "Leave that girl alone!" she cried.

Dorn produced a pair of long-handled tongs with tiny cupped ends and carefully inserted it into the gash. Ilyana's cotton gag absorbed her horrific screams. What little noise she produced accompanied the soundtrack of her vivisection—"We Used to Be Friends" by The Dandy Warhols. Dorn peeled away her flesh, slicing deeper with the knife when needed, searching for his prize. He searched and searched, prodding through her guts, pulling everything out—to no avail.

2

"Leave that girl alone!" Cat screamed. But even as she said this, the thing that had nagged at Cat all this time became horrifically clear—the thing she would have realized much earlier if not for all the fear and tension distracting her—Ilyana's large hands, huge feet—and Adam's apple.

Dorn, agitated, continued to pull pieces of Ilyana out like a child ravaging a toy box for his favorite ball. Her cries of protest grew weaker until they were barely a moan.

"Dorn, stop!" Cat yelled. "She's transgendered!"

"What?" asked Symian.

"She was born a man and changed into a woman by medical procedure," Cat explained.

Dorn's hands and clothes were covered in blood. Ilyana had gone completely quiet—her head dangled limply off the couch, her deathly stare pointed toward Cat. It was too late. From Dorn's expression, one would think his head was on the verge of exploding. He stepped away from Ilyana as though repelled by something repugnant.

"My lord," said Symian. "I did not know such things were . . ."

Dorn put up a single finger as if to say *not one word more.* "Find me a new source of magical energy," Dorn said softly, almost too soft to believe given his disappointment and precarious mental state. Cat heard what was not spoken at the end almost as clearly as if it were: *And I'll let you live.*

Symian left quickly, as though his boss might change his mind at any second. Whatever the sorcerer had intended, Ilyana was pivotal to his plans. Maybe the guardians could turn this delay to their advantage, Cat thought. The very next moment, Cat realized she was wrong. Horribly, horribly wrong. Dorn looked at her like a starving man looks at a roasted turkey leg. Whatever it was he needed from the tranny, Dorn had resolved to take it from Cat.

"I apologize, Lady MacDonnell," he said, almost sounding sincere.

Hesz grabbed Cat and pulled her toward the couch. He placed his toe underneath the front of the couch, and kicked it up until it fell backward. Ilyana rolled off and onto the carpet with a bloody splat. Hesz righted the couch with a foot again and placed Cat in the same position over the armrest. Ilyana's blood seeped into Cat's clothing, even as Kraten cut her blouse with a knife, like a paramedic in triage. She was stripped to her panties and secured; Dorn approached with a smaller, clean scalpel.

"Oh God, please," Catherine begged. She cried uncontrollably. "I'm pregnant. Please. Please!"

Dorn considered this for a second. "I have no intention of killing you, my lady. I simply cannot keep my promise not to *hurt* you."

He didn't cut all the way across her as he did Ilyana; instead, Dorn made a small, almost professional, incision on one side of Cat's lower abdomen. Cat screamed—her voice drowned out by the stereo. The cutting was agony, layer after layer peeled away until he could reach inside with a fresh pair of tongs. When he found what he wanted, he severed it with scissors and pulled it free.

"A woman is born with all her eggs," Dorn said to his men. He showed Cat her own severed ovum sac. "Thousands of them," he said, "enough for her lifetime."

"No!" Catherine wailed.

"Fear not," Dorn said. "The conceived child is safe."

Cat struggled against Hesz, pounding on his massive arms, but it was like beating on concrete pylons. "You son of a bitch! Give those back!" she cried. The pain in her abdomen was too intense and Cat thought she'd bleed to death.

Dorn produced a small vial and sprinkled a familiar white powder on Cat's wound. It sizzled and burned like a motherfucker just like the time upstate when Lelani used it on Cat's shoulder. The cut began to sew itself up. Hesz let her go.

"Why?" she sniffled. "You didn't do that for Ilyana? You gutted her like a pig!"

Dorn rolled the vial between his fingers playfully. "The ingredients of this remedy include a phoenix's feather, a basilisk's egg, and the claw of a griffon," he said. "This vial is worth more than this entire block of buildings. It is not for the salvaging of gutter rats. Being the wife of a nobleman has its merits. You and I are friends, after all."

"Friends . . . ? You cut out my ovary you fucking piece of shit!"

She spat in Dorn's face, proud of the long hard stream she was able to aim true. He smiled and pushed her spit to his lips and lapped it in.

"There's a satisfactory sense of irony in that soon, the good captain will be neck deep in his own murderous stepchildren," he said.

Dorn handed Lhars a quart-sized flask to fill with Ilyana's blood. He poured the blood into the mixture and it turned a muddy purple. Dorn read from the ancient scroll, his hands positioned on either side of the beaker like the open part of a clap, channeling his magic between them. The words Dorn uttered sounded ancient beyond time, simple, sharp, the language of men before they lived under roofs of their own making, the building blocks of all speech that was to follow. As the words exited Dorn's mouth, they took on a power and purpose of their own, fueled by a spirit within the scrolls. Something took over Dorn's voice, old beyond imagining; an intonation that could never share a world with men, released from a long sleep. Everyone in the room except for Dorn covered their ears. The sound cut through anyway, stimulating the most primal parts of the brain, the place where everyone's inner lizard still resided.

As Dorn read, the fluid emitted a phosphorescent glow. The room went dark like the passing of a storm cloud as the elixir greedily absorbed all light and took on mass. An oppressive painful pressure filled the suite, like the entire room had been expelled to the bottom of the ocean. Even the henchmen shifted about nervously.

"Dorn! Stop!" Cat yelled. But the wizard was possessed. Dorn cut his finger and dropped his own blood into the cauldron. "Hesz!" he shouted and held out his hand. Hesz produced a ziplock bag from his jacket with hairbrush, pillowcase, and little bits at the bottom that looked like nail clippings and dried skin. Dorn selected some hairs from the brush and ripped a piece off the pillowcase and into they beaker they went. Catherine realized those items must belong to the prince. Whatever Dorn was doing was custom targeted to Daniel. He chanted a last series of phrases and shut off the flame.

It was an ugly brew, not quite green or purple or brown at first but quickly morphing into a dark crimson. Catherine felt the pulsating vibrancy of life within this creation. It seemed to her that Dorn had placed enough material into the beaker to fill it five times over and yet not a drop spilled over. Dorn added one more ingredient . . . he dropped Catherine's ovary into the beaker. A part of her died as Dorn stirred vigorously, breaking up the ovary's tissue and releasing her eggs into the mix; her babies were gone forever. He poured the final brew into a conical lead-glass flask.

Hesz placed five petri dishes along the floor next to one another.

"Farther apart," said Dorn.

Using an eyedropper, Dorn deposited a single drop of the compound in each dish, and sealed the remaining elixir with a rubber stop. He poured some water into the dishes.

Cat had never been more frightened in her life. As if the aftershock of her violation and the gruesome death of Ilyana weren't enough to send her to therapy for life, there was something cursed in those scrolls, beyond evil, older than man, older than dinosaurs, that every living being across the multiverse has been programmed down to their DNA to reject. Even Hesz and Kraten wanted to be elsewhere. Magic had been around since the creation of the universe, used by beings far older than man—Aandor's stumbling across it was like children stumbling across a loaded pistol. Who decides when a race is mature enough to play with the knowledge they discover?

"Lelani said these magicks are dangerous . . . uncontrollable," Cat told Dorn. "They get away from the wizard's control. The reactions are too fast, sometime instantaneous . . . lots of wizards have died trying to do these spells. That's why your people banned them."

Cat's purpose in saying these things to Dorn was twofold: that by some slim chance, he would listen to reason, and that maybe one of his lackeys would get spooked and turn on him. They looked as nervous as she did . . . this was beyond normal spell casting. The radio droned, *"I am, I am, I am, Superman . . . and I know what's happening."*

Bad call by the DJ, Cat realized. *There's a more appropriate R.E.M. song for this day.*

Dorn approached the petri dishes with all his remaining mana stones. He chanted the third verse in that ancient language bringing back the oppressive, invisible singularity that sucked life and hope from the room to feed itself. Dorn chanted until the room shook and the mana stones cracked and splintered.

Three stalks sprouted from each dish like tentacles. Dorn looked disappointed. "Only fifteen?" he said, to no one in particular.

The sprouts continued to grow before their eyes. Plant like appendages unfolded and began to fill like animal-shaped balloons. Sounds emerged from their nascent throats; a high-pitched squeal of pain. The creatures reached five feet, eight feet, ten, dwarfing even Hesz. Dorn continued chanting and their bulk filled out, manlike shapes merged with beasts. The backward bend of wolf legs, massive arms like a bear's with downy white hair. Heavy brows hung over black deep-set eyes. The creatures lacked a true neck, their heads jutted from immense muscular shoulders. Noses like snouts pushed flat. Fangs competing for space in a mouth surrounded by thin black leathery lips, large enough to bite a human head off. Pawlike hands with black leathery palms, fingers tipped with black talons.

Dorn performed like a rapturous conductor before a symphony. He was mad. No sane person could bring forth such a thing and think it good. He motioned with his arms. Some of the creatures mimicked him, then finally all of them did. He'd made a connection, like a puppeteer testing strings. The room was filled with drooling beasts. Dorn was joyous.

Their snarls and grunts drowned out the music; when they moved, the room shook. They were frenzied for the hunt, drooling, flexing, flailing, knocking the walls behind them with their massive feral arms, yet they stayed anchored awaiting Dorn's word. Cat squeezed into the middle of the crowded space between Hesz, Tom, and Lhars. Even the ever-smirking Kraten looked unsure for once and joined them. Cat would rather have been in a room with a hundred rabid pitbulls.

"My children," Dorn cried, tears streaming down a face twisted with rapturous glee. "I can see them in my mind," he said. "Smell what they smell, hear what they hear. And they hear me. Daniel Hauer is in the city. They smell him."

A shudder ran through Catherine. *Fifteen*, she realized—fifteen of these abominations hunting the prince. And where the prince was, so were Cal and Bree . . . The last glimmer of hope left Catherine. Her rescue didn't seem as important anymore . . . but what could she do? Hesz's phone rang, and he had the wherewithal to answer.

Dorn hunched over holding his head, like his brain was growing too big for his skull. The strain of the spell while in the midst of migraines was more than he could bear. In symbiotic unity with him, the creatures roared in anguish. Dorn squeezed his nose between the eyes to drive away the pain.

"Symian has found another lay line," said Hesz.

"Yes! He will die today," Dorn said, ignoring his frost giant's message. "Danel must DIE!

"GO!" he ordered. The creatures burst from the room, some smashing through the window, shimmying down the side of the building, others bursting into the stairwell—all gone in a flash to wreak havoc at the Waldorf—to kill a boy.

The room was in shambles. *My God,* Cat thought, as Kraten restrained her.

My God.

CHAPTER 37

THINGS MEN DO

Although only days had passed, it felt like years since Seth had been back in the old neighborhood. The usual suspects were there—the shopkeepers, artists, kids, homeless—but they had changed. They were different—distant now, like a mirage of something familiar that never got clearer. His experience broadened his knowledge of himself and the world, changed expectations, but "home" remained fixed to the dimensions of his former life. If mileage took its toll on the soul, then Seth traveled the equivalent of four continents. There was wisdom in the saying, "You can't go home again."

Seth thought he had the right tenement—it was one of the ones to either side of Earl's building. Half the names were missing from the buzzer directory, and he didn't see the one he wanted. He knew it was the third floor, but not the apartment number. If he'd been a better man he'd have known . . . he'd have spent every day there doing what men did. A brightly bundled woman in a knitted wool cap with cat ears rushed out. Seth caught the door, hoping not to have his presence challenged, but she was already on the sidewalk and running down the street, probably late to an audition. It made sense that this was not a secure building since Darcy was too fucked up to get out of bed most of the time. The junk had to come to her.

He knocked on the door. A girl's voice responded.

"It's Mr. Picture Man," Seth said.

Caitlin opened the door, held at a crack by a few inches of chain.

Her single eye in the opening looked puzzled by Seth's appearance. Seth had always been a street buddy, someone to trade quips with when he walked by—maybe score money for pizza.

"Hey Sassafras. Is your mom home?" Seth said. He knew that she was.

"She in bed."

Seth's watch said 10:00 A.M. He'd forgotten what day it was, but was fairly sure it was a weekday. "It's important."

Caitlin thought about it. It broke Seth's heart when the girl granted him access. He could have been a robber or worse.

The front door led into a small kitchen area that extended into a small living room to the left of and behind the front door. The linoleum was cracked and faded under the kitchen's single circular fluorescent light. To the right beyond the kitchen were two bedroom doors side by side—one was closed.

"Nice stick," Caitlin said.

Seth handed her his staff. She ran her fingers across the grooves and etchings, examining his workmanship. The staff was almost done, yet Seth already felt a connection to the device both emotional and functional, like a child's first key to his home.

The apartment was a shambles, half empty of furniture; loveseat but no couch, entertainment center but no television, stereo, CDs, or computer. They'd been gone for some time. Caitlin had a schoolbook opened on the kitchen table with a bowl of Cap'n Crunch next to it.

Seth walked to the closed bedroom door and entered without knocking. Darcy's bedroom was as dark and cold as a tomb. It smelled musty, like unwashed laundry. Darcy was invisible in bed—black skin, on black sheets, in a black room—as absent here as she was in her daughter's life. Seth opened the blinds, allowing the sun in. On the bureau was Darcy's paraphernalia: needle, tablespoon, burner, rubber band, and a tiny plastic bag filled with what Seth assumed was heroin. In the trash were several used condoms of different makes and sizes—he stopped counting at eleven. Caitlin, he realized, remained at the kitchen table, staring into her cereal, which she stirred around in its milk. Again, his heart broke—a strange man showing up and going into her mother's bedroom was normal to her.

Darcy slept facedown, legs spread, naked. Her once beautiful, muscular body looked thin, haggard. Seth checked her pulse, which was slow but steady.

"Darcy," he said, rocking her gently.

She moaned.

He continued until she turned over and took note of him through half-open bloodshot eyes. Her small breasts sagged. Dried semen was clumped in her tuft of pubic hair. Guess some customers were just too stupid for their own good.

Darcy had been his first nude model. She was stunning when they'd met eight years ago, muscular and radiant—Naomi Campbell's heir apparent. Her father was a Maasai tribesman from East Africa who had come to New York to study at Columbia on a scholarship. There he met Darcy's mother, an African-American from Forest Hills, Queens. Darcy's skin was such a beautiful deep brown as to be a few shades short of true black. Seth couldn't believe he'd successfully seduced her even after they'd had sex. She even fell for him. He was the worst thing that'd ever happened to her.

He'd sold her nude pictures to a second-rate *Hustler* wannabe. All the work she'd put toward her legitimate modeling career went into the toilet. No designer wanted anything to do with a woman who'd appeared in a porn magazine; no mainstream agency wanted to rep her. Seth continued to shoot her nudes until she'd appeared in every trashy girlie book being published. She never made more than a few hundred dollars from the shoots. With each photo Seth consumed another piece of her soul. He paraded her at the worst parties like a trophy. It was his callous use of her, his willingness to sell out someone who meant something to him that had earned him a reputation as someone to do business with in the industry. A porn photographer with a soft spot for women was useless. Bigger industry sharks, sensing his spinelessness and insecurities, preyed on her as well, demanding their pound of flesh, promising her more than Seth could deliver, and delivering nothing except film shoots where she was passed around by multiple lovers in the most degrading videos imaginable. Darcy drank to excess and experimented with substances to shut out what her life had become. Then she became pregnant with Caitlin. So of course, Seth dumped her and washed his hands of her entirely.

Seth had felt betrayed. It was never a huge leap for him to tap into anger; it always lurked there around the corner in easy reach. He needed legs like a millipede to count his grievances in life. He'd convinced himself (and there is a distinction here from "he was convinced") that Caitlin was some porn star's spawn, some amateur cock jockey too eager to pull out in time for the money shot. But as Caitlin grew, her hazel eyes, shaped like crescents standing on their tips, and her milk-in-the-coffee coloring, offered evidence to the contrary.

Still, Seth used Darcy's parade of bareback partners to inoculate him from claiming the girl or any other part in Darcy's life. And digging down deep, parentage had never truly been the issue. It was Seth's commitment to his eternal adolescence. He'd resented Darcy for not getting an abortion. He was only nineteen at the time and there was a parade of pussy to attain. Why the hell abandon that for a used-up wife and a brat?

Seth was as bad a father as Clyde Knoffler had been to Daniel. The important difference was he was still alive. He could improve upon the past. Ben Reyes spoke to him from inside his head. *What is good?* Seth wiped a tear with his finger. The floodgates would hold for now. He had business to finish.

Caitlin ate her cereal, innocent as a cherub. Seth checked the cupboards and fridge. There was actually food where Caitlin could reach it.

"Who gets your groceries?" he asked.

"Mrs. Gomez," she said, as though Seth were supposed to know who that was. "And sometimes Sister Gladys from St. Emeric. Ain't you going to jump Mommy?" she asked.

Seth waited for his gut to reset before asking, "Are you here when men come by?"

"I stay in my room. Sometimes I sneak out. Mommy makes noise like it hurts, but she tells me it don't."

Seth pulled up a chair. He sat across from her, eye to eye with his progeny. Was it worth telling her? Would it make a difference? He'd get her hopes up, and then what? Dorn was still at large, sending people after him. What would be the point in telling her if he died a few days from now? . . . Or if he went back to Aandor? He'd just get her hopes up and then disappear.

"I'm leaving you a lot of money," he said bluntly. "And I mean *you,* not your mommy."

Caitlin's mouth created the perfect little O. "Nuh-uh," she said, disbelieving.

"Uh-huh," he said. He pulled out copies of the financial paperwork. "The money is in both our names. I set up an account called a trust, and you're going to get a little bit every month to help pay for food, clothes, and rent. And when you turn eighteen, what's left is going to be all yours to do what you want. That means you can go to college or buy a house or whatever."

"Nuh-uh!"

"Uh-huh."

"Mommy's going to take it all for drugs!" she said.

"Nuh-uh," he said, mimicking her. "Mommy's going to this place." He handed Caitlin a pamphlet for the best drug rehab center in Westchester. Stapled to it was a receipt for a three-month program—paid in full. "We're going to get her there. It's a special place for people with problems like your mom. They go in and detox, and come out better. You're going to live with your grandma in Queens until Darcy's done. And after she's better, we're going to ask Sister

Gladys to help you manage your monthly stipend until we're sure your mom won't shoot it up her arm."

"But why are you doing this?" Caitlin took it all in with the wonderment only a child could bring to such an unbelievable boon. Seth couldn't help but think she should be more skeptical . . . it would help defend herself against the bad people of the world . . . against men like him. Caitlin was her mother's daughter through and through—raised to believe in princes and magical moments—that someone someday was going to come along and make all your dreams come true. He wanted Caitlin to have the money, but he also wanted her to know what was out there.

"Your mom was my first girlfriend," Seth said. "And I'm the reason she started drinking and doing drugs. I'm the reason . . ." Seth welled up. The realizations of his actions and their effect on the lives of others fell on him like a jumbo jet. ". . . why your life isn't as good as it should be," he finished. "I'm very sorry, Caitlin."

The dam broke.

Seth wiped away tears with his sleeve. He expected her to call him stupid—to curse him for destroying her mother, for wrecking her life. But Caitlin handed him a paper towel and patted his shoulder instead. She was a seven-year-old wonder.

Cal was waiting—their business with Dorn was not yet done. But he didn't want to leave Caitlin at this time. She took his hand and led him to the loveseat in the living room where she curled up next to him.

"Tell me about my moms when she was a girl, Mr. Picture Man—before drugs."

"My name is Seth," he told her. Caitlin nodded, but made no other gesture toward the revelation. She was waiting to hear about Darcy—about the woman who would be her mother after the rehab. He called up everything good about Darcy he could remember and was not surprised that it was too much to hold in his head all at once. "Your mom was the most beautiful girl I'd ever met . . . ," he began.

CHAPTER 38
INCOMING

The sidewalk below the hotel was empty of pedestrians. A dozen creatures, white, bearlike, feral raged in frustration as they were locked out of the building by an invisible force. The police cordoned off a two-block radius around the Waldorf. Cal wished they'd make it ten blocks. They were outclassed; he didn't want any of his brothers in blue to get hurt over Aandor's affairs.

The hotel's fire alarms whooped and flashed. Hallway speakers told the guests not to be alarmed and to stay in their rooms. All the outer doors had been locked. The police had been called and were looking into the matter of the escaped animals outside the hotel.

"They can't get in," said Mal's head of security, Tom Dunning. "They've surrounded the building but it's the same everywhere."

"Lelani, will your shield hold?" Cal asked.

"Not certain," she said. "I erected it to protect against an energy or mind-control attack. I've never seen beasts affected like this. They must be saturated with magic."

"Was hoping for something more definitive," Cal said.

"Hey! Two of those things are climbing up the side!" Daniel shouted.

Lelani's eyes widened. "My lord, the shield is not a perfect envelope—it was not intended to repel a physical threat. It is a series of sheets, like umbrellas, and where they overlap . . ."

". . . there may be openings," Cal finished. "Where?"

"The roof. Several overlaps."

"I've got it," said Dunning, and he sent three of his armed men up the stairwell. Outside the suite Dunning's remaining squad set up to repel invaders from every entrance point on the floor. Cal shut the door behind him and ordered Timian and Reverend Grey to barricade it with the couch.

"Bree! Where's Bree?" Cal barked.

Clarisse came forward with the girl in her arms. She was frightened but not crying. Cal was proud of his brave little girl. "You stay with this lady," Cal told his daughter. To Clarisse he said, "You stay with this lady," pointing to Lelani. "And you protect my daughter with your life," he told Lelani. "Get her out of here if you can. I have the prince. He's the one those things are set upon, so stay on the opposite end of the room wherever he is."

"What do you mean 'set upon'?" Daniel asked. The boy's eyes were wide, his lip quivered. The most powerful wizard in the world wanted him dead. He looked scared and confused as to why this was happening to him. The boy acted so mature for his age, Cal had to remind himself that the lad was just shy of fourteen, and that all of this was new to him.

"They're homing in on you, kid," Malcolm said. "Anywhere in the world you run, they will track you down."

Cal didn't approve of Malcolm's gruff tone. The kid was already scared enough.

Cal unzipped his duffel bag. He pulled out nonstandard-issue equipment that he one day had hoped to wear in the field as a member of the NYPD's elite Hercules unit: body armor with ballistic plates, Kevlar helmet with visor, M-4 carbine assault rifle, combat boots, Smith & Wesson 9 mm with fifteen rounds in the clip and one in the chamber. Cal put on his modern armor . . . grateful it wasn't the head-to-toe steel suit he wore in battles back home. That one was fifty pounds heavier and far less flexible. He had a black lightweight ballistic shield with viewport that was more durable than any steel shield he ever carried back in Aandor. On his back he strapped Bòid Géard.

"Call the idiot!" he barked at Lelani. "Tell him we need his help now." Progress was made around the room. The barricade was up, Timian joined Clarisse and Bree, Reverend Grey stood beside Daniel, Malcolm next to them wearing a state-of-the-art military-issue special forces plate vest and wielding a fire ax in one hand and a larger, two-sided silver ax with a six-inch Kaiser spike sticking up between them in the other—everyone had a role . . . everyone except Balzac. Where was the jester?

Thunderous crashes at the room's windows, and the flying shattered glass that resulted, scared the crap out of everyone. The creatures—a mutated mingling of man and beast roared with spit-riddled breath at the inhabitants just out of their reach—they couldn't get in and their failure to attack their prey deranged them further. Sniffing at the windows, they both set their sights on the prince, but the massive paws couldn't penetrate the perimeter of the room. Their howls reverberated across the New York skyline.

Colby drew his pistol and emptied his clip into the closest monster. One of Mal's security men did the same.

"Save your bullets," Cal ordered. "Lelani, how long will this shield last?" Cal asked.

"At this level of strain, about one day. Then the battery plates run dry."

A marksman in a police copter outside their room opened fire on the creatures with a rifle. The beasts yowled, but otherwise shrugged off the attack. A third beast that they hadn't been aware of leaped upward from the corner of the building onto the windshield of the copter.

Damn, Cal thought. He couldn't see the other two sides of this building, and therefore could not account for all the creatures.

The beast on the copter smashed through the windshield, mangling the pilot with its massive jaws, and continued into the copter after the marksman. The helicopter spiraled downward, its tail smashing into the offices across the street, taking creature and crew down with it in a fiery burst. Streamers of hot metal and burning fuel covered Park Avenue like a miniature nova.

The NYPD on the ground retreated, backing their units farther from the hotel. They'd eventually muster enough manpower, but hundreds of cops might die before then.

"We need a plan to get Daniel out of the building and out of the city, possibly upstate New York or Pennsylvania," Cal said. "Mal, can you get two copters to land on the roof? Let's hope these things aren't bright and just keep up what they've been . . ."

The creatures at the window looked up toward the roof—then began to climb.

"Crap," Cal whispered under his breath.

CHAPTER 39
FROM A VIEW TO A KILL

Dorn and his remaining entourage walked into the lobby of the Chrysler Building on Forty-second Street and Lexington Avenue carrying large duffel bags filled with weapons and magical paraphernalia. People were distracted, talking animatedly about a terrorist attack at the Waldorf Astoria several blocks uptown. A mildly drugged Catherine MacDonnell barely stood on her feet by her own power—Lhars had his arm around her in an intimate embrace, looking to the few patrons in the lobby like a tired, loving couple.

The building was beautiful. Metal eagles gleaming from the corners of the sixtieth floor as they approached the building beckoned to Dorn. They reminded him of the aeries in the highlands of Farrenheil, where his father would take him eagle hunting. The lobby was a masterful execution of art deco design, and one of the few structures in this universe that impressed Dorn's aesthetics. Marble, metal, and light conspired to produce a palette of golden sheen against deep black trim. The artwork on the ceiling was simply breathtaking. As they walked, Symian proudly explained how he had found this source of magic.

"In my research to find where magic enters this world, I discovered that wherever it runs it inspires great feats," he said. "Where magic manifests there is evidence of it: the pyramids of Giza, Stonehenge in England. This building was once the tallest in the world and is still considered one of the most beautiful. It was closest to the Plaza, so I came here on a hunch and was rewarded for my insight . . . the entire building is a conductor. The lay line emerges here and pools into the building."

A security man in his fifties with graying hair and a well-tailored suit that hid his paunch stopped them before the elevator banks to the top floors. "What's your business?" he asked.

"The topmost floor," said Dorn, truthfully.

"That's just storage these days," the security man said. "We haven't had an observatory deck since the forties."

"Splendid," responded Dorn. "That will do."

"No, you don't understa—"

"Run," Cat mumbled. "Call . . . police."

The man reached for his radio too late. Hesz snapped his neck and caught him before he fell. He held the security man in such a way as to appear that he was a friend giving them a tour. They walked calmly to the elevator and headed up to the seventy-first floor.

The space was cavernous and mostly empty, the floor a mix of dark and light marble. A long wide hallway stretched from the north to the south side of the building like the cross bar on the letter H, with the elevator, stairwell, and some closets in the center on either side. On the north and south ends, the room turned west and east giving access to all four vistas. Unlike some observation decks with balconies, this one was entirely enclosed.

The ceiling on the corners tapered in following the form of the famous crown on the outside. On the walls and ceiling were painted the stars and planets of the solar system. The windows on all sides were triangular, pointed at angles outward like prongs of a crown radiating toward the heavens. A heavenly atmosphere appropriately permeated the room, perfect for Dorn's aerie of power. The magic saturated this place. Dorn drank it into himself like a man come out of the desert. He'd forgotten what it was to be continuously charged. It stayed the headache and the voices. This was what was needed, not pills. Power!

"This will do," he said to Symian.

They placed the security man's body in a storage closet and placed their oversized duffel bags within easy reach around the floor. Dorn looked down. Flashing red lights like glowing ants traveled north and east and west, converging on the Waldorf-Astoria a few blocks north. Through his link to the golems, Dorn knew of the shield the centaur had erected, but now flushed with power, he prepared to remove this final obstacle.

Dorn opened one of the triangular windows and stepped out into the open air. He floated down under his own power to the sixtieth floor and landed upon one of the eagles that guarded the northwest corner of the building. Dorn drew in the mana from the building; Symian had been right, the building was a conduit—the flow of energy was concentrated . . . richer and more plentiful than anywhere in Farrenheil.

He cast his spell and pushed the power outward in a violent thrust toward the Waldorf. The centaur's shield buckled but held. Dorn smiled and readied another spell. He would throw the world at that dwelling until Daniel was dead, dead, dead.

CHAPTER 40

MINSTREL'S LUCK

1

The building shook.

Spell upon spell mercilessly pounded against Lelani's wards. The attack went unnoticed by all except for Lelani and the cleric. Prelate Grey looked to the centaur for an explanation but quickly surmised what was happening.

"The shields are under attack!" the prelate shouted to everyone.

The protections, which Lelani had erected to ward off nonphysical attacks, had turned out to be vital in repelling the golems. They would have been dead in no time otherwise.

Lelani had read about golems, used in wars a thousand years past. Dorn had used forbidden magic to create these creatures; that was why they could not cross the protective barriers—the magic was supercharged by radioactive elements, but it was the magic that animated them that could not cross the threshold. Uncontrollable and erratic—these spells of mass destruction had been unleashed by a sociopathic madman.

Reverend Grey placed his hand over Daniel's head. His eyes were closed; he chanted in the language of his order. With the other hand, he reached for a small plastic container shaped like the Madonna, and sprinkled water on the boy.

"What the heck?" said Daniel.

"It's a blessing," Lelani said. "To protect you. Prelate, the water . . . ?"

"From a Catholic church," Grey said. "We only do full immersion at my church and I hadn't had time to make my own holy water."

"Will that actually do anything practical?" Tim said mockingly.

"Yes," Lelani said. "It changes the odds—a fifty-fifty circumstance becomes fifty-one–forty-nine in Daniel's favor. But that means someone else . . . Who?" she asked Grey.

The cleric shook his head slowly. "I drew from no one's well . . . it is the gods' choice."

The remaining golems had begun climbing up from the street. They must have had some sort of rudimentary language, and the first wave must have signaled some degree of success on top of the building. Gunfire and screams came from the roof only a few floors above them. Some of the beasts had made it through the shield.

"Lelani, will these things die?" MacDonnell asked.

"Yes," she said. Although, not easily. The captain held his carbine rifle. This felt wrong to the centaur.

"My lord, may I see your sword?"

MacDonnell unsheathed it and handed it to her without hesitation. The MacDonnells had been guardians of the rulers of Aandor for generations, probably even before recorded history. They were defenders of the truth, upholders of the law, and protectors of the innocent. Bòid Géard was an inherited family heirloom, well crafted and handed down over many generations.

Lelani suspected the sword might be unique. The MacDonnells also descended from royalty many generations removed. Though their resistance to magic was nowhere near as complete as a ruling royal, they were very hard to fool and could see through complex illusions. It stood to reason the family weapons would be uniquely suited to their vocation. She ran her fingers over the flat of the blade. Yes, it was there, she could feel it in the metal.

"Malcolm, this sword—was it forged by dwarvs?" she asked.

"Heck yeah," he said. "I could spot a dwarv weapon from twenty feet."

"Why?" asked Cal. "Is it enchanted?"

"Even better, my lord . . . it's disenchanted. The alloy contains faerie silver. It's a nullifier. This sword, not your rifle, is your best weapon."

"I was hoping not to have to get that close to one," Cal said, securing his carbine and pulling up his police shield. He stood, sword in hand, in his Hercules Unit armor and helmet, a knight for the modern age.

The building shook. Again, only Grey and Lelani felt it.

"My lord, I must reach the roof to bolster the shield. Dorn is almost through."

Something hit the hallway with a deep thud and a roar. Rapid gunfire just outside the door mingled with howls and the cries and screams of Malcolm's security detail. Stray bullets from the far end of the hall cut through the door—Cal and Lelani shoved everybody back.

"Oh fucking shit!" cried Tim. "This is all your fault!" he said, screaming at Malcolm. "You fucking forced me here! I just wanted to tour with my band! I didn't want any part of this! I should have taken off with Ball Sack."

Lelani had hoped the cocktails would bolster the musician's bravery, but instead they were detrimental to his mindset . . . only freeing Timian's inhibitions toward his own cowardice. Lelani had always been puzzled by human women's propensity to fall for such selfish, feckless creatures as minstrels. They were foppish, barely capable of building a cabin much less defending home and hearth from the ravages of invaders.

Lelani placed more stock in Clarisse's ability to handle a crisis than her boyfriend. But she and Brianna were ultimately under Lelani's protection. As always, it fell to her to wear the pantaloons, so to speak . . . even if she did have four invisible horse legs.

"We need to get up to the roof anyway," MacDonnell said. "The copters are coming, right Mal?"

Scott, holding a big fancy Motorola combat radio cell phone nodded to his partner.

"Yep," Malcolm confirmed.

The door to the suite splintered under the weight of the beast smashing into it. The men that had been screaming on the other side of the door moments earlier were silent. Malcolm with his axes, Lelani with her longbow, Callum with his sword, and Malcolm's last remaining security man in the suite with his Uzi formed the front line—behind them were Colby Dretch with his revolver and Allyn Grey holding one tine of an old iron pitchfork that he procured from the farm in North Carolina before they left. Daniel stood between them. Scott, Clarisse, Bree, and Timian stood farther back in the rear, against the wall, and Balzac . . . *Where was Balzac?*

The beast burst through the door like it was made of Popsicle sticks. Bree and Clarisse let loose a duet of high-pitched screams.

Malcolm charged with a raging howl of his own even as Lelani let loose a barrage of arrows that sailed past the billionaire's head and into the beast's left rib cage and thigh. Malcolm put his fire ax into the golem's right ankle and jammed the spike atop the two-sided ax straight up into the beast's under jaw. The creature backhanded the dwarv, and Malcolm flew over the couches, into the marble fireplace with a resounding crash, shattering the mantelpiece and painting above it. Colby shot at the thing from his vantage point and Lelani let fly two more arrows into the creature's chest and neck. The room trembled at its roar, which hit them with the force and rage of an F5 tornado.

MacDonnell and Mal's security man charged the creature. Cal managed to get his shield up before razor talons sliced him in three. The security man stood farther back shooting his Uzi point-blank into the beast's torso, agitating the monster. When the Uzi's clip emptied, it lunged past Cal toward the security guy and came down on his head with its massive open maw. An ugly crunch and a twist took the agent's head clean off at the neck.

The headless body shook with seizure before hitting the floor. The beast spat the head at Allyn Grey. It bounced off the cleric and landed before him, covered in bloody mucus. The creature took a step toward the prince, but Lelani dropped her bow, put up her arms and erected a shield between them all just in time. The creature pounded and pounded, fixated on Daniel.

MacDonnell slashed at the tendons behind the knee joint with his sword. It roared with pain and turned back toward the knight. The creature swiped at him; he ducked then stepped back just out of the way of a second swipe. MacDonnell swung at the beast's wrist, burying the sword halfway through. When the creature attacked again, MacDonnell finished the job, hacking through the rest of the sinew and bone, depriving the thing of its left paw. As it came at him, MacDonnell leaped over the couch, leading it around the grand room, away from the others. It lunged at him. He fell to the floor on his back and thrust his sword straight up into the monster's throat—using the sword to keep its jaws at bay. The beast made a choking sound, a coughing gurgle, and spit blood on MacDonnell's visor. A few more seconds of the sword in the beast drained the golem's energy until it was spent, and it finally stopped moving.

"Everyone okay?" MacDonnell asked. The prince and Bree were unharmed, Clarisse nodded yes. Only Tim looked worse for wear.

Scott rushed over to help Malcolm, who was coming around. He shook his head. "What happened?" Mal asked.

"We got it," Colby said. Everyone looked at the detective skeptically. "Uh, *he* got it," Colby reiterated, pointing to MacDonnell.

"Ow, my head," Malcolm said, as Scott helped him up.

"Good thing it broke your fall," Cal said. "You could have hurt something vital." He slapped Mal on the back and handed him his big silver ax.

2

Lelani checked the hallway outside the suite with an arrow notched on her bow. The torn and broken bodies of Malcolm's security people were strewn everywhere. Blood dripped from the ceiling; the walls were smeared with it, as well as excrement and random unidentifiable goo. They looked like they had been put through a Cuisinart.

She stepped into the stairway—MacDonnell's hand was suddenly on her shoulder, holding her back.

"I'll go first," he said. "You behind me. Mal and Colby cover the rear—everyone else between us."

They went up the stairwell single file. On the landing just before the roof another creature was mortally wounded, bleeding, but not yet dead. MacDonnell easily slid his sword into the beast's back. After a few seconds, it was dead.

They continued onto the open roof where diced and sliced remains of more security people lay about. All of Malcolm's people were dead. They found Tom Dunning's shredded torso in the mess. The top of his head had been bitten off.

Whatever Malcolm Robbe paid these people, it wasn't enough. Mal's thoughts turned inward, trying to wrap his head around the human cost of this endeavor. He brought these people into this fight—to tackle things they were never trained to handle. Scott let Mal rest his head upon his chest and he put an arm of support around his partner.

Lelani found another creature among the carnage. "That's four," she said.

"If we're keeping score, we're surely losing," Malcolm said, bitterly.

"We don't know how many Dorn sent," Cal said.

"He would have been limited by his mana reserves," said Lelani. "I'd guess twenty at most."

"I've got three climbing up this side," Colby said from the southern edge of the roof. "Halfway up."

"Three over here," Mal said, on the western side. "The same."

"Two here," Daniel said from the north. "Farther down."

Cal grumbled, irritated at his team for letting Daniel walk to the edge alone. He pointed at Allyn and then pointed at Daniel as if to say *Fetch and watch*.

Lelani suddenly turned southeast.

"There!" she said, pointing to the tall thin building with the radiating decorative silver crown and spire.

She threw her bow to the ground to ward off another attack. The force of it pushed her back, invisible hooves tearing into the top covering, toward the edge of the roof.

"Dorn's on the Chrysler Building," Malcolm said. "Why the hell would he be there?"

Reverend Grey stepped up to get a good view of the Chrysler Building. He looked around the roof, taking in Midtown Manhattan from the forty-two-story vantage point.

"My God," he said. He turned to Lelani. "Can't you see it? That building is a conduit. A segment of the lay river flows into our reality at that point, and the building is saturated with that energy, focuses it. Dorn can master all he surveys from that position."

Another attack came at them—Lelani just barely got her defenses up, but it mattered little. The attack overwhelmed her and shattered the mana stones on the roof. They were out of reserves of magic to maintain the shields. All Lelani had left was her personal supply, barely enough to protect a few people in close quarters.

Fear gripped the centaur like never before. "We have to get off this roof," she told MacDonnell.

They heard the remaining creatures tear wildly into the building from below . . . from whatever floors they'd reached when the shield dissipated—they were in the building and in the stairwells.

"The copters?" Colby Dretch asked.

Scott pulled the state-of-the-art radiophone from his ear. An ashen look descended on him. "Uh . . . this whole area has been declared off limits by the NYPD. Cops won't let any birds off the ground."

"Shit!" Mal yelled.

Disbelief and despair settled into the group. MacDonnell looked deflated.

"We are so fucked!" cried Tim.

For once, Lelani agreed with the feckless musician.

CHAPTER 41
JERSEY BOYS

1

"Everyone downstairs!" Cal ordered. "Colby, you take the rear, Mal and Lelani up front with me, everyone else in the middle." They descended single file. Cal could hear the beasts' echoes below rushing up the well. He couldn't account for the other stairwells, but there were definitely two in this one.

"Mal, do you think we should risk the freight elevator?"

"Big steel box sounds safe to me. They're coming up and we head down."

"Can't we take the regular elevator?" Daniel asked.

"She wouldn't fit with all these people," Cal said, pointing to his redheaded wizard. "Lelani and I will hold these two golems while you get to the service corridor," he told Malcolm.

Lelani shot down the stairwell, her arrows hitting their marks every time. By the time the two beasts rounded the platform below them, each began to resemble a pincushion. Lelani drew the knife she'd confiscated from Symian and together they made short work of the beasts, which were already half dead before they reached the pair's landing. Lelani retrieved her knife and showed it to Cal.

"Pure faerie silver," she told him. "I hesitate to use it because if I cut myself, I will have no magic for the better part of a day." She sheathed it carefully and secured it to her belt.

They were shocked to find the rest of the party with two more beasts—one dead by Malcolm's bloody axes, and the other growling and snapping but unable to move from its spot. It was pinned by an invisible force.

"What's going on?" Callum asked.

"It was so cool!" Daniel shouted. "Reverend Grey pointed that piece of metal and they both just . . ."

"A binding," Grey said. "I can hold one for a few minutes."

"Why is it still alive?" Cal asked.

"I'm going to attempt to communicate with it," the reverend said.

"You can do that?" asked Clarisse.

Something about the beasts disturbed Cal greatly. He hadn't been able to put his finger on it because of the frenetic pace leading up to this moment, but now, with the golem immobile, he understood that it was their eyes—gunmetal gray and almost human looking. It was more than just an element of humanity; the glimmer of intelligence had an intimate quality. He recognized that gaze but not its source . . . not the eyes of nightmares. They evoked a feeling of home to him. It must be part of Dorn's magic—causing Callum to suffer a deep sadness every time he struck a deathblow and saw the light fade from these golems—like he was eradicating pieces of his soul.

Cal hardened his heart to the feeling. As much as he'd like to pick up intelligence, it was too dangerous, and there were several other creatures unaccounted for and they needed to leave. "I'm sorry, Allyn. We can't risk it." He stabbed the creature with Bòid Géard.

The creature whimpered as its life drained, and again, Cal felt the sorrow of a loved one passing. All Cal wished for was a fair opponent and a field of battle and a good sword to fight by. "Damn sorcerers and their spells," he whispered.

"Amen," the reverend said.

The elevator had reached their floor. As the door began to open, Allyn cried out, "BACK!"

Most of the party backed away in time. Most, but not Daniel or Timian, who was still in an alcohol-induced haze. They stood dead center of the golem's line of sight as the elevator doors parted. The beast pounced on the slightly closer Tim, their momentum driving them back into the corridor wall. The sick crunch of jaws breaking bones filled the hallway. Malcolm, Lelani, and Cal were on the thing immediately, driving their weapons into its flesh.

Clarisse screamed in abject terror as Tim's limp form dropped to the floor, his neck dangling at a sick angle. She dropped Bree like a sack and ran toward Tim. Colby and Allyn held her back while the three warriors finished off the beast.

Bree cried loudly—Cal didn't know if it was the shock of being dropped, or if she had reached her limit of all the death and blood that had become so pervasive in her young, innocent life. It was not lost on Callum how much Bree needed her mother right now. The thought of his daughter never seeing Catherine again tore at his soul. Daniel comforted the little girl—drawing her to him in a hug he seemed comfortably skilled at providing. Cal remembered the boy's dossier . . . the four-year-old stepsister, Penny—left behind to fend for her herself with a newly widowed, psychologically compromised drug-addled mother.

They finally let Clarisse reach her man. She fell to the floor beside him, tears falling wildly. "Oh, my Manly-Mann," she cried. She pulled his body to him with the last of her strength and shook her head violently—her long hair whipped into a blur of despondency.

"He was—unlucky," Lelani said to the reverend.

Grey gave her a dire, yet stoic look. "We make our own luck, sorceress. It was his choice to drink five cocktails today."

"FUCK YOU!" Clarisse screamed at the reverend. "You did this! That thing is after the kid, but it went for my Manly-Mann instead. This is your fault!"

Grey would not look at Clarisse. He turned to Callum with tired, deflated eyes that confessed Clarisse was not entirely wrong.

"The luck a cleric bestows in a blessing has to come from somewhere," Lelani whispered to Cal. "They would have us believe the gods pick those most deserving of punishment."

"Please don't do that again," Daniel said. He looked shaken. "I don't want anyone cursed because of me."

They heard a door crash from one of the other stairwells on the floor. Colby and Lelani grabbed Clarisse; Daniel picked up Bree.

"Everyone in the elevator!" Cal shouted.

2

The freight elevator doors closed just as the golem leaped into the service corridor. Cal hoped that steel doors, concrete walls, and the steel box they were riding down would be enough to buy time and get to the Fiftieth Street loading bay. All of the golems should be upstairs where Daniel had been only moments before.

Metal wrenched loudly above the car. Cal knew it was too good to be true. A reverberating thud on the roof shook the elevator. A muscular talon-tipped arm crashed through the ceiling. Everyone screamed and dropped down as far as they could go.

"We're all going to die!" Clarisse screeched.

Mal swung his two-sided ax across the car, slicing the hand off at the wrist. Lelani's arrows, point-blank, hit the golem in the jugular and through the eye. Black blood rained over the group.

"Don't get it in your mouth or eyes," the preacher yelled. Everyone covered their heads with their jackets and shirts.

Cal jabbed it with his sword. The beast grabbed him and pulled Cal toward its maw, but lost strength as the magic drained out of it.

"How many of these freaking things are there?" Daniel cried out. Bree and the kid were shaking. Cal knew he was going to have to pay a fortune in therapy for the girl.

The doors opened on the ground floor. The way was clear. Mal, Lelani, and Cal led the way down the service corridor, tense and paranoid, and moved toward the loading bay. Cal went through the double swinging doors first. A catering truck filled with food and a large wedding cake was backed into the elevated dock. The bay was relatively empty otherwise.

He motioned for the others to join him. He was halfway down the stairs when a golem dropped down onto the sidewalk just outside the truck port. Cal stopped, and the group slammed into him from behind.

The beast was hunched, its massive forearms before it, knuckles braced on the ground like silverback gorilla. Saliva slobbered from its snarling mouth. Three more dropped next to it, adopting the same posture and blocking their escape. Cal was about to order retreat when two golems crept up the service corridor behind them. Lelani cast a spell that shut and bound the steel doors to the hotel. It would only hold the ones in the corridor for a minute.

The beasts closed in slowly, talking to each other in whatever passed for a language, careful not to leave any gaps. Their gaze returned often to Daniel, their programmed target, as though in anticipation of a reward, like the culmination of a sexual act.

Cal wished he'd taken Bree from the boy's arms. It was the first time he believed he'd lose the prince.

"Prelate?" Cal asked.

"I cannot bind them all," Allyn whispered back, a desperate strain nestled in his voice.

Cal prepared to attack—Malcolm and Lelani read his body language and made ready to follow.

Three black Cadillac Escalades screeched to a halt behind the creatures. Five middle-aged Mediterranean types—in retro casual bowling shirts, leather jackets, silk slacks, loafers, and pinkie rings—spilled out of the vehicles. In addition to the gold jewelry dangling from their wrists and necks, all held assault rifles. Three men armed with flamethrowers poked up through the moon roofs on the tops of each Escalade. They collectively let loose a tsunami of fire, cutting down the golems. The creatures screamed as the hail of bullets and flame liquefied them where they stood.

The golems still in the hotel finally broke through the steel door. Allyn bound them with his iron rod, and Mal, Colby, and Lelani made short work of the beasts. When all the beasts were dead, a very large man stepped out of one of the Escalades. He was six feet at least and pushing three hundred pounds, impeccably dressed in a cream-colored sharkskin suit with carnation in the lapel, had tightly wound salt-and-pepper hair that looked like the early stages of growth on a Chia Pet, and yellowed gnarled teeth when he smiled. He was smoking a thick cigar.

"Holy shit!" Colby said. "Dominic Tagliatore?"

"The mobster?" Allyn said.

"Son of a bitch!" Mal quipped.

The man approached the group, stopping before Callum, puffing on a thick Cohiba.

"You know those are illegal," Cal said.

Tagliatore shrugged in that way that said *Forgetaboutit*.

"You've changed," Cal added.

"Own a lot of restaurants," the fat man said, patting his ample belly.

"I'm confused," said Lelani. "There was no Dominic Tagliatore in the original rescue party."

"Sweetie . . . ," the fat man said, pointing his cigar at her and with a flirtatious wink, ". . . you can call me Tilcook."

CHAPTER 42
BRINGING UP BABY

Gone.

Lord Dorn could not sense the golems anymore. The last of them had been defeated. He thought for certain with the wards down, his creations would make short work of the guardians. He had underestimated his opponents. His earlier elation waned, and the pressure of the headaches returned. A dark cloud covered his thoughts. He blew apart a window, reentered the building through an empty office, and climbed the stairs slowly back to the observatory. Hesz, Kraten, Lhars, Tom, and Catherine MacDonnell watched silently as he entered, measuring his mood, which was clearly not victorious.

"How'd we do?" asked Tom.

We? thought Dorn. How fared *we*? The plan was Dorn's, its execution as well—yet Tom took it upon himself to share some of his master's failure. Since Dorn could not very well punish himself, he was grateful for a volunteer. The power of the lay line swelled within him. He said the words and made the hand gestures and shot Tom out of an east-facing triangular window. The man arched over the city before he lost momentum and plunged seventy stories into the icy waters of the East River. Everyone in the room remained quiet. And tense.

It occurred to Dorn that the problem with the attack was perhaps not the plan itself, but its scale. Symian trudged up a stairwell carrying a bag full of sandwiches, bottles of water, and soda. He stopped when he saw all their expressions.

"Did I miss something? Where's zombie Tom?"

Hesz shook his head ever so slightly and swiftly—almost a twitch. The gesture actually gladdened Dorn. His men were looking out for each other. They would need to. The pressure in his head grew—his reason slipping. It stirred in him a panic that one of these times when he descended into these episodes he would not emerge whole again. He would be lost to madness, deserving of only a dungeon cell in some wretched asylum without even a pot to piss in.

Scale.

He pulled out the flask with the golem elixir. In there were hundreds of Catherine MacDonnell's viable ova, all waiting to be born by his hand. With the power surging through this building, he could bring them all forth. But the elixir was capable of so much more—it was forbidden magic—exponential. The radiation made it hyperpotent, boundless—limited only by how much stock he could provide it. Catherine had another ovary. He leered at her. She sat bound and unresponsive against a wall on the floor staring off into another universe, lamenting the loss of her family. She noticed him observing; her back stiffened, her expression changed, and she pressed herself more tightly against the wall.

"My lord," said Symian delicately. "We may need her for an exchange. Less damaged than more. This building—this city—is overflowing with females. Let me bring you some."

Hesz and Kraten backed away from the half-troll. So much for solidarity.

In genius lies madness, and it was at this moment at the precipice of another dark episode that Dorn came up with a truly wicked thought. He struggled to retain reason and then stopped, realizing reason would only talk him out of a necessary action.

"How many females?" he asked in a rough gravely voice. His hands pressed into his temples as though the switch to turn off the pain lay beneath the bone.

"My lord?"

"In this city . . . how many?"

"The population swells to fifteen million during the day, my lord," said well-read Hesz, sticking his own neck onto the stump. "Half are female."

A smile that he knew would frighten the devil himself squirmed its way onto Dorn's lips—teeth gritted and cheeks stretched wide with dementia, he thought his face would rend itself apart. His reflection in the marble looked half mad, the veins in his forehead distinct and pulsing.

"Subtract those who are older than young and younger than old," Dorn said. It was becoming harder to speak.

"Millions," said Symian. "My lord, I don't . . ."

He turned to Catherine MacDonnell with the most devilish look and asked, "Their monthly blood . . . where does it go?"

"I don't understa—"

"The shedding of your moon blood . . . your unseeded spawn?"

"No," Catherine whispered. "Women don't flush . . . we throw it away . . . in the tr—"

"Every one of you?" Dorn said mockingly. "Every last woman in New York? Every discard, inventoried and logged!" he spat at her. The pain had become unbearable.

Dorn found the water closet. Symian held the scrolls open before his master. Dorn poured the remains of the elixir into the toilet and flushed it. As the water swirled he chanted again in that dark language that sucked the soul from the world. Only this time, it fed like a vampire on a cornucopia of limitless energy coming from the lay line. Dorn continued to chant, channeling more and more of the magic down the building and through the pipes that brought the enchanted elixir to the sewers of New York. The spell would spread through the miles and miles of mazelike tunnels, the repository of all discarded things.

CHAPTER 43

AN OFFER HE CAN'T REFUSE

Underneath the Waldorf Astoria hotel, the guardians and their new saviors caught their respective breaths under the cover of an old abandoned railway platform, away from golems or the attention of the local authorities. The station was left over from a bygone era when the Central Railroad owned most of the land that covered Park Avenue north of Grand Central Station. The remnants of track stretched east and west into blackness, beyond the meager uses of the Metro North commuter rail and Amtrak. One such spur of track stopped under the Waldorf, used by presidents and dignitaries of past eras to move about veiled from prying eyes.

"I think that was the last of them," said Callum. He looked over the group to make sure everyone was all right.

Clarisse was still in shock over Tim's demise, but physically unharmed. Daniel, Scott, and Allyn looked shaken in that way civilians do when they'd just escaped imminent death. Colby and Lelani were cool and collected as always—centaurs were a tough breed, and ex-NYPD were hard to rattle, whether dead or alive. Bree was at Callum's side, leaning against him, arms wrapped around his leg, head resting on his thigh. He stroked her hair gently, thinking of all the television he and Catherine had never let her watch to shelter her from violent programming.

Tilcook had always been a big man, even among the palace kitchen staff. In his youth, he could carry a side of beef alone to the carving table and carve it into its respective cuts expertly in under thirty minutes. No one handled a cleaver better than Tilcook. Cal wondered about the life of excess and debauchery that added the extra hundred pounds these past years.

"I got my memory back same as everyone else," Tilcook said. "I was on my way to the hotel to parley with Mal, you know, catch up on what's doing, when this thing went down and the cops cordoned off everything. Only way we could reach you was through these tunnels under Park Avenue. It's all hush-hush. Roosevelt used to use these tracks so no one knew he was in a wheelchair. Drove the car right off the train with him in it into the freight elevator and onto Forty-ninth Street. That's how we brought the cars in."

"How do you know about it?" Malcolm asked.

"Sometimes I need to move merchandise from here to there . . . on the down low. Ya know?"

"So you went from kitchen help to crime lord?" Daniel asked. The boy was a little too much in awe of Tilcook for Cal's taste. To the world at large he was known as the Debonair Don. The man flaunted the law for years, killed hundreds, if not more, in mob hits and territory battles, and was not a worthy role model for a prince of Aandor.

"Crime? What crime?" Tilcook said, gesticulating his wrist back and forth while holding his thumb against his fore- and middle fingers. "I'm a businessman. I look out for my interests. It's all perspective."

"Boss, the police are moving into the hotel now," a thin, older fellow said. He wore a royal-blue Adidas track jacket over his black retro bowling shirt and had brown eyes and slick black hair that was too uniformly dark to be natural at his age. A weak chin hovered over the cords of his neck that drooped against his tanned, leathery skin, the kind that betrayed one's love of too much sun. The toothpick in his mouth shifted back and forth when he spoke. He wore only one pinkie ring compared with some of the others and his bracelet and chain count was also tasteful by comparison.

"This is my—ah—business associate, Tony Two Scoops."

"Yeah, definitely *not* a crime lord," Daniel said to the group.

"So what do we do about this *oobatz* magician on the Chrysler Building?" Tilcook asked. "He's bad for business. I got boys working in this hotel."

"Uh, boss . . . ," said Tony Two Scoops, nodding toward Daniel.

"Later," said Tilcook, waving his lieutenant away.

"The boys . . . we gotta know our stake."

"What stake?" said Cal.

Tilcook ignored the cop and turned to Daniel. "Your Highness . . . me and the boys, we're in a little trouble. Kind of wore out our welcome around here."

"We're looking at twenty to life for some of our—uh—*business methods*," said Two Scoops, pronouncing it *mehtuds*.

"Nowhere we can go no one's gonna recognize us, see?" Tilcook continued. "So we was talkin' these past few days since I got my marbles back . . . there might be other worlds to explore, where a man can settle down and enjoy his old . . ."

"Where a man might enjoy his ill-gotten gains and escape justice," Cal interrupted. "Things are too hot here and you want to tuck tail and run back to Aandor and bring your toadies along."

"He may not have put it quite that eloquently," Mal said. The dwarv was irritated. "Jesus H. Christ, Cal—the man just saved our lives."

"Please!" cried Reverend Grey. "Do not take His name in vain."

"He robbed and murdered his way up the food chain," Cal said to his sergeant at arms. "And just when, after years of effort and millions of dollars, the law catches up with him, he wants to disappear into another universe like a Criss Angel act."

"That's about right," Tilcook said. He puffed on his cigar.

"How many people have you murdered?" Cal asked Tilcook sharply.

"Probably less than you back home," Tilcook said. "Funny thing about murder . . . it's okay to kill your stepfather with a table leg and walk away from the consequences, but if you're protecting your livelihood . . . ?"

"Self-defense is an appropriate use of deadly force," Cal said angrily. "Daniel was only in that situation because the idiot screwed up the identity spell."

"Agreed," said Tilcook, with a Cheshire cat–size grin. "I'm only in my situation because of screwed up magic, too—and I been defending myself for thirteen years. So whaddaya say? You can do worse than havin' La Cosa Nostra watchin' your back when there's some whackadoo magician gunning for ya."

A tremor shook the platform, triggering a cascade of worried glances around the group.

"My lord, Dorn resumes his attacks," Lelani said, a bit uncertainly.

"Wait a minute," said Allyn. "*Everyone* felt *that* tremor; am I wrong?"

"But with the shields gone, aren't we dog meat?" Daniel asked.

"There's so much iron and concrete insulating us down here, there's actually some measure of protection," Allyn said.

A second vibration shook the platform.

Daniel turned to Tilcook. "Yes," he said. "You have a deal."

"Now wait a minute!" Cal said. *Not this again.* It would have been much easier if the boy were still an infant.

"You wait a minute," Daniel told his captain. "I never met any of you people before last night. You're telling me some pretty tall tales, falling over yourselves to want to help me. And all these people are asking for is favors from, or a trip to, a kingdom I've never seen or even believe exists, all for some promises you all admit I have the ability to deliver, and you expect me to employ some kind of impartial judgment on what favors I accept and don't when my life is in danger?" Daniel said in one adamant, exhausted breath.

"This Dorn is never going to stop coming after me. The goombah squad usually asks for money for protection, of which, I am completely tapped out of at the moment. Do you know how lucky I am that Dominic Tagliatore and Tony Two Scoops just want a ride out of town for the privilege of saving me from an—what was that word . . . ?"

"*Oobatz,*" said Tony. "Mean's *crazy.*"

"From an *oobatz* wizard perched on the Chrysler Building, that—in your words—is 'never going to stop coming after me.'"

Cal had a head full of responses to Daniel's rebellion, but the volume of his arguments defied orderly reason and power of conviction. The kid was a survivor, and where as Callum saw Daniel's successful reclamation as the conclusion of his current mission, Daniel looked to his continued survival as an open-ended escapade. Cal couldn't make the prince accept his authority as the captain of his personal guard. And who was Cal to lecture . . . by rights, Daniel could promote Malcolm or Tilcook to general on the spot and put them in charge of his protection.

The third tremor felt like a minor earthquake. Dust and rubble dropped from the ceiling and clanked on the roofs of the cars they'd brought back down.

"The prince has spoken," said Malcolm.

"What about Dorn?" asked Allyn. "We can't leave him be anymore, Cal. He's getting more desperate and willing to hurt many people to get what he wants."

"How long can Catherine remain safely in his custody?" added Scott.

Cal grimaced. Stubbornness was his family trait as well. He hated to admit Malcolm was right. "Dorn has to die," Cal said.

They all looked at Cal in silence—the guardians fully understanding what it meant for the captain, both personally and morally, to advocate this course of action. Cal had never been one to seek violence. He was simply the best there was at responding to it.

"He can't be left alone to rain this kind of terror on people," Cal continued. "Prince or no prince, this earth must be rid of Dorn of Farrenheil."

Malcolm and Tilcook nodded in accord.

"But we get Daniel off this island," he added. "I'm not bringing the prince anywhere near this fight."

"I got a place in Upper Saddle River," Tilcook said. "Walls, security cameras, Dobermans, and a crew of jacked-up beef heads with Uzis. You have my word, Cal; me and the boys will defend the kid with everything we can throw. So long as you take all of us with you when you go back to Aandor."

"Done," said Mal.

"Wait a minute," Cal said.

"For what, Cal? For gods' sakes, Dorn's on the Chrysler Building with a river of magic to power his spells. There's no telling what he'll throw at us next. These tremors are not a coincidence."

"We can shut Dorn down," Allyn said.

Everyone looked to him, almost relieved that someone had a plan. Allyn bent down and used his iron rod to scratch a map of New York City into the platform dust.

"When Lelani destroyed the henge anchor in Central Park, she set free the lay river on its natural course through the city. I am speaking metaphorically, of course—the energy flows through multiple realities weaving in and out of universes. The main one in this area is part of the same branch from upstate where we originally came into this universe . . . we're 'downstream' of it and it runs through Manhattan island lengthwise like a braided river, splitting into offshoots, some wide and others meandering trickles. But I got a good feel of the course from the copter ride and the roof of the hotel. If I get 'upstream' of it—here," he said, pointing to the Bronx, "I can divert its flow; dry out the braid that feeds Dorn and maybe divert its course into another branch. One that would give Lelani the advantage."

The ground shook again.

This time it was followed by the sound of screams filtering through the venting grates that led to the streets above. In the blackness of the tunnel, they heard scraping of the heavy metal coverings coming off their manholes, the clang of metal hitting the tunnel walls. The familiar howls of the golems echoed down the track. Everyone looked at each other in terror.

"This plan is logical," Lelani said quickly. "If I were to take position here"—she pointed to another area in Midtown along the second main branch of the lay river—"I could counter Dorn. Forbidden magic requires a lot of power. His store would dwindle while I drew his ire, and while he's distracted, you could all escape."

"No," Cal said. "I'm going after him."

Lelani looked as close to panicked as Cal had ever seen. "My lord, it would be suicide to go up against a wizard of his caliber, much less two if you count Symian, without a wizard of your own. If we could but reach Seth . . ."

"The idiot's gone AWOL," Cal said. "We can't depend on him. Even if he were here, what good is he? Seth's been getting by on luck so far. He has no talent for magic, for fighting . . ."

"The boy's been hobbled by an enchantment," Allyn said, defending the boy.

Lelani's eyes grew to pleading dimensions. "My lord, even if what you say is true, even if Seth were incompetent and was killed in the attempt, tactically, it is still the correct move. A wizard would draw the attention of the defending wizard. He would have no choice but to address the attacking wizard, leaving the soldiers to battle among themselves with no interference. Wizards aren't omniscient, but they are paranoid about someone one-upping them when distracted. You need a wizard with you . . ."

Cal put his arms on Lelani's shoulders to calm her down. He gazed deeply into her eyes and said without words that he hadn't any choice. He had to do this as a husband reclaiming his wife, a father reclaiming the mother of his child, as an officer of the city of New York defending his jurisdiction, and as a knight defending his prince. Live or die, he would go and engage the enemy tonight.

"He will be most vulnerable when his power is used up," Lelani said. "Perhaps I can distract him when you storm the building."

"We don't even know that Cat and Tory are there," Colby said.

"Not important," said Malcolm. "We kill him, game over. I doubt most of the henchmen have any love for Dorn. We have a bigger bargaining chip than they do. They'll trade Cat for their lives. It's like chess."

Cal was not pleased to hear his wife spoken of as a game piece, and yet Mal spoke truly. Dorn would not relent. Tilcook would flee with Daniel and defend him with his life, mostly for his own interests. It was the best plan they could concoct on the fly. And it sure was about time he retrieved his wife.

"Yes," Cal said. "Til, let Colby take a couple of your men to The Plaza . . . just in case Cat and Tory are still being held there."

"Wait," Lelani said. She rummaged through her satchel for something and came up with a polished egg-shaped black stone marbled with red streaks, which she handed to Colby. "Keep this opal with you for protection."

"Prote . . . from what?"

"Symian cast the spell that made you what you are. Should he be vanquished, you might die along with him. This enchanted stone will act as a surrogate and maintain the spell just in case."

Another tremor hit, the worst one yet. More metal covers flew off their manholes and the howls of the golems shot an icy streak of fear down everyone's back. There were more this time . . . a lot more.

"Everyone move!" Cal said.

And they took off.

CHAPTER 44

NEW YORK STATE OF MIND

The streets were sheer anarchy. The golems crawled up through the manholes, service tunnels, sewer drains, and basements, smashing through asphalt in some cases—hundreds down the canyons of Manhattan's grand avenues and streets as far as Lelani's eyes could see. People ran in every direction, into each other, panicked and unsure of sanctuary and ignorant that the creatures' objectives did not involve them. The beasts, once engaged, though, defended themselves viciously against assaults whether intentional or not.

A city bus swerved to avoid a burning car—it smashed into two golems as they climbed onto the street from below, and the beasts retaliated, shattering the windshield, killing the driver. The bus careened into a diner. Police fired upon the creatures, incurring their retaliation and spurring them into a frenzied bloodlust like angry wasps disturbed on a scorching afternoon. It was worse than anyone could have imagined.

Lelani had seen anarchy like this once before—the invasion of Aandor City. It had been only two weeks since that day for her. She'd experienced enough anarchy to last her lifetime, and she wondered what offense her gods ascribed her that she should continuously witness episodes of carnage on these massive scales. And how, she wondered—how would she stop a sorcerer of her world from killing her cohorts and thrusting this city into further pandemonium?

"My God," Callum said, standing beside her and Malcolm. The captain's eyes were haunted by the chaos wreaked upon the city he loved. The three of them had traversed the tunnels below and fought their way through golems up to the surface on Lexington Avenue. There they took refuge in an abandoned bus. The captain had hoped to procure the vehicle for the trip south, but it had a busted axle. The streets were jammed in a vicious gridlock with the masses pouring through the cars like ants on a graveled path.

"How is this possible?" Mal said. "You need laboratories, gestation chambers to create this many monsters so quickly."

Lelani had been trying to find a flaw in the creatures since they first attacked at the hotel. They were a hybrid of beast and human, and all female. But whereas the first ones to attack looked identical, almost related, many of the creatures now pouring up into the streets were of different sizes and coloring, indicating their source material had become more varied. This gave credence to Lelani's theory of how Dorn created the golems.

"He dropped the catalyst for the golems into the sewers," she said. Lelani turned her thoughts inward. She did not want to think about from whom Dorn procured material for the first batch of golems. Her commander already looked haunted enough.

"As Dorn channels more energy, he pushes their creation farther and farther out. These creatures will soon rise throughout the island, from Battery Park to Inwood."

"Thousands," Cal said in horror.

"And they are confused," Lelani added. "The iron, steel, and concrete under the streets block a clear signal to the prince. The minute Tilcook's vehicle emerges from the train tunnels with Daniel, they will eventually catch his scent."

"Will killing Dorn stop this?" Mal asked.

"Most likely. Even incapacitating him would stem their further advancement. He must have some type of fealty connection with them."

"You have to get to your lay line and be ready for Allyn's switch," Cal told her. "You're much faster without us. Mal and I will head to the Chrysler Building."

Lelani nodded. "One thing, my lord . . . ," Lelani added. "Do not trust your firearms in the Chrysler Building. It is saturated with magic. Combustion science does not play well around magical energy. Your guns may jam on you."

With that said, she bolted from the bus and galloped west on Fifty-first Street, confident that everyone was too panicked to notice a girl running thirty miles an hour. It broke her heart to pass so many in need of rescue, but she could not risk it. Everything depended on her and Allyn.

And what of Seth?

Seth had ignored all attempts to contact him throughout the hotel battle. Lelani had believed her old schoolmate had changed—that he wanted to be better—mature and responsible, and address the shortcomings of his past. But he'd disappeared, and now at their hour of most need, he was nowhere to be found.

As she approached Fifth Avenue, she saw Colby Dretch and the two gunmen Tilcook sent with the detective beset upon by a beast. They had been on their way to The Plaza. Colby and the mobsters fired at the beast before them, but the creature just absorbed their bullets and growled through a fence of sharp teeth. She pulled two arrows from her quiver and let them fly into each of the golem's eyes, driving the arrows back into its brains. Colby looked over his shoulder and smiled in relief.

"Thanks, kid," he said.

"They search for the prince. Do not engage them, they should leave you be."

"Hard to avoid . . . they're everywhere," Colby said.

"Aye, and the city's response is inflaming them. Let the unchallenged creatures walk past and you should be all right."

Lelani acknowledged Colby's gratitude and bolted south on Fifth

Avenue. As far as the eye could see, it was anarchy . . . and it would only get worse. The spell would not stop making golems until it had exhausted itself, and that depended entirely on Dorn. As long as he channeled power into the sewers, it would continue to spread.

After a few minutes, she reached her destination. Lelani looked up. Gray and massive, the Empire State Building—the supreme erection of its era—pointed up at the gods like an accusing finger. She prayed silently that the elevators were still running.

CHAPTER 45

OUR "THING"

Tony Two Scoops drove the Escalade with the panache and verve of a man who'd spent a lifetime transporting contraband and evading the police. Tilcook sat in the passenger seat, cigar between his fingers and an Uzi on his lap. Behind the driver sat Daniel, Brianna in the middle, and Reverend Grey on the shotgun side. Another Escalade carrying Scott and Clarisse was right on their tail.

Driving north in the train tunnels, they had gotten ahead of the sprouting crop of golems and exited at a service ramp used to bring in equipment for track repairs and such. Behind them, columns of smoke rose through the glass and steel canyons of Midtown. The only thing to contend with in Harlem as they approached the Third Avenue Bridge was the slightly above-average gridlock of Manhattan traffic. As Tony put it so eloquently, "The day I can't outwit a bunch of civilians beating it home for *Wheel of Fortune* is the day I hang up my fuzzy dice fo-evah."

Tilcook had decided the George Washington Bridge was too risky . . . they could get locked into traffic which had been known to stay stationary for hours at a time. Instead, they would drop Allyn off at his destination and take the Major Deegan to Westchester and cross over the Hudson at the Tappan Zee.

As they drove, Allyn tried to piece together what elements he would need to build his henge. It would have to be bigger than anything he'd done before. Fortunately, his destination was currently a construction site and there would be a lot of material there. It was a really a question of manpower, which Tilcook claimed he'd take care of.

"You think Captain MacDonnell's going to be okay?" asked Daniel. "Maybe we should have sent more guys with him?"

"I ain't got three boys combined who are deadlier than Callum MacDonnell," Tilcook said. "Used to hack through a bull's carcass with one pass of his sword back in the day. I know 'cause I provided them for him from the kitchen to practice. Saved me a lot of work."

"I gotta know . . . ," Daniel continued, "how did you get to be a made man in the family when you can't possibly be Italian."

Daniel's knowledge of mafia culture bordered on fanatic, Allyn thought. The boy attributed this to his stepfather's love of *GoodFellas* and *The Sopranos*, the watching of which was one of the rare occasions Daniel and Clyde could occupy the same room and pretend to have something in common.

"When you wake up a blank slate, you kinda fill in the blanks yourself," Tilcook said. "My family over there is from the southern Kingdom of Udine—similar to Italy . . . even our language. So I gravitated, I guess, to Italian kitchens looking for work. I found a gig in North Caldwell working for Vincenzo Tagliatore. A good man . . . lonely after his wife and son died. He unofficially adopted me. He introduced me as his cousin from Sicily, knowing it would be easier to get a gig in one of the New York restaurants. I made my bones cooking for others, then opened my own place, then two, three . . .

"I really set out to do an honest business, kid. But once you get a little money, they start putting a target on your back. I ain't just talkin' Cosa Nostra," Tilcook continued. "I mean the government, the agencies, the permits, the access, the suppliers. Got to a point where I realized if I was going to keep my head above water, I needed to supplement my business with some underground entrepreneurship."

They crossed over Harlem River and onto the Major Deegan heading north.

"Don't believe the hype about makin' it in America, kid," said Tony in the driver's seat, his toothpick bobbing up and down as he spoke. "You gotta get permission from the establishment to rise beyond a particular point. Everybody with a lot of money is a little dirty. Can't be helped."

"How then did Malcolm succeed without resorting to dubious activities?" Allyn said.

The two men remained silent for all of three seconds before turning red faced with hard laughter. Two Scoops pounded on the steering wheel like a man trying to restart his own heart.

Allyn did not see the joke. He didn't like the lesson they were giving the prince. Bad enough Allyn failed to raise the boy with some moral guidance; Daniel was already enamored enough with the romance of the criminal underground.

"Padre, you jokin', right?" Two Scoops said. "People like Malcolm Robbe sell their soul to the government to get the kind of business they have. He's tight with the powerbrokers, thick as thieves with the Pentagon."

"You think he never bribed a congressman?" said Tilcook, still smiling. "One guy we own took money to pass a bill that netted that dwarf a billion clams."

"He's a dwarv," Allyn corrected.

"You don't think Mal's personal security, made up of ex-military and secret service, just opens limo doors?" Daniel said, incredulously, to Allyn.

It was one thing to hear it from Tilcook and Tony, but even the prince bought into their cynicism. How was he to rule a kingdom with these types of notions? "Malcolm has a lot to protect," Allyn said, disturbed by the implication.

"EXACTLY!" cried Tilcook and Two Scoops in unison.

"I got a waste management business, twelve restaurants, a used car dealership, and minority interest in three strip malls and two strip clubs," said Tilcook. "And a few hundred high-yield loans out to civilians trying to latch on to their piece of the American dream. I have to protect what's mine."

"What about the prostitution? The drugs?" Allyn asked.

The car skidded to a stop. Allyn's heart leaped into his throat. Did he fail to observe a rule of etiquette because of some old familiarity with the man the world knew as Dominic Tagliatore?

"We're here," Two Scoops said.

"The place you says is packed with fairy dust," Tilcook added.

So engrossed was Allyn in the prince's moral degradation, he didn't even realize they'd arrived. He stepped out of the car onto the construction lot that was being converted into a ballpark for kids. Across the street a giant sign that hung on the retro-style façade of the new ballpark read *Yankee Stadium.* But where he stood now was where the old Yankee Stadium had been for the better part of a century. This place was saturated with magic.

A well-built man in his forties with perfect black hair, brown eyes, and a Roman nose exited the car behind them and joined the reverend. Tilcook lowered his passenger seat window. "You going to be okay, padre?" he asked.

"Yes . . . I'll manage."

Tilcook waited a moment with the window down, staring straight ahead at the beautiful Indiana limestone retro exterior of the new stadium. The new classic design was an homage to the 1923 stadium that Ruth, Gehrig, DiMaggio, and Mantle had played in. There was no shortage of greatness here.

"I ain't never gone after someone's kids or spouse," said Tilcook, holding his cigar and looking at the stadium across the road. "I ain't never pushed dope in a school or encouraged any of my people to target kids. I ain't never had a man's legs broke if he only needed a week to get me my money back, and even then, I took his car if it was worth anything 'cause you can't bank broken bones. And the only bastards I ever clipped deserved it worse than I ever will even on my worst day."

He turned to the reverend, his expression saying he neither sought nor was in need of redemption. Dominic Tagliatore, aka Tilcook, was comfortable in his skin and with the things he'd done since arriving to this universe. Allyn nodded in accord. The window slid up.

Before it closed completely, he heard Daniel start to say, "He is a minister, guys. Cut him some . . ."

That the prince would advocate on his behalf gave Allyn hope. The boy had it in him to see other points of view—to be a peacemaker.

Through the tinted rear window he caught Daniel's gaze. In the boy's eyes he thought he read the question, *Do you know which god you serve?*

Allyn blinked, astonished by the thought until he realized his own eyes were superimposed over Daniel's in the window's reflection. His own troubling thoughts rebounded on him—his inner doubts, projected and multiplied as exponentially as the golems beneath Manhattan ever since Allyn remembered Aandor.

Allyn looked around this empty lot in the South Bronx. He was so far from home. He felt lost. His wife's support was gone, his home, possibly his church, and now he was at risk of losing the love of two gods if he did not choose one. There wasn't even the satisfaction of making a difference in his young monarch's life, the very reason he accepted this mission. Who did he serve?

"What the hell is going on, Johnny?" asked a ruddy-faced foreman in an orange reflective vest, blue jeans, and hardhat.

The man Tilcook had left with Allyn, Johnny Maronne, apparently had some pull with the construction unions in New York. They'd ordered all the men to stay past quitting time for a special rush construction job. Allyn looked around the park and saw plenty to work with. Concrete road barriers and tubing, piping, gravel, unearthed boulders, wood, and machinery to move it all around. But the men were reluctant, many of them having started work at 7:00 A.M. and wanting to go home to their families. The task would be highly unorthodox as well; no one built henges anymore and their hearts would not be into it.

"Introduce me to the men," Allyn said to Johnny.

"Why?" Johnny asked.

"I want to shake their hands."

As Johnny began introductions, Allyn greeted each worker with a handshake. As they shook, he infused them with a mild conversion. Instilled with the light of Pelitos, they would perform all of Allyn's requests to the letter, eager to please Pelitos's representative on earth. The sensation would last a few days, and end in a mild hangover, but that couldn't be helped. He instructed them to begin building concentric circles, to plant the concrete dividers on their ends like long towers. Shortly, with but a few components in place, Allyn already felt the river of mana shift as he closed off one braid of the stream. It would take almost an hour to complete with the help of these men. He hoped it would be in time to save Manhattan from utter destruction.

CHAPTER 46
INTO THE TRENCH

1

Seth sat in detention, the only student in an empty classroom. In the front of the class a row of teachers' chairs spanning the room from exit to window were empty except for the one by the door. The chairs seemed warm . . . recently sat in. Seth had the impression that they all had been occupied until recently, a virtual army marshaled to keep him in the room. But now, only Darcy remained, dressed like the Madonna of the Renaissance, feeding an infant Caitlin from her perfect breast.

The room was decorated with eight-by-twelve-inch pictures of Aandor above the chalkboard, like National Geographic *images. The archduke's palace and castle, the Arcadian falls and river that cut through the center of the city, the Great Library, Pentum Square, Magnus's Academy, the river ports, Golle Towne . . . and so on.*

"We were so proud of you," said a woman's voice sitting behind him. He turned. She was about twenty-eight with wavy auburn hair, hazel eyes, light skin, freckles, amply endowed, and dressed in a barmaid's apron. Seth did not comprehend why she had an Irish lilt, though. "Me and your aunties, telling all the patrons you'd gone off to the city to study magic."

"Mom?"

"I didn't think a son of mine would end up in the gutter. Would get a girl with child and throw her to the wolves."

"I was an ass, Mom. It's a deep hole to climb out of."

"Well don't tell me, lad. Tell her," she said, pointing to Darcy. "She was

a true innocent. She trusted you. You corrupted her, thrashed her dreams, polluted her body, and poisoned her soul."

"This is a dream."

"It is and it isn't," Allyn Grey said, startling him.

"Jeez, is this room empty or isn't it?"

"This room contains that which you brought into it."

"Sounds like dialogue from a Spike TV movie of the week. Why would I bring a Baptist minister from North Carolina into my dreams?"

"I cast a soothe blessing on you while you dozed in the helicopter."

"I don't like people getting into my head."

"I'm a minister. It's what we do. You needed help unlocking your potential, and since we don't have time for a year's worth of counseling sessions, I did what I did. The lady before you is the source of your blockage. She is also interacting in this dreamscape. Whatever you tell her here will remain with her."

"Maybe the problem isn't her. Maybe it's me. Maybe I don't deserve to be special or have magical powers. Maybe I feel like a phony—being set up to rise so I can have farther to fall."

"Seth, no one can control your decisions. The best things we can give each other are opportunities. I've given you a gift. Use it as you see fit."

Seth approached Darcy.

"You think that this is a dream," he told her.

"I stopped dreaming of you years ago," Darcy said placidly. Seth thought she should have been more bitter.

He got down on one knee and placed his hands on her lap. The texture of her robe felt real enough. Her legs under the cloth felt strong and healthy as they had in her youth. She had been a sprinter in high school. He looked into her large black eyes.

"I'm so sorry, Darcy. I'm in the apartment with Caitlin right now. I brought help . . . money and a chance for you to clean up. You need to do this."

Caitlin coughed and gurgled up some milk, which ran over her cheeks and down Darcy's ebony breast. Seth reached into his pocket to find a tissue and came across a cube. He pulled it out. It was a tiny blue box, with the word Tiffany *printed on the cover in black. A shiny white ribbon wrapped it. Seth knew what this was. It was an industrial strength soothe—a big pill that cured many diseases. This was the gift. But like all spiritual quandaries, the true power behind the gift lay with the choice of the bearer. Seth could use it to heal himself, free himself of the chains holding back his power . . . or he could give it to someone else. Grey could not have known about Seth's sin, but he would not have been much of a minister if he didn't recognize the quality of Seth's pain . . . that of having gravely hurt and betrayed a person who he loved. Seth knew what he wanted to do . . . what would make him happiest.*

"Nice box," Darcy said.

"It's for you," he told Darcy.

"A little late for that, don't you think?"

"It's not a ring. It's hope. You have every right not to believe me. I was not worthy of your trust the last time you gave it to me. But I'm not that person anymore. I'm here to save you."

She took the box and pulled on the string. The cube glowed a purifying light—white and unsullied as a newborn. "Oh!" cried Darcy. And she smiled.

Darcy and baby faded into the ether. The door was no longer blocked.

Seth stepped through and found himself on a low cliff face opposite an ocean that reminded him of the Pacific. The sun was bright and hot, and flecks of sea spray anointed him as the waves crashed against the cliff. A huge wave had drenched him completely, and Seth laughed. He couldn't remember the last time he breathed so freely, as though he'd been cooped up in a mountain cave and this was his first ever taste of oxygen-rich ocean air. The cool water invigorated him with possibility. He heard a piercing scream.

Seth awoke with a start.

He was on the loveseat, Caitlin asleep beside him, her head resting against his chest, both of them exhausted from his abridged tales of her mother's youth. The sun, well past its apex, had begun its descent, marking the latter part of the ever-shortening days. The north-facing room was dark despite there being some blue left in the sky.

A scream from down the block confirmed that it was not his imagination. A series of screams followed from the other end of the block, and then cars screeching, crashing—three, maybe four followed by sirens—lots and lots of sirens. The building trembled ever so subtly.

"What the hell is going on?" Seth whispered. He nudged Caitlin off and pulled out his cell phone. Eleven messages from Cal and Lelani. He regretted turning the ringer off, but with Callum's master-vassal attitude, it was the only way he'd get any peace to talk to Caitlin. Helping the prince was all well and good, but he had responsibilities to this kid, too.

A loud boom on Avenue C shook the building and rattled the windows. Seth stuck his head out and saw a black cloud billowing from around the corner, illuminated below by a flickering orange light from its source. A convoy of sirens drove past: cop cars, fire trucks, ambulances, even ConEd trucks, all heading north at breakneck speed.

A knock came at the door.

Seth slipped on the chain and cautiously opened the door. A Hispanic lady, five feet tall, in her fifties, holding two shopping bags of groceries, looked at him funny.

"*¿Caitlin aquí?*" she asked him warily.

"Mrs. Gomez?" Seth deduced. "Yes. Come in. What's happening outside?"

"Seth?" queried a groggy voice behind him. "You *are* here." Darcy stood at the bedroom door wearing a short silk robe that left little to the imagination. "I just had the strangest dream about you."

The building shook again, this time more violently, as though something were tearing through the basement.

"Aiee!" said Mrs. Gomez. "*Los monstruos!* On TV in bodega . . . Midtown is fill with *demonios*!"

Seth's phone lit up again.

"Hello?" he answered.

"EMPIRE STATE BUILDING, NOW!" screamed Lelani through the tiny speaker.

2

Midtown is built on one of the highest points on Manhattan island, a hump of solid bedrock with layer upon layer of tunnels, sewers, and other underground infrastructure rising up from the depths and culminating in the largest collection of skyscrapers in the world. That it was built on a hill to begin with adds to its ponderous height over the surrounding neighborhoods. On a normal day, from the roof of Darcy's building, Midtown looked like an oncoming wave of steel and concrete ready to crest upon the shores of Greenwich Village. Today that wave included streams of multicolored smoke billowing upward into a darkening sky. It looked like a battle zone. And that zone crept ever closer to where he was standing; the East Village was sprouting its own demons.

Lelani had said if not confronted or threatened, they would simply continue to march until they found the prince—they didn't get violent until challenged. But tell that to a freaked-out civil service. And nobody taught these things to look both ways before crossing the street.

Across the island he could see the Empire State Building. A flash of lightning arched across from the Chrysler Building to the top of the Empire State. *Son of a bitch,* Seth thought.

Seth headed down quickly. Darcy had put on jeans and a sweatshirt. "We're going to Mrs. Gomez's house," she said.

"No, stay here," Seth told them. "The monsters won't come inside."

"How do you know?" said Caitlin.

"I just do."

"Mrs. Gomez has to get home," said Darcy. "Her son is epileptic . . . stress can trigger an episode. And I don't want to stay here alone with Caitlin."

"Where does she live?"

"Two blocks west."

Seth put on his peacoat. His staff was in the living room. He was about to retrieve it when he felt the tendril of power between it and himself. His instincts told him that it had always been there, even at the very start before he made his first cut into the branch, only now it was clear. He stuck out his arm and thought of the tendril contracting, like a rubber band snapping back to default. The staff whipped through the air across the room and slammed into his hand. It hurt like a motherfucker, but he didn't let it show because it looked so fantastically cool that even the women were impressed.

"WHOA!" said Caitlin.

"Dios mío," said Mrs. Gomez, and made the sign of the cross.

"Move!" said Seth to them all.

The front of Darcy's building was clear. *So far so good.*

Two burned-out cars sat idly in the intersection between Eleventh Street and Avenue B. Seth led them to the corner. One block south to their left, a fire company sprayed three golems with high-pressured water cannons. It only made the monsters angrier. One of the beasts leaped twenty feet and came down hard on the men holding the hose. It batted them around like dominos. Seth tried to hurry the women across the intersection while the beasties were distracted. The old videogame Frogger came to mind as he scooted them across the intersection, trying his best not to get killed. But once finished with the firemen, the beasts noticed Seth and the girls, and all three began charging toward them, gnarling, slobbering, and incredibly pissed off that they'd been given a painful bath.

The phrase "hard air" circulated in Seth's brain through his panic. And he remembered: It was a spell called "hard air." He learned it his first year as a way to make dice fall more favorably when gambling. He'd never used it on this large a scale, but it was the only thing he could remember at this moment. Using his newly carved staff as a focus, he pulled energy from a nearby lay line that he swore had never been there before today, filling the staff with its force. Gripping it like a stickball bat, he swung at the beasts with all his might before they reached him and released the spell. A force swatted the creatures across the block, ricocheting them off buildings and the street like plastic soldiers kicked by a bully. The women looked at him, floored by his feat.

"Move!" he yelled.

Mrs. Gomez's building was unscathed. He saw them to the door and then turned to leave.

"Aren't you staying?" Caitlin asked.

"No, Sassafras. Now don't forget what I told you about the money in the trust—and go to school . . . every day . . . listen to your teachers . . . stay away from boys . . . eat vegetables." Seth had reached the limits of his fatherly knowledge. He turned to Darcy. "The dream was real. Don't ask me how, but the box was a second chance . . . for both of us, it turns out. I'll try not to blow mine . . . you have to make the choice for yourself."

"You're not staying?" she asked. She seemed upset at the idea of his leaving them . . . despite everything that she'd been through because of him.

"They actually need me to stop all this craziness. Don't ask me how or why. If I survive today, I'll find you again and tell you the whole story. You need to find the strength to stay off the junk—for Caitlin's sake. Get better—and stay indoors until this monster thing is over." He turned to leave before he lost his conviction, and did not look back.

Seth co-opted an abandoned scooter with Chinese menus in a

basket and great-smelling food oozing through grease-stained paper bags clapped to its rear. Traffic, as he approached Midtown, had ground to a halt; abandoned cars lay all over Fifth Avenue. People still exited office buildings, desperate to get home. No one wanted to die at work—*We want to be in our Barcaloungers in front of the TV when the world ends,* he thought.

Many of the creatures were happy to leave him alone on their march north. It was the challenge that triggered them. Don't shoot it, hit it, bump it, or snarl at it and there was a good chance it would leave you be. They were programmed to find and kill the prince. Of all the cities in the world Dorn could have chosen, it had to be New York; the most condensed cluster of aggressive, type-A fuckheads on the planet. The regulars in the pubs alone could have set off World War III. If this had gone down in Portland, there'd be a lot fewer fires.

Seth made it to the Empire State Building. A beast driven to frenzy from multiple bullet wounds charged at him. He didn't have time to charge up another hard air spell—he held his staff before him, holding it horizontally at the middle with a single fist and recalled another spell, one that he'd already used successfully down south. This was the first time he cast it on a living thing. The creature was a patchwork creation saturated with magic. Seth perceived the arcane seams holding it together. As the creature leaped at him, Seth "unzipped" the sorcery and repurposed the freed magical energy toward his spell—the beast disassemble into purple blossoms, starting with those paws reaching out toward Seth, until all that was left was a dense wave of flowers that broke apart on him like a chandelier hitting marble. Seth had learned flower conversion to impress barmaids. As he recalled more of his lessons, it was obvious that his repertoire of spells consisted of tricks that helped him cheat at gambling and get laid. Redemption was going to be a long, long road.

CHAPTER 47

FOOD FOR WORMS

It took Lelani two elevators and ten minutes to reach the observation deck on the eighty-sixth floor. The sun was over New Jersey, turning the western horizon a faded turquoise even as indigo blue painted the opposite horizon over Long Island. The sirens echoed upward along the surrounding buildings in a frenetic monotone chorus. She sensed the power in the building, even that high above the city. A strong lay line flowed through New York—robust as any in Aandor, concentrated and swift like a stream after first melt.

They had stopped sending tours up when the golems first attacked, but a few stragglers hoping to avoid the chaos below still loitered about. This would not do.

"Everyone, please head for the exits," she said as authoritatively as she could. "It is not safe here." It certainly would not be in a few moments.

An officious looking African-American man approached her. "Excuse me, I work here, and I don't know who you are."

Lelani searched her pocket for the enchanted silver flower Cal had returned to her at the hotel. She pinned it to her lapel. "I'm from Homeland Security," she said. "It is vital that you clear this deck immediately, including yourself." The man herded the visitors toward the emergency stairs, where a few floors below they could access the elevator to the ground level.

Alone at last, Lelani started to secure her station. She pulled dream catchers from her satchel made of Rosencrantz's wood and woven from strands of her own tail, and hung them in all four corners on the iron suicide gate that surrounded the deck. She placed two more, one in the center of the east face and one on the north, to reinforce the shield on the side facing Dorn. Ideally, one used unicorn hair to weave the strongest catchers, but there were no such creatures in this reality. It was Rosencrantz who suggested she use her own hair; Lelani had never considered herself a magical creature before. She also placed a tiny catcher hanging from a leather cord around her neck.

Next she placed soft clay eggplant-shaped objects on the stone ledge around the deck. They were for magical ailments, diseases, and gas attacks. Lelani didn't know what Dorn's spell book contained, but she was determined to prepare for every contingency. The small holes at the eggplants' bottoms made them look like miniature beehives. Once done with the wards, she planted herself at the northeast corner of the deck gazing out at the Chrysler Building across the skyline. The western sun gleamed on that building's silver crown and windows; she was more beautiful than the Empire State Building.

When Lelani first arrived in New York, in awe of the city's majesty, she saw the two spires as a princess and her knight protector—one lean, a graceful dancer topped with a silver coronet and reaching toward the heavens with a slender arm—the other, the stalwart gray sentinel, armored, spear-bearing, guardian of the realm it surveyed. Little did she realize how right she was—the Empire State Building was indeed Lelani's staging area for the city's defense. Across town, the dancer's beauty belied the dangers within her. Captain MacDonnell would soon engage Dorn regardless of whether Prelate Grey had managed to stop the flow of mana along that branch of the lay line.

Lelani needed to distract Dorn, get him to concentrate on her; maybe even send Symian over to deal with her. That way MacDonnell could engage Hesz and Kraten freely. *Damn it!* she thought. *She* should be there with them. Dorn was Lelani's responsibility. Outclassed or not, she could never have sent Seth against that madman in her stead. She could still make a difference, if only Seth hadn't abandoned them.

Lelani felt betrayed. She'd believed in him . . . that he wanted to make up for his mistakes. She defended him against MacDonnell's distrust. Was he was dead? One of Dorn's minions could have ambushed Seth, and he lay bloody in the gutter somewhere, another casualty of this horrid war.

She used the cell phone MacDonnell had provided to call Seth. Four rings and it went into voice mail, again. She tucked the device into her belt and focused her disappointment on drawing power through the building. She pulled at it like someone drinking a thick shake through a straw. It had to go somewhere though, she couldn't just keep pulling in magic with no release; people were not equipped to be mana batteries and it would consume her. Lelani would use a new spell that Rosencrantz had taught her—a cousin spell to her phosphorous balls. She chanted the words for an orb of fire. She poured the tremendous amounts of energy she had access to and added more of herself into it, visualizing it, asking the energy to form a globe of intense heat, and whipping up the biggest, most powerful sphere of fire she'd ever created. Like a twin to the statue of Atlas holding the world just up the street at Rockefeller Plaza, she stood on the corner of the observation deck, one leg raised against the stone wall with arms wide holding her creation, a miniature sun under the transitioning twilight sky. It illuminated the building behind her and the tops of buildings below with its radiance.

Lelani prayed that Catherine was nowhere near the southwest corner of that building. Helicopters buzzing around the city suddenly turned toward her. She waited for a clear line—when she could put no more energy into the flaming globe, she uttered the release and shot it across the Manhattan skyline at the Chrysler Building. It exploded on the Chrysler crown like an errant firework, bringing back the daylight for an instant over Midtown. The flash subsided and the smoke cleared, there was not too much damage that she could see—just singed metal and several blown in windows.

"Knock, knock," she said to herself. Despite the stupidity of picking a fight with Dorn, Lelani was quite please with herself. That was the biggest attack spell she'd ever cast.

This was it—all was set in motion. There'd be no hiding now. She was in a duel with one of the most powerful sorcerers of her world. If only Seth had turned out truer and willing, then she need not face him alone. She whipped out her phone for one last try. As the phone dialed, the magical net she'd woven around the deck lit up in a multicolored pattern mimicking the webs on the dream catchers, only on a scale that covered the entire deck. *You'll not turn my mind today,* Lelani thought, fingering her necklace.

"Hello?" answered Seth on the other end.

He is alive!

Elation and irritation struggled for command of Lelani's voice. If Seth could replace her on the observation deck, Lelani could go to MacDonnell. "EMPIRE STATE BUILDING, NOW!" she yelled, into the tiny device. Did that come out desperate or angry? She hoped she hadn't scared him off.

A Fox News helicopter suddenly rose before her. It hovered between her position and the Chrysler Building. A cameraman tried to get footage of her. *Get out of here, you fools!* Lelani thought.

A spark, like glint off a mirror, lit the top of the Chrysler Building. Less than a second later, a sizzling bolt of white-hot lightning nicked the helicopter and seared the observation deck, blowing out several windows behind Lelani. She escaped Dorn's retort by mere inches. The copter flew off erratically, leaving a trail of smoke behind it. Tendrils of excess lightning slithered up the dirigible docking mast and diffused into the antenna and then the open air. Her phone was less fortunate; pieces of melted slag smoked upon the ground. Dorn would need a moment to prepare the next charge. Hurled lightning was an incredibly taxing spell that even Lelani had yet to master—a much more intense and focused spell than fire. Knowing she had protected herself from mind control, poisons, curses, and such, Lelani expected more direct attacks from here on in.

She charged up her second fireball, lest Dorn think she escaped to find cover. Lelani hoped that if death had to come, it would be swift, and that her gods would somehow find her in this strange and far-off land.

CHAPTER 48

A DISPROPORTIONATE RESPONSE

Catherine sat tied and bound on the marble floor of the old Chrysler Building observatory. She was not herself. Drugged and still wearing the remnants of her torn blouse and skirt, Cat looked very much the victim Dorn had made her. It tore at her. What that man stole was not any man's right to take. The very foundation of life itself was cut out of her and perverted—perverted to make the most horrible monsters she could ever imagine. There had to be a special place in hell for Dorn. Alone, afraid, and powerless—the few coherent thoughts Cat strung together did not dwell on her loved ones but on what she would do to Dorn if the opportunity presented itself.

It was cold in the observation deck because of the broken window Dorn had put Tom through. Cat was at least grateful Kraten hadn't gagged her. She leaned against the wall for balance, shifting from cheek to cheek to relieve the ache in her glutes.

Kraten, Hesz, and Lhars guarded the entrances to the observatory as Dorn, sitting lotus style in the middle of the floor, poured his energies through the building into the sewers below Midtown, pushing the magic of the elixir to the ends of the island. The sorcerer looked pale—sweat beaded on his face and he ground his teeth as he worked. It wasn't just the spell . . . the man was fighting his illness as well. Every act now was one of desperation. A random thought occurred to Catherine: If Dorn died, would the golems as well? Would his men surrender? She prayed for the chance to put that theory to the test.

Through the open window, Cat heard the distant wails of many sirens, gunfire, passing helicopters, and, even though she thought she imagined it because of the height, screams.

The authorities don't know, she realized. Didn't know that the cause of all this mayhem was a madman sorcerer up here in the Chrysler Building. How could they? This world was not equipped to deal with stuff like this.

Pressing her back against the wall, she tried to worm her way to standing. Kraten observed this and stepped toward her.

"Not trying to escape," she said. "Just want to see outside."

He grabbed her by the cuff, pulled her the rest of the way up. He jerked her the few feet to the window. Forty-second Street was a sea of flashing red lights. Even from that high up, she could make out the golems among the people. *So many,* she thought. It was bedlam out there, made worse by this happening so close to rush hour. Even the skies were filled with police and news helicopters, buzzing about Midtown. *Midtown.* Not downtown. Dorn's efforts had not reached the fringes of the island yet. If only there was something she could do to stop him now.

To the southwest, a bright hot light formed near the top of the Empire State Building. It grew unnaturally blazing like a miniature sun on the corner of that building.

"My lord," said Kraten, also looking at the bright light. "Perhaps you should see this?"

Dorn was in an irritable state. Hesz helped him up and the sorcerer leaned on the giant as they approached the window. He looked far worse, now that Cat saw him up close—veins running close to the surface, lines around his eyes and mouth. Dorn looked as though he'd aged ten years since before casting the golem spell. Kraten pulled Catherine away from the window to make room for his master. She'd lost her balance, and tried to regain it, but felt herself teetering forward with each tiny hop. Symian caught her just before she hit the floor. Even through the fanged grin, grayish skin, and yellowish eyes, Catherine sensed warmth coming through his smile. He'd saved her when Dorn wanted to use her remaining ova for the second golem batch. Why? They were the bad guys . . .

Symian smiled at her tenderly—but this same man had tried to kill Cal and Lelani on multiple occasions. He left her by the middle window to check out the light show with the others at the southwest end. She squirmed her way up until she could see the Empire State Building again. The ball of light suddenly grew bigger in a much different way . . . before it was fixed in its location—now it blocked the view behind it, as though it were . . .

"Oh shit," Cat whispered. She rolled on the floor as far away from the southwest window as she could get.

Hesz shoved Dorn and Kraten away from the corner, shielding them with his massive back as the ball of flame hit the building. It wrenched a gaping, smoking hole in that corner of the observatory, shattering the glass, and ripping apart the frame of the window it hit. The temperature rose from the hot glowing debris along the hole's edge as tendrils of fire and smoke came into the room.

The crown's metallic skin shielded them from the worst of the blast. It was not a very effective attack but had garnered Dorn's attention.

"That bitch!" Dorn cried out. His temper had turned dark, and he forgot about powering the golem spell. The smoke soon dissipated, and as the observatory was mostly empty space, nothing actually caught fire. At the edge of the floor, using the new opening, Dorn raised his right palm toward the Empire State Building and his left palm down toward the floor. He uttered phrases alien to Catherine. Moments later, tendrils of light glimmered on the Empire State, like a pulsating fiber-optic spider's web.

"She's erected wards," said Symian.

"I can see that," Dorn said, transfixed on the other building across the city. "Go deal with her," he ordered his apprentice matter-of-factly.

Symian, usually upbeat and positive, turned sullen in an instant. A quiver in his lower lip confirmed to Cat that Symian did not approve of this order. Kraten, Hesz, and Lhars observed quietly, each with dour expressions. Hesz's posture betrayed a hint of anger.

"My lord, the streets are filled with vicious golems," Symian said. "Surely you can . . ."

"I cannot send them on a new task until the prince is dead," Dorn said. "Not even if I wished it. That is their core purpose for existing."

"My—my lord," Symian pleaded. "The centaur has bested me. Twice."

Dorn turned to his apprentice with the most placid of expressions. "Is the centaur a match for me?" he asked.

"No, my lord." Symian's response smacked of politics.

"Yet she attacks me anyway!" Dorn pointed out. "Show me similar resolve, Symian. Or go be a mummer's apprentice and pull weasels from your fool's cap." Dorn pondered his command for a moment and then added, "I care not for fair fights. Use your blade . . . stab the bitch with faerie silver and throw her from the roof. I've always wanted to see a centaur fly."

Symian went from sullen to stunned in the blink of an eye. He was in open disbelief that this was actually happening.

"You may take Lhars with you," Dorn added, satisfied with his own generosity.

Lhars closed his eyes in silent deliberation. Symian turned to Hesz and Kraten—both men looked at the floor solemnly and said nothing.

Dorn grabbed at his head again as though someone hammered an invisible spike into it. Cat didn't know enough about magic battles to tell if it was something Lelani did or if Dorn's headaches were reaching an all-time new pain threshold.

Symian put on his coat slowly, as though waiting for a last-minute reprieve—but Dorn was focused on his own pain, holding on to the wall to brace himself. Symian looked like a dog that had been kicked and banished by his master—waiting for Dorn to remember how loyal he truly was and see the error of his strategy. He shuffled to the elevator with Lhars, flipped his hoodie, and pressed the button for the lobby. And they were gone.

Dorn sounded like a man tortured on the rack. His eyes were wild—his breathing in perfect rhythm with Cat's Lamaze method when she had Bree. He took off his suit jacket and tossed it on the duffel, loosened his tie, and rolled up his designer shirtsleeves with their fancy French cuffs.

Cat studied her captor's strong profile, thick wrists and blond hair tied back—a Norse god come to earth. Dorn chanted in a foreign tongue again that sounded very much like German, but wasn't—around his balled fists blue electricity snaked like St. Elmo's fire around a ship's mast. Cat could feel the static charge in the room . . . her arm hairs stood on end as power borrowed from the lay line hummed through the building to this hidden aerie.

Dorn stood at the edge of the newly formed precipice and let loose a drum-shattering war cry as an arc of intense hot light crackled from his hands and whipped across the darkening sky like an angry lash, colliding violently at its terminus—the eighty-sixth floor of the Empire State Building.

CHAPTER 49

RIDE THE LIGHTNING

The lay line energy that enveloped Seth in the lobby of the Empire State Building was the purest magic he'd experienced to date—it charged him like refined sugar juicing a man that never eats sweets. The building was a conduit, a long metal pole in a lightning storm drawing power from everywhere. The magic was familiar—imbued with a presence similar in that way a scent can bring back long-ago memories and transport a person into yesteryear. The magic filled him, pouring into reservoirs he had long forgotten existed within. He was different in that way . . . it was what Magnus Proust most liked about him he now recalled—a rare talent. Not all mages could store magic within themselves the way that Seth could. One teacher called him "the camel"—an anomaly among anomalies.

Elevators were only bringing people down. Seth found an idle lift at the end of the hall that would take him toward the observation deck and tapped the control board with his staff to activate it. As the elevator climbed, he wished he'd brought some gum to pop his ears against the pressure change. On eighty, he transferred to a second bank to take him to the eighty-sixth floor. Staff at the ready, he didn't know what to expect when he stepped onto the deck lobby. Strong gusts buffeted him when he walked out of the car. Normally the lobby was enclosed by thick glass walls and filled with tourists, but the floor was empty and the east-facing windows shattered, broken glass pushed by the wind skittered around the floor, glittering weakly under the waning sun.

The smell of soldered metal and ozone saturated the air. A four-foot-high stone wall marked the perimeter of the outside balcony, topped by a suicide-preventing steel and iron grate that curved inward at its highest point like a breaking wave with jagged tips. Lelani huddled on the New Jersey side of the deck, farthest from the Chrysler Building. She crouched behind the concrete slope of a handicap ramp that led from the lobby to the balcony. This side of the deck was in better shape—windows still intact. Burns, cuts, and smudges all over Lelani told of a long, harrowing day.

"Hey," Seth said.

"Hey," she responded. She looked glad to see him—something Seth had little experience with overall.

"What's going on?" he asked.

"Distraction."

"How's that working out?"

"Not well."

Lelani reached up, grabbed Seth's lapel, and pulled him down on top of her just as a streak of lightning shattered the windows above them and electrified the metal fence surrounding the deck. Electricity sizzled and spat off the fence in pieces where the bolt hit, like white-hot embers off an industrial welder. Seth and Lelani brushed the hot sparks off their clothes quickly and crawled to the southern side of the deck.

"Holy crap!" Seth cried. "We're going to fry up here! Who's doing that?"

"Dorn."

"Dorn? Why are we up here?"

"I miscalculated. I thought with enough power I could deflect his attacks and draw his focus until his mana depleted at the Chrysler Building."

"You picked a fight on purpose?"

"We need to draw the bulk of his ire here to stop the spread of the golems and to distract him from the captain and Malcolm, who are even now storming his position."

"Jeezus! I'm gone for a few hours and we're suddenly on the offensive."

Another bolt came through the lobby of the observation deck and hit the grating. The smell of ozone permeated the air and the hairs on Seth's arms stood on end.

"We got to get off this deck," he said. "We're going to die up here."

"Seth . . . ," Lelani started. She paused a moment looking uncharacteristically uncertain. "I have to go to the Chrysler Building. I have to take on Dorn directly."

"Are you nuts?!" he scolded.

Far from it, her look said she was deadly serious. Seth gained a little insight into the lives of wizards at this moment. They all lived in fear of one another . . . like the era of mutually assured destruction before the Berlin Wall fell, wizards inherently understood there was no sure way of telling who was more powerful than whom, what tricks the other had, what the other knew that you didn't, and that the only certain way to stay alive was to always strike first and strike hard. Even during the best of times, they were like college professors perpetually in fear of the competitor's paper that would disprove a life's work; only in wizards' cases there were temporal powers involved—means to control and manipulate the universe. *What a mad way to live,* Seth realized.

The sky darkened from more than the setting sun. A true cloud had formed over Manhattan, above the collective black haze from all the fires and explosions, to block the few stars the city laid claim to. The breeze picked up, cool droplets fell intermittently chilling Seth's cheeks, threatening to become a steady drizzle. A flash in the clouds startled them, thinking another bolt had landed on their deck, but it was nature's power, outlining the ceiling's linty bulk, like blue-gray balls of cotton crushed in a bag.

"Powerful magic affects weather patterns," Lelani said. "It's never good to draw out so much in one place. Dorn has used a lifetime's worth of spells against us."

"What do you need me to do?" Seth asked.

"Stay up here and throw anything you can at him . . . anything that will make him believe he still battles me. By the gods' good graces, I may make it there in time to engage Dorn when Lord MacDonnell assaults his stronghold. If he can dispatch the remaining henchmen and escape with Catherine, it would dispirit Dorn—perhaps enough to give the malady that ails him time to run its course."

Seth grabbed her arm. "Wait. Why don't you just kill him? You sound . . . like you don't expect to be around to see Dorn go down."

She gently put her hand on his and forced a smile. She leaned in and kissed him on the cheek, and headed into the lobby. Seth followed her with a million questions. He couldn't very well throw hard air or turn things into flowers across a city. Before they reached the elevators, one dinged and its doors opened. Symian and a large heavily armed henchman stepped onto the deck.

Lelani grabbed Seth and hurdled them both through the broken panes back out onto the southern balcony. Bullets whizzed overhead, flying out over the unsuspecting city. Lelani whipped up two phosphorus balls and chucked them back into the lobby. She didn't have time to put too much energy into them, but they flashed brilliantly. The trick worked because the henchman now shot wildly, and like a blind man with a gun managed to hit everything except what he wanted to. They heard Symian yowl in pain. Seth recalled that the troll's skin was flammable.

Seth worked up the spell for hard air. "Get behind me," he said to his partner, and swung his staff toward the lobby intending to blow both assailants completely off the deck. A spray of glass and rubble, souvenirs, pamphlets—everything not nailed down—blew out the eastern side of the building in a cloud of debris that looked very much like the sky over a ticker tape parade. The lobby was emptied.

"Well done," said Lelani, impressed. "You must teach me that."

They entered the lobby again, slowly. The henchman was on the floor of the east balcony, moaning, saved from flying off the building by the suicide grate. He reached under his coat. Lelani approached, and as the pistol emerged from the coat, she kicked him in the head, caving in the henchman's skull like a ripe melon.

Symian was still missing.

They looked at each other, wondering if the troll now lay splattered on some lower rooftop. They walked through the lobby, carefully searching.

Suddenly Lelani waved her arms in a pattern and the air around them flashed brightly, crackling like a bug zapper in summer. "You'll not catch me twice with that spell, troll!" she shouted.

"What'd he do?" Seth whispered.

"He tried to place us in stasis."

A few moments of silence felt like they stretched into years. Unexpectedly, Symian walked out, hands up where they could see them, waving a white handkerchief. He walked slowly past the elevators in full view. Lelani put up her own hands in a defensive posture and Seth raised his staff. The right side of Symian's jacket and hoodie was burned through. His right shoulder and neck blackened. Apparently, he'd learned how to put himself out when afire.

"I can't beat you," Symian said.

"It's a trick," Seth said.

"I wish it were," said Symian. He looked dispirited, like he had no fight left in him. "I returned one faerie silver dagger to Dorn—he believes I still have the other knife and therefore the advantage. I could not tell him that I had lost it to you. I cannot beat you in a fight, fair or otherwise. He sent me regardless, knowing that . . . to my death." To Lelani he said, "You offered me mercy once . . . I choose not to die. I have that right, do I not? To live?"

"Just like that?" Seth said.

"He's mad," Symian said fearfully. "The headaches have driven him to desperation. Look at how many of our company are dead. What he did to Tom—to Lord MacDonnell's wife . . . We are undone. Even his own childhood friend, Kraten, believes we're on the path to our doom under Dorn—but who dares confront a deranged sorcerer? He's too scared to go home defeated. He's despera—"

Symian fell to his knees writhing in a struggle against an invisible force. He grabbed his head and made choking sounds. "Nooo! Stay out!" he cried.

"Mind spell!" Lelani shouted. "Some of my wards are down!" She shot a phosphorus ball at the troll.

Symian caught it with no effect on him and threw it back at her a hundred times more powerful. Lelani erected a ward just in time, but the blast blew her and Seth back out the other end of the lobby toward the Jersey side. White spots in a white haze filled Seth's vision.

Symian approached them with a confident swagger. Something was wrong with his eyes . . . they moved independently, in different directions.

"I thought I'd help my apprentice since he has such high regard for your talents," Symian said. His speech pattern was different, his voice gravelly and forced.

Seth cast another hard air spell, only to have Symian-Dorn throw it back at him. The force slammed him into the wall and he lost consciousness . . .

. . . It was the second time in a day that someone spoke to Seth while he lay in a subconscious state. This time, it was the tree wizard Rosencrantz, who it turned out, was the familiar presence in the magic at the Empire State Building. The lay line that ran through New York also emerged in the tree wizard's meadow, and Rosencrantz was capable of sending out a tendril of consciousness along the stream. The tree wizard was already familiar with Seth's mind. It cost Rosencrantz greatly to communicate in real time. The tree had to cast its own time warp to speed its reactions to human levels, and it aged rapidly as it did so. Seth could not tell what language the communication was held in, or what the tree wizard's voice even sounded like, or even how long the conversation lasted. He just knew that all these things happened. Rosencrantz healed his concussion through the stream as they communicated.

Seth opened his eyes to a throbbing pain clamoring on his skull. A steady drizzle had arrived and its coolness helped revive him. Symian-Dorn had a hand around Lelani's throat and the other pulled at the dagger on Lelani's belt. Not long had passed since Seth had been struck unconscious.

"What's this?" Symian-Dorn asked the centaur.

Despite blurry vision and a throbbing headache, he had to take down Symian now or Lelani was finished. It had to be fast and simple. *The simplest spell.*

He got up quietly, moved behind Symian, and cast the spell to separate the bonds between all the salt molecules in the troll's body. Symian-Dorn screamed and dropped the dagger. Salt was a vital component in any carbon-based creature; Seth didn't think he could kill Symian quickly this way, but he had his attention.

Seth poured it on. *That's right,* he thought. *Who's your daddy? Take your focus off Lelani so she can whammy you into next week.*

Instead, the possessed troll called up a powerful gale and threw Lelani into it. The gust carried her over the protective grating around the deck. Lelani reached out at the last minute and grabbed the curved top of the suicide grate with both hands before she went over. Seth thanked God the top of the grate curved inward to create a bit of a platform at the top that Lelani could lay on, otherwise, she would have been impaled by steel rods sticking straight up. Seth continued to wreak havoc with Symian's salt levels until the troll slumped to the ground dazed. Silvery smoke rose from his body. His eyes were straight, though. *Elvis has left the building, folks.*

Seth ran over to his partner, who was struggling with all her strength to stay atop the grate and fall inward toward the deck, not slide off the outer curve. Her hands were bleeding from the strain of her weight.

Shit . . . she weighs as much as a horse! Seth realized. She began to slip backward, the edge of the grate cutting at her fingers. He dropped his staff and jumped up to grab her shoulders, pulling back toward the deck with all his weight. His added weight allowed Lelani time to brace her invisible back hoof on a support piece that ran horizontally along the fence, and leverage by which to stabilize herself.

A very expensive sounding piece of metal pinged, as it was unsheathed behind Seth. He was not at a good angle to see behind him, but Lelani's expression said Symian was on his feet and opportunistically revoking his surrender. From the corner of Seth's eye, Symian shuffled slowly toward them through puddles on the deck with the silver dagger in hand, still dazed by his master's mind puppetry and Seth's salt attack.

"Fucking bad guys," Seth grunted.

As if things could not get worse, a flash emanated from the Chrysler Building. Time slowed for Seth—everything in the world looked trapped inside a gelatin mold, but whether it was a true magical effect or his mind's natural reaction to impending death, he could not say. He did know that a bolt of lightning hurled toward them across the sky—whether it hit true was irrelevant, Lelani could not get off the fence in time—she would fry. Her fear-filled expression locked with his in mutual understanding that there was not enough time for whatever sentiments still remained between them—her hands too vital in keeping her from falling off the building to raise a counter spell.

An epiphany filled the ex-photographer, a possession of his consciousness by his own knowledge of a thing. As the bolt approached, he dropped from the fence, put out his hand toward his staff and called it to him, whipped it before him to tap Lelani through the grate, and aimed the back end at the troll. The lightning hit Lelani dead on; it passed through her, painfully, but safely, into the staff and shot out of the rear at the troll. Symian simultaneously ignited and was blown through the grate on the opposite end of the deck by the powerful bolt. He shrieked in anguish, a bright screaming star hurtling down with the rain toward Horace Greeley Park.

The lightning blast had short-circuited Lelani's illusion spell. With Seth's help, she clamored back onto the observation deck, slightly smoking, in full centaur glory. Her hands were bloodied, her clothes torn, and her bright red hair a mess, but still, she was beautiful. Seth had forgotten how stunning she was. He'd been in shock when she dropped her illusion at the MacDonnells' home, with barely enough wits to appreciate what a striking creature Lelani Stormbringer was. Without the illusion, she abandoned her crouch and stood at her full height, topping out at six foot three. He drank her in, determined not to let another opportunity pass him by.

"Thank you," she said.

"Thank you," he responded. "For putting up with me. For saving my life when you got to New York . . . for being my friend when I was so undeserving of it."

She grinned devilishly. "Well . . . I will deny this if you repeat it, but as much as you were an annoying pain in the ass back in Aandor—you were also the most fun student we had at the academy. If you hadn't kept challenging the limits of common sense, it would have been a lot duller."

Seth laughed.

They headed into the lobby—the elevators were completely blown out.

"I guess it's the stairs," Seth observed.

"Not exactly," Lelani said. They walked to the eastern side of the building. Lelani used a spell that mimicked a blowtorch to cut through the grate. "You have to challenge Dorn. He is unaware that his power dwindles."

"He probably thinks we're dead."

From her satchel Lelani retrieved a small dream catcher necklace, similar to her own, and placed it around Seth's neck.

"You should disprove Dorn of that notion," she said.

Seth knew just what to do, too. Rosencrantz reminded him while he lay unconscious . . . the nature of lightning. And having channeled it, he understood it better now, knew how to use magic to manipulate its essence. Standing on the northeast corner of the observation deck, he dug in his heels, knees bent. He brought up his anger—anger of the injustices in his life; anger at himself for ruining Darcy; for taking his friends for granted over the years; for Ben Reyes, who deserved better than to die protecting his home; for all the men and women who died in this city tonight who would never have a chance to redeem their own mistakes because of Dorn—years of accumulated shame, fury, and pain. This time the magic did not avoid him, he had threaded the needle . . . he knew how to draw it to him, bind it like a cowboy knew how to rope five hundred pounds of angry bull.

Seth focused all this emotion into a white-hot line in his head that he named redemption, and thrust his staff toward the Chrysler Building with both hands. A bright hot streak of lightning emanated from its tip and whipped across the sky battering the other building's silver crown.

"That felt great," he admitted.

Never one to let a challenge go unanswered, Dorn responded in kind, but before his bolt reached the Empire State, Seth met it halfway with another one of his own. The two lines collided over Thirty-ninth Street struggling for dominance, illuminating the Manhattan skyline for miles. Dorn's push was strong, but Seth pushed just as hard and held the midpoint of the dual bolts at bay.

"GO!" he grunted. "I don't know how long I can stay toe to toe."

Lelani closed her eyes. With hands opened, palms up and thumbs and index fingers forming circles, she chanted in a language Seth now recognized as Centauran. She entered a trancelike state as she cast this enchantment upon herself. A faint black glow appeared on the edge of her body then brightly flickered out like the blowing of flame. Lelani opened her eyes, pulled her composite longbow and quiver from her bag, and, with a smile, vaulted over the edge of the balcony.

CHAPTER 50

NO SOUP FOR YOU

The last column of the henge was about to be put in place. The highly experienced and able men of Local 20 had made fast work of it. Allyn wondered why then it took so long to get construction projects finished in New York. The same highways were still under repair since he had last visited two years earlier.

He looked toward Manhattan; flashes of lightning cut the deep blue sky. This was wizards' doing . . . heavy columns of gray smoke billowed up from Midtown and joined the rain clouds above. What price to pay for the life of one boy. How many dead? Injured? Scarred for life? Americans were not used to fighting battles on the home front. War was something we exported. In so many ways Aandor was similar, Allyn thought. Like New York after 9/11, Aandor, too, had lost its innocence . . . its confidence of its own indestructibility.

What Farrenheil had done to Aandor was an abomination. The rules of chivalry kept wars on battle plains among armies. But once the dogs of war were let loose, few could restrain their bite. Soldiers did not fight for weekly pay . . . they fight for the opportunity to pillage, to make themselves rich in one fell swoop by raiding the fine homes of the enemy, to plant their seeds in their adversaries' wives and daughters. Now, Farrenheil has taken its pound of flesh from this beautiful metropolis as well—a city that had suffered so much already. There would be a reckoning. No one listens to the pacifist pleas of ministers and priests. Cycles like this were hard to break.

Allyn stepped onto a crane and motioned upward with his thumb. It rose ten stories, giving him a better vantage by which to see Midtown. He could just make out the Chrysler Building from where he stood. It was still saturated with the mana. But he spotted what he had hoped for, a cutoff point near its middle. As Dorn used more energy, the mana rose but did not replenish from below—it drained from the building like penicillin plunged out of a needle. Soon, Lord Dorn will have nothing to draw on but the smoke and ash of his own destruction.

"We done here, Rev?" asked Johnny Maronne.

"Yes. It's up to the warriors and wizards now."

"Okay boys, wrap it up!" cried Johnny. You'll have some special bonuses in your next pay. Don't spend it all in one place."

"Where to, now?" asked Allyn.

"Boss says to bring you to the compound in New Jersey."

Allyn debated heading back to North Carolina. He missed his wife and daughter greatly, even if Michelle wanted nothing to do with him at the moment. But the boy . . . so much potential; Allyn would stay, just a little longer to see this episode through. If Callum and Malcolm failed, if their wizards were killed, the prince would have only Allyn and Tilcook to help him. He did not want to leave that impressionable young man alone in the hands of a mobster.

"Lead the way," Allyn told Maronne.

CHAPTER 51
A CRIMSON BLUR

Lelani Stormbringer galloped down the side of the Empire State Building with the speed of a thoroughbred—defying gravity as her hooves stamped their imprints into its slick stone façade. Her scarlet hair billowed behind her like a torch in defiance of gravity, random blond streaks bestowing her with the illusion of a flaming crown against the building's gray, dark countenance. The enchantment held her firm to the granite and Indiana limestone as though it were the earth itself.

The cool rain purified and revived her. People at their windows witnessing the mayhem below turned their heads to the unlikely sound of a gallop on their walls. They gasped as she passed. Such was the height of the building that Lelani thought she had run miles before she was close enough to discern man from beast for her purposes. She raised her bow firing at golems as she hurtled toward the street. From the onlookers, a roar of cheers came forth from the windows, loud as any sports stadium, quashing the sirens and gunfire below. Each arrow hit their mark, straight through a monster's brain.

The beasts had collected below her, enraged by her attack and raring to engage her. Lelani grasped that as long as they were focused on her, they would leave the civilians and civil defenders alone. A few began to climb up the Empire State Building, impatient with her progress toward them. At the fifth floor, with the more advanced golems only feet away, she pushed away from the building, leaped over the beasts, onto the roof of a coach bus. Looking north, a locked-in sea of coach, city, tour buses, and trucks presented the path of least resistance to Forty-second Street. The golems shook the bus and climbed to get at her—Lelani took a running start, avoiding their grabs, and leaped to the next bus several feet away, and not stopping, ran for the next one after that.

She was soon past Thirty-fifth Street with a sea of golems on her tail. She vaulted the metal bars that held the streetlights aloft. Where there were no busses she leaped to the nearest truck, where there were no trucks, a cab, an SUV, whatever vehicle gave her the highest elevation until she again found herself on the highest point possible.

Spotlights from the helicopters above had found her and struggled to keep pace as she dashed above the streets of New York, her tail flapping in her wake. The air vehicles were careful to stay out of the lightning battle's line of fire, still raging overhead. Lelani fired arrows continuously, wherever she thought it would do any good: a family cornered—arrow to the beast's head; policemen under siege to her right—arrow to the head; a besieged double-decker tour bus in front of her—arrow to the head; two beasts on the left chasing school children—two arrows to the brainpans. Lelani transformed into a whirlwind of deathly grace, with a growing mob of golems behind her laboring to keep pace. She had made herself enemy number one to this newly minted race.

Better her than the prince of Aandor, she thought. She had finally met the boy, and deemed him worthy of her sacrifice.

At Forty-second Street, Lelani cut a hard right onto a double-decker Gray Line tour bus and headed east toward the Chrysler Building. Above her the lightning storm still raged, illuminating the streets in an eerie strobe of blue-and-white flashes and intermittent darkness. There were power outages in this section of town, probably power lines severed when the golems rose up through the infrastructure. The Park Avenue Bridge that circumvented Grand Central

Station came up ahead, and she had no clearance for it. She leaped onto it, crossed the road, and resumed her bus hurdles on the other end. The monsters were not deterred. All the beasts on Park Avenue, seeing their enraged Fifth Avenue brethrens' stampede, quickly joined in. Each street she passed brought other hordes of growling, snarling beasties toward Forty-second Street. Lelani was sure the majority of the Midtown golems were now converging on her. When she reached the Chrysler Building, she came to a defensive position made up of police and military units behind tanks and quickly assembled hodgepodge perimeters made up of trucks and trailers. Hovering loudly a hundred feet above these units were two military helicopters armed to the teeth. The men on the ground tried to stop her advance. She hopped onto a tractor-trailer parked next to the Chrysler Building and then jumped onto the building's façade to begin her gallop upward in the reverse of her Empire State Building descent.

With more pressing matters upon them, the military copters opened fire on Lelani's collected mob of golems with everything: autocannons, rockets, 30-millimeter M230 machine guns.

The hordes turned into a virtual stew of fur, blood, and talons. More heavy weapons fire came to bear on adjoining streets, and then the tanks and ground units moved in under the cover of the helicopters. They shot anything still moving dead on the spot.

Several high-up news copters had kept pace with Lelani and tagged her with spotlights as she made her gravity defying upward run. She'd just cleared the sixty-first floor when she felt her traction begin to slip. Lelani tried to pull more magic into her enchantment, but to no use—with Dorn sucking in every last joule of mana in the edifice, the building was drained of mana—her enchantment was dying off. She considered using her personal reserve, enough for one large spell, or several smaller ones, but held off in case it would be needed against Dorn.

Gravity suddenly reasserted itself. She slid down several feet and landed hard on the corner balcony next to a metallic eagle gargoyle. For better or worse, this lay line was shutting down. She kicked her way into an office, and made for the stairs.

CHAPTER 52

IN THE END, THE HATE U MAKE IS = TO THE LOVE U TAKE

1

Cal and Malcolm arrived at the Chrysler Building whole and intact. It was a grueling slog, but as soon as they realized the golems would ignore them if not confronted, they made better time. This was very hard for Cal because of the beasts' primary objective, to find and slaughter the prince, and he felt that each one they left alive might be the one that killed Daniel. Mal convinced him of the folly of fighting hundreds of monsters instead of the random few that charged them in a rage. They would never have made it to Forty-second Street. In the thirteen years since Cal last saw his sergeant, Mal had become adept at seeing the big picture.

For safety reasons, the Chrysler Building elevators had been shut down. Callum tried to use his pull as an NYPD officer to get them to start one car, but everyone was in a state of disarray. It wasn't a matter of authority; this was a full-fledged panic. The Chrysler Building was ground zero for the rise of the golems, and most people had fled. A few tenants hunkered down in their offices and would not leave.

"I guess we take the stairs," Cal told his sergeant.

A look of resigned acceptance came over Malcolm. Callum opened the stairwell door. They looked up the well and Malcolm sighed.

"I'm wasted on a marathon of this type," Mal said. "Dwarvs are natural sprinters, very dangerous over short distances."

Mal positioned his shield on his left arm and they climbed, soon running into people huddled for safety in the thick concrete well. These folks were scared, not sure of whether to leave the building or stay. The military force building up outside their building on Forty-second Street made staying in their offices just as dangerous. Down the street from them was the United Nations, and around the corner, embassies from all over the world. Pretty soon there'd be tanks, mobile infantry, and probably a few Apache attack copters hovering above them. Contingencies like this—well, maybe not exactly like this—were planned for among the top brass in the police, FBI, and Department of State.

A few of the stairwell huddlers were startled by Mal's elaborate ax.

"NYPD," Cal would assure them.

By the thirtieth floor, Mal was winded; he had to rest.

"Gone soft," Cal teased, breathing a bit harder himself. "Billionaire's life is good?"

"Those damn Washington dinners," Mal said. "Generals and senators love to eat richly."

"Can't have you going into cardiac arrest soon as we get up there."

"I'll be fine," Malcolm assured him, panting. "Though I've a bad feeling I'm going to end up fighting the giant."

"I'm more worried about attacking a wizard without a mage of our own," said Cal.

"Any luck getting that kid on the phone?"

"Stopped trying once we hit the stairwell," Cal responded. "Too much concrete and steel for any reception." Cal took a sip of water from a Poland Spring bottle and handed it to Malcolm. "He's an idiot, anyway. Bringing him is almost as bad as having no wizard."

"Okay—but maybe you can fight the giant? There aren't any dwarv victory songs about fighting frost giants. Lots of victory songs against the quarterlings of Fhlee, though."

"They're two feet tall and avid pacifists."

"Yeah . . . well . . . before my time."

"Hesz is the easier battle for you," Cal told his friend. "You can turn your short—uh, shorter stature to your advantage with the right tactics. I don't need you to beat him, just keep him occupied while I take on the Verakhoon. Kraten would cut you up in less than two minutes. He sword trained in Farrenheil under Schweinaufklebera when he was a ward of the archduke's."

"That the guy from the Hodonin wars . . . the one who won the Red Tourney."

"Yep. Anyway, Kraten's a knight, or whatever passes for one in that mockery of a desert kingdom he hails from. You wouldn't last two minutes against him."

"Right. So I'm going after the eight-foot defensive lineman with tusks jutting out of his mouth instead."

"You have a pretty big ax," Cal assured him.

They heard a crash several floors above them, followed by howls and screams. Dozens of footsteps rattled the well as a stampede of civilians rushed past toward the lobby.

Golem? mouthed Mal.

The beast rounded the landing with blood splattered on its fur and shreds of the last person it tore apart still in its teeth. Cal clicked the safety on his carbine and the stairwell exploded with gunfire. Cal poured a hailstorm of bullets into the golem. A few seconds in, the gun jammed. The beast was severely wounded, but not enough to stay down. It lunged at the cop, who got his shield up between it and him. Cal dropped the gun for his sword and thrust it into the creature's gut. It wailed, then whimpered, and eventually died.

"She wasn't kidding about the guns jamming around magic," Mal said.

"Break's over," he told Malcolm. And they climbed.

Cal didn't know what to expect when they reached the top, but it seemed more and more like there were no guards on duty—not heartless minions, golems, or goons from the fatherland . . . just a partly open door to the observatory deck, which he spied from half a landing down using a mirror.

The only internal light came from a single round lamp hanging from the ceiling with metal bands mimicking Saturn. The room was mostly dim with patches of darkness in corners where the light didn't reach it, accented by soft light from the surrounding city coming through the windows. The ceiling was dark, except for areas of reflection where white paint or gold leaf was used in the pattern of the cosmic motif.

Cal really didn't know how to proceed next. A sorcerer of Dorn's caliber knew a dozen ways to neutralize people quickly. Symian probably knew a few as well.

Suddenly there were raised voices in the observatory, followed by the booming crash of windows. Flames and smoke flew by the open doorway. *Cat!* Cal thought. In a panic for his wife's safety, Cal rushed up to the landing with Malcolm at his heels. Mal grabbed him by the back of his utility belt and shook his head *no.* It was too dangerous to just rush in. His sergeant was correct, of course . . . If Cat was dead, there was no sense in throwing his own life away revealing himself. And if she was unhurt, she deserved a better rescue than a husband half cocked with fear.

The observation deck was hazy with smoke—blackish tendrils wisped into the stairwell pushed by the cool Manhattan air blowing into the observatory. With the mirror, he spotted Cat's feet bound on the floor near the southeast corner of the building. Coughing and nearby voices held Cal back from a blind rush at that moment.

Dorn was telling Symian to go to the Empire State Building with one of the Farrenheil soldiers to handle Lelani. Cal indicated to Mal that they wait until those two left. That would leave only one sorcerer and two men to fight.

One elevator still worked for Symian, and soon they were gone. Kraten and Hesz walked past the stairwell door to the other side of the deck to open more windows and get a cross breeze going. Using the mirror, Cal placed Dorn at the blasted-out southwest window. The sorcerer was ensconced in the act of hurling lightning bolts across town. He hoped Lelani survived the attack. He turned the mirror around to check on the other two, and two bright blue eyes in the mirror reflected right back at Cal.

2

Hesz smashed through the door with a huge studded mace. The force of it launched Callum into the air until the stairwell wall abruptly stopped him. Had he not been wearing his police armor and helmet, he would have been knocked out from the impact. Hesz filled the door frame, appearing too large to fit through, but fit he did, turning his shoulders to squeeze into the stairwell. Malcolm immediately charged with his ax, only to have it blocked by the mace. Hesz made a backhanded swipe at the dwarv with a large fist. Malcolm ducked; the giant's fist landed on the iron guardrail where it wrenched metal.

Cal charged the giant, swiping with his sword, and drove Hesz back into the observatory, much to his preference. The stairwell was too confined for swordplay. A pang of fear that Dorn would notice him and cast some sort of sorcery ran through Callum, but the sorcerer was half mad with his battle against the Empire State Building. Kraten, however, noticed and ran toward them. Mal charged out of the well and got between Callum and Hesz, swinging at the giant's legs and yelling, "GO!"

With his police shield in one hand, Cal and Kraten closed the space between them rapidly and greeted each other with clashing steel. The desert warrior's form was good; vertical cut followed by a downward swing, and then a horizontal swipe. There were few thrusts to the midsection, and of those, none were sloppy or desperate. Cal parried blow after blow, alternating his blocks with his shield and sword defenses.

This type of fight was very different from the all-out carnage of a battlefield. In war, very few of your assailants actually knew what they were doing with any weapon. Cal usually cut through an enemy company like they were aged veal, sparing only seconds for each man he ran down. In a melee such as this, your opponent had more finesse than the average soldier.

Sword fights were not as graceful or elaborate as the ones in the movies. There's an economy to your attack and defense—moves are measured and calculated. Real weapons and armor tired you out quickly, and there was no director waiting to yell, "cut" so that you could retire to your trailer for yogurt and a massage.

Malcolm seemed to be holding his own against Hesz. The giant had cuts on his hands and legs, and each time Hesz brought his mace to bear, Mal no longer stood where the giant had aimed. The Dwarv rolled and leaped with the agility of a gymnast, avoiding the lumbering giant who was determined to squash this annoying bug. Mal always had a reputation for being extremely hard to kill.

Cal's reputation was that of the raging warrior—a berserker-killing machine finely tuned to the art of war. Such was his lot for daring to survive, for if he were not efficient at it, he would have come home in a cold box long ago. It bothered him slightly that this was how soldiers, maidens, shopkeepers, tradesmen, and children saw him. Everyone assumed he was a hyperaggressive warrior, weighing heavily toward violent motions like this bronze-skinned opponent employed against him now.

But Cal's father had filled him with age-old wisdoms handed down through the generations, and James MacDonnell stressed the defensive moves over the offensive. There were seven primary zones a swordsman had to defend: the head, neck, shoulder, elbow, wrist, gut, and legs. Cal had developed his blocking and parrying expertise to a degree where he could afford to wait out his opponents in a melee with little danger to himself. It wasn't so much that he'd wear out his adversary as he was studying the person's style of attack.

Cal kept a corner of his eye out for Dorn, lest he deign to recognize enemies in his presence. Dorn was dancing in his burned-out corner of this metal aerie. He made the strangest motions, as though manipulating an invisible marionette. Kraten intensified his attack, trying to push Cal back to the center of the floor.

"I have waited for this duel for years," Kraten said, as he sliced unsuccessfully at Cal. "Callum MacDonnell, captain of Aandor, defender of the House of Athelstan, defender of the realm. A bloated reputation if ever there was one."

Either Schweinaufklebera's reputation was overrated, or the training had been wasted on Kraten. To hear his opponent speak so boldly would mean he hadn't a clue Cal had been taking his measure since they began their fight. Unless Kraten himself had a similar ploy, Cal thought the man would have been much better in a life and death struggle.

Kraten was aggressive on offense, showing creativity and speed on the attack, but exhibited only four defensive maneuvers so far. His arrogance and attitude stemmed from his overly aggressive offense, which, no doubt, along with his fierce appearance, has served him well in all the fights of his life. His boasting reminded Cal of Lelani's own desert sorcerer in the meadow upstate. Cal let Kraten attack him thrice for every halfhearted cut he made. The captain learned much about the desert prince in the time they sparred and recognized openings and patterns that would not be obvious to the untrained eye.

Arrogance appeared to be a national trait of the Verakhoon. Its rulers would do well to bite their tongues and curb their boasts in future council meetings. Aandor had not fought Verakhoon directly in a war for hundreds of years, but if Kraten represented the cream of their military, it would be a rout. Perhaps that was why the archduke of Verakhoon behaved more like a vassal to the lord of Farrenheil than an heir to the empire in his own right.

"Your partner put up a better fight before I took her head," Kraten said, with an oily grin. "I only wished I'd had more time to teach her a woman's duties before I dispatched her."

He lies.

Erin was killed in the most cowardly manner—she never knew what hit her. The mention of Erin's decapitation ended Cal's patience. *This is the bastard that took Erin's life . . . that stole my wife in front of my daughter.*

Cal dropped his shield and gripped his sword two-handed. He cut and sliced in unorthodox combinations Kraten was not prepared to defend against. Cal was like a car that had shifted from third gear to fifth; the new tactics threw Kraten off his balance and a worried look spread over the desert warrior's face as cut after cut sliced and nipped at him. He tried but failed to predict Cal's moves. The cop drove him back along the hallway toward the north side of the hall with a whizzing flurry of swipes—the gleam of the sword became a marriage of poetry, dance, and light. Kraten lost his footing on several parries and then also a big chunk of his long raven-hued hair.

Cal had him against the wall—Kraten attacked hard, like a batter who'd lost his timing and swung for the fences. Cal uncharacteristically parried to the inside of his own body, something all are taught never to do because it leaves the pointy end of your opponent's sword within reach of your unguarded midsection—but Kraten was not expecting it, and not only couldn't take advantage of the opportunity, but he overextended and lost his balance. The tip of Kraten's sword scraped the floor—Cal put his boot on the blade's center and snapped it with a ping. Kraten, hand still on his hilt, was unable to withdraw fast enough when Cal wound back with his sword arm like a recoiling spring.

With a twist of his torso, Cal sliced through Kraten's neck like hot butter. Kraten's head popped off, hit the open triangular windowsill behind him, and bounced out the seventy-story room while his corpse hit the floor at Cal's feet.

Cal said a prayer for Erin and headed back to the other side of the floor to see how everyone else fared.

3

Cal was mostly still concerned about Dorn. A new lightning battle had replaced the marionette dance—a far more fevered pitch characterized this duel.

The Empire State Building gave back with equal fervor. Cal was never more proud of Lelani. Dorn was unhinged and completely oblivious to the goings-on behind his back. Cal thought about attacking the man, but the lightning looked dangerous beyond his capacity to tolerate and he couldn't pass up the opportunity to get Catherine out of the observatory first.

Hesz and Mal were nowhere to be seen in the main hall that spanned the length of the building. Cat had crawled from her spot beneath the window to an area closer to Dorn, just behind him next to a large duffel bag on the west side of the floor.

What the heck . . . ? thought Cal.

She rifled through the duffel bag with hands bound and pulled out a dagger that she then tried to unsheathe with her teeth.

Cal rushed over, praying Dorn wouldn't notice them. When she looked up at him, he took her face in his hands and kissed her passionately. She melted at his touch at first, then put her fists on his chest and pushed back hard.

"Are you okay?" Cal asked.

"That depends," Cat said.

"On what?"

"Will your *fiancée* mind our kissing?" she said coldly.

"Really, Cat? Now?"

A frigid wash cascaded over Cal—like a winning coach under the bucket after the Super Bowl. No magic scared him more than his wife's wrath. He preferred to be sword fighting—killing stuff was easier. As if in answer to his wish, Hesz and Malcolm crashed through the ceiling, landing with a loud thud beside them. Cal didn't even realize there was another floor above them.

Cat flattened herself in time as Hesz's mace whooshed over her and smashed the wall next to her head into dust. Callum shot up looking for an angle of attack that wouldn't compromise Malcolm. He thought he'd found it, but charged into Hesz's backhanded swing. It was like hitting a wrecking ball, and he flew across the room smashing against a wall. This was the second time Cal's armor saved him from disaster, but his Kevlar helmet had suffered a huge crack.

Hesz's backhand maneuver gave Malcolm a much-needed opening. The dwarv raised his ax above his head and with a hard vertical swing, buried it deep into Hesz's left calf. The giant roared in pain and swiveled back toward his attacker. Mal couldn't free his ax in time to avoid Hesz's grasp. The giant took him by the scruff and held the diminutive billionaire away at arm's length. Mal tried to grab his other ax, but his arm wouldn't bend enough with his shoulder pinned under the crushing grip. Hesz hobbled to the north corner window that somehow remained undamaged through all the fighting and hurled Malcolm through it with tremendous force, smashing glass and frame. Mal's screams faded into the night as he plummeted.

Cal recovered, though he still saw spots dancing about him. His leg took the brunt of his crash and fiercely ached. He tried to still his grief over Malcolm's sudden demise, enough to keep his wits for the fight ahead. Cat was almost through her bonds, her knife wedged between her knees as she rubbed her wrist ties against it. Hesz was oblivious to her, despite being only a few feet away. The giant was lost in deep contemplation.

Sword in hand, Cal cautiously shuffled toward the bruised, bleeding frost giant. Hesz effortlessly pulled Malcolm's ax out of his calf. It was a toy in his gargantuan hands—albeit a very sharp toy. Cal was alert—Hesz could chuck the weapon like a no. 2 pencil—but instead Kraten's headless body by the window engrossed the giant's attention. Hesz turned to Dorn, consumed by madness and mesmerized by his lightning war, hurling tremendous power across the city at his unseen antagonist. Then the giant looked at Kraten's corpse again.

Some complex thinking occurred in the brute's mind, which Cal found fascinating. Hesz turned back to MacDonnell with the most somber expression, his sky-blue eyes piercing out at the captain from under the heavy ridge of his brow. These were not the eyes of a man intent on violence.

"The people of this universe have done nothing to offend me," Hesz said sedately, with a deep voice like rolling thunder mixed with gravel. "They've not affronted my race or my kingdom. They did not deserve this—madness," he said. Hesz dropped Malcolm's ax. "I yield."

"You what?" Cal said, incredulously.

"Whether in madness or desperation, Dorn has squandered our advantages," Hesz explained. "Our mission is done. I do not hate the people of this world enough to continue this chaos. I do not even hate the prince. Life is difficult enough without the whims of wizards and kings to muddle through."

Hesz limped toward the stairwell leaving a line of blood in his wake. "Dorn will be dead soon enough . . . ," he continued as he hobbled toward the exit. "Whether by your hand or by the illness that has plagued him. If your impatience steers you toward the former, I bid you good fortune, MacDonnell; I truly do. I ask only one consideration for this terse peace . . . if you capture Symian, show the boy mercy. He is not evil . . . we all must earn our fortunes some way."

Hesz turned his back on Cal, a compliment that Cal's reputation for fair play preceded him and he would not attack the giant from behind, and slowly walked into the stairwell. Cal heard his descent, one slow lumbering step after another.

Cal was stunned. He couldn't really let the giant go . . . not after what he did to Malcolm. But there were more important tasks at the moment than picking a fight. He was alone now, and Cat's safety was paramount. Of all the ways he imagined how his fight with Hesz would play out, this was not even close. He hadn't even known the giant was that articulate.

The floor was quiet. Too quiet. He turned slowly. Dorn stood before the gaping hole in the wall facing him. Cat was still on the floor to the wizard's left. The sorcerer's pallor had whitened; he had cold dead eyes . . . windows to his dementia.

"They've left me," Dorn said. He looked overcome, drained . . . like a faded shirt that had been washed too often. "All of them." Dorn pulled out a small locket that opened on a hinge. "Even Lara has abandoned me." He held out the locket to show Cal the picture. "And they've turned off the magic." Dorn sounded like a kid who just received a time-out for something he didn't do.

"What kind of a world is it where you can turn off the magic? WHO SAID YOU COULD TURN OFF MY MAGIC!" he screamed, animated.

His eyes looked like they had been flushed with salt water, crimson and webbed, his face filled with hatred one moment, then confusion the next, followed by the softness of sorrow. He put the tips of his fingers against his right temple, picking at the roots of his blond hair even as he pressed. Dorn's emotions ran like the colors in a spinning kaleidoscope—melding and blending without start or end.

Cat did not dare move or even take a breath, her eyes conveying her fear at the wizard's mental breakdown. Cal locked eyes with Dorn, willing him not to notice anyone else in the room. It wasn't as hard as he thought . . . Dorn was suffering terribly and looked to be able to concentrate on only one thing at a time. Cal squeezed the hilt of his sword, which made the leather-wrapping squeak, and took a small step toward the sorcerer—then another one. By the third step, he could not move—not at all.

"Tsk,tsk," said Dorn, waggling a reproachful finger at MacDonnell. "There are spells, you see," he said, unfolding his arms in a grand gesture to encompass the room and its murals of the heavens. ". . . And then there are spells." He made the universal symbol of small things with thumb and index finger close together. "I have enough magic left to keep you a well-behaved statue. Do you know what you've cost me, MacDonnell?"

Cal thought it a rhetorical question, in light of what Dorn and his ilk had cost the Kingdom of Aandor.

Dorn shouted, "DO YOU?!"

The shouting exacerbated Dorn's migraine. Dorn pressed the butt of his hands into his temples hard enough to crush coconuts. His arms trembled with the effort.

"Before I go, I will see an end to you," Dorn promised. "Good bye, MacDonne—" Dorn suddenly yelped in pain.

Cat, crawling on her stomach behind the lord of Farrenheil, had stabbed him in the ankle with her knife. Dorn kicked her away. He pulled the knife out of his foot and waved his other hand toward her—Cal dreaded what would happen next.

Nothing happened, though. Dorn waved his hand at her again. Still nothing.

The stasis spell had begun to unwind. Cal struggled against it, like wading through saltwater taffy, but it became easier with each moment. Dorn noted Cal's progress and looked utterly confused, but there was sanity in his confusion. He no longer seemed plagued by migraines, and some of his color returned. He studied the knife in his hands.

"No!" he whispered in horror. The blade upset the sorcerer greatly. At the same time, he looked relieved, like a great pressure had been taken from him.

Cat got up and ran over to her husband. "What's the matter? Why don't you move?"

"S p e l l," he said. "W e a r i n g o f f."

"Not fast enough," she said.

Dorn went to the duffel bag. Cal tried to get to him, but was still moving in slow motion. Dorn retrieved two swords, one long, one short. Before he unsheathed either, Cat took a running jump and lunged onto Dorn's back, pounding his head with her fists. She bit his ear and scratched at his face like her namesake.

"You fucking son of a bitch!" she screamed. Cat tore the cartilage off his ear.

Dorn punched her behind his head. She fell off, dazed by the blow, and the ear fell out of her bloody mouth and plunked on the floor with a wet smack. He turned toward Cat—she rose and came at him again. He slapped her hard then backhanded her on the return. She went to her knees.

"You're no lady," he said, grabbing Cat by the throat. He pulled her off her feet.

Dorn shook Cat violently, throttling her, cutting off her air. She swung and kicked, but he blocked her blows. Cat tried to kick him in the groin several times, but Dorn twisted and weaved. She turned blue from asphyxiation, but instead of finishing her off, he threw her across the floor toward the gaping hole. Cal's heart stuck in his throat as Cat's momentum took her toward the open air. She grasped a piece of jutting wreckage at the last second as most of her body went out the hole. With legs dangling in the rain, Cat held on for dear life.

Dorn unsheathed his long sword and limped toward Cal. Blood from his ankle trailed the floor behind him.

"What irony, MacDonnell," he said. "The very weapon that rendered me common also stays my ills. My thoughts are clear, the migraines gone. I never would have thought to try this. To think, a cure has been in my possession all this time." He swished the swords before him gracefully, his thick wrists rolling like ball-bearing joints.

"I was Schweinaufklebera's best student in Farrenheil, MacDonnell. But his teachings are wasted against a man in your condition right now. I doubt you could race a snail."

It was true, Cal had half his mobility back, but it wasn't enough. He braced himself for the thrust, ludicrously trying to get his sword into position, while Dorn literally could run circles around him. Dorn locked onto Cal's eyes, determined to see the killing blow on his face. A shadow to Cal's right distracted the lord of Farrenheil—something that clopped on the vintage marble floors like a—

Rearing hooves smashed into Dorn's chest. The sorcerer skittered into the wall from the force. Lelani moved into Cal's field of vision, a true sight for sore eyes. He tried to tell her to help Cat, who was struggling to climb back into the building, but his speech was still affected.

Lelani put her hands on Cal's chest, sang words in her native language, and drew the stasis out of him the way cold hands drew heat from a hot body. He could move again.

He was about to spring to Cat's aid when the sound of a dagger cutting the air ended with a thud in Lelani's back. The tip of a silver dagger pierced through Lelani's chest where her pectoral met her deltoid muscle. Blood surged from the severed brachial artery. She screamed and tried to grab the knife from behind, but the hilt was out of her reach.

"Schweinaufklebera's fourth rule . . . ," Dorn growled, clutching his chest where she hit him, but getting back on his feet. "Even the playing field."

Lelani thrust her arms to cast a spell at the sorcerer but nothing happened—she, too, had been neutralized. It was the same silver knife Cat used to cut Dorn. Lelani, dizzy, went down on her front knees as blood spurted faster out of her wound.

Dorn charged MacDonnell. The knight raised his sword just in time to keep from being cleaved. The clang of metal again reverberated through the art deco aerie. But unlike Kraten, Dorn's aggression was artful, balanced—his feet placed perfectly shoulder width, his stance relaxed despite the wound to his ankle. His strikes were smooth and rapid. Dorn's powerful quadriceps bulged against the fine wool of his custom-made pants.

Cal would not last five minutes on a routine of parries and observations with this man. Dorn was the finest swordsman he'd ever encountered, and Cal was thirteen years out of practice.

The sorcerer drove Cal back up the center hall to the north side, out of sight of Cat hanging on for dear life. Lelani, still in view, was bleeding out on the floor. She would die soon without attention. Cal tried to think of a way to help them, but Dorn's barrage forced him to concentrate on the fight.

Behind Cal was Kraten's body by the window, and nearby was his police shield. Cal cursed himself for having dropped it. He really needed it now, but there was no way to pick it up without exposing himself.

Dorn did not need sorcery to feed his arrogance; had he been a common knight, he would have won tourneys and glories by his art with the blade. Cal's defenses were crucial. Each blow was crippling. If he failed to block or parry once, it would be devastating. And still, half his mind was with the mother of his child dangling seventy stories above the city. Dorn drove him back with perfect form, elbows slightly bent, never overreaching: cut, swing, cut, thrust, swing, parry, parry—the two men danced, graceful as the ballet but without the fancy flourishes. This was pure business.

Cal's armor saved him on a few strikes, whereas Dorn fought in his custom-made Façonnable dress shirt and was not touched once.

"Yield and I will give you a quick death. You have my word," Dorn promised.

"You're still a little demented, Farrenheil," Cal said, trying to sound less winded than he actually was. "I'm still standing. Why quit now?"

Dorn renewed his attack, switching effortlessly between the two blades. He'd turn suddenly for a deeper reach with the long sword and a thinner target as he presented his profile to the captain. Every time Cal tried to take advantage of that pose, Dorn would prance out of the way. It was like trying to skewer a lively wiggling worm. Cal was mindful of his distance to his opponent . . . their swords were roughly the same length, but Dorn was not shy about coming into Cal's guard. Cal kept trying to get some range on the man, but he continued to pull and push, manipulating Cal like the moon influences the tide.

Dorn faked a horizontal cut that turned into an impossibly quick downward swing. He caught Cal's brawny wrist in a compromising angle, spun the knight's blade and unarmed him. Cal's sword fell a few feet away. Dorn immediately went for the thrust to the gut. Cal jumped back, and Dorn's blade only glanced his armor, but it put the cop off balance and he stumbled backward. Dorn lunged and swung—Cal hustled backward on arms and legs as sword strike after strike smashed into the floor next to his limbs. He was running out of floor when he heard the sweetest sound come from behind Dorn.

"Turn around and face an armed man, you pribbling, dog-hearted, flax wench," said a voice that sounded very much like Malcolm Robbe.

Dorn swiveled quickly out of Cal's way to reveal Malcolm, busted up, bloodied, broken nosed, and broken armed, but still holding a big ax in his good hand.

"A dwarv?" said Dorn, dripping with contempt.

"Malcolm Robbe, you're lordship," Mal said in mock etiquette. "I see your magic's gone . . . I thought I'd shove my ax up your arse."

Run, you fool, thought Cal. Even in the best of health, Mal was no match for Dorn, magic or otherwise. As though reading his thoughts, Mal backed away quickly instead of engaging Lord Dorn, drawing the man away and giving Cal the second he needed to reclaim his sword.

Dorn easily caught up with Malcolm, who blocked a vertical thrust with his ax. Cal attacked Dorn from behind, and the sorcerer switched into a new pattern, fighting them both off with impossible grace and accuracy. Malcolm and Cal spent as much time on defense as they did attacking the bastard.

"I'd hate to see what he's like without the bloody injured ankle," Mal shouted across the room. They maneuvered until Mal and Cal were together again and Dorn backed both of them up against the north wall.

"Nowhere to go," Dorn said, victorious.

"I wouldn't say that, exactly," Mal quipped.

They heard a twang, whoosh, and a thud. Dorn cried out as an arrow lodged into his right shoulder blade.

Lelani clopped into view from the hallway. Another arrow was notched to go, but the bow shook in her hands under the tension. She was drained of color and struggling to stay conscious. Dorn shifted his defensive stance, rotating to keep all three in his sight. Mal spread to Dorn's right and Cal to his left.

"How?" asked Cal.

"You didn't think I came back, saw the girl bleeding out and your wife hanging by a fingernail, and would help you first?" Malcolm said incredulously. "I knew you'd hold it together."

"That's flattering," Cal said.

Cat came out of the darkness of the corner behind Dorn. A shot of fear went through Cal, and he was about to tell her to get out of the building, when he noticed the automatic in her hand—likely something she found in Dorn's duffel bag. She slid the rack to chamber a round. Dorn turned with a start when he realized someone was behind him. She pointed the pistol at him. He looked like a trapped animal.

Dorn began to laugh. For a moment, Cal thought the insanity had returned, but it turned out to be the laugh of prideful superiority in the face of defeat.

"You think you've won?" said Dorn. "Vanquished the evil villain and saved your kingdom. But you've lost. You come at me with mongrels—centaurs and dwarvs. You don't know it yet, but soon enough you will—again at the mercy of others who will not care about your high-minded notions of brotherhood and peace. Ten thousand years of progress—of safety in our own homes—squandered away to these . . . these ANIMALS!"

"Hypocrite," said Mal. "You have gnolls, frost giants, and a troll working for you."

"As my vassals! Not my equals! Symian despised his father's people. He would have worked harder to destroy the trolls than any man in my indenture. They are not peers. They were a means to an end."

"Where are they now?" Cat said, eerily monotone. "You're all alone. None of them wanted to stay . . . to be loyal. They were afraid of you . . . needed a paycheck. They failed you because you utterly failed them. You treat others like pieces on chessboard. How can you lead when you don't respect those who follow you? How can you govern when you don't look after all your people? You treat everybody like shit. Despots—trash with money and thugs."

"Silence!" Dorn barked. He took a step toward Cat.

The gun cracked. Dorn went down on one knee and dropped the sword from his good arm to brace himself. She had put a bullet in his thigh.

"How dare you!" Dorn cried. "Wretched commoner! You are not worthy!"

"Cat?" said Cal, with some alarm.

"Our villages are filled with refugees because of your treachery," Lelani chimed in. She was shaky and the loss of blood gave her flesh a sallow tone. The shaft slipped out of her grip and into Dorn's other shoulder blade. He cried out again. Dorn looked like a deformed angel with very long wing scapulars with tiny feathers at the ends.

"Pardon," she said, in anything but sorrowful tone.

"You are not worthy to strike the likes of me!" Dorn cried. "I yield to Captain MacDonnell." He dropped his last sword with a clang on the ground and placed his hands in open surrender.

"Yield?" asked Cat. "What does that mean?"

"He surrendered," Cal said. "Put down the gun," he asked cautiously.

"What?" Cat said.

"The man yielded."

Cat's face screwed up to defend from what she was hearing. Her eyes were red and tears streamed down her cheeks. "If he gets his hands on magic again, he will kill us all."

"My lord," Lelani said. "The golems." She indicated out the window.

"I can't live like that," Cat said.

"You said incapacitating him would stop them," Cal said to Lelani.

"This is forbidden magic. One cannot be sure how many will live on. But if he were dead . . ."

"Yes, MacDonnell," said Dorn scornfully. "Take orders from your centaur witch. She has you thinking you command here, but really, no. I hope you like the taste of hoof. Get used to it."

Cal thought about what Dorn knew . . . the size of Farrenheil's invasion force, the wizards involved, and the strategies. The man had yielded. He was due privileges of protection. Cal turned to Malcolm, who was using his ax for support at this point.

"We're barely standing," Malcolm said. "He wouldn't think twice of slitting any of our throats. The minute he has magic—"

"Spare me!" cried Dorn, disgusted. He looked to MacDonnell. "A dwarv, a centaur, and an alien woman that you unwittingly married are compelling you to turn your back on your chivalry—on your HONOR—to kill a nobleman that has yielded to you in battle. Are you a captain of Aandor, or a whipped, befuddled fool MacDonnell?"

Cat grew agitated. "You kidnapped me—separated me from my

family . . . ," she said through gritted teeth. "Murdered Erin Ramos, threatened my daughter, wrecked my house, blew up half of Manhattan . . ."

"Cat . . . ," Cal warned.

"He *stole* my *babies*!" Cat screamed, rubbing the spot on her stomach where Dorn had cut into her. "Those first monsters you killed—they were part of me!" she cried.

Cal identified with his wife's rage. For all that Cat had been put through . . . the violation to her body, it was his own rage as well. Cal felt her suffering and struggled to not execute Dorn at that moment. It went against all he believed in. "But . . . in cold blood," Cal said weakly.

"He is cold blood," Cat said. "Mutilator of helpless children. He's a reptile."

"Kind words, Lady MacDonnell," Dorn said. "This is the price I pay for showing you mercy? For not taking the unborn child in your womb?"

"Mercy . . . ?" Cat said, in shock.

Dorn picked up his short sword and pointed it toward Cat. "If you'll not protect me from your wench MacDonnell, I'll do so myself. I should have ripped all the life from your bowels and left you for dead when I had the chance!"

Cat shot Dorn in the forehead right above the eyes. The side of his head bloated out with a crunch as the bullet pushed brain tissue outward. He crumpled to the floor on top of his sword. His leg jittered for a moment, and then ceased along with the rest of him.

"That should cure your fucking headaches," Cat said. She was still pointing the gun at him, shaking.

Cal walked over to her slowly and gently took the gun away. He clicked the safety on and put his arms around his wife. She rested against him.

"You going to arrest me?" she said, as her legs gave way. Cal bore her weight on his arm. He sheathed his sword and lifted Cat in both arms like a child.

The three rickety cohorts slowly shuffled to the stairs, then exhausted and thinking better of it, decided to risk the elevator. It dinged on arrival. The doors opened, and a very scared Seth Raincrest was in the box, holding his staff before him like a spear.

"Holy shit," he said, upon seeing the four of them. "When Dorn stopped fighting back, I thought for sure you guys were dead." Seth saw Cat in Callum's arms and added, "Is she . . ."

"She's fine," Cal said. "Finally crawled out from under your rock, huh? Thanks for nothing."

"What?" Seth said. "Are you fucking kidding me?"

"My lord, Seth is the one who engaged Dorn with the lightning," Lelani said.

Cal looked at Lelani, then Seth, with disbelief. "The idiot?" he said.

Seth aimed his staff at Cal. "That's it! I'm done . . ."

Lelani jumped between them. Annoyed, she said to Cal, "Seth was brilliant. I could not have fought off Dorn's attack. He saved my life. He saved all our lives."

"Good work, kid," said Mal, and slapped Seth on the butt, sports-style, as he got into the car.

Cal didn't like the awkward position he found himself in. Gratitude to the idiot . . . ? What was the world coming to? He softened his glare and nodded to Seth. "Well, okay then," he said. He joined Seth in the elevator. "Thanks."

"Are there a lot of beasties still on the ground?" Malcolm asked.

"They're falling apart—dissolving into some kind of gas," Seth said.

"A few golems may escape Dorn's death to become beings in their own right," Lelani warned. "The random nature of exponential magic."

The three men and Cat headed down; Lelani remained behind, waiting for an empty car.

"Mal, don't take this the wrong way, but why are you still alive?" Cal asked. "Hesz threw you out of a seventy-story window."

"Never hit bottom," Mal said. "Eagle broke my fall . . . one of the chrome nickel-steel guardian gargoyles on the corner of the sixty-first floor. Steel has always been a dwarv's best friend. I nearly bounced off the damn thing, but managed to get my small ax into it and held on for dear life. I'll have to cut the owners a check to repair it."

"Why not just buy the whole damn building?" Seth joked.

"That's not a bad idea," Mal quipped, seriously contemplating it. "It's quite lovely."

CHAPTER 53

WITH APOLOGIES

The blood-red graphic read ATTACK ON NEW YORK as the reporter tried to explain the fantastic events of the day. Every conceivable explanation was thrown at the viewer: terrorist attack, hallucinogenics in the steam that seeped out of the streets, wilding gangs gone feral . . . all other television programming had been suspended as every channel with a news department plastered the airwaves with coverage of the chaos in Manhattan. Strangely absent from that coverage were actual pictures of the golems themselves.

Lelani and Rosencrantz took an already existing sorcery that removed ink from parchments—mostly to remove spells from grimoires, signatures from contracts—and built upon it until they were sure it could work on digital and photographic sources. It was a testament to Lelani's genius that she was able to concoct such a thing, as Rosencrantz had never heard of video or television. Rosencrantz contributed the global reach of the spell, ensuring that every device be affected. Add to that, no physical trace of any monsters and what you had left looked like mass hysteria and peoples' bad behavior. The centaur and the tree wizard would stay on top of the situation and neutralize any forensic proof of magic or the creatures as they popped up. It might take weeks, but she assured Cal that it could be done.

Mal's people were busy at work cleaning up sites where the battles took place and the suite at The Plaza. And by cleaning, everyone understood leaving as little evidence behind of magic and golems and their presence there. With the whole city on alert and thousands injured, the authorities didn't have the resources to launch a proper investigation into the cause of the events. They didn't know where to look. Sorcerers? Wizards?

The prince's guardians sat exhausted in the recreation room of Tilcook's North Jersey compound, watching the news on a fifty-six-inch television. They were licking their wounds in style surrounded by a huge roaring fireplace, pool table, full bar, baby grand piano, plush couches, high-definition television, and a neon jukebox containing every Frank Sinatra and Tony Bennett song ever recorded. Mal recounted the battle in the Chrysler Building to a captive audience of Daniel, Scott, Tilcook, Seth, and Tony Two Scoops over some draft beers. Daniel slurped on a root beer ice cream float.

"Anyway . . . I got back upstairs and first thing I see is Lelani bleeding out on the ground," Mal said. "She has this vial in her shaking hands, but they're so bloody it's too slippery to get the top off the tube. So I help her, and I realize it's knitting powder—I'd never actually seen it, but everyone's heard of the stuff—worth, like, four sacks of platinum standards. So I pour it over her wound and it starts to fizz . . ."

Cal drank his beer alone, away from the others, on a stool at the corner of the bar. A speaker on the wall above him played Sinatra's "All of Me." Cal looked over at Daniel contentedly; after thirteen years, the prince was once again among them, safe and whole.

Getting out of the city after the fight had been easy . . . Lelani had taught Seth her cloaking spell, which, though flawed, didn't need to be perfect with all the confusion and hysteria in the streets. Seth, it seemed, had the ability to store some amount of magic in him, a fact that utterly fascinated Lelani and made her a little bit jealous. After a stop at the Empire State Building to recharge, Seth recast her illusion spell, and they blended into the chaos and joined the masses piling onto the Hudson ferries, which were overloaded to get as many people off the island as possible. They co-opted a van at a used car lot in Union City. Mal left cash for the vehicle in the office mail drop.

Cal studied the large room in the really big house, calculating the rewards of a life of crime: four-car garage, ten acres, eight bedrooms, swimming pool, panic room, and security room where all the cameras from a half-mile of perimeter fencing fed. If Cal were caught in here on a federal raid, his career in the NYPD would pretty much be over. At the same time, he could walk into Tilcook's study and probably find enough evidence to put the crook away for years. They'd won, though, and people wanted to celebrate and relax before deciding what to do next. Even Cal agreed, planning was better left for tomorrow.

Bree played a videogame in the far corner with Tilcook's daughter, Paradise, a spoiled brat of a girl with curly black hair and a heart-shaped face who, unfortunately, had the name of a stripper stamped on her birth certificate. Tilcook's wife, Gina, with her teased hair, overdone fingernails, and blue-collar vocabulary, practically stepped out of an episode of *The Real Housewives of New Jersey*. She was not happy to have all these strangers in her home.

Notably missing was Cat. She was not in a celebratory mood, as Cal fully understood. Killing a person, no matter how justifiably, haunted you. It took Cal weeks to shake it the first time he'd killed a man in battle. Even though you knew you had to do it, the power over life and death for mere mortals was disconcerting. One had to be a sociopath or megalomaniac to handle the act with no ramifications. Coping involved desensitizing yourself to the sanctity of human life. It also involved time, which was by its very nature not a thing to be rushed.

Cal left the recreation room for the bedroom floors. The house was done in a neo-roman style—white columns, multicolored marble floors, vaulted dome ceilings—the kind that only Mediterranean types would call classy. In the first bedroom he passed, he heard Allyn and Colby's voices. He knocked and entered. With the two men were Lelani and Colby's son Tory.

"Any progress?" asked Cal.

"Yes and no," said Allyn. "The boy's eyes were severely gouged. They will take a long time to heal, months perhaps; I'm essentially regrowing them."

"Can't you use the knitting powder?" Cal asked.

"The healing powder works best on simple repairs, a torn artery, vein, or skin cells," Lelani said. "To rebuild a human eye would require a pound of powder. Even if that much existed, the cost would bankrupt a kingdom. The powder is made of ground horns of a unicorn and white rhino, beak of a gryphon, hooves of a satyr, a garlic clove from the garden of a white witch, blood of an executed innocent, phoenix feathers, and a few other ingredients just as rare. And the ingredients are only half the effort."

"Jesus Christ," said Colby.

"On a positive note," added Allyn, with a scowl toward the detective, "we mixed Lelani's healing powder in a solution of isotonic saline and injected it near the break in Tory's spinal cord."

"Hurts like a mother . . . !" said Tory, grinding his teeth.

". . . which is a great indication that the nerve cells are knitting," Allyn added. "With rehabilitation, Tory will one day walk again."

"That's wonderful news," said Callum with a parent's sincere understanding. "And Colby's problem?"

Allyn and Lelani balked on explanations.

"Yeah, we hit a snag on that one," Colby said.

"It's very complex magic," Lelani said.

"It's almost sacrilegious," said Allyn.

Cal was shocked. "Allyn, don't tell me you're refusing to help this man. The prince would be dead if not for Colby. It's not Colby's fault that Dorn . . ."

"No, no . . . ," Allyn said. "I will honor our agreement with him. It's just that, this is not a blessing that is readily done. I have never performed it, none of my brothers in the order have either, and I know of only two prelates who claim to have done it, one in Farrenheil and the other in Moran. We know it can be done, but I have yet to figure out some aspects of it. And Lelani is not herself sure of her end. Wizards can only do this with the help of a cleric, and you know what relations between clerics and wizards are like back home. There's not a lot of communication."

"So it's a logistics problem?" Cal said.

"Maybe we can call UPS," Colby quipped.

Cal locked eyes with the detective. "Colby, I swear, we'll . . ."

"Settle down, Cal. What you're doing for my boy . . . that's more than I could ever dream of. For him to walk and see again . . . being undead is a small price to pay."

"Yes, well, far be it from me to quit so easily," Lelani said. "In anticipation for the time we are able to make you whole again, I've cleaned your heart's arteries of plaque buildup, and used the powder to knit holes forming in your aorta and right ventricle. The organ should last another fifty years—far longer than your lungs if you continue to . . ."

Cal took Allyn outside into the hallway as Lelani and Colby argued the health risks of cigarette smoking.

"What's going on at home?" Cal asked the reverend.

"Michelle is being Michelle—stubborn as a bull. But it's my home, my family, and my church, and I will deal with it. I'm staying in this universe, Cal—and like all good things, my life here is worth fighting for. I can do tremendous good. Restore people's faith."

"But . . . Allyn, what about your clerical order? Pelitos? How can you preach Christianity knowing what you know?"

"What do I know, Cal?" Allyn said.

"But . . ."

"Cal, have you ever heard the story of the blind men and the elephant?"

"Not that I remember."

"Three blind men were shown an elephant and allowed to touch it so they could 'see' what it was. They each grasped a different part and soon began to argue. The first man grasped the trunk and declared it was a snake; the second felt the animal's leg and insisted it was like a tree, and the third man held the elephant's tail and claimed it was like a slender rope. They were all wrong, and yet, all right. I have an enlightened view of the universe now, as is appropriate for all travelers. It does not exclude Yahweh or Jesus. And I truly believe the Christian path, when celebrated without prejudice and false airs, will lead people to a happy and moral life."

Cal mulled over the sermon, suspecting it applied to his life as well. He gave the reverend his blessing and promised to let him know when they were planning to head back home so that Allyn could give him letters and photos for his siblings.

Cal walked down the hall and stood outside his bedroom door for a few moments. He breathed deeply and knocked. The light was still on, so he entered quietly, but Cat was awake and rolled over on the king-sized bed to face him. She wore leopard-skin spandex pants and a Bon Jovi T-shirt that Gina had lent her.

"You look lovely," he told her sarcastically.

"You have to see this woman's closet," Cat said. "It's as big as our living room and there's not a single tasteful item in the entire thing. This whole house looks like a patrician villa in Pompeii before the eruption. I chose leopard skin out of desperation. If you prefer tiger or zebra . . ."

Cal stopped her with a wave of his hand. "That's okay, thanks. Thought you'd be asleep."

"Can't sleep."

Cal sat on the bed next to her. He rubbed her arm softly. "Lot on your mind, huh?"

She nodded.

"Is it what Dorn did to you, what you did to him, or what I did to you by not telling you about Chryslantha?"

Cat nodded.

He whistled. "All of the above. No wonder you can't fall asleep."

"I'll make my peace with what I did to Dorn . . . eventually. After what he did to us—to me—it's not as though he didn't have it coming."

"I see. And the other thing?" Cal asked.

"Do you still love her?"

It was the question Cal had dreaded ever since his memories returned. He could not lie to Cat, not even if he wanted to. "Yes," he said.

Cat was being brave, holding her reaction at bay even as tears welled.

"That doesn't mean I don't love you, Cat. I just . . . Chrys and I didn't decide to go our separate ways. There was never closure. She's still in Aandor, hopefully unharmed, praying that I'm not dead and waiting for me to come get her. She still believes we have a future together. She's such a good . . . a good . . ."

It was Cal's turn to well up; emotions he didn't allow himself to feel while he searched for the prince tore through his constraint. It wasn't just what he'd put his wife through with the revelation. He experienced true bereavement—the loss of a loved one. It was as if Chrys had died—he could never go back to her. It was worse, actually—after all was resolved, after all the pain he and Chryslantha were slated to experience when he tells her of his marriage, Cal will have to bear the thought of her marrying another man—some choice of her father's to bury the shame of his daughter's carnal indulgence. Another man will make love to the woman he still cherished and who had been his best friend for his entire youth.

He took solace in his vow to Catherine; he very much loved her and Bree. Cat didn't realize yet how much he would need her to help him through this tragedy. But before that could happen, he had to make amends.

"I didn't know how to bring it up," he told her. "There was never a good time. I hadn't even worked out what the betrothal meant to me. Part of me thought if I died trying to save the prince, it would have been better for everyone. Then I wouldn't have to break anyone's heart. Not until I learned Dorn had you hostage did everything crystallize. I was so afraid, Cat—so angry. Not just for you but for myself as well—the thought of living my life without you in it."

She sat up and wrapped her arms around his neck. Cal didn't know where such a small woman got all her strength, but he thanked gods in both universes that she was on his side.

"You should have trusted me," Cat said.

"Yes . . . yes—I'm not making excuses. Please, forgive me. You're my wife. I'm taking you, Bree, and the new baby back with me, and we'll deal with the consequences when we get there."

"When?" she asked.

"A year, maybe two. What we're considering . . . it's ambitious."

"Guess I should change my masters program then," she said. "Medieval anthropology or animal husbandry."

They laughed.

"We're a little more sophisticated than medieval," Cal said.

"Really? That why you hack each other up with swords and axes and call each other 'my lord,' and curtsy?"

"Well . . ."

"I just feel bad about my mother," Cat said. "She's going to have a much harder time with that kind of life."

"You're mother?"

"Yeah."

"We are not bringing Vivian," Cal said.

"The hell we're not," Cat said.

"There's no room for her. It's a small castle."

"I'm not going up against your mother without mine at my back." Cat cast him a determined grin.

Cal swallowed his response. He was too tired to fight, and had over a year to talk Cat out of the insufferable notion. He smiled back and kissed her. She pulled him down on top of her.

"Wait, the lights," he whispered.

Cat smiled devilishly, clapped her hands twice in quick succession, and like magic, the room went dark.

EPILOGUE 1

Daniel sat under a blanket in a lounge chair on Tilcook's back patio. The pool was covered for the season and the sky dark with a bright smattering of the stars. Daniel's breath painted the air white before him despite the fire burning in the stone fire pit next to him. The wood cracked and spit as the fire consumed it, the smell of mesquite soothing to the boy's senses. Seth Raincrest also sat beside the fire pit with his staff beside him. Daniel guessed that it was for his protection. Callum didn't want him outside alone until they could account for all the golems and the few remaining bad guys. Daniel felt a bit like a prisoner. Tilcook had a lot of security on the grounds—dogs and roving groups of family soldiers—he thought having a shadow on top of that was overkill.

Seth was fiddling with the big stick. A lit cigarette hung from his lips as he stroked the wood with ultrafine grade sandpaper.

"How much more you got to do?" Daniel asked.

"Not much. Going to stain it with some water seal. Lelani says it's not necessary. The magic protects the wood, makes it hard as steel. Only another wizard can shatter it in a duel at this point. Still, I think I'm going to go for a wheat or golden maple color—kind of like a Louisville Slugger."

Daniel had an off-color joke about the guy being overly obsessed with his staff, but it was not princely, and he decided against it.

These people—these utter strangers—looked up to him. They

admired him, despite the fact that he killed his stepfather and ran away from home. They considered him strong and possessing leadership qualities—they executed the decisions he made in Manhattan. Daniel had said in the rec room that he missed his friends Adrian and Katie and wished he could see them again. They all set about trying to figure out a way to get them up to North Jersey for a weekend without tipping off the cops. And Malcolm hired some heavy-hitting New York lawyers to get the Baltimore prosecutor's office to drop the murder charges against him, based on circumstantial evidence of self defense. A New York City cop, a billionaire industrialist, a mafia capo, a Baptist reverend—all working toward his benefit and taking his suggestions seriously, like they were required to listen to him. It was surreal.

"They think I'm your half-brother," Seth said, out of the blue. Daniel didn't expect that.

"Really?"

"Yeah, it's how they justify my having been sent on this mission. I'm the reason you got lost in the first place, though—put into foster care. I was a bit of a fuckup."

"I thought it was because the guy taking care of me had those interdimensional bends like Dorn and drove our car into a truck."

"Galen and Linnea should never have been alone that night. The group was supposed to stick together. The plan was to buy up an entire block of houses somewhere and live tight-knit. My faux parents might still be alive if we did that. Lita, the woman pretending to be my mom, had the migraines, too, and set our house on fire in an act of madness."

"Yeah, I'm not too crazy about getting migraines that cause me to become a homicidal maniac. Does anyone know why that happens?"

"Nope. Lelani says it's just random."

"Hey, is—she really a centaur?"

"Yep."

"If I ask her to show me, would she do it?"

"Probably. She needs you to save her race. She'd probably jump your bones if you asked her. Might want to spritz on some Calvin Klein Obsession first."

"Ewwwww! That's like screwing a horse!"

The two of them sniggered.

"Could be worse . . . ," said Seth. "She could be a mermaid."

They both said, "Ewwww!" and chortled harder.

When the laughing died down, Seth turned to him, all serious, and asked, "Do you want to go back?"

Daniel thought about it long and hard. There was no Xbox in Aandor—no baseball, comic books, movies, airplanes, NASCAR, or even electricity. They still had to repel twenty thousand enemy soldiers from the homeland first. At the same time, his parents—his *real* parents—were back there. He'd be running the kingdom eventually. And even if Mal's lawyers could get them to drop the murder charges, it would hang over him wherever he went, the rest of his life. Clyde Knoffler was not worth going to prison for.

Daniel looked at the man that might or might not be his half brother. Seth seemed like a fun guy, in a seedy sort of way. This was a good crew to hang with. They loved their kids and each other—as good a lot to throw in with as any.

"Yeah, I'm ready," he said. "It'll be fun. Bring it on."

EPILOGUE 2

Hesz entered Balzac's small basement university office by crouching under the door frame. His head just cleared the ceiling, and only in places where naked pipes did not run along it. The professor looked up from his back-leaning swivel chair, where he graded the latest term papers at his desk. He wore a wool sweater vest and his reading glasses hung at the end of his nose.

Hesz closed the door behind him and locked it.

"Dorn is dead," said the frost giant. "As are Kraten, Symian, and all the rest in our party."

Balzac put down the paper he was marking and folded his hands across his belly.

"I told you things were heading in that direction, my friend," Balzac said. "My information gave you several advantages, none of which you exploited to your fullest. Instead of waiting to conjure magical golems with forbidden spells, you could have used your vast wealth here to hire some local human thugs to go to the hotel and shoot them." Balzac threw his hands in the air in defeat. "Even when not suffering debilitating migraines, Dorn always had an arrogant, entitled streak running through him. Kraten, too. The type of men who were born on third base and think they hit a triple. Comes from a childhood of having everything done for you. Always others to pick up your . . . In this case, Dorn would have been better off delegating the whole matter to you, my friend."

"I'm bothered by your lack of concern for our cause . . . our well-being," Hesz said.

"Concern?"

"Surely by now they know of your betrayal. Lady MacDonnell will likely reveal . . ."

"What of it? Are they going to go to the authorities, where an interview with me will reveal that they have as little place in this world as I do? None of us are of this universe. Will they murder me in cold blood? Am I not a citizen of the United States, a tenured professor of good standing? I took no part in any murder. I simply visited two hotels to talk to friends in town. Gossip is not illegal. My treason was in Aandor—Aandor has no reach here. We are out of their jurisdiction."

Hesz sat on a small loveseat against the wall, worrying his hat in his massive hands. "That is all well and fine for you, Balzac. What of me? I have no place in this world. I am not so inconspicuous that I can blend in and disappear. My cause lies in that other reality, and I have no means by which to get home."

"Fear not, my friend. We shall see home again."

"We? Are you a sorcerer as well?"

"Not at all. They will bring us home with them."

"You are mad, Balzac. They will never trust us."

"It's not so much a matter of trust, my gentle giant, as it is of need. We possess information that is invaluable to them. Troop strengths and positions, fleet sizes, targets, number of wizards, spies, the spells used to undermine their security."

"They will place us in chains," Hesz protested.

"Yes, and bring us back home in them. The key point being we will get home. Once home, chains can be broken, deals can be made. And they will have their hands filled contending with Lara. She will be none too pleased to hear of her nephew's demise. They thought Dorn was mad . . . his beautiful aunt makes him look like a choir boy.

"As for playing the royal court . . . MacDonnell will believe his wife's accounting of my attempt to kill her, but the generals and court flotsam in Aandor will not put as much faith in the opinions of a woman. Aandor is not an enlightened society by any realistic measure, and my story will carry as much weight despite its fabrication.

"No, my friend . . . having failed to indoctrinate the prince to my own personal beliefs, the key is to get home by any means necessary and wait out this generation. Daniel's heir will be the true emperor after all, the blood of twelve kings. I will appeal to these high-minded egos, placate their whims, and find myself in a position of influence again. And then, we shall reshape the world, by iron, by fire, and by blood."